THE RIGHT WRONG PROMISE

A GRUMPY SINGLE DAD ROMANCE

NICOLE SNOW

Content copyright © Nicole Snow. All rights reserved.
Published in the United States of America.
First published in December, 2025.

Disclaimer: The following book is a work of fiction. Any resemblance characters in this story may have to real people is only coincidental.

Please respect this author's hard work! No section of this book may be reproduced or copied without permission. Exception for brief quotations used in reviews or promotions. This book is licensed for your personal enjoyment only. Thanks!

Cover Design – CoverLuv.

Proofread by Sisters Get Lit.erary Author Services.

Website: Nicolesnowbooks.com

ABOUT THE BOOK

I inherited a freaking family.

Thanks, Gramps. I expected the lake house, the repairs, and the weird little secrets you left behind.

But sharing this place with Kane Saint and his kids?

Holy potato.

Don't laugh at his name.

There's nothing holy about a man this guarded and growly and scary fine.

He's at war with everything except his adorable munchkins.

It's a classic standoff the instant I let him stay after an awkward mix-up.

I go to work looking for my grandfather's final cryptic gift.

Saint Dadzilla goes to work on *me.*

A helping hand I never asked for.

The warmest laughs over breakfast feasts.

And when one stolen kiss claims my soul, I forget this is clinically insane.

I'm in shambles.

Every flaming night whispers promises we can't keep—especially when Gramps' legacy has teeth.

What happens if playing house with the wrong man feels like coming home?

I: MAKE YOURSELF AT HOME (MARGOT)

It's a long drive up to the lake house from Portland. Over three hours on the road where city comforts bow to marching mountains and tall forests as thick as my memories.

I make the entire trip with the windows down, though.

It's fall, and the wind streaming through my hair gives me a sense of freedom I've been missing forever.

Why does this feel like a new beginning when it's really just a working trip to assess the mess I've been handed?

Thanks, PopPop. You always did love to send me on scavenger hunts.

By the time I pull up the gravel driveway outside my grandfather's secluded lake house, I think I'm ready.

I tell myself I've braced for the emotional sucker punch.

I'm sure I'm old enough to handle this like a grown-up and not a hurt little girl who still desperately misses the old man who held her entire universe together.

Ha, no.

This is the first time I've seen the place since Gramps died. Honestly, since my first year of college.

Half a lifetime ago, we'd head up here every summer as kids for deliciously lazy weeks lost among the country greenery and an infinite canopy of stars.

It's been a hot minute since I've made the trek up the long, dark, winding path through the tall pines and vibrant maples.

The old house's exterior certainly doesn't match the memory in my head.

"Ouch," I mutter, wincing at the worn blue paint.

The short steps leading up to the porch are a little overgrown along the sides. We're talking weeds poking through the slats like they're scheming to trip you.

The handrail looks like it's a heartbeat away from falling over the second you grab it.

With a heavy sigh, I linger in the car, just taking it in for a second.

Dead, black windows stare back at me. The nostalgia trapped inside this place suddenly feels gloomy.

The old blue house has certainly seen better days.

So have I.

But at least it's a warm, sunny day for September.

One of those breezy autumn kisses that likes to pretend it's still summer. Cloudless blue sky, rolling breeze, gold splashed everywhere.

It makes this house feel picture-perfect even if it's looking more rustic ruin on the outside.

Makes coming here feel a little less morbid, I guess.

In the will, PopPop left me the lake house and vast land around it. The only real estate with my name on it.

The rest of his sprawling empire went to my brother, Ethan, and that's fine.

There's still some big secret waiting in the wings for my little cousin, Cleo, too.

For me, it was a generous addition to my trust fund I didn't really need, plus this property.

But now that I'm here, I'm more confused than ever.

Why did he leave me a place that probably needs a hundred fixes to shine again?

My hands grip the steering wheel, turning my knuckles bone-white. I release them, blowing out a long, slow breath.

Then I put on my game face and climb out of the car.

My arrival disturbs a few big crows on the porch. They erupt from their roost cackling, and a couple of them nearly take my head off in their rush to leave.

"Jeez!"

I almost drop my sunglasses as I throw up my hands. Before I can curse them, they're gone, spiraling into the sky like a plume of black smoke.

Great. At least I'm alone if this place has gone to the birds.

I snort, shaking my head.

If Ethan saw me freaking out over a few bouncy crows, he'd never let me live it down.

Whatever. It's expected.

Jitters.

That's part of the journey when you come back to a childhood stomping ground that's basically haunted. Memories can be just as scary as ghosts.

For all I know, a few real ghosts moved in while it's been abandoned, barely checked by locals and Gramps' old bodyguard, Holden.

With my luck, I'll need to look for psychics along with contractors to make this place decent again.

I snatch the unopened letter off the passenger seat and pat the back pocket of my jeans to make sure I've got the keys before stepping through the tall weeds crowding the old stone walkway to the back of the house.

The rickety stairs are sturdier than they look. They only creak a little as I climb them.

It's *weird* doing this alone without my dumb brother charging ahead of me, or my bestie, Hattie, by my side.

When we'd come here as kids, we'd always run in through the back.

"Front's for guests. The back, that's for family," PopPop would always tell me with a wink.

Old habits die hard.

Same with people, and *God, I miss him*.

It's been almost a year since he left this world, but every time I think about it, my heart aches bitterly.

My grandfather was more like a third parent to Ethan and me.

So much crap has come out about his life and his complicated relationship with my mom that I don't even know how I should feel about coming here.

But that's the thing about feelings. Sometimes they decide for you.

The letter in my hand almost vibrates, waiting to be read.

I put the key in the lock and turn. It's a little stiff from disuse.

Then I walk inside, inhaling the living past.

Oh, I forgot this smell.

There's still a hint of brine in the air from the nearby ocean, mingling with the staleness of abandonment. The lightbulb in the hallway blows out the second I flick the switch, so I head to the living room.

Surprisingly, the blinds are open, revealing the glittering lake sprawled out in front of me. Fall colors dye the water twenty shades of red and orange.

It's freaking beautiful in a moody kind of way.

There's a little beach down there, all rocks and pale sand,

along with an old dock jutting out into the lake. The water laps against it gently.

I smile before I catch myself.

It's *weird* being here with so much silence.

I keep imagining Ethan will jump out from behind a door to scare me or PopPop will come stomping downstairs and tell me to unpack the damn car before he has to do it all himself.

Now, just whispers.

The wind whistling lightly against the house, floorboards creaking, secrets frozen in silence.

At least the house has been maintained on the inside. It's actually clean in here, with nothing obviously broken besides the light.

The appliances all work, supposedly.

Might have to thank Holden for that. He still makes the rounds periodically at all the old family properties, making sure they're safe and secure. It keeps him employed and gives us one less headache until we decide what to put on the market.

Still, it almost feels like there's someone else here.

That's silly.

Today it's just me and the breeze and whatever chaos PopPop left behind in this letter.

I mean, it can't be worse than Ethan's surprise, right?

It's not like I have to *marry* some dude just to get my inheritance. Never thought in a million years it would lead to Ethan and Hattie tying the knot, but here we are.

Not much comfort.

PopPop was a strange man, and adventure was practically his religion. He loved to live, and if he had to prod you along to do it, that was no sin.

My stomach churns at the thought of opening it.

His last words.

The last little fragment of him I'll get in this life. And after that, I'll have nothing but grief.

More grief.

Nothing but sadness and ghostly jump scares from my own brain. Melancholy and mysteries I'm not sure I need.

There's a real possibility he's left me something else here, something crazy.

I might be safe from any freak engagement clauses, but so what? He gave my brother the kick in the butt he needed to find true love. In PopPop's eyes, Ethan needed it.

But what about me?

Is he just waiting to upend my life with some weird lesson while he chuckles from beyond the grave?

Only one way to find out...

My stomach twists again and I bite my bottom lip.

No, luggage first. Then I'll read it.

I head back outside to my luggage waiting in the trunk.

When I packed my bags, I wasn't sure how long I'd be staying, so I brought enough stuff to last a month. Just in case I need to do more here than take a good, long look at my property and figure out what to do with it.

Too bad I'm not a light packer.

I'm a material girl, okay?

It takes me three trips. By the time I've lugged the third bulging roller bag up the old staircase to my room, I'm sweating.

I'm a runner, so I don't lift much, and it shows.

This is way more intense than the workouts my personal trainer puts me through back home.

I leave the remaining luggage by the back door and don't bother locking it as I head into the living room again. It's not like I'm worried about anyone breaking in.

We're in the middle of nowhere.

Reasonably close to Bar Harbor but tucked back and

secluded from the main tourist rush which is tapering off around this time. Just twenty or so miles northwest of the rocky shore that starts in Acadia National Park, but it might as well be on another planet.

It's the kind of place you visit to escape.

Right now, I'm not feeling it, though.

With the steady breeze and the isolation, I keep hearing noises upstairs.

Footsteps, almost, and even though I know it's just my imagination running wild, it has me on edge.

Or does the letter just have me so worried I'm hallucinating? Is that a thing?

Deep breath, Gigi.

I've never been one to shy away from the important stuff.

But this letter is pure dread.

Probably because I never imagined how many dark secrets were swirling around this family until Ethan's whole drama arc played out.

No more putting it off, though.

The lawyer released it for a reason once I told her I'd be making a trip up here. But even when Jackie Wilkes turned it over with her usual stern, polite lawyerly smile, I didn't dare open it.

Not there in her posh office on those nice chairs that came straight from an Instagram photo.

Not when I could stall and put it off until I'm alone and vulnerable.

Idiot, a little voice in the back of my head whispers.

It's not wrong.

Now that I'm here, I'm out of excuses.

Time to put on my big girl pants and read.

Whatever he'll throw at me, I'm ready.

And even if I'm not, I'm alone.

At least I can cover my face and scream.

Holding my breath, I slide a nail under the sealed flap before I can overthink it. The lake ripples out the window as the paper tears.

This must've been written close to his death, judging by the shakiness of his handwriting. The thought makes my eyes sting, but I blink the tears away.

My eyes flick over the first few words.

I can almost hear the fondness in his voice, the same gentle tone he'd use with me. Ethan used to tease me that the girls were his favorite, but like Cleo and Hattie, I was just less complicated.

Less trouble in my teen years than the overgrown punk Ethan turned into.

Dearest May,

By the time you read this, I'll be dead, and you'll be grieving me, if I should be so lucky.

Please don't mourn too long. There's only so much life to live, and there's a hard limit on wasted tears, especially for a worn-out old man.

You cannot waste time. I know that better than anyone.

The truth is, while I've accomplished many wonderful things, there are other sins I'm less proud of. Many sins.

By now, perhaps you know a few.

Others, I've kept closer, hidden away from troubling you and Ethan. In his case, more than I already have.

There's nothing quite like regret, dearest Margot.

It's a corrosion on the soul, and in time, it will rust your heart shut.

You don't realize it's there at first. Not in the cruel hours ruminating, chewing endless what-ifs. But it builds.

It builds and devours until all you're left with is a pile of dust.

My life was filled with too many regrets I failed to bury.

No great success ever came without a destructive ego.

My life was a balancing act, and I'm sorry to say I rarely found a way to even the scales.

I never had the time to find the right footing. A hundred more years couldn't have helped me recover the right shoes.

You and Ethan and Cleo, you're better than me. And I'm prouder of you all than you'll ever know, but more worried than you can fathom.

It's too easy to fall down the same pit I did.

Now that I'm gone, I hope you'll find the path I tried to walk, buried on this land. I hope you'll trust me for one last scavenger hunt, just like the ones you and Hattie adored.

Find what I've left behind. Use it as a lesson.

Let it be your compass, your muse, and the first step on a journey of a thousand miles.

Let it sing the only truth that ever mattered.

Let it be my final judgment—but only after you've walked in my shoes.

Your foolish old PopPop

That's it?

I stare at the letter blankly. The words replay in my head like an unwelcome earworm, ominous and eerie.

Too many regrets.

A corrosion on the soul.

I mean, that's how it was with my mom. His own daughter disowned him after he pushed her to do the unspeakable, and all the Blackthorn billions could never make it up to her.

Ethan was crushed.

Without Hattie around and the little push I gave him, he might still be locked up in a cabin, drinking himself to death.

Ugh.

PopPop kept the truth locked up until it was too late.

That was months ago now and it had a happy ending, but it still stings.

One more bout of aching confusion added to the pile.

But this letter, this regret, it hints at something else.

Also, a lesson?

What the hell kind of lesson does he mean? What does he mean about walking in his shoes?

My mind spins with dark possibilities.

I fight the urge to start tearing the house apart, prying up floorboards and punching through walls to find—

I don't know.

The letter isn't helpful in the hints department.

For all I know, it's not a physical thing at all, and I'll just wreck this place looking for an invisible needle in a phantom haystack.

"PopPop, whyyy?" I groan out loud. "Why can you never make it easy?"

The man was tricky like that.

I think he loved putting us to work. That's why he'd spend hours walking his big house back in Portland, planting little toys and treasures for us to find.

I fold the letter back up and stare at the lake, wishing he hadn't left me a dime, much less this old eyesore turned guessing game.

But before I get too deep into my pity party, there's a scream behind me.

Sharp and high and piercing.

Holy shit!

I'm up before I even know I'm moving.

Heart pounding, adrenaline gunning through my veins.

I act on instinct, sprinting into the hall as footsteps pound the staircase going up to the next level.

Just as I reach them, there's a blur falling down the steps.

And there's only a split second.

Just enough time to throw out my arms to break the intruder's fall.

I'm expecting to be bowled over when we collide.

That happens a second later, after I've grabbed the small wrecking ball plowing into my chest.

We both go down screaming.

Oh, crap.

A short, soft grunt of pain rattles my bones as my grip tightens on the bulk that's crushing the air from my lungs.

No big, scary intruder at all. Not an adult one, at least.

A tiny *person*.

One look at the girl makes me gasp and release my hold.

She rolls off me, coughing, flopping across the floor.

She's young, still in that gangly phase before kids grow into their arms and legs, but she's almost a teenager.

I blink slowly, taking her in.

Big green eyes behind glasses that dangle from one ear, miraculously intact after crashing against my boobs.

Blonde hair falling loosely around her shoulders.

Her mouth quivers like she's on the verge of tears.

What the actual hell?

The girl looks as bewildered as I feel, just staring back at me like a startled fawn.

If I had to guess, I'd peg her age around ten, with the kind of delicate bone structure that says she'll be stunning when she's older.

But holy *shit*, what just happened?

Why is she here?

We both start scrambling to our feet like wary animals.

I extend a hand to help her up. But before she can take it,

there's a single clipped word behind me. A growl so low and vicious I'm not sure it's a word at all.

I spin around, stepping back out of instinct as I see a man who could shame my darkest intruder fantasies.

He's tall. Absurdly tall. Like fee-fi-fo-fum territory.

His jaw looks clenched so tight it's a wonder his teeth don't snap.

And he shares the girl's jade-green eyes, bright and flashing with anger.

He glares at me like he wants to murder me on the spot and it's only sheer willpower that's stopping him. His hands open and close by his sides.

His face is set to *murder*.

Ah, just my luck.

I stumble across the biggest, scowliest, and scary-hot man I've ever laid eyes on, and he wants my head speared on a pike.

God help me, I can't stop *staring*.

Broad shoulders.

Short, dark hair and sensual scruff around a mouth pinned into a violent, flat line. Cheekbones made to cut you to ribbons.

His face has a craggy look, Henry Cavill-level on the hotness meter. No baby-faced, sweet-eyed celebrity here. He's all storming testosterone and bristling muscle.

And boy is he *pissed*.

II: THIS OLD HOUSE (KANE)

What the *fuck* am I looking at?

No, more like who?

This strange woman folds her arms as she stares up at me in shock. Sophie's still behind her on the floor, giving me that kicked puppy look I know too well.

There's murder in my veins, even if the intruder looks harmless enough.

What the hell is she doing in my rental, grabbing my daughter?

The second I heard my little girl scream, I came running like any father tuned to his kid's distress call.

Now, I'm ready for war to protect her, if that's what it takes.

"Don't move," I bark at the stranger.

Her face tightens.

At least she listens, allowing me to storm past her and take Sophie's hand. I get her off the floor and shield her behind me.

"What the hell are you doing here? What did you do to

my daughter?" I demand, sizing the woman up, raking my gaze over her.

Her blue eyes flash with anger.

For a second, I realize she's young, maybe double Sophie's age.

She's also effortlessly gorgeous, even without makeup. The oversized shades perched above her eyes push her bright blonde hair back from her face.

Her jeans are faded, clinging to shapely legs and hips designed for sin.

In another life, I might keep staring, drinking her in like the tall sip she is.

But in this one, where I'm a father, this prowler has hell to pay.

"Well? Talk," I demand.

She clears her throat loudly.

"First off, I didn't do *anything* to your daughter. Oh, besides break her fall when she came tumbling down the stairs. You're welcome," she adds, rolling a shoulder.

She winces, sucking in a sharp breath.

I don't feel sorry for her.

For all I know, she's playing it up for sympathy.

My eyes flick to her pockets, her hands, just to be sure she isn't hiding a weapon. Old habits die hard.

She doesn't look that threatening, no, but appearances can be deceiving.

You never know if Little Miss Indignation will morph into Little Miss Switchblade in the blink of an eye.

"You have five seconds before I call the cops," I snarl.

Usually, people wilt at the ice in my voice when I get pissed.

I'm a big guy. I know how to throw my weight around, and my voice, too.

When you're my size, people know you don't back down from a fight. Animal instinct.

No matter how much we like to think we're higher up the monkey tree from all the other creatures, humans still respond viscerally to beasts with size and attitude.

Not that I feel very beastly after years hacking spreadsheets down to size and trying to stay awake during long video meetings with investors.

Have I lost my edge?

Right now, this woman doesn't seem to give a shit.

Interesting.

Her chin tilts up, high and sharp. She glares at me like she's trying to decide if she can run or maybe go straight for my eyes with those long, manicured nails in pastel pink.

"Whatever," she says finally. "Call them, dude. Then they can arrest you for trespassing on *my* property."

"Trespassing?" I spit the word back. "You're the one who barged in and tried to take my daughter!"

"Take your dau—" She hisses furiously and rips the shades off her head, freeing her gold-spun hair. "Are you serious right now? Like, is this some sort of fucking joke?" Her eyes flick to Soph and her face screws up. "Um. Sorry, kid."

"It's cool," Sophie says, brushing my sleeve as she steps forward. "Dad, she was just—"

"Not cool, Soph. Let me handle her."

The woman rolls her eyes, brazenly unafraid.

Fuck.

For someone who just shamelessly broke into my rental house, she's bold as hell, and I feel a grudging twitch of respect.

Doesn't change the fact that I can and *will* have her blonde ass arrested if she doesn't give me one good reason why she's here—and fast.

"Don't hold back on my account." She folds her arms, the sunglasses still dangling from her fingers. "What are you going to do? Pick a fight? Punch me through a wall? You don't scare me, Dadzilla. And you're not dialing the cops yet, either."

"Dadzilla?" I stare through her, wondering if she's mentally younger than my daughter. "Are you being funny right now?"

"No, actually. I'm being pretty serious, considering you're treating me like I'm a criminal and I own this place."

"You had your hands on my daughter," I growl.

"I was *catching* her. How many times do I have to say it?" She gives Sophie another quick glance, her brows drawn together like she's worried Soph will flip any second, trading her fear for my attitude. "Have you tried being decent? Maybe thanking me instead of threatening to have me arrested? You're welcome."

Sophie tugs my arm again, and I finally look down at her, reluctantly pulling my attention off the woman.

"Daaad," she whispers. "It's true. Everything she said. I was leaning over the railing to look down because I heard a noise, and it broke. The lady caught me."

"You're *welcome*, girlie. That's better," the woman says too brightly. "But I'll admit it was lucky I broke her fall. We scared each other out of our wits. Either way, we're both miraculously unharmed."

For the first time, I notice the large splinters on the floor. When I glance up, there's a gaping hole in the railing.

"You fell from up there?" I confirm quickly with Sophie, my eyes still fixed on the woman. "Are you okay?"

"I spun around too fast. But yeah, I'm fine, Dad."

"See?" the woman prods. "Now, maybe you won't mind explaining who *you* are and what you're doing in my house?"

"*Your* house? Come on. Take the comedy act somewhere else." I snort.

"Yes, my house. Why do you think I'm here? How do you think I got in?" She gestures around the entire room, turning a full 360. "You think I just go around breaking into people's homes and scaring their children for fun?"

"How would I know, woman? No clue who you are." I fold my arms right back, glaring at her. "I know for a fact you don't own this place. I did my research before I booked it. It's a Blackthorn property, and you don't look like Leonidas Blackthorn."

Her face changes, so fast I almost miss it.

A flicker, the flame dimming in her eyes.

A second later, it's back, though, and dialed up in intensity.

"Obviously," she clips. "I'm his granddaughter, Margot Blackthorn. He died months ago—didn't you know?"

I *was* aware, but I didn't think that she would be.

I just assumed—

Shit.

In New York, you'd have to live under a damn rock to avoid hearing the name Blackthorn. That goes double in New England, especially in this small town, Sully Bay.

The Blackthorns are one of the heavy hitters on the Eastern Seaboard, and easily the wealthiest family in Maine. Even national journals covered his death and the company's aftermath for weeks.

Now I'm face-to-face with this woman, who's claiming to be one?

Fucking doubtful.

Where's her entourage? Her staffers and bodyguards?

I give her another stone-cold look of frosted skepticism.

Designer sunglasses.

Blonde streaks in her hair, almost certainly from a high-end salon.

Black leather jacket, molded to her body, and jeans.

Casual enough, but the way it sits on her frame tells me that she chose this outfit deliberately. And that leather isn't some cheap knockoff material. It's the very expensive real deal.

Before I can grill her, she's moving.

"You know what, screw it," she mutters, brushing past me and stalking to the back door where apparently she's dumped a collection of her stuff. There's an oversized rollaway parked next to a green leather bag resting on a chair, and she starts rifling through it.

That's probably designer, too.

I don't have a problem with luxury goods, even if Daria killed the shine.

Then again, Daria wouldn't be here with a dust-covered ass and a bare face, moving like she doesn't give a shit about how she looks.

That's more appealing than my ex-wife's carefully contrived appearances and public freakouts whenever she lost a single fake eyelash.

The supposed Blackthorn woman retrieves a small wallet from her purse and stalks back to me, yanking out a card and handing it to me.

"My license," she announces. "Happy now?"

Happy isn't the right word for this fuckery, but yes. A quick scan tells me she wasn't lying about her name.

Margot Blackthorn.

The picture matches, too—and she's somehow just as damnably pretty in that awful ID photo as she is in the flesh.

Just a few years younger.

Rounder face, the same sultry hooded eyes she has now,

but without the same tiredness. I wonder if the past few years have been hard.

According to the license, I wasn't far off with her age.

She's only twenty-five.

Still not a reason to roll out the sympathy train.

"Margot," I say, looking back at her like I'm a bouncer checking her ID.

"Awesome. You can read," she says impatiently. "So do you believe me now?"

My jaw clenches.

Unless this is an excellent fake, I have no grounds *not* to believe her. And if she's a Blackthorn, then chances are she really does own the place.

Which means—

Nothing fucking good.

I scratch my head, processing.

I'm stumped.

Mrs. Griffith assured me this place was vacant since it needed a little 'fixin'' in her words. Even so, it was still pricey for a vacation rental at the edge of the offseason.

I blamed that on its size and location, just steps from an awesome lake, the whole reason we're here.

"Satisfied?" she clips again.

"Yeah," I say. She looks ready to slash my throat with the license I've just passed back to her.

"Uh-huh." She shrugs and returns her wallet to her bag. "So, now it's my turn. Why are *you* here?" she asks over her shoulder.

"We have a reservation," I say.

She turns, frowning until her pretty pink lips turn down.

It's a normal expression I shouldn't notice so much, but dammit, I do.

The lushness of her lips, the way they make her face more

sensual than sharp, balancing out the point of her nose and slight point of her chin.

Blackthorn or not, she rocks supermodel good looks.

Not at all the type of woman I expected to find in this sorry, beat-up house.

"You're renting it?" she clarifies, worry lining her face.

"From Mrs. Griffith, yeah. That was the plan."

"I mean… in this state?" She coughs.

"Obviously." My voice is dry. "I didn't know you were coming or I'd have tidied up. Mrs. Griffith said the place was all good on the inside."

She looks around again and winces at the dated wallpaper and a few long scuff marks on the wooden floor.

Possibly left by Leonidas himself. Or someone moving furniture around after his death, maybe.

Who knows.

Either way, this place isn't rental-ready. Mrs. Griffith's impression was a brutal understatement.

But we booked it. I have the emails to prove it.

"Oh. Well, I haven't spoken to Mrs. Griffith since right after the funeral. Gramps' lawyer was handling the rest," Margot says slowly, like she's piecing everything back together in her head. "I didn't realize—I just assumed you knew the lake house was only being rented as a temporary thing. Had I known the house was this rough, we would've vetoed it."

Yeah, shit.

"That makes two of us," I grumble.

Mrs. Griffith didn't say anything about temporary when I spoke with her last month. Or any of the times since.

Hell, I just picked up the keys when we rolled into town and no one said a damn word.

Fuck this day.

"Regardless, I paid good money for this place. I'm not looking to walk away just yet."

"You did?" She frowns as she looks around again.

There's no denying the 'rough' condition here after my daughter could've snapped her neck. I wouldn't have paid so much for it if it hadn't been the *only* thing available in the area.

Sully Bay stays busy deep into September with the spillover from the Bar Harbor crowd and Acadia leaf-peepers not far away. That's what I found out when I went looking for the perfect fall getaway in driving distance.

Not Vermont with its bad memories in the wake of the divorce.

I thought Maine would be safer for the kids, and for me.

I pinch my nose, trying to keep my cool even though we drove up from New York this morning and I'm *exhausted*.

The kids are already unpacked in their rooms. This was supposed to be the break we needed, the kind I promised them for *months.*

But if Margot Blackthorn really is the new owner like she seems to be, that means she's in charge.

Which should also mean she's obliged to hold up her end of the contract I signed.

My brain works.

I'm no expert on rental agreements in the state of Maine.

Still, if she makes us vacate now, after the shit day I've had, it's going to be a long haul back home in the car.

What other choice is there? Sleep in the vehicle?

Frustration curdles my breath.

"Mrs. Griffith assured me it was available." I try to be gentle, though honestly, I don't want Margot taking it up with her.

Mrs. Griffith is a nice old lady, and she's also the wrong side of seventy. Exactly the type you'd expect to deal with in a small town like this for a last-minute rental off the beaten path.

If she's behind this mistake, it was an honest one.

"I didn't tell her I was coming up. I forgot." Margot frowns. "Guess I didn't realize she was still actively renting the place out."

"And I didn't know she wasn't supposed to be."

We stare at each other in shared confusion.

"Look," I say, shaking my head. "Obviously, there's been a mix-up."

"Yes. Obviously."

"But this was the *only* place available, Miss Blackthorn. That's why I snapped it up in the first place, rather than staying down in Bar Harbor."

All she does is blink at me. The silence, weighty and damn near suffocating.

She's waiting for me to say something else incriminating or to justify our presence here. Or hell, maybe to say I'm going to pack up the kids and my bags this instant.

No chance.

If she's going to evict us, she can ask properly.

Her name means nothing to me.

Margot Blackthorn can't just sail in, snap her fingers, and throw us out when we had a legitimate agreement. And even if she can as New England royalty, I'm ready to put up a fight.

Her nostrils flare.

Her heart-shaped lips press together—dangerously seductive for a woman raking me over the coals.

She's a tall woman, even without heels, and I'm sure she's used to looking down on her problems.

Not today.

I'm not some cockroach she can step on, and neither are my kids.

I tower over her, and my eyes never flinch, locked on hers in a silent challenge.

Go ahead, rich girl. Make my day.

Make my whole damn year.

Then the front door whips open, startling everyone.

"What's going on, Dad?" Dan calls, his arms full of more bags he's pulled from the SUV I parked in the garage.

Odd that Miss Blackthorn must not have parked there or she would've realized she wasn't alone.

My boy gawks at Margot, and her eyes flick from him back to Sophie again.

Familiar scene.

Most folks do a double take when they see them, like twins are a rare species. They've grown and developed into their genders as they've gotten older, yeah, but when they were little, they were almost identical.

Now, Sophie's glasses and Daniel's broad shoulders hide their similarities, along with the hair styles, but the resemblance is unmistakable.

Um, I thought there was only one of you? I can practically hear Margot's thoughts.

"Oh." She blinks again, wiping her expression clear. The microsecond shock she allows herself fades.

"Who's she?" Dan sticks out his finger.

"Don't point, Son. Not polite."

"Excuse me for a sec. I need to make a call," Margot says awkwardly, digging in her purse for her phone.

Whatever.

If she sees trouble, she'll handle it like most billionaire's spoiled granddaughters.

She'll call someone and demand to know what the fuck is going on. Then they'll bring out the big guns and evict us.

I just hope she's not bothering Mrs. Griffith. Especially if the look in her eyes promising hot death is anything to go by.

Dan watches her strut away, bewildered as she exits through the back door to the kitchen. Then he notices the dust and splinters on Sophie's clothes from the broken railing, and his eyes widen.

"Hey, what happened to you?"

"N-nothing. I'm fine," she says defensively, pushing her glasses up her nose.

Also familiar. My girl's embarrassed at having fallen, and even more embarrassed at falling on Miss Blackthorn.

The shoes make her self-conscious as hell, and her condition saps her confidence. If she stumbles like any kid her age, she always assumes the worst.

I fucking hate it.

"How's the foot, Soph?" I glance at her right leg.

Her orthopedic shoes are huge, black, clunky things, but I'd like to think they do their job.

"I said I'm *fine,* Dad. Really." She avoids my eyes.

My lips twist sourly.

She's not limping, no, but that doesn't mean jack shit.

She's a proud girl for her age, and she'll go to great lengths to play tough, even when she's still my fragile hummingbird. At nine years old, she's becoming an expert at hiding her limp.

"Bruh!" Dan runs forward, eyeing the splintered wood on the floor before he looks up at the shattered railing. "Dude, what *happened?*"

Sophie flushes. "Nothing, derphead! This house is just old."

"Yeah, right! You fell down the stairs, didn't you? Come on, Soph, fess up!" He doesn't look worried, just impressed. "And you didn't even break anything? For real? Holy—"

"Daniel, enough," I bite off.

He flashes me a sheepish smile.

The last thing I want right now is rehashing *why* Sophie

isn't hurt to my overly curious son, so I nod and ruffle Sophie's hair until she laughs and pushes at my arm.

"Dad, *staaahp*."

"If anything hurts, you tell me, shortstack," I whisper. "We'll go get it checked out."

"Nope. All good," she insists, frowning until her glasses slip down her nose again. She's straining to see the back of her arm. "But I think my elbow might bruise."

I take her arm gently and take a look while Dan paces around.

Nothing too serious, but she's probably right.

This could've been far worse if Miss Hospitality wasn't around to break her fall.

"So, who's the lady, Dad?" Daniel wants to know. "She looked scary."

"She owns the house," Sophie tells him. "She was pretty mad that Dad's here with us."

"She wasn't expecting us, that's all," I say flatly, but I doubt they believe me.

Soph isn't kidding.

I can't shake being looked at like a chunky, unwelcome spider she wanted to stomp. Why, who knows, considering the condition of this place.

Maybe she has big plans. A demo job to lay the groundwork for a new resort or a proper rebuild down to the studs.

If there's one thing Blackthorns do, it's empire, though I thought her brother inherited the real estate biz.

"What's gonna happen next?" Sophie whispers excitedly.

"Yeah, that lady must be pissed! Soph broke her railing," Daniel says matter-of-factly.

"I did not! It was already broken, or it never would've crumbled when I pushed on it."

"I dunno," Daniel mutters. "But Dad, are you gonna tell her to get lost?"

I smile wryly.

In my kids' simple world, it's an easy solution.

I'm always the big man in charge.

They've seen me say no to people so often, they assume it's the default.

"We're talking. I'm not going to tell her anything," I say. "Just stay here with our stuff while we get this sorted. Don't go marching around until I can check this place out. It's an innocent mistake, guys, and we'll get it sorted. Obviously," I add.

"Obviously," Sophie echoes, still frowning.

I drag a hand over my face.

So much for peace and fucking quiet.

I wonder what will happen if we do leave.

We brought tents as backups—the kids love camping, even if it's a bigger risk for poor Sophie. Loving the great outdoors with a bum foot is a recipe for disaster when it comes to hiking on uneven terrain.

Still, if she had her way, she'd spend all night wandering around in flip-flops, staring at the skies with her telescope.

It's not the end of the world if we have to rough it in a nearby park for a night before we head back to New York.

But fuck.

They've been looking forward to this place, warts and all.

Honestly, so have I.

After the mess with the company—never mind the divorce, the months of stress—I haven't taken them on a real fishing trip since they were knee-high.

My boy hasn't said it, but I know he misses being on the water. Now, knowing we might get kicked to the curb, the disappointment on his face knifes me in the gut.

One more letdown.

One more cruel punt from life, which hasn't been kind lately.

"It'll be cool. I bet we go camping," he tells Sophie, tugging her toward the stairs to sit on the bottom step.

He knows it bothers her to stand for too long, so he sits to give her an excuse to sit as well.

Damn. They're such good kids.

How do I figure this out when I've kicked a nest of bees?

The past few months have been hectic.

Difficult.

This was supposed to be our hard-earned break with the world.

Even that's slipping through my fingers by the second.

A door closes and the sound of footsteps on wood announces Margot's return to the kitchen.

I wipe the brooding off my face and go to meet her near the pantry.

One look at the expression on the cold, hard, annoyingly beautiful line of her lips says my fate is sealed.

Boned.

I don't have the energy for this, especially if I don't have a leg to stand on legally and this is her property now.

I've done enough arguing for one lifetime.

I clear my throat.

"All right, I get it. Nobody needs more trouble. This is your castle and you expected to find it empty. We haven't even unpacked much yet—just give us an hour and we'll hit the road. Deal?"

Her pale brows arch.

An oddly elegant gesture, more put together than the suitcases piled haphazardly in the front room suggests.

"Where will you go? You said it yourself, Bar Harbor's booked like crazy this time of year."

"There's always somewhere. It's not your problem." I shrug.

"But... do you even live in Maine?"

"New York, Scarsdale. Long drive back, but I'm sure we can crash somewhere."

Her face drops.

"Sounds pretty rough with kids." Her tone isn't unsympathetic.

The empathy catches me off guard.

Do we really have a chance?

I fully expected the ice princess treatment until the second we rolled down the driveway, and probably a parting 'fuck you' for treading on her little kingdom.

"We'll manage," I say gruffly.

Her frown deepens. "There's nowhere else... You said it yourself. How long did it take you to get here?"

"Eight or nine hours with a couple stops. Got a real early start."

"Oh, crap." She sucks her bottom lip.

Like I need a reminder.

"What else do you suggest, lady? I'm offering to get out of your hair." I'm losing my patience.

"Dad, can we stay?" Dan calls impatiently from the other room.

I look back just as I hear Sophie smack him.

Margot leans against the wall, her arms folded, her face lost in contemplation.

"Why not," she says with a sigh. "I know how hard it can be to find rentals in these parts, especially in the fall. This place is massive anyway. I won't use all four bedrooms."

"So we can stay?" Dan whoops from the great room.

"Weren't you listening? We can stay!" This time, it's Sophie.

She claps her hand over her mouth like she's shocked at the sound of her own voice.

I am, too.

It's not often she gets this worked up, especially in front of a stranger.

That tells me this place means more to her than I realized, and it slams my heart like a brick.

"You can stay," Margot confirms. "As long as you don't mind sharing a room and the kitchen."

"That's very generous—" I start, but the kids leap up from where they're sitting on the stairs and sprint for the back door.

Dan flings it open until it bangs against the doorstopper.

He holds it open for Sophie, and they're already gone before I can tell them to slow down and be careful.

Lovely.

"That won't happen again," I promise quickly. "If I can, I'll patch up a few things around here."

"No, don't put yourself out. They're nice kids," she says, watching them as they go bounding across the lawn to the lake. "Sophie and…?"

"Daniel. Dan for short."

"They look like twins!"

"They are."

She shrugs and pushes off from the wall.

"Well, feel free to settle in and unpack. I don't need more than a room, really."

"Thank you," I say cautiously.

This is fucking new.

Sharing our vacation rental with a strange woman who owns the place wasn't the plan, but it's sure as hell better than being turned out with nowhere to go at the last minute. The place is huge, and as long as it's safer than that staircase, we can handle a little extra company.

"You're sure about this, Miss Blackthorn?"

"Totally." Margot waves a hand. "How could I disappoint them? I remember how excited I'd get when I was that age.

Anyway, I'm just here for work and to check in on the property. I'll do a full walk-through to make sure there are no other hazards lurking around."

Fine.

Time to make the best of this crisis-averted situation. I stick out my hand.

"Thank you. I mean that sincerely. I'm Kane Saint."

"Saint?" She snorts with amusement. "I like Dadzilla better."

My brows pull down.

That makes one of us.

After a second's hesitation, she slips her fingers into mine.

Slim, smooth hands, slightly cool to the touch.

My blood sparks at her touch. I drop her hand like she's four hundred degrees.

"That's my name. Even if I'm more of a sinner at heart," I say flatly.

She laughs again, blushing.

I wish I were joking.

"Sorry. I didn't mean anything by it. But your name sounds familiar."

"I get that a lot." I look away, hoping she doesn't connect my name to my career. Hell, *any* of them.

She cocks her head slightly, staring more intently than before.

"I dunno. I feel like I know you from somewhere. It'll come to me, though."

I hope it doesn't.

If I have my way, she'll never figure it out.

I came here to keep a low profile.

I've had enough fame and bullshit pity I don't deserve for one lifetime.

"Do you have a favorite room? We'll give you top choice,

of course," I say.

The kids have already picked theirs, but they can move if we need to reshuffle.

"Nah." She picks up one of her suitcases with a small groan.

"Let me." But the second I move forward to help, she pierces me with a protective glare.

"I've got it. You're a paying guest, not a bellhop."

"Yeah." I back up a step.

Okay. So this woman wants little to do with us besides sleeping under one roof.

Fine, that's her right.

No skin off my nose.

Though it might make sharing this house awkward. On the other hand, awkward can be managed if we're just sleeping here and having a few meals.

"I'll just take whatever's free. No worries," she says once she's partway up the stairs, looking like she'll barely make it to the top.

Another section of the railing bends when she lays her hand on it, and I grit my teeth.

"Careful. Tomorrow, I'll get that hammered back into place and something over the gap," I tell her. "And I'll do my own sweep through the house, if you don't mind. Looks like nobody's been living here for some time."

"They haven't," she agrees. "PopPop wasn't exactly coming around the last few years of his life, and we didn't rent it out until recently. We've had a few people checking in and handling maintenance, but I guess they missed a few things. Sorry again for the crappy condition."

She gives the railing a good shake to test it and glances over her shoulder at me. The entire structure wobbles like a licorice rope.

"Like I said, I'll deal with it."

Her shades are back on top of her head, threatening to fall down her nose. "No need. I'll have someone drop by soon and patch it up."

"Why bother? That could take days and I'm here."

"*Technically,* you're a tenant, and I'm the landlord. And I've already put you guys in danger." She's reached the landing now, and she rolls her shoulders as she sets the bag down. What does she have in there, bricks? "That makes it my responsibility. My house, my rules, Dadzilla."

I snort.

Stubborn as hell and twice as infuriating.

"I mean it," she calls.

Sure, she does.

Only, by the time she brings some handyman in, even if they're local, I could've had this mess fixed.

Also, I'm pretty sure I saw a toolshed out back. Might not even have to go into town for supplies if there's any surplus equipment in there.

That also reminds me to quit glowering and check on the kids.

Maybe I'll stick my head in the old shed, too, assuming it isn't locked, just to scope it out.

I head outside through the back and cross the large green lawn to the lake, following their excited yelps down the beach. They're already skipping rocks on the lake.

When I glance up at the house, a curtain swishes over one of the second-floor windows.

Margot's face disappears from view in a puff of beige, a split second ahead of her hand, making a pointed gesture.

I try not to grin, especially in front of the kids.

Was she seriously flipping me off?

I can't believe my luck, and just when it seemed like it was turning around.

This is going to be a special kind of torture.

III: HAPPY HOUSEWARMING (MARGOT)

What a freaking *day.*

I spend the evening holed up in my room, or what counts as my room now.

I haven't had much time to make it mine yet. Little Sophie took the old room I used to claim when I'd come here as a kid, and the décor in this barely used guest room is way too beige.

With an old family photo on the desk I swiped from downstairs and lights strung around the mirror on the wall, it's finally a bit brighter.

I make a mental note to buy some furniture ASAP on the off chance I decide to keep this place. Maybe even if I don't.

A splash of color never hurt anyone.

But PopPop liked his old-world rustic charm. He was onto the organic earthy look before it ever became a modern trend.

Thankfully, there's a desk in the corner.

I throw myself into the office chair in front of it, one leg tucked under my rear. Gramps' cryptic letter sits off to one side like a taunting demon.

Or is that my tablet tonight?

It's perched in front of me, the screen blank. With my stylus in hand, I halfheartedly try to finish up my latest shoe design with a little AI-assisted variation.

None of the two dozen options it spits out feel right.

It's not vibing.

And I'm not relaxed, my anxiety soaring as my creative spark wimps out.

Before, I hoped I'd get to chill by coming up here.

Nope!

Below, there's a steady beat, like someone's doing a drum solo, banging away like their life depends on it.

The little boy, maybe.

Dan.

He looked like the kid musician type. All gangly preteen and fresh-faced mischief in his eyes. Athletic, too, which probably means he's into drums when his school band made him choose an instrument.

Back when I was in high school band, the rowdy boys into sports always picked the biggest noisemakers. Drums, trumpets, saxophones, you name it.

I'd be surprised if the little girl was into something so obnoxious.

At least the family's all settled in, I guess.

Even if their dad *could* use an attitude transplant or three.

Ugh, Kane.

This must be the tenth time I've thought of him since I shut myself away.

The expression on his face when he thought I was kidnapping his daughter...

So ridiculous.

Total overreaction.

How is that a reasonable assumption when you see a strange woman helping your kid off the floor?

Then again, what do I know about parenting?

But didn't he *see* the splintered wood?

The obvious fact that his daughter fell?

Nah.

Dadzilla just *had* to jump to conclusions, right off the cliff.

He had to assume the worst, thinking I was some wild-eyed gremlin coming to carry his little girl off to my gingerbread house in the woods.

Who even thinks like that?

Is there something about me that seems threatening?

Gawd.

Also, this whole situation sucks more because he's hot.

And why not?

Normal, well-adjusted guys are often so mid. Probably because they're confident enough to avoid becoming cyclones of testosterone who treat gym like church.

I stare into empty space, scowling at his hotness.

If he could just be the bastard offspring of a garden gnome and a gargoyle, I wouldn't dislike him so much. You can understand why someone so ugly might have a chip on their shoulder.

But Kane has the looks that set your life to easy mode—and that makes his bristling rudeness far less acceptable.

There was something jarring about those jade-green eyes, too.

Almost like he could see right through me.

Obviously, he couldn't if he thought I'd ever lay a hand on his sweet girl.

Stupid overgrown ego.

Still, those mile-wide shoulders stick in my mind. I hate how tall he is, how easily he can look down on—well, everyone.

The man is a freak of nature. He must've been a beast at

some sport when he was young, back before his well-connected daddy handed him his quant finance job.

Just a wild guess.

And I know, I should talk.

Doesn't change the fact that I'm dealing with a giant daddy's boy who's used to getting his way. All self-propelled, pure entitlement.

Although when he figured out he was the intruder in my home, he backed down, didn't he?

Surprise.

That, plus the sad, worried look on the kids' faces was what convinced me to let them stay. I'm not in the habit of crashing with strangers.

And I'm still not sure if I made the right call.

At least it saves me a potential legal flap, though. After I saw the rates Mrs. Griffith was charging, he had every right to be pissed.

Maybe I don't like him, but the man has kids.

Why should a goofy mix-up ruin their family vacation?

I glance at the photo on the desk and sigh.

PopPop and his whole 'summer crew'—Ethan, Cleo, Hattie, and yours truly. Probably about twelve years ago.

We spent the day hiking the woods, wandering overgrown trails just a few miles from the lake. Ethan tried to scare us with bigfoot stories until PopPop put an end to it.

I'll never forget the way my grandfather snuck up on him and growled like a cave bear.

The shock knocked the cigarette Ethan shouldn't have even had right out of his mouth.

I catch myself laughing and shake my head.

This house is a time capsule. Made for memories, not living in the present.

Besides, it's not like having the Saints here will be a big problem.

It's a massive place.

I have a feeling they'll be out during the day plenty, leaving me lots of space and quiet to poke around.

Honestly, the fact that Dadzilla wasn't livid over the safety tells me a lot.

If it was me, and I'd paid Mrs. Griffith's princely sum, only to wind up with my daughter falling, I'd be furious.

I'm still embarrassed.

If I knew this place had deteriorated so much in the years since our family trips ended, I'd have had contractors lined up. And I would've politely told our kind local property manager to pull the place off the market.

It's crazy the Saint-devil didn't threaten to sue.

Huge relief, really.

And drumming aside, his kids don't seem like they'll be too awful.

I push back from the desk with a deflated sigh and find my phone, pulling up Jackie Wilkes' contact. It's pretty late for the lawyer to be at the office, but we pay her too much not to be available on short notice.

I can't imagine her at home. She's a legal killing machine who lives and breathes documents.

Exactly the kind of woman my grandfather would leave in charge of his estate.

"Miss Blackthorn," she greets me. Her voice is brisk and efficient, no hint of any irritation at calling past eight o'clock. "What can I do you for?"

"I made it to the lake house," I say, neglecting to mention my guests. "And I've read the letter."

"Excellent. I was going to call you in a few days to make sure you had."

Yep. Detailed to a fault.

"But I have a few questions... He said there's something

hidden here to find? I'm not sure how to take that, but I wondered if you know anything else about it?"

"Did he? Can you be more specific?"

I wince, remembering the letter was for my eyes only. That probably means Leonidas Blackthorn left no other hints with his lawyer.

"Wish I could. It didn't really say. Not explicitly, anyway." I roll my eyes, but a wave of fondness overwhelms me. PopPop had his flaws, but I still love him. "He talked a lot about regrets and he called it his 'greatest truth.'"

"Curious," Jackie says. "Well, I have a recent inventory of the house's contents at the time of his death, and regular updates from the last few months, courtesy of Holden Verity. I can send them over, but I've gone through the lists myself. I doubt you'll find anything too useful there."

Damn.

If it made Jackie Wilkes yawn, there's zero chance I'll find anything helpful.

"I thought you might have a guess what he meant?"

Silence.

I'm sure she's secretly laughing at me. This woman is so not the guessing type.

"I'm afraid I can't speculate, Miss Blackthorn." Her voice softens. "You know your grandfather was notoriously private with family affairs. He didn't provide me with any long explanations—not in your brother's case and not in yours. My only role ends with executing his last wishes. If I could read his mind, so much would be less complicated."

Believe me, *I know.*

But it doesn't answer my questions, and they gnaw at my belly.

Not her fault, though.

So I just doodle my signature in the corner of my shoe design.

"I get it, just thought I'd check. Thanks, Jackie."

"Certainly. Is there anything else I can help with?"

Unless she has a time machine so I can ask my grandfather what the hell he meant, no. I shake my head, even though she can't see me, and lean back in my chair.

I think the drumming downstairs has stopped.

"No, but thanks again. I'll let you know if anything else comes up."

"Understood." Jackie hesitates, then adds, uncharacteristically, "Good luck with the hunt, Miss Blackthorn. I sincerely hope you enjoy your stay. He loved the old house passionately."

"Yes, he did. Thanks," I mutter, trying not to tear up.

I disconnect and slump down in my seat, boneless.

After everything Ethan went through to inherit Blackthorn Holdings, he's the only one who could understand what I'm feeling.

It must be bad when I start wishing my dumb brother was here.

If only to help me survive Gramps' last game, without the Saints complicating everything.

* * *

THE OLD HOUSE might be worn down, but it's surprisingly noise resistant.

When I wake up in the morning, eye mask still on, I discover that even though I forgot my earbuds, I slept pretty well.

Soft gold sunlight streams through a gap in the curtains.

My body has that warm, pleasant feel after a deep sleep. Given how I've slept recently, it's probably overdue.

Just weird that it hit here of all places.

I swing my feet out of bed and listen.

Nothing.

The only sign I'm not alone in the house is the tantalizing scent drifting through my closed door.

My stomach rumbles. I realize I skipped out on dinner yesterday between getting unpacked and everything sorted after so much drama.

First thing's first—I need to get showered and dressed.

No way am I walking in on family breakfast time before I'm ready to face the day. Plus, my cami and tap-pants pjs don't scream family-friendly.

Sticking my head out of the room, I make a dash for the bathroom across the hall and lock the door behind me.

It hasn't changed much since childhood, everything's charmingly old-fashioned and in good shape. The bathrooms might be a decent selling point for the house later.

They're not bad, even with the shower sputtering with disuse before it stays on hot. By the time I emerge, I feel like I've had a spa routine.

I tie my wet hair back and head down, carefully running my hand along the railing.

The first thing I notice is that it doesn't try to throw me to an early death today.

Huh.

Actually, it's weirdly sturdy, not bending at all.

I give it a good push to test it, just like I did yesterday. It doesn't budge.

I grit my teeth, noticing the gap torn out of the railing is gone too. There's fresh, unstained wood there, smooth and nailed into place.

So.

Mr. Saintly Dadzilla thinks he can sneak around behind my back to play fix it after I point-blank forbid it.

I ignore the tiny spark of relief that no one's at risk of falling anymore.

There's no denying he solved this problem faster than anyone else, but—

Ugh.

I take a few seconds to swallow my pride before I face them.

The kitchen is bright and cheery, barely used since the last big renovation. It's the main room PopPop made a point to update over a decade ago.

Unlike the bathroom, it's sleek and modernish. U-shaped marble counters around a huge family table with a hint of Tuscan colors, the style in vogue well over a decade ago.

The twins are busy hauling plates of food to the table, enough to feed a small army, and there are four places laid out.

Four?

Oh, boy.

My stomach lurches.

I don't let myself think about what that means.

The way our family mealtimes at home always came with some agenda in my parents' house, especially as Ethan and I got older.

"Hi." The boy looks up cheerfully. "I'm Dan, remember?" He points at his sister. "That's Sophie. You saved her yesterday."

I laugh and shake my head.

"I do remember. And that's a little dramatic, kiddo, but thanks."

Unable to help myself, my eyes flick from their smiling faces to where Kane huddles over the stove. By the looks of it, he's wrapping up his feast prep.

He's dressed casually in a hoodie that might be a size too small. The fabric stretches across those massive shoulders, and when Dan mentions me saving Sophie's life, he sends the kid an annoyed glance.

Guess he still doesn't like me.

Fine and dandy, it's mutual.

But he turns, holding a frying pan with sizzling bacon, and nods at the table.

"Have a seat," he says. "You like bacon?"

"There's scrambled eggs too. Dad makes the best with the butter—oh, and toast!" Dan announces.

Sophie pulls a jar of Nutella from a bag on the counter and plunks it down on the table.

This is the most indulgent, classic American breakfast I've seen in ages.

Possibly the first time I've seen one outside a sitcom. Definitely not something I'm used to.

If I even bother with breakfast these days, it's fast and healthy ninety percent of the time. Usually a grab-and-go yogurt parfait with chia seeds or an açai bowl or maybe just a banana on the way to getting on with my day.

I don't skimp on coffee, though.

Life would suck without caffeine.

Like he can hear my thoughts, Kane pushes a button on a small sleek-looking coffee machine off to the side. It's too new for this house, so it must be something he brought, and that convinces me to slide into my seat.

"Pancakes?" Daniel offers. He's a miniature version of his dad, although he's mastered the art of smiling. "We have maple syrup, bananas, and blueberries."

"And Nutella," Sophie chimes in. Her eyes are big behind her glasses as she looks at me shyly, then away again. Adorable.

"Berries and a little Nutella sound good," I decide. Both their faces light up, and I know I've said the right thing. "Did anyone else notice the elves who fixed the stairs overnight?"

Kane snorts as he brings the bacon over and takes the

final remaining seat. His sharp green eyes land on me like swords.

"I wasn't about to risk another accident. Those old stairs are steep. Somebody could break their neck if they're not careful."

"Chill, Dadzilla. I said I was going to call someone." I grip my butter knife tighter than necessary.

The kids giggle.

"No need. I saved you the trouble." He looks away pointedly. "I'll replace the burned-out bulbs, too, and start sanding down some splinters on the old dock. I noticed it's a little rough this morning, but it has good bones."

"It needs cleaning—that algae, yuck!" Dan wrinkles his nose. "It's all covered in black stuff. It got all over my hands yesterday."

"And your jeans," Kane says with weary patience, but he sends Daniel a wink that makes the boy smile. "Looks like good weather to make it shine. Think I could get a little help?"

"You're not my maintenance guy, Mr. Saint," I remind him.

He glances at me quickly, then looks away before I can read any layered meaning behind that broody expression.

"And you can stop fussing. Consider it a perk of keeping us around," he says firmly.

But I can hear what he doesn't say. *Let's not argue in front of the kids.*

Fine, idiot.

"Yeah, Dad, I'll help," Dan says. "Do you wanna start after breakfast?"

"Isn't there something else you need to do first?"

"Huh? Like what?" The boy tries to sound innocent, and he isn't fooling anyone.

I can't help smiling, remembering when Ethan would do the same thing.

"You can come help out *after* you've finished your homework, little man. You promised me you'd start this school year strong before we left, and I'm holding you to it." Kane gives him a knowing look.

"I'll help you with math," Sophie volunteers. "It'll go way faster."

It's hard not to laugh at the way the boy scowls. So familiar.

Not that my brother was ever much help with homework.

Certainly not when he turned into a teenage punk, but when it came to family drama and friend group fights, he always had my back.

"Aw, do we have to do it now?" Daniel asks.

"Yes, Bud. The sooner you hit the books, the sooner you can hit the docks, and the faster we can all hit the water. Get moving and we might make it out on the lake today."

Sophie's face lights up.

The difference is stark.

When she forgets to be shy, she's a pretty girl, radiating light. I bet she'll be gorgeous when she's older.

"You promise, Dad?" she asks excitedly. "Can I take my telescope? The little one?"

"Only if you let me make sure you've got the solar filter on first. I'm not letting you burn your eyes out staring at the sun," Kane says, frowning as he crumbles more bacon on his pancakes.

"Yeah, I know!" Sophie chirps. "I actually just want to look at the scenery. No sky until after dark."

"Well, bring it. As long as you promise not to look near the sun, Soph."

"I'll be like a pirate queen," Sophie says, turning to me. "What about you?"

My heart skips a beat.

"What about me?" I pause, forkful of food halfway to my mouth.

"Are you like the landlord lady?"

"Yes, something like that," I say awkwardly, determined not to look at Kane. "I mean, it's not my real job."

"What's your real job?" Dan demands.

For a second, I hesitate. But they're just kids.

Harmless, I hope.

"I design shoes," I tell them. "It's a work in progress, I mean, but that's what I'd like to do."

The interest in Dan's face drains away, but Sophie looks at me in awe. "Shoes? You design *shoes*?" she whispers with reverence, like she can't imagine anything cooler. She looks under the table at my feet. "Like, the kinda shoes you're wearing? You have people walking around with your shoes?"

I laugh.

"Are there any other kind? Mine aren't good enough to be worn just yet, but a girl can dream. I can show you some designs, if you want. Do you like shoes?"

Her cheeks flush.

"Love them, but I don't really get a chance to—aw, never mind," she mutters.

When I look over, Kane watches with a hawkish intensity.

Perfect segue to the question I've been wanting to ask since we met.

"What about you, Mr. Saint? What do *you* do?"

His gaze slides over my face.

I get the impression he's sizing me up again, just like yesterday, and my shoulders tense.

"Nothing as glamorous as shoes," he says, nodding at Sophie, who's still watching me.

"No, but come on. Is it top secret or what?" I joke.

He sits back and shrugs, stuffing a forkful of food into his mouth, offering nothing.

Um, okay.

When my gaze intensifies, he finally says, "I exited a start-up recently. Still planning my next move. Looking for my next big headache, I guess."

Start-up, huh?

That is a surprise.

He's a certified dick, but he doesn't exactly strike me as the dorky tech bro type with their head in the clouds—or just their bank account.

That's also not much of an answer.

I want to poke him, but before I can fire off more questions, there's a knock at the door.

"I'll get it." Kane levers up from his chair, but I wave a hand.

"No way. You enjoy your breakfast. It's my house, remember?"

It's a relief to get away from the table, even if I'm not sure why.

Maybe because it felt so warm with the kids making easy conversation. A far cry from the stuffy, formal dinners I had at my parents' table as a kid.

They make it too easy to feel like more than an awkward stranger crashing their family getaway.

Thank God for the adorable kiddos, really.

Sitting next to Kane Saint feels jarring enough. If it was just him, I'm not sure I could stand sharing the house.

Still, I find myself breathing easier as I walk to the front door and turn the bolt.

I blink dumbly at the unfamiliar couple waiting outside.

They're older and kind of worn-looking, all wrinkles and leathery tans that must come from years in the harsh sun. I'd guess they're in their late forties or fifties, squarely middle age.

The woman immediately sticks out her hand and cracks a smile too large for her face.

Her blonde hair looks unnaturally bleached, but there's a healthy earthy vibe to her greeting that puts me more at ease.

"Hi, there! Are you the new owner?" Her smile looks bone-white next to the tan of her face and the sharp lines around her eyes. "I saw the car parked out front and I couldn't help dropping by to say hello."

I accept her handshake.

"Close enough. Margot Blackthorn, nice to meet you," I say. "I'm Leonidas' granddaughter, actually."

"Oh, poor Leon." The woman makes a sympathetic face.

Leon? I blink at her.

I've never heard anyone call him that.

"It was such a shame to hear about his passing. I'm Viola Babin, and this is my husband, Joseph. We own the big old blueberry farm next door."

Ohhh.

I do have vague memories of the distant property, backing up to a farm many acres away, but I hadn't given it much thought until now. There's a lot of natural privacy around here from thick tufts of forest.

As kids, we spent so much time on the water or tromping through Acadia that we never strayed too far off PopPop's land and onto anyone else's.

"Neighbors, that's nice. Glad to meet you," I say. "How can I help you? Did you know my grandfather?"

"Oh, we just came by to introduce ourselves and see how you're settling in. Lord knows this old place sat vacant for too long, and Sully Bay doesn't get a lot of new faces, even seasonal ones." Viola's rattling laugh clashes with her tired cheeks and no-nonsense faded denim jacket. "And yes, Leon was such a good neighbor to us. So humble for being stinkin' rich and famous."

I wonder if my strained smile says I'm a little weirded out.

I've never heard anyone call my grandfather Leon in his life. It's not even a proper nickname like Leo.

But... I *can* imagine him spending time with this denim-clad couple, inviting them in for cider on the back porch or maybe that Greek ouzo he loved.

He didn't mind reminiscing about quiet country life, away from the buzz of business in the cities. When my grandmother was still alive, they might've had a very active social life here once.

The thought makes me ache, like there are parts of PopPop I never truly knew. Especially the days when Grandma was around, before I was born.

"So, are you moving in?" Viola asks, undaunted by my weird expression.

"Not yet. Right now, I'm just kind of feeling it out. I came up from Portland to look the property over since it's mine now," I say. "The place needs some work. I'm sure you've noticed."

Her husband nods briskly, a quiet lump of a man with a bushy mustache. He looks like he's been dropped from the French countryside into northern Maine, but he carries himself like a lifelong Mainer from the sticks.

"I'll be heading home in a few weeks or so," I say.

Living here permanently was never the plan.

"Just in time to beat the cold," Joseph huffs agreeably.

"Well, if you need anything—anything at all—you let us know." Viola glances at her husband, who flashes the same wide smile like he's on a delay. "We'd be happy to lend you a hand with clearing brush, raking leaves, patching up buildings, you name it. Wouldn't we, Joe?"

"Sure would," he says flatly.

Huh.

I fight the urge to squint at them.

Why does this feel oddly rehearsed? Like they've practiced their lines a few times before showing up here.

But why? If they knew PopPop, then they should be past the weird intimidation with the Blackthorn name some people feel.

I want to shake myself.

This is old habit, assuming the worst about everyone.

Hattie calls me out for it all the time. She's one of those impossibly upbeat, sunny people who only see the good in the world.

"Thanks, I'll do that," I lie.

Joseph grins at me again, and I can't help forcing a smile back.

"Actually, Miss Margot, we did come here with a little agenda, if you want to know the truth." He clears his throat. "If you're not thinking about moving right in, we wondered… any chance you're selling?"

I wait for an emotional kick that never comes.

"Maybe," I say quietly. "Honestly, I don't know what I'm planning yet. I just got here yesterday. There's been a ton to sort out with Granddad's estate the past year and I'm taking a good look around."

"Of course, ma'am. It's all so new and there's a lot on your plate." Joseph nods sympathetically. "Anyhoo, if you decide the old place is too much and you want to unload it, we'd be very interested."

"For the land!" Viola interjects. "Not the house or the other buildings. We wouldn't bother you with any fixes—it would be a simple teardown job. Makes it quick and easy for you."

Tearing down the lake house?

There's that delayed gut punch.

In theory, it makes total sense, but the sentimental value finally hits.

This place belonged to PopPop and I think his ghost still visits.

No, I haven't been here much since I was a kid. Whatever ties I had earlier in life were dissolved.

But imagining everything gone?

The house erased and the path going down to the lake overgrown with blueberry fields?

That's heavy.

"I haven't made up my mind," I tell them. "But if it goes that way, if I decide to sell, you'll be the first ones I'll call."

"That would be amazing! Thank you," Viola gushes. She bends down, picking up an enormous basket behind her I hadn't noticed. It's filled with packaged blueberries and jars of jam. "Here ya go, sweetie! And welcome to Sully Bay."

Holy crap.

The basket nearly breaks my arm.

There are so many blueberry goods tucked in here they're almost overflowing, straining the basket itself.

I stagger backward and set the basket down in the house. I watch them climb into an old, beat-up pickup truck to leave as I shake my arm to limber up.

How weird.

I don't even know why meeting them feels a little freaky, but it was.

They were just—a bit too friendly?

Then again, I'm a New York girl at heart.

Even Portland feels small-town friendly with its cozy old cobblestone streets and gaggles of happy seasonal tourists.

I've spent a lot of time in the Big Apple and later on in places like Scottsdale, where people keep their distance and posture a lot.

They don't do small talk.

They aren't *neighborly*, not by nature.

This is country living as an adult, I suppose.

Having people pop in with gift baskets and random offers to help with housework.

That can't be a bad thing, I guess.

The basket digs into my chest the second I hoist it up again with a grunt. I balance it on my knee as I twist around to kick the door shut behind me.

The weight of the heaping basket eases, and I spin around so I can march it into the kitchen.

But I only take two steps before I collide with a very hard, very firm, very *present* wall.

Okay.

Not what I expected.

Kane grabs the basket as I bounce off his chest with a slight *oof*.

His other hand flies out to take my elbow, helping steady me.

The next second, he's releasing me again, his face totally blank as he holds that ridiculous pile of blueberries like it's fresh laundry.

Show-off. Him and his big stupid arms.

Enormous, Hercules arms.

I try not to notice, but it's like staring at the sky and pretending the sun isn't there.

Who else has biceps big enough to threaten popping out of that oversized hoodie, anyway?

And his eyes, holy—

For a hot second, they drill through me.

They're so effing *green*.

I didn't know human eyes could rival the forest, but here we are.

There's still something familiar about his face, too.

Like I've seen it before.

The hard lines, the way he goes from stormy to soft as cotton candy for his kids, the square jaw that looks like it could break the fist of anyone stupid enough to throw a punch.

He's imposing in the way guys get when they've spent too much time working out and posing behind an Instagram filter.

Not that he strikes me as the model type, or even the type to want attention.

I just can't figure him out and it's infuriating.

Behind him, the kids zoom upstairs for their homework.

If it was me, I'd be dragging my feet and sulking, but they're laughing now. Dan takes Sophie's arm and drags her up faster.

I notice the chunky shoes she's still wearing in the house while her brother goes around in his socks.

I didn't pick up on them yesterday. She moves like she's used to them on her skinny legs.

And I wonder if they're the reason she shut down earlier.

I look back at Kane, who's still staring at me. His dark brows draw together and his mouth slashes into a pointed frown.

"Thanks, but I've got it," I say, gesturing to the basket. "Go enjoy your breakfast. Clean up. Whatever."

He doesn't let go.

Asshat.

"Dude," I hiss. "I've got it. Back off."

When he won't relent and turns his back instead, I roll my eyes and follow him into the kitchen.

As tempting as it is, a scuffle in the hall would be undignified and possibly dangerous with such a heavy basket. I think he knows it, too.

I also think he knows I *will* fight him on this.

I don't care if he fed me breakfast.

He sets the basket down on the counter and doesn't look at me, grabbing a roll of paper towels instead.

"I know your ears work. I told you to let me handle the blueberries," I bite off. "You know, just like I told you not to fix the railing."

"You know, you don't have to do much to this house if you're selling," Kane says from the stove, where he's cleaning up the grease from cooking.

"Apart from how it's falling down around us, you mean?"

"I can fix it."

"What, you're a builder and a plumber and electrician?" I huff loudly.

He shoots me a tired look.

"If there's anything I can't do, I'll let you know. But I might as well stay busy while we're here and the kids are occupied."

So he can't sit still.

Why am I not surprised?

I'm curious, though, and I lean on the counter as I watch him, against my better instincts. The muscles in his back flex deliciously as he scrubs.

Damn him.

"What *do* you do?"

"Huh?"

"Your job. What do you do besides stomp around, acting all saintly? I know you come by it honestly with the name, but you must work."

His shoulders stiffen.

"I told you, I'm between jobs right now. All the more reason to keep busy, and there's a lot I can do around here."

For a second I just stare at him.

I'm trying to decide if I should be glad I have a free handyman or yell at him for being so mute and walled off.

"But you'll still need supplies."

"There are plenty of tools around in the shed. I went poking around when I got up and fixed the railing." He stops and turns, bracing his hands on the edge of the stove behind him, big and imposing even in this large space. "Look, I can handle the basics. Tell me that railing wasn't tighter than a drum."

I can't. But I glare at him.

"And I overheard you've got interested buyers. Where's the harm in giving you a head start on polishing this place up?"

"You were eavesdropping?"

"Yeah." His face has no shame. So annoying. "No matter what you decide, the fewer issues here, the better."

He's not wrong.

I *hate* that he has a point.

Yes, I could hire a few guys to come here and help out. It's not like I don't have the money. But if I'm being offered free repairs, what kind of idiot would I be to turn him down?

"You really take the Saint thing seriously, don't you?" I feel a slight thrill of victory as he snorts and rolls his eyes.

If he wants to keep barging into my life, I'm going to annoy the crap out of him.

"Brilliant, Miss Manners. I've never heard that shit before."

"What else do you do? Help schoolkids cross the street? Rescue kittens stuck up trees?" I stack a few plates from the table to lend him a hand. Impressively, the dishes were cleaned, nothing but crumbs left behind.

"You say that like it's a bad thing. Are you always this damn judgmental over a guy helping out?"

Ouch, somebody's sensitive.

"Only when a guy gets all secretive and gives me a good reason to figure him out." Reaching past him, I open the dishwasher. Thankfully, it was barely used when the house was abandoned and still works. As I load it, I feel him eyeing me with pure ice. "What? I just think it's important to know the details about your renters."

"Technically, I'm renting from Mrs. Griffith."

"And technically, she works for me. She's also the reason we're in this mess. But I bet you know technicalities get you nowhere."

He almost smiles.

Almost.

Probably a trick of the light.

The next second, he's right back to resting scowlyface.

"And what about you?" he asks. "Would you stop to save a kitten if you saw it on your way to drop a few thousand on designer shoes?"

"Well, yeah! I'm not a monster. I'd call the fire department. You seriously think I could climb a tree in heels?" I hold out my leg, shaking my bare foot.

His gaze scorches my flesh for a frenzied second before he looks away, muttering under his breath.

"Yeah," he growls. "That's exactly what I thought. I wasn't about to let you break your neck, stumbling around with forty pounds of blueberries. For some reason, you're pissed I didn't leave you to your fate."

God.

How can he be so grouchy after eating half his weight in bacon?

But maybe it's a crude defense mechanism.

It's just him and the kids here, I notice.

No wife.

Curious.

Is she just too busy girlbossing it up somewhere else or is there another reason she's MIA?

Either way, I do not *want* to give Kane Saint free rein to do whatever he wants in this house. Even if it helps me.

Especially if it helps me.

I'd take the broken bones by blueberry mishap over feeling like I owe this man *anything.*

"If you're looking at repairs that would cost a thousand bucks, just run it past me first, okay?" I tap my foot impatiently, waiting.

He stares at me for a long second.

"Okay. Assuming you're done throwing hissy fits over the basics."

Dick.

I hate the term 'hissy fit.'

Like I'm some hysterical creature who can't check her inner bitch before it eats someone's face.

If only I could melt him through the floor with a glare.

"Yeah, fine. I'm going to trust you to live up to your name and respect my property, Saint."

"Fair enough," he says unexpectedly, wiping down the table.

I stare at the bulging basket of blueberries, wondering what the hell I'm going to do with them.

Make twenty blueberry pies?

It's not a terrible idea.

I love baking and it's the only thing in the kitchen I'm any good at, so this would be a great excuse to sharpen my skills.

Kane catches my eye again as he works around me silently.

I chew my lip, doing my best not to watch him too long.

I'll admit, if you look past the good looks and rancid attitude, there might be a semi-decent human underneath.

My mind drift's back to PopPop's letter and whatever he

hid in this house. Only, now it feels like I have more than family secrets to find.

What's Kane Saint hiding?

Why does he need to occupy every waking second so badly?

What kind of demons is he trying to tame?

IV: HOME SWEET HELL (KANE)

*T*oo much goddamned bacon.

I've got the meat sweats in spades, but that's not the only reason I'm burning up on a crisp autumn morning like this.

Only our first morning here, and while the kids are inside doing their homework, I'm out here scrubbing the hell out of this dock, erasing years of grime and mildew. I want to see how the boards look underneath.

It's a pleasant autumn morning, the sun still as warm as a summer's kiss but the air cool. The leaves are unholy, tinged with every shade of red, and the reflections on the water make me feel like I've stepped into a watercolor painting.

Maine is fucking incredible at its peak.

For a second, I stop working the brush, tilting my face up to the sun. I breathe out half my soul, feeling the stress melting away.

That's rare as hell, especially considering the situation.

This morning at breakfast, I should've known nothing would come easy with this strange woman around.

And now some neighbor wants to buy this place. That

couple talked like they wanted to start negotiations immediately.

So much for a peaceful vacation, let alone figuring out what's next.

But there's a lot to love about this moment, just me and the whispering lake and not a video conference with people I hate in sight.

It's an excuse to get outside and do nothing important.

Best of all, despite the coolness in the air, my old leg injury isn't flaring up.

I usually dread the cold when temperatures plunge.

Like always, I stretch it out, but something stops me from going through the entire stretch routine my physical therapist drilled into my head.

No, not something.

Her.

Margot damn Blackthorn.

There's a prickling sensation at the back of my neck. I resist the urge to turn around.

If I do, I know I'll catch her watching me again.

She's up there now, creeping away from the big bay windows on the first floor, making me feel like the unwelcome party crasher I am.

Just my luck we're stuck with her—a dash of extra chaos the Saints didn't need on their first real family trip in *years.*

I call her type the Evil Blonde.

Bratty, affluent, annoyingly hot in that cool, sophisticated way, with long legs and big blue eyes that hypnotize men who let their guard down.

She's a human cobra masquerading as a minx.

The sort of wicked witch who breaks hearts and doesn't think twice about it before moving on to her next sucker.

She's also an heiress to billions, which does make her different.

I'm no slouch in the money department, but I'm damn sure not old Blackthorn money. Much less Maine royalty.

Danger, my mind warns.

All my nerves bristle with the knowledge that being stuck with her has the potential to get all kinds of shitty.

Hell, the way she looked at me after breakfast when I rescued her from a blueberry bone fracture keeps replaying in my mind.

"Fucking stop that," I growl, slapping my cheek.

She's taking up too much real estate in my brain.

Annoying.

Everything I've been through, and the dumbass boy inside me still simps for a pretty face.

But she's attractive in all the wrong ways, like she was made to wreck my defenses. That extra splash of feistiness that hooks under my skin doesn't help.

Thank fuck the kids are around.

If I'd come up here on my own, just me and Little Miss Fancy Heels, it could've been catastrophic.

Exactly the kind of drama I don't need.

Not after Daria, the divorce, and ten thousand glass shards ripping my life to pieces. If I have my way, I'll be a monk for the next few years.

Absolute celibacy.

If that goes well, we'll see about the rest of my life.

I turn my attention back to the dock, still feeling Margot's eyes on the back of my neck.

By the looks of it, plus a few good stomps, the structure feels sound, though it'll need some fixing before it's totally safe.

I grab a cloth and run my hand over a rough-looking board.

Splinters peel off from a small rotted area around a nail, trying to jam into my skin.

Damn.

This thing needs a full sand and restaining, plus maybe a few boards replaced for good measure.

And all these nails—some are popping out after years of neglect.

I'll tap them down, I decide.

It's quicker and easier than trying to put new ones in, and although they're rusty, the structure feels solid enough to keep anyone from falling through it.

Especially with Sophie and Dan around.

Trouble is, the kids won't look for splinters or uneven nails before they go pounding along on the wood barefoot.

Somebody will wind up hurt if I leave it like this.

New rule: no screwing around on the docks until I've fixed it up. If there's time, I'll treat it, too.

Winter's coming.

Future proofing never hurt.

That's a mistake I'm never making again. I yank at some splinters, ripping them from the docks and leaving fresh, pale wood behind.

At least Dan and Sophie can get some fresh air out here.

They've always wanted to live somewhere like this, born lovers of the great outdoors, just like me.

For now, that's fantasy, but this getaway should be good for the soul.

Grabbing this rental was spur-of-the-moment, and it was the right call. The best call to take the sting out of the past couple years leading to our divorce judgment.

But fuck—if I could've prevented that sting in the first place, I would have.

If I could've spared them the pain, the anger, the uncertainty, I would've given up my next fifty vacations.

My chest cramps, and I grit my teeth.

No matter how much Daria's bullshit hurt—*and yes, it*

fucking did—the thing that kills me the most is how the kids were caught in the middle.

How couldn't they be?

Their mother went out ugly.

There's only so much you can do to protect two intelligent nine-year-olds from the wreckage. They've heard the fights and felt the long absences for years.

They knew what was coming, and although they seem fine lately, I can't let anything slide.

My phone buzzes in my pocket, dragging my mind up from the pit of despair.

I shouldn't turn down the distraction.

But when I pull out my phone, I see the number on the screen and stop cold.

Why the fuck didn't I block her already?

I frown at the screen, wondering if I should even answer.

Every muscle goes rigid with the urge to break something. Starting with this iPhone, which I'd love to skip over the water until it disappears forever.

Still, curiosity gets me by the throat. I snap and swipe the green icon.

"What?" I snarl.

"Hello, Kane. Do you have a second?" Her voice is pleasant and razor-sharp, just the way it always is. Nothing's changed, and it takes me right back to failure.

"No." My voice is stone-cold.

"Aw, come on. Just for old times' sake."

"You know I want nothing to do with old times, Mallory. Much less the present."

"Kane." My name lashes me in the face as her voice softens. "It's the Harley-Farview conference," she hisses. "Look, I know it's a lot to ask, but it would be *so* deeply appreciated if you'd make the briefest appearance to—"

"You're right. It is a lot, and the answer is no."

"You... you wouldn't have to be there physically," she stammers. "I know you're out of state. Just a video call will do."

"To do what? Trick your investors into believing I haven't dropped this shit show? Because in case you forgot, I *have*." I inhale sharply, shaking my head. "What the fuck is this, anyway? Calling and asking for a favor?"

"I'm sorry if I'm interrupting you," she says, placating. "And I know things didn't end on the best terms, but—"

"No. No more buts, Mallory. How many times do I need to fucking tell you? I'm done with OptiSynth, and you're done using me for PR puff horseshit."

She sighs, the rush of static going straight through me like ice.

"I'm not asking for the world. It would just be one little brief—"

"*No*," I snap. "Not today. Not tomorrow. Not fucking ever. Not after the shit you pulled."

"Now listen, we had a sincere difference in vision and—"

Bullshit.

I hang up, swiping with more force than necessary. I miss the days when you could demolish a phone by slamming it back in its cradle.

Breathing roughly, I stare at the trees on the other side of the lake, adrenaline pelting my veins.

Why did I think they wouldn't have the *gall* to contact me?

Especially like this, cold-calling out of the blue to ask for a favor they sure as hell know I don't owe them.

"No, *you* go back and shut it!"

Sophie's voice.

I stuff my phone back in my pocket, trying to shake my anger.

Just in time to see the kids racing downhill to the docks.

The back door swings shut as Dan closes it, then races toward me, right behind his sister.

"Careful!" I call, my arms splayed wide to catch Soph. She stumbles into me with a squeal, and I grab her, swinging her around before setting her back on her feet. "What have I told you about running down hills?"

"Only run if you wanna fall over?" She grins, her glasses tilted. "But that's why you're here, Dad! You're my brakes."

Munchkin logic.

That's why it's impossible to stay mad at my angel.

Luckily, Dan brakes himself and bumps into my side dramatically.

"We finished our homework. English is easy. Can you believe they let me pick *Narnia* for the dumb paper?" he yells. Birds erupt from the nearby trees, and Sophie giggles.

"Pipe down, we're not the only folks here," I say, even though from here, it looks like we are.

Another reason I picked this place when Bar Harbor was a bust.

"It's just birds." Dan settles beside me. I steer them both away from the dock. "Are we taking the boat out? Or do we have to clean first?"

"Yeah," Sophie says, beaming up at me. "You promised you would."

The explosive pressure in my chest eases as I look down into their faces.

The prickling sensation of being watched has faded. If I look up, I'm sure I'll see Margot drawn back behind the earthy curtains.

This is what I need after that call, though.

An excuse to get us out on the canoe, away from the world.

"I guess I did promise, huh? And you're lucky I took care of the worst with the dock. I won't keep you guys waiting, but you step where I tell you." With my hands on their little shoulders, I steer them toward the small shed that's sitting by the water, where I've hauled our canoe.

Sophie holds up the small telescope in her hand, making a big show of playing pirate, swinging it around.

"Arrr, I'm ready, Captain Dad!"

"Keep it straight, little matey. Remember what I told you about where to look with that thing?"

She rolls her eyes, mouthing, *"I know."*

Just like I know I'm going to have my hands full with her in a few years, especially if she turns out a fraction as spoiled as Margot Blackthorn.

Stop thinking about her, idiot.

"Okay," I tell them. "Let's get the boat into the water."

***

It's heaven on the lake.

The kids turn into dynamos, both of them talking my ear off about the scenery and pointing out damn near every bird nestled in the trees. When a young moose bolts into the woods after taking a drink, it takes half an hour to calm them down.

Sophie spends her time after that staring at the opposite shore with her telescope, moose hunting, while Dan helps me paddle.

At least I can put *one* of them to work to help burn off some energy.

By the time we return to the house and pull up the canoe, they're exhausted and damp from getting splashed on the way back up onto the dock. I send them upstairs to change as I get started on lunch.

Thankfully, the kitchen's empty.

The sigh of relief slams to a halt in my lungs when I see

the plate in the middle of the counter under a glass cake dome.

Blueberry muffins, courtesy of Miss Blackthorn.

There's a note beside it, too, written in the pretty, flowing handwriting of someone who went to a private school. Probably the only place on Earth where they still mint kids who care about their cursive.

I pick it up and read.

Breakfast hit the spot and I thought I'd return the favor. Help yourselves!

Fucking great.

Like Sophie needs another excuse to fangirl over Margot Blackthorn.

She only mentioned her about a dozen times out on the water.

No surprise when Margot's pretty, shoe-obsessed, and visually successful.

Everything I worry about my little girl trying to idolize. I grew up comfortable, not stupidly rich, and there are dangers to spoiling her too much.

I don't want blue-blooded young women with Instagram model looks setting her standards.

Then again, doesn't every kid need a positive role model?

Someone who *isn't* her mom.

However much Margot annoys me, she let us stay. Plus, she has a profession that isn't modeling in obscure locations with a string of revolving boyfriends.

Fuck.

I don't *dislike* her, necessarily.

Maybe my cave bear instinct just comes out because I don't want more trouble. We've had our limit.

"Are those muffins? Score!" Predictably, Dan's the first one back in the kitchen. His hair is still damp from his shower, sticking up in all directions like a human cactus, and there's a redness in his cheeks I haven't seen in a while.

"Just one before lunch," I warn as he rips the glass cover off. "If you're still hungry, you can have another one after we eat."

Sophie gasps as she clatters into the kitchen, stumbling against the counter in her excitement. The ortho shoes aren't always great for a kid's balance, either.

She flushes, but her beady little eyes are fixed on the muffin stack.

"Margot made these?" she asks.

It seems obvious.

Yet I still have to pinch my jaw to bite back my irritation.

After our morning on the lake, it's a godsend to two hungry kids, and even I have to agree it's homey.

Damnably so.

The room still smells like a bakery, all sugar and berries and batter.

"See? I told you she was cool," Sophie says, taking an enormous bite. Her eyes roll back in her head. "Yum! Her baking game's on point too, Dad. Try it."

"Yeah, she could teach you a thing or two," Dan tells me, smacking his lips.

I snort loudly, snagging one on my way to the fridge.

We'll just see about that.

"Keep talking like that, Bud, and you'll be making us lunch."

Dan's eyes bulge and he shakes his head.

"Okay, okay! But why not just have the muffins instead?"

"Absolutely not. You need nutrition. When you're older, you'll appreciate your old man caring about your macros and glucose levels."

I bite into the muffin, expecting to be overwhelmed, but—

Shit.

A blueberry cake rainbow floods my mouth.

I'm not sure I've had anything baked this good in ages. That includes the best places back home, and even the times when I'd pop into the Sugar Bowl on trips to Kansas City in my younger days. I think the old lady who owned the place then did black magic with a mixing bowl.

Unfortunately, this muffin tastes too close for comfort.

And now I have to add *outrageously good baker* to Margot Blackthorn's mile-long list of red flags.

I'm just glad she isn't here to see her stupid muffin make my eyes roll.

And she doesn't butt in to disturb us as I throw together chicken salad on whole wheat bread for lunch with heaping bowls of those fresh blueberries as sides.

The muffin offering doesn't help Sophie's budding obsession with her new friend. I count fifteen separate mentions of Margot in the twenty minutes it takes to eat lunch together.

Daniel's less interested in her, thank God.

Then again, Dan's focus wanders like a puppy if it isn't directly related to sports, military history, or music.

Margot isn't a drummer and she doesn't play soccer. Right now, she's just winning him over with food.

Whatever.

He's too young to have a crush on her. *I hope.*

Because I'm way too fucking old to feel the weird spark of jealousy if he does.

After lunch, I head upstairs for a few minutes of privacy, leaving the kids to read and talk in the kitchen. Music plays gently on the portable Bluetooth speaker we brought along.

We'll see how long it takes to start a fight.

Sophie loves to play the same pop lists ten times in a row.

I think Dan wants to burn everything Swift or Milah Holly related on sight.

They bicker damn near daily over what's on Spotify when they're in the same room. It might be the most tired and worn-out argument in our house.

I swing the door to my bedroom open and freeze.

Margot stands in the corner, her hands flat on the wall and—tapping?

What the hell is she doing?

The door creaks and she swings around, bright color flooding her cheeks. Sunlight streams in through the windows, adding a golden glow to her hair and making her blue eyes glitter with a rush of emotion I can't quantify.

Then it fades as she squares her shoulders, trying to project calm.

Goddamn, she's gorgeous in the deadliest ways.

All pouty lips. Softly appealing without any artificial puff.

I'm pretty sure she's all natural, despite the salon highlights in her hair.

Her leggings cling to every line of her long, trim legs. The oversized tee over the top gives her a casual look today.

Plain and relaxed, but the way she wears her clothes makes them look like they were designed just for her.

"Miss Blackthorn," I say her name like a gunshot.

Her eyes flare as they meet mine.

Sparks.

A second later, she's bolting, stepping away from the wall with her hands in the air before she tucks them behind her back.

But it's too late to play it cool, and I think she knows it.

"Shit!" She looks away for the first time. "I'm sorry. I thought you were still downstairs."

I raise an eyebrow. "Yeah? Because that makes it okay to go pawing through my room?"

The hellfire red on her cheeks returns and deepens, extending down her neck until it lines her chest.

I can't tell if she's flushed from sheer irritation at having been caught or genuine embarrassment.

Hot anger boils my lungs.

Sure, she let us crash here, but that doesn't mean we can trust her, and it damn sure doesn't give her the right to go rifling through my room.

"No," she says quietly. "Of course not. But I wasn't going through your stuff!"

"Then explain. What the fuck are you doing in my bedroom?"

"Right, I—" She gestures uselessly at the wall. "So, I know this looks bad—"

"You're damn right. So does my patience." I step closer, and she eyes the space between us warily. "Tell me what was so important you just had to invade my privacy, duchess."

She stops and stares at me.

Fuck it, I know. I'm erupting and I'm past caring.

"I'm sorry!" she sputters. "But do we have to do the name-calling? No one's called me that since middle school."

Not an answer. Also, no sympathy.

The stubbornness on her face doesn't weaken my resolve.

"Kane, I didn't go through your things. Honest. I never touched a single drawer or your bags."

My eyes scan every corner, cold and assessing.

At a glance, she might be telling the truth.

I haven't had time to unpack much and make the space too personal yet, and my bags are right where I left them.

But that wasn't the question and she knows it.

Margot Blackthorn isn't stupid.

I fold my arms and wait.

Her gaze bounces off my chest.

Again, there's a challenge in her eyes. Like she's sizing me up in a very physical, visceral way.

When she inhales, her shoulders tighten.

"It's my house," she says.

"I'm aware. Just like I'm sure you know there are laws on the books that say you don't barge in on paying guests unannounced. Blackthorn or not, you're not goddamned royalty, duchess."

Her face goes crimson as she pinches the bridge of her nose and sighs.

"I know that. You don't enter without probable cause. It's just... it's my responsibility to look over everything and make sure it's safe. Structurally sound. I wanted to check everything after that mess with the stairs." Her voice is cool and composed, confident, and she doesn't look away.

She's a decent liar, I'll give her that.

Only, the fact that she's bluffing kicks anger through my gut.

If there's one thing I hate, it's bullshitters.

"Uh-huh," I say, matching her tone. "You didn't tell me you were a building inspector."

"Oh, I know some basics."

Like hell.

"So is it, in your words, 'structurally sound'?"

"Yes." Her eyes skitter away from my face. "Couldn't find anything too concerning when I knocked around."

"Good thing you checked. It's nice knowing the walls won't erupt with rats who'll eat me in my sleep."

She laughs too hard at that.

Her shoulders are still stiff, but she offers me a smile. "Well, I'll get out of your hair."

I don't move from blocking the doorway.

"Not until you tell me what you were *really* doing."

"Are you calling me a liar?"

"I sure as hell don't think you're being real."

For a second, the corner of her mouth twitches before she wrestles it back under control. "I guess you got me there."

"Guess I did. So what are you really up to, Margot?"

Her nose wrinkles as she sends a wry glance at me. "It's embarrassing..."

"Try me."

"It's like you said... mice."

"Mice?" I turn the word over like tasteless chewing gum.

"Yep. Big dumb mice. I haven't been here in a while, but years ago there used to be some issues—not just this room, most of this floor sometimes. I had to make sure they didn't come back."

I blink at her, wary.

There might be some truth to it.

I can believe this old house has had mice over the years, and there's an edge of sincerity in her voice that her last pathetic excuse lacked. That also explains the tapping on the walls—but not everything.

The way she holds herself gives away the half-truth.

The prolonged eye contact.

The self-deprecation that's supposed to be shame and worry but feels like another way she's covering.

No, I don't trust this Blackthorn brat.

And if she's going to be any kind of role model to Sophie, however temporary—whether I like it or not—then I need her to knock it off.

Just like I need to know how much I can trust her while she's sharing a roof with my kids.

Right now, the only thing she's done that screams good faith was allowing us to stay, and she could have any number of reasons for that.

Not all of them pure.

Everyone's allowed their little secrets, fine. Hell, it's not like I don't have them falling out of my ears.

Only, the second you start compromising my privacy and acting sly about it, you cross a red line.

Margot hasn't just crossed it.

She's trying to erase it with both feet.

"If any pest issues turn up, tell me right away," I demand.

Her eyes widen.

It's like someone hooked a live wire straight into my gut.

Everything tenses.

I want to see it in her eyes when she realizes what messing with me could cost her.

I'm not a man you dick around with, and I don't care if it's a pretty face doing the dicking.

Instead of backing down, her chin tilts up as I step forward, and a shadow crosses her eyes.

Awareness, maybe. A frosted hint of defiance.

"Kane," she whispers, moistening her lower lip with her tongue. I stare at it for a fraction of a second that's already too long.

Goddamn.

"I mean it, woman. If there's a mouse problem big enough to send you knocking around my room, I deserve to know. They carry diseases. I can help get rid of them."

"Okay, yeah. And again, I didn't touch any of your stuff," she says quietly.

"Not the point."

She's hiding shit, acting suspicious as hell in my private space and in a house my kids are staying in.

She holds up her hands, trying to look harmless.

For a second, it looks like she wants to put them on my shoulders, trying to be reassuring. One good look at my face makes her think better of it, though, and she lowers her arms.

"Look," she says, and I start getting flashbacks of my call with Mallory from OptiSynth. "You're already working for free playing handyman. Chasing around rodents should be the least of your worries when you're on vacation and—"

"No. If I can't handle my worries, you'll know. I'm not getting spooked by a few fucking mice."

I roll up my sleeve for proof and she shuts the hell up.

Her eyes dart to the tattoo across my bicep.

Yes, it's a power play.

A message of fearlessness that goes beyond vermin.

I'm not afraid of them, and I'm in no mood for your bullshit.

From the way she sucks in a breath before we lock eyes again, she knows it.

Her face glazes over as she looks back down at my arm.

The tattoo is a skull with a US Airborne unit insignia. The eye sockets are wide and dark and staring, the shadows intricately inked.

A fucking cool piece of art, heavy with meaning, and something I'm proud to wear on my skin.

A reminder that no matter what life throws at me, I'm equipped to handle it.

And considering everything that came after I returned to civilian life, I'm damn lucky I know how to handle myself.

"Listen, Margot," I say, my voice low.

She flinches. Her lips part as she waits for me to finish, and—

Shit.

I tear my gaze away from her mouth, riveting it back to her eyes.

It doesn't help that I'm both pissed at her and very aware of her proximity.

The featherlight brush of her breath, the faint scent of blueberries. Her headier perfume, something floral and sweet.

"Listen, I've seen enough shit in my life to handle a little mouse. What I can't tolerate are people who lie to me."

She rocks back like I just slapped her.

The distance is good.

I need her to understand whatever game she's playing won't fly, and I've had enough dishonesty for this lifetime.

It was bad enough with Daria and the way everything imploded after her affair started.

Margot swallows a few times, like she's suppressing whatever emotion I just drew out of her, and she takes another step back.

"I'm really sorry again," she says one more time, her soft voice a little flat. "I won't come creeping a second time."

"Or the kids' rooms," I warn.

"No." The way she shakes her head seems a little mechanical, but I detect a trace of indignation before she squashes it. "This was my mistake."

Her gaze flicks to my tattoo again, my sleeve still pushed up.

The intimidation factor suddenly doesn't make me feel as good as before.

"In case you hadn't noticed, I'm not great at this landlord thing. That's why I had Mrs. Griffith." She moves past me to the door. "I read you loud and clear, though. No more surprises. No sign of mice yet either, so just… yeah, just enjoy your day."

I can feel the burning intensity in my eyes as I watch her go.

V: HAUNTED HOUSE (MARGOT)

*Y*ou're looking at the smoothest girl ever.

Ha.

That couldn't have gone down worse if I'd decided to make a blueberry pie and whacked him square in the face with it.

I lean against the wall of my room, hand against my chest, heart still racing.

Honestly, it might've been better if I *had* pied him. It might've distracted him from finding me obviously creeping on his turf.

If he wasn't suspicious before, he sure is now.

He was also a total domineering asshole, up in my face, angry tattoo bristling, but I can't even blame him.

The man had Army written all over before he flashed his ink and storming testosterone. A riptide of violence in his eyes, like he'll do *anything* to protect his kids.

Yes, I had it coming.

I should've waited until they left to go into town or something before sleuthing around. Getting caught was hilariously preventable, especially when I had an inkling of how he could react.

Very badly.

And again, completely justified.

I think he saw right through my little mice story.

There *was* a mouse problem here in the past. That just wasn't the reason why I went poking around.

Ugh.

Why couldn't PopPop have just *told* me what I'm supposed to be looking for?

Or at least hinted where it is.

Now, I'm shooting in the dark and missing every target.

I've retreated to my room with the fairy lights on and the fading sunlight streaming in.

I feel ridiculous for ever thinking there might be some trapdoor or secret passage in the house.

I mean, I wouldn't put it past Gramps to make a big show of whatever he's hiding. I still don't know what kind of 'priceless memento' he left my little cousin Cleo. But I'm glad that's her problem, considering how stressful this house is.

I slide down the wall and crouch on the floor, my hands in my hair.

God, if he was here right now, he'd laugh at me.

"Don't give up so easy, May. Where's your curiosity? It doesn't kill the cat; it gives it a reason to live."

Seriously. I can't count the number of times he'd say that with the same warm rolling chuckle.

Always when Hattie and I were kids, and he'd send us on his big scavenger hunts out here or sometimes at the big house in Portland.

Back then, it was fun. The stakes were lower, and the prizes were candy or books or sometimes little silver lockets and bracelets.

Tromping around the gardens out back or the lakeshore never made me feel like a sneaky weirdo either.

No wonder Kane wishes I'd fall off the earth. It doesn't excuse his assholery, but he has good reasons.

I hate that he had to forbid me from going into the kids' rooms. That was a sucker punch, like I'd go snooping around for no good reason.

...but isn't that what I did?

Shit, this is so pathetic.

I stand up and go sit on the bed.

Whatever, it's fine.

I'll just stay in my room guessing until the Saints aren't here, hoping whatever that crafty old man hid isn't perishable.

* * *

THE REST of my day goes by about as well as my encounter with Kane.

Ethan doesn't know anything about the lake house or any secrets Gramps hid here, and he's also notoriously bad at texting me back.

But that's what happens when your older brother's too busy being all lovey with Hattie.

I can't be mad.

At first, it was weird, but they're such a good couple. When the chemistry hits right, there's no stopping it.

And now they're both so happy it might be sickening if I didn't love them both to death.

I only wish the chemistry wasn't flatter than a day-old soda with my latest shoe design.

I sit down at the desk in front of my tablet with an iced matcha and try to focus, moving elements around, trying to find the magic combination.

Colors that vibe with the vision in my head.

Patterns and laces and straps that make sense, that will make people gasp with delight.

But nothing here feels cohesive, and after over an hour, it starts running together.

Everything I touch is crap today.

Flat, tired designs that wouldn't wow anyone back in the eighties.

Nothing fresh. Nothing exciting. Nothing new.

It feels like slapping paint on a canvas and hoping you wind up with a pretty portrait by the end. But art doesn't work that way and neither does product design.

When I close my eyes, I can see it so clearly.

Something elegant and understated.

Shoes that scream *classy* and *chic* without being ridiculously flashy or some minimalist heel horror that bites your feet until they turn purple.

Just a nice, everyday shoe that still makes a statement. Bold without being brash.

Sigh.

I flick through pictures of Pinterest boards and AI mockups, trying to find something that kickstarts my creativity.

A line, a color, an idea that grabs me by the hair.

But there's nothing here that hasn't been done to death.

I sooo need a new direction.

The thing is, it can't be *mundane*.

It can't be ordinary.

Fashion is a moving stream and it's never the same twice. It has to tell a story other folks want to hear and be part of.

My stomach growls and I glance at the clock, tossing my stylus on the desk.

It's late—hopefully so late they've eaten downstairs.

The sun set over an hour ago and the sky has that pale blue-grey shadow as night falls on the lake.

A rush of nostalgia punches me, and I breathe through it, gripping my tablet.

For a burning second, I remember what it was like coming here as a kid, before life got so complicated.

I remember the excitement, the way we'd feast on Gramps' beef stew or seafood pasta before fighting over the best places in front of the fire for story time.

He'd read us the classics, Greek mythology or modern myths he just made up. The man never had a TV on in this house until we were half-grown.

I remember how carefree the woods would feel at night with chirping crickets and bellowing owls.

I remember how good my heart felt in this house, before he died and our little world shrank like a fading puddle.

I stare at my tablet and my stupid designs, wrinkling my nose.

Yeah.

The only thing as frustrating as a dream you can't remember has to be a memory you'll never relive. They both feel like if you just push a little harder, you'll get there.

And yes, I know this isn't healthy.

I need to get out of this room and my own head before I drive myself crazy.

It's a cool evening, so I grab my light jacket from the closet and sling it over my shoulders as I head downstairs into the kitchen. My stomach growls like a wildcat.

The old house is dark and silent around me, the only noise the floorboards creaking underfoot.

Perfect.

I'm planning to grab a drink from the fridge and head into town to see what's still open, but as I flick the light on, my attention snags on a sandwich off to the side, neatly packaged up in foil.

For the only smartass mouse I want to keep fed, the note beside it reads. *Come clean with me when you're ready, duchess.*

Holy crap.

Oh, he's good.

I want to hate him for mastering the art of contradiction and showing off.

Everything would be easier if he was a hundred percent asshole.

But this note is a whole lot of nice and I—

I don't know how to deal with that.

So I stare at it, my heart lodged in my throat, ticking oddly.

I knew he never bought the mouse thing for a second, but I guess he isn't too mad. He just wants my confession.

The sandwich feels like a peace offering of sorts.

One I'm tempted to accept in my sappy, hangry mood.

It's been ages since anyone really looked out for me.

I glance out the window to the other side of the house out back, where there's a patio and firepit, right next to the old hot tub.

The flickering light says they've got the fire going. The night darkens with every minute, more stars poking through the indigo-blue sky.

It's the kind of evening Hattie and I used to love outside, buried under blankets as we talked about school and books and crushes.

Another pang of nostalgia.

I have the weirdest urge to tear up.

But that's way too much emotion for a sandwich, and I need to eat.

So instead of blubbering, I pick it up and wrap my coat more firmly around me as I head outside.

Little Sophie sees me first. Her face lights up like Christmas morning.

The firepit blazes, and the corrupted Saint himself relaxes against the cushions of his chair nearby, his arms outstretched with a beer loosely clasped in his fingers.

The star of the show, though, is a large, fancy-looking telescope perched in the middle of the deck on a tripod.

It gleams in the firelight, and there's a stool positioned next to it.

"Margot!" Sophie chirps, coming toward me in those oversized shoes and waving her hand. "Wanna have a look through my telescope? The skies are so amazing out here. Nothing like back home."

There's no way I can say no to this adorable request.

Actually... I don't think I've ever looked through a telescope before. Certainly not something this big and fancy.

"She's obsessed with the skies because nothing's cool enough for her on the ground," Dan tells me with the familiar superiority of a cheesy older brother, even though they're twins. He still pretends like he's older and wiser, and that makes me grin.

"Am not!" Sophie sticks out her tongue at him.

"Are."

"Guys, enough," Kane barks. "No bickering on the patio or we're packing it in."

"We weren't fighting, Dad. We were *debating*," Dan says.

"A debate has nuanced arguments. You just brought an argument, boy."

Dan rolls his eyes as he sinks back in his chair, putting earbuds in as he prepares to play his little portable drum pad. Quietly this time, thank God.

"Did you know you can see Jupiter tonight?" Sophie asks. "It's super bright. Come look."

Kane's eyes never waver, tracing my every movement.

Don't feel anything.

Pretend he isn't there.

That's insanely hard when his emerald stare rivals the fire, and there's something like a whisper of a smile toying around his mouth.

At least I was right—he doesn't seem mad.

I don't want to think about what else is running through his head as he watches me.

Sophie practically pulls me down on the stool in front of the telescope's eyepiece, and Kane's smile deepens.

"This is a serious telescope, Sophie. Really nice," I tell her.

"Dad got it for my birthday. It's real easy to use, that's the best part. No wasting time trying to aim it just right."

She holds up her phone, opening an app with a star map that matches the sky. She punches in 'Jupiter' and the telescope moves automatically, positioning itself to capture the planet.

"Amazing. I've never even used a basic one before," I say.

She beams.

"Hey, Dan," she says. "Margot's never used a telescope!"

"What?" Dan pulls out his earbuds.

"I said she's never used a telescope!"

The kid looks at me with mingled shock and that twitchy excitement kids get when they know something an adult doesn't.

I don't hold it against him, though, because he immediately launches into a mangled explanation of how telescopes work.

"That's wrong," Sophie says firmly. "They use mirrors."

"Mirrors, yeah, duh." He rolls his eyes. "That's what I said."

"You said glass, and that's different." She looks up at me apologetically, her eyes shining behind her glasses. "Have a look. You might have to adjust the zoom a little."

She shows me how to change the focus, her fingers moving deftly.

I put my eye to the little black eyepiece and squint.

I'm not sure what I expected, but it adjusts my expectations like a chiropractor snapping bones.

I know what Jupiter looks like.

It's a big gassy planet with cake-like stripes and swirly orange spots. I've seen the pictures.

But instead of the pristine NASA portrait in my mind, I get a field of really bright stars.

And there, right in the middle of my field of vision, is one that's brighter than the rest. At this magnification, I can see the light and color, a fuzzy smear of a planet with several small moons dancing around it.

Okay, so it's not perfect.

But for a second, I'm gobsmacked with wonder that's hard to put into words.

I'm still looking at a *planet*.

Something hundreds of millions of miles away.

Talk about feeling small, but tonight, that's kind of comforting. What are my worries and frustrations and hair-ripping frustration with my grandfather's secrets against the vastness of the universe?

I exhale slowly.

"Pretty cool, huh?" Sophie says.

"Fantabulous," I say. "Super cool, Soph. Can we see Mars?"

"Not right now. It comes up pretty late this time of year. I wish they were up around the same time. You'd have to wake up really early or stay up real late to see it."

"Oh, sure. That's the only planet I've ever really noticed in the sky," I say.

"That's because it's so red. Venus is easy, too, but it's just bright," Sophie explains. I can't help smiling at the way she schools me. "It's way cooler through a telescope. If Dad lets us stay up, I could show you."

"Unless she's sick or jet-lagged, my girl should always be asleep at four a.m." Kane nods gruffly, telling her it's settled.

God help me, I smile.

"This is a great place for stargazing. No question," I say.

And no lie.

The light pollution sucks in New York.

Even Portland can't compare to what's up here on the nights when the Atlantic isn't smothering the city with clouds.

Here, the night sky sprawls as far as the eye can see with only the faintest light to one side where Sully Bay is.

"Wow, you can see *so much*." Sophie sounds so happy.

I glance at Kane with his eyes half-closed in the chair. I think it's the first time I've seen him relaxed.

Even so, I can feel his attention on us.

And I wonder why they picked here for a getaway.

"So, am I speaking to the future head of NASA?" I tease, looking at Sophie again.

She blushes so fiercely I can see it even in the shadows.

"I really like space," she says.

"Being an astronaut would be cooler," Dan says.

They bicker for a few minutes about what's more impressive—a scientist discovering a new planet or an astronaut walking on Mars—while I take another peek at Jupiter.

Honestly, the clarity isn't nearly as impressive as the high-res photos you can pull up online.

Still, it almost looks close enough for me to reach out and touch.

But when I pull back and squint up at the night sky and there's nothing but that small bright pinprick of light, the universe doesn't feel like a massive empty room.

A cool wind blows in and I shiver.

"Right, guys. You still have a lot of people on both sides

who'll agree," Kane interrupts a new debate about how 'mean' it is that Pluto isn't a planet now.

"But if Pluto's a planet, it means we have a *ton* of planets in our solar system. It's not that special. There are lots of frozen balls just like it out there. Do you really wanna memorize thirty more planets?" Dan challenges.

"Why not? Just wait till they start imaging other stars." Sophie turns to me. "They can't do it yet. But Dad sent me an article where they're trying to use AI with the closest stars. Won't that be crazy? Seeing brand-new planets up close?"

I think Sophie is patiently trying to educate me, but she keeps getting derailed by Dan.

Kane actually chuckles.

I throw him a knowing smile.

Seeing them fight like that brings back memories. Ethan was way worse than Dan when he was a kid.

The pranks we'd pull on each other were legendary.

Sophie and Dan don't have quite that dynamic.

They bicker just like we did, but my brother would've called me out for being a dork with a telescope or talking about sci-fi stuff. There's a warm friendliness to Dan that brings a pang to my chest.

They're such sweet kids.

"It's getting late, guys. Start wrapping up."

"*Daaad*," Sophie whines, giving the telescope another longing look. "It's not even that late yet."

"Going on ten o'clock," he says, tapping his smartwatch. He sets his bottle on the ground and stands with a bearish stretch. "Come on. You know we're heading into town tomorrow."

I try not to listen too closely, sliding awkwardly off the stool and heading over to the sofa, wrapping myself in blankets.

The night sky unfurls above us, so vast it takes my breath away, as Kane finally ushers the protesting kids inside.

It's been forever since I sat in front of a fire like this.

I tip my head back, letting the fire's warmth sink into my skin.

The day's frustrations melt away into a low hum of discontent I can handle.

It's not just the fire, I think. A little company doesn't hurt. And yes, maybe Kane doesn't hurt tonight either with the note and the sandwich.

He's back a few minutes later, picking up his beer bottle and sinking into the other end of the sofa.

We're silent for a few heavy seconds.

It should be uncomfortable, but it feels weirdly easy.

Not many people I know wear silence as gracefully as Kane Saint.

"Nice night, huh? The air's almost perfect with its bite." He takes a long swig from his bottle. I do *not* look at the curve of his throat. "Should get the hot tub going one day. The scenery's made for it out here and it's the perfect season."

"I'm not sure how much work it'll be. Old electrical and all, plus I bet it needs a new pump. It's probably been years since it was last turned on," I say too quickly.

Hot tub has certain connotations.

The sexy kind I totally don't need right now.

Kane doesn't strike me as the sort of guy to do casual anyway, and I'm a hookup kinda gal. Almost exclusively.

It's just tidier without any tangled feelings or lofty expectations.

Also, I don't have space in my life for commitment, much less a relationship, even if I'm not getting any younger.

That makes me think of PopPop and my stomach knots.

Grief is weird.

"I could make it work. Let me take a look," he offers.

Ugh, no.

But I can't scold him for being so handy when my little lie eats away at me. After spending time with them again, the guilt gnaws me to the bone.

Come clean with me when you're ready.

I'm not a chronic liar, I swear. But I'm also not a loyal truth teller.

Kane isn't exactly an open book himself.

But secrets are in the Blackthorn blood, and to tell people all those grubby little facts about yourself, you have to get close to them.

You have to trust them.

The past five years or so, the only people I've felt close to are Ethan and Hattie. Though I guess there's a first time for everything, including trading half-truths with a stranger who stirs me up in ways I don't want to deal with.

I shift around so I'm facing him, wrapping the blanket up to my chin.

He twists, too, blanket-free, though he's wearing a gorgeous burgundy sweater that looks soft enough to sink into. Our breath spirals out in white puffs.

Oh, this is harder than I thought.

But we're sharing space—something I haven't really done since Hattie ran off and married my brother.

For whatever reason, I don't want him thinking the worst of me, like I'm some lying spoiled brat who can't be trusted around his kids.

"Hey, so... I got the sandwich. And your note."

Awkward. I almost regret the words as soon as they're out.

He nods, sipping his beer again before setting his bottle down.

It lands on the wooden armrest next to him with a slight

clink. "I shouldn't have gotten in your face like that. My bad, duchess."

"You're going to keep doing that, aren't you?"

"If the glove fits." He shrugs, biting back a smile.

I should be furious. The last boy who called me that dumb nickname tried to copy my book report. I guess it was his way of 'getting back' at the class princess, all thanks to being a Blackthorn.

And I kinda proved the point by telling the teacher and getting him suspended for three days.

"It's not a bad thing," Kane whispers. "It's how you carry yourself. Very regal. You see how Sophie looks at you. Dan, too, and I'd like to keep it that way. That's why I'm over what happened earlier—even if it doesn't mean I'll drop the duchess part anytime soon."

I swallow a laugh, shaking my head.

It's not quite an apology, but it's close.

Now, I might have to give him the truth.

"You're right, though. I wasn't being strictly... open, I guess."

Deep breath.

His eyes flash, this feeling that's there and gone in an instant.

Not vindication.

More like an acknowledgment he was right. Plus, an intense flash of disgust because I lied to his face.

But then he looks at me, green eyes like jade in the night, the firelight playing across the shadows of his face, and I know he's waiting.

Come clean.

Right. Dear God.

I clear my throat. "The thing is, I don't know what to say. Or how to explain it. My grandfather was—I guess you'd call him eccentric."

"Leonidas?"

"The one and only. When I inherited this place, he left a letter saying there's something important here. Something that belonged to him. But I don't have a freaking clue where to start."

Kane goes silent, like he's taking his time thinking, slowly digesting the news.

The opposite of me.

I'm a knee-jerky kind of girl who likes to get things done. When my brother was spiraling, I practically shoved him back into the world.

"Was that so hard, Miss Blackthorn?"

I narrow my eyes at him.

"Don't push your luck, dude. I'm telling you because yes, I invaded your privacy and I feel pretty crappy about it. And yes, you're also living in this house, but let's not forget who owns it. And would it kill you to call me Margot for once?"

The corner of his mouth twitches.

"Gonna kick us out, Margot?"

"If you piss me off enough… yeah. But the kids can stay. They're *nice*." I cock my head, ignoring the warning in my belly that says this feels like flirting. "They make me think you must be doing something right. Don't prove me wrong."

That half smile he's wearing blooms into a smirk.

"Just you wait until Sophie tells you how many Earths can fit in the Sun for the thousandth time. Or when Dan starts his drumming at eight o'clock on a Sunday morning," he says dryly. "You wouldn't believe how much laundry these kids can make. Mount fucking Everest."

I'm laughing.

It's so jarring, thinking of this tattooed, self-propelled ego who rarely cracks a smile running around and trying to keep up with his kids' laundry.

The thought relaxes me, and I settle into the blankets.

"I stand by my decision," I say.

The other corner of his mouth tips up to join the first. "Guess I'd better do my best not to piss you off then, duchess."

"Guess so. You could also help with the big mystery, since you're so handy." I must be desperate if I'm asking Saint Lucifer for help.

But I'm seriously at my wit's end.

"I could. Any idea what it is you're looking for? What he might've left here?"

"Not one." I sigh. "I'd kill for a hint, but nobody has one yet. Not my brother, not my parents, not my grandfather's lawyer who was handling the estate."

"I'll keep an eye out for anything out of place."

The sincerity in his voice surprises me. Here I am, dumping one more chore on him, yet he's handling it like a gentleman.

"Thanks." I smile.

"And hey, seeing as I'm heading into town tomorrow, why don't you come with? There might be a place we can rent a metal detector or get some other tools to poke around."

It's not a bad idea.

The last thing I expected from this grouchy lump of coal.

Then again, he doesn't seem so awful now.

It's a small smile and a few kind words, sure, but he's acting human. Maybe the beer loosened him up.

"Have you tried anything like that yet?" he asks.

"No. Can't believe I didn't think of it until now." Even if it's a shot in the dark, it's better than nothing.

"The kids went through a phase where they were obsessed with finding buried treasure. We used to bring a metal detector out to a few local parks. Never scared up anything too interesting besides a couple old silver quarters."

From ancient treasure to the stars. I can see the connection.

It makes sense.

I also like that he indulges the kids. It's undeniable how much he loves them, and he's not afraid to show it.

"Sure," I say. "Why not?"

He nods, but there's still that ghost of a smile on his lips. It sparks just enough confidence to ask a question that's been bugging me all day.

"So, if you don't mind me asking, what had you so upset on the phone? I saw you take the call. You looked like you were ready to chuck your phone in the lake."

The smile disappears.

His eyes become black glass as he shuts down, his gaze dropping to a point past me. His mouth hardens into an angry line that tells me more than any words will.

"How damn long were you spying?"

Ouch.

Clearly, he worships his privacy.

Just like when he found me in his room.

Why does it feel like we've taken one step forward and two steps back?

"I had the window open. I wasn't spying. Your voice just carries." The fresh air was nice, that soft fall breeze I was so sure would help my muse. "I wasn't even paying attention at first, but you got a little heated and—and it was hard to ignore."

"Right." His body language is all coiled irritation. "It's nothing, just some old work business that's not my problem anymore. They just don't know when to leave me alone and figure it out on their own."

"Did you quit?"

He hesitates.

"Close enough." He twists away from me then, fixing his eyes on the dark trees beyond the lake.

I don't press him. Not when he's obviously done with this conversation.

I just join him in companionable silence, staring at the distant, dark waters under the moon and wondering.

What sort of life does this Saint have beyond his kids?

How many storms are raging behind his guarded green eyes?

VI: TOO CLOSE TO HOME (KANE)

Now that Margot's confessed—and this time I believe her—I don't mind her company, or the influence she has on my kids.

If only I could blunt her curiosity.

The day dawns clear and bright, and when she comes sailing into the kitchen for breakfast, blonde hair piled on her head and dressed casually in jeans and a grey sweater with a red stripe running across her breasts, she doesn't look so skittish.

She's adjusted to our presence.

"No breakfast today?" she asks, hand on her hip. "Didn't anyone tell you guys it's the most important meal of the day?"

"We're eating out today." I nod at the SUV parked outside the house. "There's a little diner Sophie spotted on the way in. I promised we'd get breakfast there."

"It smelled *amazing*. Like cinnamon rolls or something delish," Sophie says.

Margot laughs, jamming her shades into her hair like it's old habit. I doubt I'm the first man ruined by that look.

"Jenny's, right? Best place in town! Not that there's much competition in Sully Bay, but it's a cute place with good food. PopPop used to take us there all the time when we were little."

"Are we ready yet? I'm starving." Dan yawns impatiently.

"You're always hungry, little man. Guess I'm screwed in a few more years when the growth spurt hits and you eat twice as much. Come on." I gesture at the door with my thumb.

The diner's only a ten-minute drive away, and by the time we're on the road, all I can smell is Margot's perfume.

She makes the morning brighter still.

Don't know whether her smiles are meant to make up for the awkward end to last night when she pushed too far, but I don't mind them.

I'm a morning person by nature and the kids are at that age where they drag when it's early.

Having a woman around who can keep up with my energy, that's a welcome change.

"Table for four?" the waitress asks when she sees us. "Right this way."

"She's been working here as long as I've been coming." Margot laughs. "Must be at least twenty years."

"Wow. Does this place ever change?" Dan asks.

"Nope! That's the beauty of it."

The seats are sticky old leather, but the table's clean and there's a mini jukebox fixed to the wall.

Dan starts fussing with it the second we sit down, trying to find an Elvis song.

Margot entertains Sophie with stories about the pranks she and her brother used to trade on their summers here.

Mostly harmless kid stuff, even if her older brother sounds like a damn punk.

I'm only half listening as the food arrives, watching as

Margot smothers her eggs in hot sauce and takes big, hungry bites.

The girl can *eat*. And she doesn't mind her spice, which surprises me.

When she's done, she blots her mouth daintily with a napkin. Sophie copies her so closely I want to snort and roll my eyes.

The food's surprisingly tasty for a place that looks like it's been cooking with the same bacon grease for fifty years. Even Dan wolfs down his pancakes without any complaints.

Being a bottomless pit doesn't stop him from getting picky sometimes.

I ignore the way he's drenched them in so much syrup they're practically see-through.

Across from me, Margot tells Sophie about her best friend.

"...we've been besties since we were about your age," she says. "Hattie was always my partner in crime. Once, we put frogs in all of Ethan's shoes and he squished one. I don't think he forgave me for *months*."

Sophie groans and pretends to retch.

"Sucks for the frogs," Dan says.

"It did, yeah. We were no angels," Margot assures him, and the corners of her eyes crease as she grins. "But I wasn't thinking about the frogs. I was just thinking about how I could pull my brother's tail and rage-bait him into getting grounded. My granddad had this bodyguard around, Holden, and he was a total bulldog if we stepped out of line."

Bodyguard, huh?

"Why's that? Did old Leo upset that many people?" I ask carefully.

"No, not really. I mean, not that I was ever aware of." Margot's smile turns sad. "Just typical safety stuff, I think. It's pretty common when you have his money. Honestly, a lot of people wanted PopPop to have a whole detail of armed guards the older he got, at least for the trips to New York, but he wouldn't have it."

"So, nothing worth guarding at the house?"

Her eyes flash as she realizes what I'm really asking.

She shakes her head.

"Nope. I doubt it. Holden was like a second shadow. He followed PopPop everywhere."

Damn.

Probably no help in the hidden treasury department, then.

"You should hit him up, if you haven't yet," I say. "Couldn't hurt to ask about the house, just for old times' sake."

"I suppose," she whispers.

With a pleasant weight in my gut, I wave the waitress over for the bill, and she gives me an indulgent smile.

The woman must be in her fifties, wearing the apron like she never takes it off. There's a warm, motherly glow to her face.

"How was it, honey? Everything good?"

"Never fails, Bekah. Thanks so much," Margot says. Her voice slips, almost back to a comfortable drawl, like she's lived here for decades, born and bred in this backwater town.

"You're welcome, darlin'." She looks across at Sophie and Dan, and her smile widens. "And I hope you don't mind me saying, but you have a lovely family now. The big man must've been so proud before he passed."

Oh, shit.

Margot blinks, batting her eyes as raw shock rushes over her face.

"Uh, it's not like that," I rumble, hating the edge in my voice.

It's an innocent mistake. No need to chew the poor

woman's head off when she must deal with finicky customers every day.

Still, I sure as hell don't need people thinking I'm *with* Margot Blackthorn.

I know rumors fly faster than the speed of light in small towns.

Like thinking this little group outing is a *family* breakfast.

That's a good way to get gossip kicked up online, and then this trip's truly fucking blown. Maybe eating out was a mistake.

"We're not together!" Margot's syrupy laugh comes out thicker than the sugary slickness of Dan's pancakes, brushing over my rudeness. The waitress' face relaxes. "We're all just —" She hesitates, glancing at me before she says, "Friends. Just friends grabbing a bite."

"Oh, of course. Didn't mean to assume anything, hon. You disappeared for a while, so I just assumed you—yeah." The waitress holds up a finger. "Be right back with that bill for you."

"I've got it," I say firmly when Margot pulls out her purse.

Her eyes meet mine, all sky blue witchfire, and she slides her card across the table.

"It's fine, Kane. I don't mind paying when you've helped out so much," she says firmly.

While it's instinct to push, to pay for this woman like I always do, even if she's just a friend, I realize it's pointless.

A cheap breakfast is nothing for a billionaire heiress.

"Fine. Thanks for the food, Margot. Kids?"

Sophie and Dan eagerly rush their thank-yous as we head outside a minute later.

All the way to the car and then to the hardware store, the waitress' assumption sticks in my brain like a barb.

Never thought I'd be grabbing a meal with the kids and

another woman this soon. Not that it's like that, fuck no, but still—

I've never had to worry about anyone assuming they have a different mother.

Shit.

The thought makes my stomach churn.

Especially because Margot would've been like sixteen when they were born. Don't even ask what that would make me.

Another damnably good reason to keep my distance.

If we stroll around this town too much—just like we're doing now—the local yokels might spool up some really wild stories.

When we pull up and park in front of the little hardware store, Margot's face lights up.

"You didn't forget," she says happily.

"No. Can't hurt to pick up a few more tools for the house anyway." I cut the engine and head inside.

It's barely the size of a gas station, but it still looks like it has everything we need. Any residual tension from the diner fades.

Margot ties her hair up like she means business, and the kids split up, wandering the aisles.

"Stick together, guys," I call after them. "Don't leave the store without me."

"Dad, we know," Dan calls back, rushing down an aisle with drills and power tools.

I wander alone down another aisle, only halfway paying attention to what I'm looking for as my mind wanders.

Naturally, it goes back to breakfast.

I'm overreacting.

I shouldn't have gotten so revved up over a random waitress thinking we're together. It was a natural assumption really.

And it's my baggage blowing it up into more.

I push my thoughts aside and focus on what I'm supposed to be doing.

I do my best not to think about Margot, all long legs and miles of trouble.

Bad, bad idea.

I'm still brooding like the moody sack of ice I am when I meet her and the kids in the paint section. They're chattering excitedly as she looks up and taps her fingers against a can on the shelf.

"What do you think?" she asks.

"Broad question. Generally, I think a lot."

She slides me an unimpressed look as Daniel groans and covers his face.

"Smart-ass," she says. "Do they start teaching Dad jokes at the hospital when your kids are born or does it just come from getting old?"

"Uploaded to my brain the day I signed their birth certificates," I say. "Like changing a lightbulb."

She laughs.

"You're so cringe," she mutters, chewing her lip as she moves along the aisle. "But I figured I'd get some paint to freshen up the house while we're here. I've already got a power sander."

That'll definitely come in handy, considering the walls could use some light touch-up and a fresh coat or two in places.

"Sure. We can probably get a couple rooms done."

"What color do you think? More beige maybe? Organic style's pretty in." She tilts her head adorably as she thinks, sucking at her lip.

"I like pink. The light creamy one," Sophie says.

Margot nods seriously. "So do I. An accent wall maybe?"

"What about green?" I venture, eyeing the dark green-black colors. "It'll bring the forest inside."

"Mmm, the dark ones are very moody. But a nice viridian green overlooking the lake... that might look cool. We could even throw some red in to pop with the fall colors and winter sunsets." She pulls out her phone. "I took a couple pictures earlier. I wish I'd taken more. There's this sweet app that simulates colors and styles on real rooms. It's a game changer for home renovations. You upload some pics and it'll take the options and put them into a full 3D model, like walking around your new house. Here, let me find it."

My spine locks.

It's like some asshole just punched me and I'm retraining my lungs how to breathe.

"*So* useful," she says, tapping her phone and flicking through her apps.

"*No,*" I spit.

She glances up, surprised at my sharp tone.

Fuck, I'm giving too much away.

But I know it's hardly as useful as she thinks.

"Come again?" Her eyebrows draw together in confusion.

I force my throat to relax a little.

"I just mean I've seen them before," I rush out. "Yeah, it might be useful, but the AI engines give you too many options and not enough good ones. Why don't you get a real opinion from a contractor? If Sully Bay doesn't have an interior designer, surely there's one somewhere down in Bar Harbor."

"But that could take a week or more. I thought you wanted to get this done?"

That was before she mentioned the app.

"I can help you get started, yeah. Besides, these painting projects usually take longer than you think. Whenever I didn't hire it out back home, it could take me days to do a few rooms."

She puts her fist on her hip like she's gearing up for a fight.

"I've painted a bedroom before, you know." Her voice is teasing, but I just stare at her.

"Never said you couldn't. I think it's a bad idea to go bolder like this without an expert weighing in, that's all."

"Well, okay. I guess." Her hand falls back to her side and her posture softens.

Like my lack of humor has knocked the wind out of her sails.

I'm sure she expected something more constructive or maybe for me to join in with her teasing, considering the almost-flirting last night, but the app soured the mood.

If she knew who owned that technology, she'd understand.

"The metal detectors are back this way. Think I even spotted a thermal tool for seeing behind walls," I say, nodding at the kids to follow us.

"Can we rent them both? That would be super helpful." She jams her phone back in her pocket and follows me.

Relief cools my blood, knowing we've moved on from AI bullshit.

"I think so. If there's anything behind the walls to worry about, we'll find it." I play it cool, not saying much more in front of the kids.

If they get one whiff about hidden treasure in the house, they'll howl until I start knocking holes in the walls.

Margot looks at me but doesn't comment on the *we* part.

Just like she doesn't say anything else about shooting down the app consultation. I'm sure it comes off as weird and old-school.

Who *isn't* embracing AI-powered everything with wide-open arms to make their lives better?

I need to do better.

Keep it the fuck together, man.

She insists on paying for the tools, and I allow it.

Technically, she's the homeowner, after all.

The sun feels warmer as we step outside, burning away the last of the morning mist by the time we head back to the vehicle.

The kids rush back to our SUV. Margot sees a poster on the side of the hardware store before we leave.

"Farmers and crafts market today?" Her expression lights up. "Okay, now we have to make another stop. It's just a couple blocks away."

Her eyes shine like she's one with the sun.

"Seriously?"

"Seriously," she echoes. "It'll be fun. Don't you like a little spontaneity, Kane Saint?"

I grit my teeth.

"If you think spontaneity means tromping around a farmers market when you're already struggling to eat up half a ton of blueberries, you should redefine fun," I growl, but I'm already following her, waving Dan and Sophie over.

"It's not *just* a farmers market. It's a farmers and *crafts* market." She holds up a finger. "Important distinction."

In this town, she isn't wrong.

Sully Bay isn't a big place.

It's one main street cutting through the business district, a couple eateries, and one or two touristy stores selling tacky souvenirs. The market takes up the whole center of town, tents and stalls set up all along the sidewalk.

It's the epitome of small-town excitement.

A band plays covers of eighties hits, which is perfect for the crowd. There are a few younger people in their teens and twenties wandering around, but most of the folks here look middle-aged, if not pushing into their senior years.

"Awesome," Sophie declares, pushing her glasses up her nose.

"See? Listen to your kiddo." Margot flashes me a knowing smile.

Most of the stalls are hawking local produce, honey, and more blueberries like they're the local currency.

Of course, the quality is obscenely good.

Sophie pops into a craft stall, looking over a row of birthstone necklaces. Dan hovers at the next one over, keenly scanning some intricate wooden carvings of animals.

Margot struts around like she was born for this.

For a billionaire's granddaughter, she's no oversophisticated snob.

I fucking hate how refreshing that is.

She flicks her hair back over her shoulders, dazzling the stall owners with her breathtaking smile, pausing to make polite conversation with a few artists.

Still, nothing grabs her until she comes to a stall filled with ceramics.

I'll admit, they're impressive. Artisan quality like you see at the fine shops in New York or whenever I've traveled to the West Coast art malls.

Huge urns, bowls, and cups bursting with colors and a glossy finish that makes them look museum-grade.

Some have swirling blue and green patterns, the edges fading to a darker brown. Others look like stone on the outside, with muddy red or dark-purple accents inside.

"Wow!" Sophie's eyes go wide behind her glasses as she peers in for a closer look at a bowl. "How do you think he did this?"

Margot touches the tip of one finger to the rim of the

bowl, her lips pursed in thought as she looks up. "Why don't you ask him?"

"Um. I dunno. Can you?" Sophie shakes her head so adamantly her glasses slide down her nose.

She's such a shy girl and she doesn't strike up conversations with strangers easily. Especially when they impress her.

"Go ahead. I bet he'd love to talk about his art. I'll get you started." Margot leans over the table, catching the eye of the man in the corner. She flashes him her showstopper smile. "Excuse me? My friend here has a question about your work."

I don't miss the way Sophie's lips turn up.

My friend.

Damn, this woman has a knack for making kids love her.

Shame it's so complicated with adults like me.

Then I remember last night, the way she looked at me under the stars.

Not like I was some monster getting in her face with his tattoos and damaged history, but like I was a person she wouldn't mind getting to know.

Even after I tried to intimidate her.

Then again, she's never laid on the charm like she's doing for this guy.

Jealousy rips through my gut like a storm of needles as I listen in.

"Um, I just wondered, mister… how'd you make them so colorful?" Sophie's voice is a whisper.

The man steps up without a smile, tall and grim-faced, wearing the typical five o'clock shadow scruff a lot of artists do.

"Trade secret, my dear. I'm afraid if I told you, I'd have to kill you in the worst ways." Then his face breaks into an enormous grin.

Sophie gives back another tiny smile.

Margot laughs politely, breaking the tension.

That should annoy me, too, but it doesn't.

"These are unbelievable. You could sell them for three times as much to rich people in New York," Margot says. "Did you make them all yourself?"

The man's eyes flick to me and then to Sophie and Dan, then back to Margot, like he's memorizing us.

Besides being a human beanpole, he's broad-shouldered and lean, with a shock of reddish-brown curls that makes him look younger than I suspect he is.

He smiles, his gaze lingering on my face for a beat before he looks at Margot again.

"Every piece on the table is mine from start to finish," he says with an easy charm I can tell Margot likes.

Her body language changes, relaxing and moving closer.

The way she looks at him makes my fist tighten.

What the fuck? I have no business feeling this urge to break one of those fancy bowls over this clown's head.

"Amazing. Have you been at it long?" she asks.

"Just started my shop, actually. I only moved here earlier this year." He sends me another glance, a flash of what might be curiosity or annoyance that I'm here with a woman this beautiful.

"Oh, that's recent." She waves a hand at the street. "And how do you like it? Such a lovely place, right? I bet it's perfect in the offseason for your work. Lots of quiet to focus and get things done."

"Lots of scenery," he corrects gently. "A man can't help feeling inspired when he's surrounded by beauty everywhere."

He looks away from me and back to Margot so pointedly I want to laugh in his face.

Fucking worm.

If he thinks that's a good pickup line, he's clearly been spending too much time with his pottery.

But Margot doesn't wince at what he says.

She bites her lip a little as she glances away, though I'm sure she's no stranger to being called beautiful.

"What made you move here?"

"I came up looking for a fresh start, I guess. About like half the people around these parts if they weren't born and raised here." We lock eyes again, as if I'm the one who asked. Some weird, standoffish challenge in his eyes. "And what about you, miss?"

"Oh, I used to come here as a kid." She stops in front of a collection of bowls in sunny autumn colors. "These are freaking gorgeous, by the way. I'm in love with your designs, Mister...?"

"Lee." He smiles. "Lee Glazkov, and thank you. It means a lot to hear that."

"No, I'm serious. You have some serious talent. You must have a website or something online?" She picks up another object shaped more like a mountain with a grooved path running down to a small basin at the bottom. "And this incense holder—fabulous!"

"If you're hoping flattery wins you a discount, it's working," Lee says.

She bites her lip and bats her eyes.

Shit.

Again, flaming hot jealousy knifes me in the chest.

"So generous, I'd love that. Not sure I'll be here long, though. I'm basically just here on vacation," she says. "If I buy something now, can I get it shipped home?"

"Absolutely. And thanks for showing me how kind Sully Bay can be, even if you're not a regular," he says with an easy smile. "Take your time, and please don't worry about hogging anything you like. They're all one of a kind, and no one else stopping by yet has appreciated this stuff like you."

Why do I doubt that?

Could've sworn I saw several other people fluttering around his stall earlier. I think one older lady walked away with a mug, smiling from ear to ear.

But I don't think Margot notices or cares.

She just smiles at him gratefully as she browses, running her finger absently along a few pieces.

Out of curiosity, I pick up a black mug and turn it over in my hand.

There's no denying quality when you see it. Sturdy with an artistic flare that makes each item stand out with deep, rich colors and a glossy finish. His stuff feels high-end without being pretentious.

He has a good eye, this Lee.

That's why Margot loves his work, I suppose.

"What about you?" Lee asks, stopping in front of me, separated by another table featuring his ceramic wares. "Did you also come here as a kid?"

"No. First time in Sully Bay, actually." I turn the mug over again, keeping my eyes riveted to it. There's a faint signature scratched into the bottom. "I'll take three of these. Black, red, and that dark-green color." I nod at the row of mugs in front of me.

"Excellent choices." He takes the black mug back and starts wrapping it up with the others in thick brown paper. "You planning on hanging around here long?"

My eyes narrow. My blood stings.

It couldn't be fucking clearer he's after Margot.

I fold my arms, already regretting the purchase.

"Maybe. We're flexible with the kids just starting school," I lie.

So what if I emphasize *kids?*

Let him think whatever he wants.

From the way his face falls, he must think she's off-limits, and that's goddamned fine and dandy.

"Oh, yes. Playing it by ear, huh? It must be nice for the young ones this time of year. I could never sit still in a classroom, especially with big piles of leaves to romp through." He holds up the card reader with the amount on the screen, offering a tight smile.

I don't even look at the screen as I tap my card.

"Guess so," I say flatly.

"Hey, Lee, can I get a few of these bowls?" Margot interrupts, pointing to the autumn-colored dishes.

He quickly moves over to wrap them up for her.

There's a lull in the conversation as she pays, and we accept our paper bags. They're nondescript, no logo on the side or any fancy branding.

At least Lee stops leering as he checks her out.

"Your work shines," I say, just to show him there are no hard feelings. "Honestly, I wasn't expecting to find anything this high quality here. That's getting rare, even back in New York."

For a second, his eyes glint.

"Handcrafted will always be king, my friend. Nothing will ever change that. The machines won't come for ceramics for a while. I hope I'm dead by then if they do."

Huh?

Margot steps back, flashing me an odd look. She's as shocked by the sharp edge in his voice as I am.

Every word drips bitterness, and there's this odd anger in his eyes as he looks back at us.

Then he rakes a hand over his face, smoothing it away like he's peeling off a mask.

"My apologies," he says with an embarrassed chuckle. "I've been reading about a lot of AI platforms replacing artists lately. It's just sad. Remember when we always heard technology would take on the hard work and free our creativity? Now we're living the opposite, more with every passing day."

"Unfortunately. Hate that shit," I agree, feeling a growing knot in my gut.

Lee stares right through me.

Just a little too long for my liking.

Then again, aren't the best artists usually a little off?

Margot frowns next to me, staring like she's trying to decipher coded words that aren't there.

"Are we ready?" she asks eagerly.

"Yeah, let's go," I say.

She doesn't complain as we usher the kids back through the crowd.

After a quick stop for some fresh apple cider at another stand, we head back to the vehicle, and I deliberately forget about AI and the bullshit it brings.

VII: HOME RUN (MARGOT)

A few days pass and I'm no closer to finding whatever big secret PopPop might've left in this house.

That cuts deeper than it should.

It feels like I'm failing him on the last great scavenger hunt he'll ever leave behind.

I imagine his ghost in the corner, shaking his head, his white hair waving as he smiles sadly and whispers, *"Try harder, little May."*

Try.

That's all we've been doing.

Oh, sure, the metal detector and thermal scanner did confirm there's nothing unusual tucked behind any walls or floors. And the kids have been having a grand old time playing with them when we're not using them.

Sophie took off with the metal detector the second we were done, with Dan close behind her.

They're convinced they'll find some lost Viking gold along the lakeshore.

Dan gave me a whole rundown on how ancient

Norsemen made it to Canada and northern Maine isn't 'that far' in his humble opinion.

I actually wish their curiosity and innocence could help me.

I'm starting to wonder if there's anything left for me to find.

After the last home inventory, Holden packed up the few remaining valuables to bring back to Portland for safekeeping before this place turned into a short-term rental. Nothing notable left behind besides a couple miscellaneous art pieces and a china set.

But what if something was taken that should've stayed?

Then again, I'm positive Gramps knew that could happen after he died.

He wouldn't leave anything out in the open that could be grabbed by his loyal and meticulous servant or anyone else if he wanted me to find it.

With every room, every day that passes without finding anything, the anxiety wound around my throat tightens.

At least I'm not alone in the hunt.

When he isn't tightening doors and cabinets or touching up little dents in the walls, Kane helps out.

He's better at this than I am, too.

Even if he cracks his dumb Dad jokes while I'm turning blue with frustration.

The way I groan or laugh painfully forces me to take a break, to breathe, to stop myself from ripping my hair out over nothing turning up again.

"Thanks for roughing it up here with me," I tell him now as he wipes dust off his chin.

It's hard to breathe without coughing thanks to decades of accumulated particles thrown into the air by every footstep.

A single bright bulb dangles from the middle of the attic, which we're searching a *second time.*

Yesterday, I poked my head up here for the first time and started pawing through old furniture and boxes of broken toys I haven't seen since I was five. I gave up and didn't bother with another pass.

But this is the last major area we haven't picked to the bone and it's a natural storage space. So yes, it warrants a second sweep.

Incredibly, Kane hasn't complained once while we're stumbling through fifty years of cobwebs. All so he can help me comb through family debris he's not even connected to.

His eyes meet mine over a pile of boxes we've turned out.

"I'd say it's my pleasure, but we both know that would be a lie."

And we all know how he feels about lies.

"What? You mean you're *not* having the time of your life?" I wipe my forehead, smearing dust everywhere. "Need some water?"

He holds out a hand for the bottle, which I toss to him.

His throat moves when he rips the cap off and drinks, and his eyes close.

Ugh!

A man drinking water has no business looking this erotic.

"Think we're almost done. We're getting to the end of that last stack," he says, lowering the bottle and glancing at the pile of books he was flipping through.

Gramps was an avid book collector and I think my grandma was too. There are a ton of old overflow books from the fifties packed away up here. Mostly editions of old classics, American lit, and some thrillers from the eighties with fun cheesy covers of explosions and bloodied hands gripping knives.

My book crazy bestie and sister-in-law would die from joy.

I just want to shower off all this muck. We'll talk about donating the books later.

If I never have to smell musty pages again for the next decade, I'm cool.

Over in the corner, behind the boxes, there's a painting propped against the wall. I've noticed it a few times, but I doubt that's the awesome secret.

I shuffle over and shake away the worst of the dust before I remove the grey tarp and gently turn it over.

I'm confronted with a picture so pretty I gasp.

It's a striking scene: brilliant blue sky, lively yellow flowers, and lavender rioting across green grass.

In the center, next to the flowers, there's a pair of little white shoes. They could be kids' shoes, judging by the small size.

The big grey tabby cat sprawled out next to them adds to the sense of size, sleeping in the shade of a tree at the edge of the flowery field.

The Maine countryside.

Possibly a familiar place, if that's the same lake I think it is in the distance.

It must be this house, a long time ago, back when it was full of love and life with perfectly maintained gardens that stretched down to the water.

"What did you find?" Kane joins me.

"Just an old painting."

"That's a stunner. Damn, those colors—looks like it was just finished yesterday. What's up with the shoes? Sophie had a pair almost like that when she was a baby."

"No idea. It's a little odd."

I tilt my head, studying the scene.

There's something familiar about the style, too, though I can't pin it down.

Did they hire someone to paint the backyard?

I gently wipe more dust off the glass frame, revealing the signature, and frown.

Where have I seen this before?

Another painting at Mom's house comes to mind. But this one was a close-up of vibrant red flowers in a tall white urn with wavy blue stripes.

It might've had the same signature.

No, I'm sure it did. Just like this one, it's gold, and I've seen that art a thousand times.

"Huh," I mutter, sinking down on my knees.

"You think this is it? Your holy relic?" Kane's gaze sharpens.

"No, but... I think my grandma might've painted this. I never knew her. She died a long time ago."

I look closer at the corner and wipe more stray dust until a gold signature pops out.

May Blackthorn.

My heart skips.

Gramps called me May until his dying day. Because I reminded him of my late grams in spirit, he told me.

"You think he wanted you to give her painting a good home?" Kane asks.

"I mean, probably. It couldn't hurt. But I don't think this is everything." I brush my fingers over the gold frame, feeling this odd longing. "I wish I'd known her. Things were never the same with this family after she was gone."

He nods silently as he admires the painting.

"It felt familiar when I saw it. There's another like this at my parents' house."

"Part of a series?"

"Could be. Mom still has a few here and there, hanging

around the house. I should probably take this back to the fam."

"Why don't you ask your mom if she knows what you're looking for? Might speed up the search," he suggests.

His eyes scan my face as it heats.

Oh, if only it were that easy...

The truth makes my heart hurt, which isn't new.

It's been this way for as long as I remember.

"My mom and grandfather were pretty estranged before he died," I say. "She wouldn't know. She wanted nothing to do with him."

"Harsh. I'm sorry," he rumbles gently.

"But I bet she'd love this painting. It was her mother, after all." I pick it up and tuck it under my arm. "At least we didn't just get mummified in cobwebs for no reason. Sorry you wasted your time."

"No waste if it's important to you, duchess. We'll keep looking."

"Hopefully!" I snort.

"Don't give up. If it takes effort, it must be worth it."

Yeah, we'll see.

I've had my doubts, but he could be right. Whatever Gramps left has to mean something if he decided to be this cryptic, right?

Right???

He knew me better than my own parents. Sometimes, it felt like my childhood was only real when I'd stay with him.

Losing him tore away a piece of my soul. Especially when he went out as stubbornly as he lived, hiding his illness until the bitter end.

We didn't even get to say goodbye.

This summer was the first without him, and so many things have changed in less than a year since he's been gone.

Mostly good things. Hattie and Ethan tying the knot, that

was a huge happy surprise, and it's all thanks to Gramps playing cupid from beyond the grave.

Unlike Ethan, I'm not getting a spouse out of this deal. No way.

For me, this is it.

The very last piece of him, and whatever's hidden away was something he thought was important enough for me to have.

I desperately want to push through and *find it.*

Like maybe it will somehow shake me out of this slump with my designs, my life. My entire world after Leonidas Blackthorn.

I'm almost at the pull-down staircase when a loose board splinters.

"Whoa!"

I stumble.

Scream.

My foot pitches into the sinkhole, which makes me drop the painting.

And I'm bracing for a rough landing before my brain catches up.

The impact never comes.

Strong hands grab my waist, swinging me back up before I can face-plant on the floor.

There's a huge wall of a chest in my face instead and a cloud of pine-scented man.

When I open my eyes, I'm safe in Kane's arms.

He's above me, scanning my face, breathing hard.

Holy shit.

"W-what was that?" My mouth goes dry and I lick my lips. My heart hammers like mad. My fingers tremble.

I'm lucky I didn't break a few bones. That sinkhole could've snarled my ankle and sent me crashing down at a nasty angle.

"Loose board death trap," he growls. "You're lucky I was right behind you."

No argument there.

I nod fiercely.

"You okay? Did you hurt your ankle?" He brushes stray hairs from my face. For such a big man, he moved like lightning, and now he's so gentle as he holds me.

He envelops me, anchoring me to him with one big arm around my waist.

I'm trembling now for a different reason as adrenaline whips through my body.

"I'll survive. Jesus, that was close," I whisper with a shaky laugh. "I'm fine, just—how did you get here so fast?"

"I used to play hockey when I was younger." His voice scrapes my spine like sandpaper, rough but reassuring.

My heart won't slow down, even though the shock of my near-death experience has faded.

"Hockey? That explains a lot."

He snorts. "Nothing special. It's all muscle memory now."

"Sweet. That must come in handy with saving clumsy women all the time."

"No. Just you, duchess." He gazes down at me with a hardness in his green eyes and, behind that, so much heat I shiver.

I could take that statement in so many awful directions, jokes and innuendo with devastating consequences.

But I don't dare.

He hasn't moved his hand from my waist. His free hand lingers in my hair, his thick fingers moving idly, gently tucking a loose strand behind my ear.

"Hockey," I say again. I'm almost squeaking.

What a sight that must've been.

Kane Saint with his ridiculous height and barrel chest tearing across the ice.

I can see the hockey stick clenched in his hands, murder in his eyes as he confronts the other team.

His animalistic focus on the puck, ready to plow his way through a solid line of huge men.

I'm not a big sports girl, but that I could watch.

Then I see a faceless woman in the stands, cheering him on.

Hot jealousy bolts through me.

She must've been something to hook herself a hockey beast, even if it didn't last. Were they high school sweethearts?

Stupid, I know.

I have no clue what happened to the kids' mom, but now it eats at me, almost as much as finishing Gramps' little treasure hunt.

I'm guessing they're not together anymore.

He hasn't worn a ring this whole trip and there's no sign of a woman in the picture, no mentions from the kids, no calls back home.

But once, she could've been his everything.

"Hockey," I whisper again.

"Don't tell me you just learned the word?" He smirks.

"No, I—I'm just surprised. And I wish I could've seen it."

His smirk widens. "Why's that?"

"Maybe it would've been nice to see you a little less buttoned-up and more spontaneous."

"Maybe?"

"*Orrr* maybe I just want to picture you being good at something besides swinging a hammer when I beg you not to."

His gaze drops to my mouth. "Woman, I'm good at a lot of things."

Oh, no.

Another image crowds my senses now.

One with his smirking face between my legs and his green eyes on mine as he slides my panties off with his teeth.

My heart jackhammers.

There's no ignoring the ache in my belly.

My hands find their way to his chest on their own, palms flattening against wall-to-wall Kane.

"You going to keep giving me shit for helping you or what?" he asks.

"Only because you're fun to tease. But for real, I'm glad you're here," I admit, a little too breathlessly.

"Yeah?" His voice is just as quiet.

He must be single.

Surely.

There's no other woman, and he certainly hasn't been here long enough to date.

If he even *does* date.

Who knows.

Somehow, that feels more foreign than seeing him dominating the ice.

This human brick, walking into a classy bar to meet a girl from an app with butterflies in her eyes.

He's too intense for something so mundane.

And there are so many mysteries, so many questions burning the tip of my tongue like a match.

But he hasn't let me go since I stumbled.

There's this fierce hunger on his face that sends lava to my fingers and toes.

No one looks at me like this.

Not in a long time.

Maybe never.

There's a promise in his eyes that says total ruin.

He shifts his weight, fingers flexing. I get this awful feeling he'll pull away then and make some flimsy excuse to stop touching me.

"Y'know, I might've twisted my ankle after all. Feels a little sore," I tell him.

"Your foot went pretty deep," he agrees.

"Yeah. I don't think you should let go just yet."

His lips curl up. I swear he's suppressing a growl.

The hand in my hair drifts down to my neck, over soft skin, and his thumb traces my pulse.

We're a human rubber band stretched to its limit, and it's too much to bear.

Screw it!

I kiss him.

Hard.

For this crazy heart-splitting second, he doesn't kiss me back.

His lips tighten, his rough mouth stone under mine, his grip on the back of my neck tightening.

Did I just fuck up?

Maybe he never wanted this.

Maybe he only wanted the fantasy, the flirting, to look without tasting.

Then he truly *grabs* me.

His kiss turns ravenous.

Possessive.

His hot growl pushes into my mouth until I'm vibrating.

His tongue sweeps the seam of my lips, not asking, and God, I let him in.

His kiss is a blazing red brand, claiming and soul deep.

If I thought I was on fire before, this—

This makes me Margot chocolate, helplessly melting.

All I can do is thread my fingers through his hair, tugging him closer, begging him to continue.

He retaliates by pushing me against a wooden beam.

The roughness tickles me through my t-shirt, and I whimper.

He replies by biting my bottom lip.

Holy shit!

Whatever this thing is between us, it's explosive.

Desire burns just under my skin.

I want to get closer, to inhale him, to surrender myself to a mouth made for dark delights and saintly sins.

My mind spins.

Dizzy with want, right down to the heavy wetness between my legs.

From the way he's kissing me back, I guess he feels it too.

Unrestrained lust.

Like a dormant volcano waking up.

And I was the tectonic call that made him erupt.

I'm the ground made to burn, ready to be reshaped by his passion.

That's hot and satisfying and deliciously heady.

His hands linger on my hips, holding me steady as he grinds against me, making me feel his erection.

Absolute battering ram.

No surprise, but it *is*.

He makes a ragged noise in the back of his throat, so sharp it makes me gasp.

God.

I've never needed a man like I need him now.

Right here, right now, dust and darkness and worries be damned.

His hand slides up my shirt, grazing bare skin.

His hands are so hot, incandescent, and he inhales softly against my mouth.

"Fuck, duchess. The things I want to do to you could put me in prison."

I bite my lip like the thirsty little deviant I am.

His dirty talk must be devastating.

I raise a leg and he catches my knee, pulling my legs open, and shit.

Holy flaming shit, I'm losing my mind.

"Dad?" Daniel's voice shakes my vision.

Kane freezes against me.

His hand squeezes my thigh almost painfully. I can practically taste his reluctance.

"Daaaad!"

Yep, we're dead.

I'm grateful he doesn't rip himself away too fast or I'd hit the floor again. There's a tent pitched in his jeans as he shifts his belt.

Scrambling, I finger comb my hair and tug my shirt down, pressing everything back into place and trying not to look at him.

Oh, man.

These *kids*.

Two very big little reasons why secret attic kissing should not be happening.

And one of those reasons starts coming up the ladder, stepping on the bottom stair and straining to look up.

I wipe a shaky hand over my mouth, grateful I didn't bother with lipstick today, trying to pull myself together.

Dan will be a distraction, at least, and I need one ASAP.

If Kane keeps looking at me like that, all dark and dangerous, I'm going to lose my calm.

We can't, we can't, *we can't*.

The boy pokes his head up through the small door a few seconds later, bewildered. He gets a lungful of the dusty attic and grimaces.

"Oh, yikes! It smells like Grandma's garage in here," he says, coughing. "And we're getting hungry. Is it almost dinnertime?"

I'm already moving, brushing past Kane, who remains stock-still.

I don't dare look at him, even as my body drifts past his.

If I could just rewind time and—

No, don't think about it.

"Great timing, Dan. We were looking for you," I say brightly. "Any chance you want to help me get this picture downstairs?" I retrieve the painting and hold it up.

Dan eyes it suspiciously. "You wanna keep that?"

"My grandmother painted it."

"Oh, cool. Yeah, no problem." Clearly no art connoisseur, he just holds out one hand. "Ready when you are."

"Go slow, Bud," Kane urges, hovering over us and ready to step in if it doesn't look like we can handle it.

"Be careful. Let's see…" I pause, counting the steps on the ladder. "Why don't you stand at the bottom and we'll just pass it down?"

Safety first.

If I'm the reason Kane's kids get hurt, won't that be the cherry on this awkward hot-shit sundae?

"Sure," Dan huffs. "Then will you guys come down for dinner?"

"Have some patience, little man," Kane grumbles behind me.

"It's fine, we're on our way." I don't look at Kane directly, but I'm sure his stance has relaxed a little. "We're done up here anyway."

My voice cracks a little on the last word as I scoot up, slowly dangling the painting down through the opening.

Dan reaches up and grabs it, then sets it on the floor.

"Coming?" I whisper over my shoulder.

I won't let my eyes focus.

Seriously, if I see him right now, I just know I'll see the disgust in his eyes.

"Right behind you. Take your time and watch your step down." His voice is so neutral, so flat it hurts.

Watch your step.

A little late for that, dude.

How do we coexist after trading wildfire kisses?

* * *

As soon as the painting gets tucked away safely in my room and I've cleaned up, I head outside.

Zero need to stick around for dinner.

If Dan caught one whiff of what was happening, then everyone knows I made out with Kane Saint by now.

Technically, my tenant.

Definitely my latest disaster.

My heart drums a messy rhythm, still lodged in my throat.

If Sully Bay has a town idiot, I've just stolen their place.

Nothing much to show for Gramps' huge riddle, and now I've gone and kissed a near-stranger.

Practically in front of his kids.

Yeah, there's no way I can face him again and ever look normal.

It's not that it's the first time I've kissed a stranger.

When you don't date much and you had the wild college phase a lot of girls do, accidental kisses happen.

But before, it was always in an upscale wine bar or after a short hike in the park. Or maybe after watching an Arizona sunset too perfect for life while some cute dumb Scottsdale boy invites me on his dad's private jet.

That's happened often enough over the years.

Men like me, and I like men.

I just don't really *date* them.

I've stayed away from lethal older single dads for good reason.

Messing around with a guy casually, that's one thing. But when kids are involved—oof.

And I've been happily keeping my distance from men ever since Kelso Tully cheated on me just when we were getting serious.

Fending off fuckboys, that's normal and boring. Old habit.

Then along came Kane Saint with his panther-like bedroom eyes and hockey body and big heart behind barbed wire.

Down went my shields.

Now, I'm cut to ribbons.

Stupid. So, so stupid.

This actually feels worse than college. I'm grown now, not innocent and naïve and forgivable because I haven't learned how to keep my hands to myself with guys who bring nothing good.

What was I *thinking?*

The obvious answer is I wasn't.

Goddammit.

Thankfully, it's early enough for me to pop next door and see the Babins. That's what I decide to do.

I could use the distraction, and the excuse.

If the kids ask why I wasn't around tonight—I didn't give a reason, I just fled—then I'll have a real alibi.

I also text Hattie in a panic, firing off messages until my thumbs hurt.

Hattie!!!

I did something dumb. help

What would you do if you kissed a guy you're accidentally living with?

And by what would you do, I mean what should I do

Because I might've kissed my renter
And it might've been really good
And his kids might have walked in on us
And now I am freaking OUT so text me back when you finish laughing. Thanks and bye

She doesn't reply.

I'm sure it'll be a while, now that she's living a normal life with my brother and running the best bookstore in Portland.

I pace the driveway, waiting for an answer.

This always happens when I don't want it to.

The second I let my guard down just an itty bit.

Historically, I'm drawn to terrible men.

I fall too hard, too fast, and get stupid fast.

Then comes the cannonball to the heart.

Kelso, the only prick I truly dated for years, just played me for my looks and my name.

I didn't see it at the time, but looking back, it was so obvious.

The way he had Margot Blackthorn in huge letters on our assigned seats at this stupid crypto conference with his venture capital friends should've been a dead giveaway.

Back when I thought he liked me for me, I thought he saw past the Blackthorn mystique.

I thought he admired the real me.

But all he wanted in the end was my name next to his, my smile plastered on his Instagram, and eventually, my money backing his dumbass investments in a questionable start-up.

Ethan warned me off him more than once, but I was lovestruck and I thought I felt something.

Stupid and in love?

That's a miserable place to be.

In the end, the way he broke my heart was vicious, getting so careless with his cheating it didn't matter if I found out.

He couldn't just end it like a normal human being and spare me the agony.

Especially not after I said *no* to a ten-million-dollar investment in crypto-backed meme tokens for public toilet access.

Even now, my heart stings a little, the way it always does whenever I think about him.

If I hadn't been so easily charmed, so obsessed, I would've seen it coming.

I'm not close enough to Kane to be damaged like that—not yet—but we're definitely close enough for me to *do* some damage.

He's a father.

And I still know basically nothing about him.

Hattie's obviously busy, so I give up and drive to the Babins' place next door.

I've never been here before, but it's nicely marked with a big sign in blue letters with hand-painted blueberries surrounding their name.

It's charming in a rustic way.

The house itself looks like a large cottage, a little worn but in an endearing way.

A bit like the owners, I suppose.

Soft lights gleam from the windows through the curtains, and I tuck my hair behind my ears as I approach the front door.

Calm. Sophisticated.

They were probably used to dealing with Gramps. He could make business deals in his sleep, and he never lost his head in a professional setting.

I knock gently and hear footsteps a few seconds later. Then the door swings open, revealing Viola Babin.

She looks more casual this time, wearing an oversized

grey hoodie with a pair of blueberries on the front. When she sees me, her fraught expression dissolves into a smile.

"Joe, get over here," she calls over her shoulder. "It's Margot Blackthorn!"

"Invite her in!" Joseph calls from somewhere in the house. "I'll put on some blueberry tea."

Dang, do these two have a life beyond blueberries?

Viola holds the door open wider.

"I'm so glad to see you again," she says, welcoming me inside.

The air feels warm, slightly dough-scented like they've been baking. The interior is just as quaint as the exterior, very much old farmhouse style before it became a modern suburban thing.

I step around the long vine-like leaves of a potted plant and into the kitchen. Joseph stands by the stove, beaming at me.

"What a surprise." He wipes his hands on his apron before approaching. "How are you, Miss Margot?"

"I'm good, thanks. I didn't have much going on this evening, so I thought I'd stop by to talk about the lake house."

"Of course," Viola says warmly. "Make yourself at home, please. We'd have tidied up if we'd known you were coming."

She laughs. Kind of a worn cackle, like it's been smoothed down by years of disappointment, not quite a comfortable sound.

"Don't put yourself out for my sake," I say honestly.

The kitchen has faded yellow walls and looks dated. Like it was put in twenty years ago and not updated since. And sure, there are dishes piled on the sides from dinner, but in general, it looks pretty neat.

Homey. Warm.

The kind of kitchen I always pictured my parents having

if we were normal and didn't have hired help cleaning dishes spotless the instant we finished eating.

"That's mighty nice of you to say," Joseph says over his shoulder. "Blueberry tea? We've got fresh honey too."

"Sure." I'm surprised these people haven't turned into Smurfs with their blueberry rich diet.

But I can't complain.

It's admirable to devote your life to something with this much passion.

"How are you settling in, dear?" Viola asks. "I heard you all went to the craft market?"

"News travels fast in these parts, huh?"

"Like the wind," Joseph says, setting a mug down in front of me and taking the seat across from me. "If we're dry on gossip, well, that's worse than running out of beer in Sully Bay."

He winks at me.

"I bet. You're lucky to live in a town where a few tourists passing through can make news instead of real problems."

"Just the famous ones, mostly, Miss Blackthorn." Joseph smiles.

I smile back, trying not to seem too awkward.

"We're truly blessed. It's a gorgeous season in a pretty place," Viola gushes. "And your granddad's lake house always was the crown jewel in these parts as far as land goes."

She talks on about the way they used to fly kites as kids and ride horses with their cousins when they were older, right up to the edge of Gramps' property.

And sometimes they'd catch the odd hiker wandering up from Acadia, which still happens to this day.

I can't imagine PopPop or Holden chasing people off like they did, but the Babins boast about their barbed wire, big dogs, and No Trespassing signs supposedly posted every thirty feet around their large farm.

"Like we said before, if you ever feel it's time to part ways with the old place, give us a holler!" Her smile fades. "Only thing is, though, I'm afraid we might not have the cash to buy it outright. But if you were flexible on financing…"

Oof.

I figured there were a few strings attached.

Then again, it's not like I need the money.

I can afford to be generous and patient with folks who need a little breathing room, especially when I'm not sure the blueberry business is making them rich.

This house is big and warm, but it's outdated and a little musty, the longer I'm here.

My eyes flick over a couple old water stains on the ceiling, not well painted over to blend back in.

"That could work. If I decide to sell," I say carefully.

The thought makes me sadder than I expected, and I don't know why.

They could give the old place a second life, couldn't they?

The Babins are farmers. There's probably a ton of untapped potential in the soil, but that would mean losing the house forever, sooner or later.

That stings when I can still feel PopPop in every room.

Joseph leans back in his chair with a sigh that seems to come from his feet.

"Would be nice to do something useful with that land again. It's been ages going to waste with rich people owning it, just rotting away." He snorts with disgust.

Um, what?

I jerk my face up just in time to see Viola shoot him a sharp look.

That sting in my chest deepens.

"Dearie, I apologize. My Joseph doesn't always think before he yaps. He meant no disrespect," Viola says hastily.

"Yeah, uh, sorry 'bout that. Ma always told me I was born

with foot-in-mouth fever. You Blackthorns always had a knack for keeping things pretty around here. There's a reason your family's so loved in these parts." He grins uncomfortably.

That's not what he implied a minute ago.

I sip the blueberry tea, which tastes more like syrup with way too much sugary honey.

Joseph shakes his head. "I just meant—aw, it's nothing, but my family owned that land once."

"*Extended* family," Viola corrects.

"Extended relatives, yes. A long, long time ago now—almost a hundred years, way back in the 1930s. Rough time for the country and for Maine, too. Huge floods drove the Babins out one year. For a while, that lake was a giant swamp." His mouth twists in what could be a smile or a grimace. "The land was pretty useless till Leonidas came in with his money in the sixties."

"Money talks with a loud mouth," Viola says, like she's trying to lighten the atmosphere. "And your granddad had a lot of it, bless his soul. He put in a modern drainage system and hired a bunch of contractors. Took a few years to get everything cleaned up with state-of-the-art stuff. He brought the land back to life."

"Money don't just talk, sometimes it punches," Joseph says. "I'm just saying, Miss Blackthorn, we're good for it. We'll work something out whenever you want to get this ball rolling, whatever it takes."

When.

The word lands in my lap like a cactus, sharp and heavy.

This is not what I came here for.

I wanted a distraction.

I wanted to get out of Kane's sight and breathe again.

I wanted to think about the future, but now that I'm stuck

here in this bizarre conversation, I'm not sure I actually *want* to sell the old place.

Not this soon, anyway.

I'm also a little creeped out, and I'm not sure why.

They've been perfectly nice, even if they're a little too honest for their own good.

But the way they're watching me...

It feels like hawks scanning the fields for mice.

Hungry. Impatient.

A little ruthless, maybe.

Hardly the nice easy chat I expected.

If I announced I was selling this minute, I'm sure they'd shove a contract in my face to sign away my soul.

"It's been fun, guys, but I should probably head back for dinner," I lie, pushing my mug back toward them. I barely touched it. "I'll get back to you about the property before I leave town. I haven't made a final decision, either way."

"Of course." Viola's smile feels forced. "You haven't been here long, Miss Margot. Take all the time you need."

Yeah, okay.

I give them a halfhearted little wave as I head back into the cool night. My car is right where I left it, waiting to make the short drive.

Nightfall swept in while I was at the Babins' house, and when I pull up and park in the long driveway, there's an autumn silence shared by the tinsel stars overhead.

So calm.

So peaceful.

So worry free—except for the human grizzly in the house I couldn't keep my hands away from.

Sigh.

I let out a long, hushed breath.

The shock mortification after the kiss has faded, sure, but there's an afterburn that smells like anxiety and shame.

And it's so overpowering I have no clue how to face Kane again.

Or Dan with his adorably unfiltered mouth.

Or little Sophie and her cherub smile.

Holy hell.

Hopefully the kids didn't catch on to what was happening in the attic, but it doesn't make it any less cringey for me. Or clinically insane. Or—

Yeah, no.

Time to stop thinking about it.

My phone buzzes, and I grab it, relief flooding through me.

"Oh, thank God," I mutter as I pick up. "Hattie? Has Ethan had you chained up?"

She laughs so loud I have to hold the phone away.

"Oh my God, no. But I need to hear everything right now. What guy did you kiss? When? How hot is he on the Dornan to Hemsworth scale?"

"Take a breath, girl."

"Not a chance! You were on a dating fast. What happened?"

Great question.

"...I'm still figuring that out," I admit. "You know the family I mentioned who turned into surprise roommates? Well, Renter Daddy wanted to help me out. We were up in the attic looking for whatever Gramps left—we didn't find it—but then I tripped on a broken board and he caught me and there was just *so much* thirst."

"The dream." She sighs fondly.

"Holy shit, if you're about to mention my brother and *thirst—*"

"You're getting distracted, Gigi," she interrupts. "Back to the deets."

"*Fine*. So he's hot. Like so hot it's scary. Horrible attitude, of course."

"See? You're living a rom-com dream."

"I don't *have* rom-com dreams," I remind her.

But her banter makes me feel better. Like maybe I can finally walk into the house without turning into stone the second Dadzilla lays his eyes on me.

"Okay, fine, you're living *my* rom-com dream. What are you going to do now? Have you seen him since?"

"Nope. I kinda ran away and he didn't stop me."

"You mean you've been avoiding him?"

"Did you miss the part where I mentioned he has kids? And they basically walked in on us?"

"Minor detail."

Despite myself, I laugh.

My shoulders relax.

"Not minor, Hattie. But what am I supposed to do now? We're stuck under the same roof."

"The only thing you can—let him make the next move," she says immediately.

Brutally good advice.

Ever since she tied the knot with Ethan, it's clear her confidence has improved dramatically.

"…that's a whole lot of nothing on my part."

"Exactly. Just walk in and pretend it never happened. The sitcom remedy." She laughs again.

"Yeah, I don't know. Do you really think—"

I don't get to finish.

A shadow bursts from the trees, large and blurred, yet shaped too much like a man.

He nearly smacks into the front of my car, the silhouette bright and unmistakable for a split second against the dark horizon.

I scream.

A heartbeat later, he's gone.

The darkness swallows him like he never existed.

"Holy shitballs!" I spit the words as I lock the car pathetically.

He's gone, he's gone—but just gone from sight.

With my hands shaking, I put the car in Reverse and back out so fast my wheels kick up stray rocks.

Did that just happen?

But it did.

It was a man.

An intruder, illuminated in the headlights.

He came charging at me, straight past my window.

"Margot? Gigi, are you there?" Hattie's worried voice floats up from the floor where I dropped my phone. "What's going on?"

I need a few panicked seconds to catch my breath.

A sob rattles my chest.

"H-Hattie, I should go," I strangle out. "Someone's here who shouldn't be… and I think they were watching me."

VIII: HOUSE RULES (KANE)

I'm convinced I need a muzzle.

No bad-mannered mutt ever did worse than the shit I pulled.

Yes, I expected pure torture from the moment we met, but I never thought it would go down like this.

I never thought I'd let one charged kiss melt my brain like an ice cream cone dropped on a sidewalk in July.

I've barely finished cleaning up dinner—left a plate for her in the microwave again, if she comes back—when Margot bursts through the door.

Blue eyes wide, blonde hair whipping around her face, and that gorgeous face—

She's gone bone-white.

This isn't the same woman who wouldn't look at me when she fled the house after my biggest mistake since the divorce.

"Kane!" she yells as the door slams against the wall. "Kane, thank God."

The panic in her voice activates pure instinct.

I'm already moving before I process what she's said. My hands grip her upper arms and she gasps.

She stares up at me with stark fear flashing in her eyes.

"What the hell happened?" I whisper, iron yet gentle.

Her eyes flutter shut and then open again as she breathes roughly.

Her throat tightens.

"I... I was in the car, just pulled up at the end of the driveway and—there was someone there. A man, watching me, slinking around in the shadows. When I saw him, he freaked. He went flying right past my car, and I—" She's trembling now, and I guide her into a chair.

"Sit," I tell her. All my old military instincts sharpen, and a familiar icy calm settles over me. "Start from the beginning. What did you see?"

"Not much. Definitely a man. He was hiding in the brush, I think. I was only there a minute before he just sprinted past the car, and—"

She breaks off as the kids come barreling into the kitchen.

"A man? What man?" Sophie squeaks.

"A bad guy! Don't worry, I'll find him." Dan rips a drawer open in the key drop by the back door, rifling through it until he finds a flashlight.

"No, you won't." I grab him before he reaches the door. "You're staying put and I'm going out there."

"But—"

"No buts, little man. Lock the back door after me."

The severity on my face says there's no argument as I pry the flashlight out of his hand.

Dan nods, his face falling a little.

Margot slumps down in a kitchen chair, watching me through damp blue eyes while Sophie looks on, bewildered.

"Hello?" a tinny voice says on the other end of the phone

clenched in her fingers. "Is everything okay? Did you make it back?"

Slowly, mechanically, she raises the phone to her ear and speaks, looking at me the whole time. "Yes, I'm okay, Hattie. I'm with Kane and the kids now."

"Kane? Is that the guy who—"

"Bye!" Margot ends the call.

"Stay with them while I investigate." I grip the flashlight in one hand. It's one of those long, sturdy tactical flashlights built for the outdoors. The hard, all-weather shell built around it makes it double as a small club.

Possibly left behind by Leonidas' bodyguard or maybe the old man himself.

At close quarters, it's a makeshift weapon, which might be useful. Can't rule out anything the second I step outside.

Adrenaline tosses my heart like a tumbleweed, but I wrestle back the caveman instinct to go rushing out there in the dark.

First, I need to make sure these guys stay safe and the area around the house is clear.

"Sophie," I say. "I need you to stay with Margot and Dan, okay?"

She nods, her small green eyes wide.

Dan brushes past me, grinning in triumph. "Ready to lock it when you are."

"Good. I'll wait until I hear that click," I tell him. "Now what do you do if someone comes to the door and it isn't me?"

"Call 9-1-1," the kids say together.

"And hide," Dan adds.

"Right. You head upstairs to our room and lock the door. Push the heaviest thing you can find in front of it." I glance at Margot, grateful to see her color returning. "Will you stay with them? I won't be long. Exactly where did it happen again?"

"That section with the overgrown brush," she says.

So they were lurking near the house, then.

That's fucking grim for intentions, knowing that brush is thick.

Also tells me they were probably around long enough to figure that out, which means they could've scoped out the entire place.

Shit.

I nod firmly and make sure my phone is still in my pocket, brandishing the flashlight in my other hand.

"Anything else I should know?" I lock eyes with Margot.

"I don't think so. Just—be careful, Kane."

"Don't worry about me. If I find anybody poking around, worry for them."

The color fades from her cheeks again.

I'm not trying to scare her, but I'm deadly serious.

Asses will be kicked to the moon if I find anybody on our land.

Her land.

What the fuck ever.

"Stay put, guys," I warn once again, looking them over. "I'll be back soon."

***

THE DRIVEWAY IS long and dark, one long cold shadow when the temperature drops.

I can see my breath in my flashlight beam. It's not that late, but it's pitch-black under the tall trees near that brush. I get why she panicked.

Fuck.

I expected trouble in the wake of the kiss, yeah, but not chasing a prowler.

At least the kids seem more excited than scared.

Dan's having the time of his life playing superhero. The boy's too young to have a real sense of danger and old enough to think that a few summer karate classes turned him into a lethal machine.

Sophie only panics when she's alone, and I'm glad as hell there's plenty of company for her.

A twig snaps under my shoe.

I swing my flashlight over the path, checking for any movements, any rustling on the horizon that can't be blamed on the trees.

Nothing.

It doesn't take long to get to the spot where Margot parked and claims she saw the shadow man.

There are tire marks on the ground from where she squealed away and kicked up gravel. Then there's the brush, where she swore the man was lurking.

I approach warily, my senses on high alert.

If he's smart, he's long gone.

Only, she didn't stick around to find out if he was alone. Or if he came back.

The leaves seem bleached in the light as I circle the brush, reversing direction every few seconds to avoid anyone getting the drop on me.

Nothing and nobody.

Just dead autumn silence.

My lungs heave with tension.

Loud frogs croak in the night. A few thin branches sway in the breeze.

It's an eerie night even without any mysterious prowlers. I wouldn't be surprised if a coyote came slinking out of the brush.

As I look closer, my flashlight catches something glinting in the grass.

There are several broken twigs and a patch of flattened grass like someone was camped out here for a while.

And right in the middle, an unlit lantern.

Shit.

Fury knifes through me as I pick it up, examining it in the light.

This isn't the sort of thing you'd pick up from a store—it looks weirdly homemade or modified. Stained glass, maybe, it's tinted dark blue to dull the LED light inside.

Whoever did this knows a few tricks.

No trail, no trace of them at all except for this fucking lantern.

How long was he here? And why?

Did Margot startle him when she parked, flushing him out of the trees? If she was this close, he might've thought it was just a matter of time until she saw him and bolted.

But who the hell would come snooping around the place this late?

I search the area one more time, but there's nothing besides this ghostly blue lantern.

I head back to the house and knock.

Margot appears in the doorway a second later. Her eyes widen when she sees the lantern.

"What's that?" she whispers.

"A present left by our friend. Found it abandoned in the brush."

Dan and Sophie appear by her side, crowding in to get a good look.

"Whoa!" Dan gasps. "Dad, what is *that*?"

"Just a lantern some careless idiot threw together. Let's not get carried away, okay? We could've just had a stray camper who decided to crash on this land."

Yes, I'm playing up the mundane possibilities.

I don't want them worried sick.

I'm also reasonably confident any imminent danger has passed. The average burglar or rural squatter is more skittish than a deer.

There's no good reason to come back now that they know this place isn't vacant, or an easy target.

"So... we're not in danger?" Sophie asks softly.

"No," I say emphatically. "And if we were, they'd have to get past me first. Bad day for any clown who tries."

Sophie smiles as I wink at her and ruffle her hair.

Margot gives a whisper of a smile too. I hate that it feels like a weight off my shoulders.

"You're lucky you guys have a scary dad," she tells the kids, still watching me intently.

"Sure are." I flex my guns like a bombastic wrestler until they laugh.

The corner of her mouth dimples. "And if there was someone creeping around out there, I guess they can't see much now. Not without the lantern. It's so dark tonight."

Sophie pushes her glasses up her nose and looks at Margot with clear relief.

"Why don't you guys go watch TV? Just to be on the safe side, I think we'll stay in tonight. It's too cloudy for much stargazing anyway," I say.

Dan already has the remote in his hand. I wait until he's bickering with Sophie about what to watch.

Then I wave Margot closer.

"Hey, you mind heading upstairs with me for a minute?"

Her expression freezes over, but she nods, threading her fingers through her hair. Her phone stays in her hand as she follows me up to my bedroom.

After everything that happened between us earlier, this feels like another mistake in the making, but I force away the thought as I push the door shut, leaving it open a crack to hear what's going on downstairs.

"Tell me if you're good. For real," I growl.

"I'm... yeah, I've calmed down a bit." She clears her throat, glancing at the wall I caught her tapping on before. "I'm really sorry if I freaked you guys out."

"You didn't scare me. And Dan's always desperate to prove he's just as tough as his old man, so you didn't scare him, either." I fold my arms. "Soph, she's stronger than she looks. But we'll file a police report in the morning."

A line forms between her brows.

"A police report? Really?"

"Better to have something on record in case it happens again."

"Hmm. Doesn't that seem..." She shrugs. "Just a little like overkill? I dunno, what if it was just a drunk camper who strayed too far or some local kids screwing around?"

"Then the cops will know it's a camper or some little hellraisers. If it is, they probably came stomping around other people's properties, so we'd be doing a community service." I hold up the lantern again. "Hate to say it, but this doesn't strike me as a wandering drunk. Somebody made this thing carefully so they could prowl around without being seen. The glass really dims the light."

"But *who?*"

I shake my head slowly. "Your guess is as good as mine. But I damn sure intend to find out."

She sighs and her shoulders slump as she sits on the edge of the bed.

"God, I'm glad I wasn't here alone," she says. "And you're right, filing a report might make sense. Just in case they come back."

"Exactly." I crush the protective feeling that rises when I see her hunched over like this, a small sparrow of a woman seeking shelter. "I don't want this rattling you more than it has. If you're not okay, you tell me."

"Just shocked, I think. If someone was watching me..." She trails off and holds out her hands, examining her nails. Her fingers are trembling. "The Babins were being weird, too."

"That's where you went? Their place?"

She nods.

"I said I'd drop by, and it seemed like as good a time as any." She glances at me, then looks away quickly. "But they just felt overeager or something. I knew they wanted to buy the place, but they were super strange about it. Too enthusiastic. A little snippy. I dunno, it's hard to explain."

I drop into a chair next to the bed, facing her until she looks at me. My mind works, wondering if they would've had time to sneak over here after she left.

They could have associates, too. Someone told to come snooping while they knew she was occupied.

"Try me," I say.

"Um, well." She tucks a lock of hair behind her ear. I force myself not to think about the way it felt like silk when I kissed her, just like her skin. "It's like they wanted to hide how desperate they are for me to sell. They were pretty open about needing some leeway with financing, too. But it also felt like they wanted all their cards on the table."

I feel the hair on the back of my neck rise, thinking back to when they dropped by the house.

I didn't think much of them then, when I was more annoyed by Margot than anything else.

They seemed like your average overly friendly, slightly eccentric rural folk who've lived in the sticks for too long without much socializing with strangers.

I lean forward, my forearms braced on my legs.

Margot's gaze darts over me before it settles on the floor.

"Why do you think they're so interested?" I ask. "Do they want the house or the land?"

"The land for sure." She sucks her lip as she thinks. "It just felt like they were trying too hard, y'know? A little too twitchy about the whole thing. I think they expected me to sign it over right there. It weirded me out, so I left."

"You drove straight back here? How long were you parked outside?"

"Yeah, pretty much. My friend Hattie called and I was talking to her when I pulled in." She runs her fingers along the duvet idly. "I don't know how long I sat in the car. Ten minutes or so, maybe? It wasn't a long conversation."

Still, that's enough time for either Babin or a sneaky friend to come creeping if they decided to go full psycho.

Why, who knows, but when she tells me something's up with the Babins, I believe her. The timing feels suspect as hell.

I've never been a big believer in coincidences.

"I'll keep an eye on them," I promise, leaning back in the chair. "Also, we should talk to other folks in town. Find out more about the history, if your grandfather ever left anybody with hard feelings."

"It shouldn't take too long with the gossip train here. The Babins knew we went to the hardware store." She blushes.

"We'll be careful. Last thing we need is them suspecting anything."

"Yeah," she agrees. There's a shy tilt to her thin smile I haven't seen before. "Uh, so, about earlier..."

Earlier.

The kiss.

The attic fuckery, hot and heady and hungry.

Her lips on mine, stirring a thirst that had me kissing her back like I wanted her for breakfast, lunch, and dinner.

"That was a fuckup, duchess. All mine," I growl before I remember how good she tasted.

"Well, yeah, but that's not fair." She tucks her hands under her thighs. "Technically *I* kissed you. Remember?"

I wish to Almighty God I didn't.

"You wouldn't have done it if I'd kept my distance. That was my fault, and I don't mean breaking your fall."

The moment I caught her, I should've set her down and stepped back.

My hesitation cost us dearly.

"So what? You think that means I have no autonomy?" She cocks her head, her hair spilling across her shoulder. "A girl can't make her own choices? She's just helplessly dickmatized by the amazing Kane Saint?"

I snort loudly.

"I wasn't thinking. I invited trouble," I tell her. "It's been a long damn time since I shared a space with a woman."

Her blue eyes flare.

I have to look away before she starts asking too many questions.

Hell, before I'm tempted to answer them.

"We lost our heads. That's it. Doesn't have to be more complicated," I finish, nodding for emphasis. "We were overwhelmed. It was a long-ass day, and—"

And her body was pure velvet against mine.

So inviting, calling my hands to every curve.

If she hadn't put her mouth on mine, I might've erupted anyway.

I might've grabbed her bottom lip with my teeth and thieved every moan.

Her jumping me, that was a relief, if I'm brutally honest.

But it calcified my brain like an expired orange.

I can't forget that.

She's nodding with almost as much irritation.

"Never again," she whispers.

"Never."

Then she smiles, a little awkwardly, and looks out the window, into the night. But instead of stepping back and giving her space, my eyes stay glued to her.

The way her lips purse, the shyness on her face, the wicked thoughts that must be swirling in her head.

Margot Blackthorn isn't innocent or introverted, but there's hesitation there now.

And it's fucking adorable.

Same for the way she glances at me, a little too fast, like she wasn't expecting to find me watching her.

Damn.

But I'm a man who learns his lessons, and it's time to fucking *go*. I stand up.

No more getting deep in her business, helping her look for whatever it is her gramps left behind now that we've scoured the attic. I'm sure she can reach the other places in the house.

No more getting too close.

No fucking more fantasizing about ripping her clothes off while I take my teeth to her skin, marking her from head to toe.

Good luck.

Not sure I can control that one when she's around, looking like a wet dream made flesh, but I can try.

And if sharing an isolated house with a beautiful woman and only *occasionally* getting hard to dirty thoughts about her is the worst of it, that's a victory.

As long as it doesn't become reality.

From the relief in her eyes, she knows it, too.

We don't need to drag this out when we're on the same page.

Dan almost walking in on us mid-kiss was the wake-up call we needed.

"All right, I have some reading to do," I say, jerking my thumb at the door and stepping back. She nods. "I left you a plate. You can heat it up later if you want."

"Again?" Her confusion melts into something warmer. "Dude, you have to stop doing that."

"What? Leaving you to starve for no good reason when we always have leftovers?"

"No," she says, still a little soft, a little gentle. "Taking care of me, I mean."

Oh, that.

That's one more sign I really am the idiot who's making this so hard.

Keeping her fed isn't putting distance between us, is it?

And even if that's another fucking fumble, even if I'm making our lives more intimate than they should be, we both know I'm not stopping.

Not as long as we're under one roof, two prisoners to our own depraved desires.

IX: HOMEWORK (MARGOT)

*A*fter the day I've had, there's no freaking chance I'm getting any work done on my designs.

But I sit down at the desk anyway, stylus in hand. My tablet waits blankly in front of me like a mirror to my soul.

I want to focus on pretty shoes. Delicate heels and strappy sandals and pumps made with Cinderella-worthy class. Boots with so much sass they turn heads on a swivel, making every footstep a statement.

Wouldn't boots like that fit Maine perfectly?

I'm not sure my heart will ever match my head when my muse whispers quietly. Right now, she's being drowned out.

Kane.

Kane.

My unexpected white knight. Eighty percent devil and part-time gentleman.

Would the creeper have scattered for good without that big man charging out the door to protect us?

I wonder.

And I can't wait to file a police report now, because even

if I hadn't seen him run past, the look on Kane's face when he came back in, holding that lantern...

I shudder, even though I'm toasty warm in my purple robe.

...but what if he's right?

If someone put in the effort to make a discreet lantern, who's to say what they were up to?

I swear, they were *watching me*.

But along with the fear churning in my stomach, there's a different jitter when I think about Kane Saint.

At first, he was all bravado. More eye-rolling rather than intimidating, even if he had that authoritative spark from the very beginning, when *I* felt like the intruder barging in.

Now, knowing he's just a few doors down, ready to tear the heads off anyone who breaks into this house, it makes me feel safe.

Am I really such a shallow girly-girl?

The thought makes me snort.

Never, in all my twenty-five years alive, have I felt like I needed a *protector*.

When you're a Blackthorn, there's always someone watching your back.

Hired security at private events dripping with money. Or Holden Grumpface when I was little, always somewhere when PopPop was around, quietly making the rounds like a loyal guard dog.

The man could give Kane a run for his money, all sharp edges and hidden secrets.

I'm pretty sure he's a single dad these days, too.

Looking after myself came naturally, though. Especially with parents who were more concerned about their next luxury stay in the Maldives than my emotional well-being.

But this feels different, a threat I've never known.

This isn't some ass-clown trying to get close to me

because they think I'm an easy in with Blackthorn money. I've lived and breathed that since I turned sixteen.

This person was *stalking* me.

Not online.

Not with cringey texts or unsolicited dick pics.

They invaded a special place very few people know about.

Of course, it's no secret locally that I inherited this place after Gramps died, and we went into town where word travels fast. But there's no one here with a grudge against me specifically.

Right?

Gramps on the other hand...

What did he do here alone? What was his life like in Sully Bay with my grandma, long before he ever brought us here as kids?

There's a knock on my door, and my heart jumps up my throat.

Small miracle I don't scream.

My legs tremble as I push up to stand, wrapping my robe tighter.

Kane again?

My heart starts humming for a different reason.

This late seems unlikely, and if it is, does it mean he's rethought his whole mistake speech?

Is he about to storm in here bristling, ready to smother me in kisses and throw me on the bed?

When I open the door with my breath stalled, there's a blank space where Kane's head should be, towering above me.

Instead, I look down and see a munchkin.

Her hair's messy and she's wearing cotton pajamas with sheep on them.

"Sophie?"

"I can't sleep," she mumbles, swaying forward like I've already invited her in.

I glance up and down the hall.

Still and silent, just the way it should be.

Uncertain, I push the door open wider.

"What's up? Did you hear something?"

"No, it's not that." She shakes her head and shuffles in as I close the door.

"Oh." A quick glance at my smartwatch tells me it's almost midnight. "What is it, then? Do you need your dad?"

She stops and looks at my desk with my tablet propped on its stand.

Her little eyes flash with a familiar light I've seen in Kane's eyes.

"No, um… I just wanted to talk to you. Because you make shoes."

Well, not really and not yet.

But she seems so serious, I don't dare disappoint her with inconvenient facts.

"Sure, Soph. What's up?"

I invite her to sit with me on the bed.

"So, I was thinking… could you help me get rid of these?" She flops down on the bed and holds up her black heavy shoe for inspection. I didn't notice them in her hand earlier. "I hate them. I never get to wear anything pretty, not like other girls. Not like you."

My heart pinches.

Poor, sweet baby.

The ortho shoes *are* ugly. They're built for function, the aesthetics an afterthought, drab and clunky with thick straps laid over the top.

They also look too big for her feet. I guess that's the point medically to give her extra support and protection.

But if I was stuck wearing these things, I'd be sad too.

I take my time, leaning in to examine them from every angle, turning her foot gently. "How long have you worn them?"

She pushes her glasses up her nose.

"This type, a few years. When I was little, I didn't mind the others so much, but now... They're like braces, but your teeth never get any better!"

My heart.

This is so wildly out of my scope as a designer, and I'm not even a real designer yet.

It's just a wild dream backed by a fashion degree I was lucky to get. Designing something with medical considerations, that's a whole different ballgame.

But she's watching me with trusting green eyes and I can't tell her no.

I can't just explain away her hopes and dreams with lifeless logic, even if it's the normal, adult thing to do.

"I'll see what I can come up with, Sophie. Just give me some time," I say firmly.

She leans forward and hugs me.

"Awesome! Thanks a ton, Margot. You rock."

I rub her back, a little self-conscious.

I don't deserve this little girl.

She's already thanking me for a miracle I probably can't deliver, and with so much gratitude you'd think I just made it rain puppies on parachutes.

But at the same time, warmth blooms in my chest.

I'm not used to kids hugging me. It's surprisingly nice, and her skinny arms around my neck feel reassuring.

I give her a parting squeeze.

"I'll definitely help out if I can, but just know, I can't promise anything. Are you cool with that?"

"Oh, yeah, I *know*," she says earnestly. "But that's better than no one trying at all, right?" My surprise must show on my face, because she adds, "Dad's cool and all. He just doesn't get wanting to look pretty."

No, I don't suppose he does.

Dadzilla might be an expert at a lot of things, but that excludes his little girl's style and self-image.

Sophie watches me a second longer, her small face pinched in thought.

"You know, it's okay if you wanna kiss him," she says slowly.

What?

I sputter, my fist banging my chest as I try to parse what she said. Surely, she didn't actually mean—

"Kiss? Honey, are you talking about me and… your dad?"

She gives me a dull look. "Well, yeah. Who else?"

I can't breathe.

"Why would you say that?"

"Dan said he saw you guys kissing in the attic."

Holy shit!

I freeze.

"No, that was—" I stop before I hit a new low point in my life.

Dan did see. Or he's smart enough to add it up.

I'm mortified.

"It's cool, Margot," Sophie whispers gently.

"It's not cool. Not even a little." My voice is so faint. No version of this fact will ever be okay. "It was a mistake, really—an accident. We weren't thinking and we're never going to do it again."

What else can I offer her but the truth?

I think she'll be relieved, or at least she'll pick up on my humiliation and back off, but it turns out I've misjudged her.

She just folds her arms and looks at me stubbornly.

"You should."

"I can't believe we're having this conversation." I stop

short of burying my face in my hands.

"Dad *needs* a girlfriend," she hisses.

It's so comical I could almost forgive her for springing this on me.

"I doubt he'd agree. And besides, Sophie, um…"

Where do I even start?

How do you explain to a child that a kiss doesn't mean two people want a serious relationship?

Especially two people like us.

Kane Saint couldn't be more different from everything I know.

Kids. Baggage. Big homemade breakfasts instead of croissants and coffee or green smoothies from a grab-and-go café.

Nothing says he even *likes* me enough to want to kiss me again beyond our shared thirst.

When I tried talking to him about it like a normal human being, he just bowed up and denounced what happened.

Probably for the best, honestly, because I've already decided it should never happen again.

But still.

There's a difference between knowing something and having the man you kissed in a stuffy attic tell you what an awful move it was.

Especially when I'm the one who kissed him first.

Arrogant prick.

If it was a ginormous mistake—and yes, we both agree on that—then it was *mine*.

"Dad hasn't been with anybody since Mom," Sophie confesses with wide eyes.

I hate that I'm interested in this little nugget of news.

"Your mom?"

"Oh, she has *loads* of boyfriends. I barely remember their names." Sophie's voice is scathing. "Dad, he should get one lady friend, at least. It's only fair."

Oh, man.

I have no earthly clue how to interpret that statement, but my heart skips anyway.

So their mom is still in their life, but things are strained.

I mean, he has the kids here for fall, which must mean he has primary custody?

Not that I know much about how all that works. But I can't pass up this opportunity to find out more.

I draw my legs up under me and face her like we're two besties at a slumber party.

"What's your mom like, anyway? Apart from the boyfriends, I mean."

Her face screws up as she thinks, but she doesn't tense up, which makes me think the question isn't awful. Hopefully, talking about her mom isn't a sore spot.

"Dad says she's not very down-to-earth, and I guess he's right," she says eventually. "He needs somebody more grounded."

Oof.

Let's steer this conversation away from our dating potential.

"When did they split?"

"Last year. But it wasn't great for a long time before that."

"Are you okay? Do you need to talk to someone about it?"

"We did that for a while." She shakes her head and her glasses slide down her nose. "Actually, it's better now that we don't. It's starting to feel normal again."

"How do you mean?"

"When Mom and Dad were married, they'd get mad at each other a lot and fight. But now when they talk to each other, they're just nicer." She twirls a strand of hair around her fingers. "I can live with that and so can Dan. And I think he's happier since he left the company too."

So much to unpack there.

"Company? What company?"

"Uhhh, yeah." She wrinkles her nose as she thinks and it's adorable. "I think it was called Opti-something or other. Studios."

Okay.

I make a mental note to Google it later.

"But I don't think he ever liked it," she confides. "He used to come home all grumpy."

"Huh. Can't imagine *that* when he's a big shiny cinnamon roll." I only mean it half-sarcastically.

And I can't help smiling as I think about the Kane I've gotten to know.

When he forgets to be all up his own ass and relaxes, he can be fun. Chill. Smiley even.

The rest of the time?

Pure beast.

Her large eyes shine behind her glasses. "He wasn't as grumpy when he played hockey, though."

Oh yeah, how could I forget?

My mind was glued to him owning the ice when he mentioned it after breaking my fall.

And then what happened next, with the kiss...

No, don't think about it.

"Was he a good player?" I ask.

"So good!" She beams. "He was really famous once. Like people used to beg for his autograph. I remember one time we were at the store and this lady wanted to take a picture with him. Dan and I were really little."

"I bet. How old is your dad?"

"Thirty-six," she says proudly. "Pretty much Jurassic old."

"Yeah, that's super old." I laugh.

"How old are you?" she asks curiously, hugging her knees.

"I'm twenty-five."

"That's old too. Just not *ancient*."

"Thank you," I say flatly.

"You're only prehistoric after thirty."

"Yeah?" I remember when I was her age, and even twenty felt like it was light-years away.

I was sure that by the time I turned twenty, I'd have my shit together.

Gorgeous, brilliant career.

My own money that doesn't come from a trust.

Over the issues that come with being a Blackthorn.

But then I hit the age and I was still a rich brat, learning how to grow into the name I grew up with. Ignorantly thinking people would love me for *me*, and not because of my grandfather.

I've always been attractive though, so at least I had that.

The past five years have taught me a ton.

Mostly about who I am, what I want.

Just one freaking winning shoe design, for example, though what she's asking for is way out of my comfort zone.

"Dad said thirty was when he started getting grey hair."

I think back to his dark hair, the tiny hints of silver by his ears. If that's all natural, he's doing well.

"On *that* note," I say, giving her a little push, "I think it's time for bed. Try to get some sleep, before your dad finds out what you told me. I don't think he'll want people knowing he's going grey."

She giggles. "But you can *see* them!"

"Only if you're really close." And I have no intention of getting that close again. "Come on, bedtime. It's late and I'm only five years away from being old, so I need my rest before they shuffle me off to a home."

She giggles maniacally.

"But you'll remember the shoes, right?" she asks anxiously as I walk her to the door.

Even the most stonehearted person on the planet couldn't resist that pleading look. And I'm far from granite.

"Absolutely, baby," I promise. "Sleep well."

She gives me a little wave as she leaves, and I close the door, leaning against it.

It feels like a bomb just went off, blowing my life to confetti.

The shoes.

Kane Saint, (in)famous hockey player.

The awkwardness around his life, his career at—Opti-something.

But Opti-what? And why is it so Opti-weird?

My phone waits on the bed.

I throw myself down and snatch it up, bringing up a new tab to start some deep sleuthing.

* * *

I'm positive I'm going to beat Kane downstairs the next morning, but by the time I step into the kitchen with the sun barely peeking over the horizon, he's already laying his ingredients out on the counter.

This man brings a whole new meaning to 'morning ritual.'

For a second, I just stand in the doorway, staring like he's a ghost.

My Google sleuthing paid off last night.

Few answers and a lot more questions, gaps in his history I never would've guessed, some turning into gaping chasms.

Like the company he was involved with, *OptiSynth Studios*. He was a co-founder and on the board for years before he left it abruptly earlier this year.

According to the tech articles, he stepped away due to

'differences' in vision with the rest of the company's executive team.

I can read between the lines.

In money and business circles, that means there was a blowout. Then he either walked away or they shoved him out.

I can't guess which.

All I know is, the former co-founder of a premier AI design studio is standing in my kitchen, whipping up blueberry pancake batter along with the cheesy eggs and hashbrowns I'd planned to make.

It doesn't feel real.

Eventually, he senses me and looks up.

His green eyes blaze when we connect, burning like lanterns before he turns back to what he's doing.

My stomach flips.

My skin feels too hot.

My toes scrunch like every bad rom-com movie.

God, we should keep our distance.

But I have questions for Kane Saint that desperately need answers.

And it's awfully hard to look at him the same way now that I also know he had a big ugly public breakup with Daria Purty. I stalked her Instagram for over an hour last night.

Of course, his ex-wife is gorgeous.

All sun-bleached blonde hair with a fitness freak figure, shiny skin, and teeth so white they rival porcelain.

And she's basically famous. She does a *lot* of product ads and modeling for the big brands, jumping around the globe to breathtaking places.

Judging by what Sophie said, that means jumping through a lot of men, too.

Her current bae seems to have stuck around for a little while, judging by the photos. He's just as polished and pretty as she is with wiry muscles and an old-blood jawline straight from a cologne ad.

Nothing like Kane, who comes by his good looks with rugged honesty.

I wonder what brought them together.

Sure, he used to be a hockey star—he was an ice king in his time—but that doesn't explain what they saw in each other.

If they ever saw anything at all.

In my world, people marry for leveling up their reputations or their money all the time. Love, who cares?

It's more important that your spouse is a minimally fuckable powerhouse.

Also, nothing ever stays the same.

Maybe Daria's taste in men has evolved. Maybe Kane's taste in women shifted, too.

If they got together almost ten years ago, a whole lot can change.

"You can come join me, you know. Unless you want to keep creeping," Kane says, glancing up again. "I don't bite, duchess."

Maybe I want you to.

The corner of his mouth curls up like he can hear my thoughts, but he stays grounded on what he's doing.

Those strong hands are so, so capable as he cracks eggs and briskly whisks them around in a small metal bowl.

"Something on your mind?" He looks up from his stirring.

See? Mind reader.

"Sophie dropped by late last night," I say, pulling milk from the fridge.

"Is she okay?" He stops what he's doing and fully looks at me.

"Oh, yeah, she's fine. I thought she was freaked out about

the commotion last night, but she actually wanted to talk about something else."

"Yeah?"

I hesitate before I say it. "You."

"What about me?" His eyes narrow.

"Well, mainly that you're really old and decrepit at the grand old age of thirty-six." I bite back a giggle. "And the fact that she notices your grey hair."

"Little snitch," he mutters.

"But also… she told me a little about your past." I eye him hopefully.

He grunts as he greases the pan with butter and clicks the stove on, offering nothing.

"You weren't just a hockey player. You were famous."

"Unfortunately. Nothing worse than having a name folks recognize, but I think you know something about that."

"Um, yeah. She also mentioned Daria." I say the name carefully, watching his face. "And she said you worked for a place called *OptiSynth*."

That last word does it. His playful half smile flattens into a hard line of war and his face goes rigid.

"What else?" he growls. "She's at that age where kids love to overshare."

"Nothing bad, dude. Relax." I step closer. "You don't need to hide so much about your life. I'm not here to judge you."

"Like you already have? You're not stupid, Margot. I'm guessing you've found out what you needed to."

"Well, I Googled you," I admit sheepishly.

That whisper of a smile returns for a second, accenting his lush green eyes. "Hell, I'm just surprised you waited and didn't dive in the first night."

"I didn't know you were a star then. You should be proud of your career."

He snorts loudly.

"Nah. That part of my life's over and I can't say I miss it." He shakes his head. "You hurt my feelings the first day. Couldn't believe you'd never heard the name Kane Saint."

"I don't follow sports obsessively," I say, patting his arm in false reassurance. "But you could've said something. It's cool knowing we have an ice king in the house."

"*Former* ice king," he says dryly. "Like I said, that's over and done with."

"Never coming back for an encore?"

"Not after you retire," he says. "As Sophie pointed out, I'm an old dude now. They wouldn't have me back even if I tried."

"You sure? You mean you'd never show up for younger players or charity?" I know how demanding professional sports can be, and how it's not meant to be a lifelong career.

But when I take a good, long look at him, he's strong. Big and fit and honed.

If he's lost any of his former superpowers on the rink, it doesn't show one bit in that punishing body.

"I'm sure. It's not the chapter of my life I want to revisit. I'd rather be dead than turn into one of those guys who never shuts up about the 'good old days.' Like life just ended the day I hung up my stick. You start talking like that, you'll believe it, and then you really are boned."

Wise man.

His gaze sharpens, and I do my very best to keep the admiration off my face.

"I left hockey and that's that. There's nothing else to know."

"Okay, okay. No fame and fortune for you. Got it." I grab his dishes from mixing and place them in the sink to soak. "Maybe someday people will finally stop recognizing you, too."

"That's the hope," he clips.

Man.

I desperately want to ask about the company he helped found after his sports career, but I can tell he's on edge.

His voice seems wary, on edge, and I like his easy, whimsical side too much.

"Probably a shit idea hanging around you if I want to keep a low profile," he jokes. "Everyone in Sully Bay knows who you are, huh?"

"Well, yeah. I used to come here a lot."

"You're a Blackthorn, you mean."

"It's just a name," I say, starting on the dishes. "And it's not like I'm famous on my own. Sure, I go around to big events and people get all giddy to shake my hand. But it's not like I'm a movie star or famous model."

"Too modest." He leans across to bump shoulders with me. "Everyone in New England and New York have heard of the Blackthorns. You're damn near royalty."

I raise an eyebrow.

"Oh yeah? Is that why you went all bouncer and made me show you my ID?"

"You're mad about that?" He throws his head back and laughs.

"Can't remember the last time I had to show it. Not since I turned twenty-one," I tell him.

And yes, when you're a Blackthorn, the security at high-end clubs and restaurants rarely checks. I was carded more in Scottsdale and LA than anywhere else.

The rules are different when you have enough money to buy out entire VIP areas for a girls' weekend.

"I thought you were trespassing. Simple as." Kane's shoulder nudges mine again. Warmth blooms from the contact and my arms tingle. "You could've been some crazy asshole's accomplice, waiting to snatch my daughter."

"My *point* is, I'm not that famous. You had no idea who I

was."

"No, but I knew the name. Your grandfather was a legend." He flips the pancakes and puts the hot ones on a plate, piling them up like he's done this every day for years.

I wonder if he has.

I get started on the hashbrowns. Might as well contribute something.

"So, what's next for you?" I ask. "New career? Retirement? Early grave?"

"Very funny," he deadpans. "I told you, I'm not looking to die like some guys do when they leave the arena."

"I mean it. What's next for the great Kane Saint? Another wildly successful start-up? OptiSynth sounds like it's doing pretty well."

His shoulders stiffen.

The atmosphere in the room dims.

One second, we're teasing and laughing. Then we're dropped into this tense, eerie pit where he looks down at the pan like it's his life ebbing away.

"I'm out of that game, too. Last company didn't work out," he mutters, his eyes still riveted to the sizzling pan.

"So that's a no?" I whisper.

"Fuck no. The corporate world doesn't suit me. All that cutthroat cloak-and-dagger shit gets old. If I wanted that, I would've gone into politics like my old man wanted."

Oof. Now we're getting somewhere.

I noticed his father served a few terms in Congress when I ran my little background check.

For all the talk about *my* family's lofty achievements, the Saints are no slouches.

There's a bitterness in his voice I don't quite understand, though, and before I can ask, there's a banging upstairs, followed by blunt, rhythmic tapping.

"Dan's awake. Watch the stove for a second, will you?"

Kane peels away from me and walks to the base of the stairs. "Dan, keep it down! Too early, kiddo," he calls up.

"He really loves to practice, huh?" I say, seizing the opportunity to change subjects.

If Kane shuts down every time I mention his old company, I guess I shouldn't push it.

I don't want him stressed every time I'm in the room.

"He's addicted, that kid. Can't even count the days he's woken up the whole house." He shakes his head affectionately as he comes back into the kitchen. "But I guess it's a good thing. Music builds discipline and it keeps him out of trouble."

"Yeah. I played the oboe and I was pretty awful," I confess, wincing. "I'd like to think it helped me with school, though. Chemistry was a breeze after squeaking my way through an hour of sheet music with the band teacher turning red."

"Margot Blackthorn, defeated by a damn reed? I can't see it." He chuckles.

"Be glad!" I say back brightly.

We fall into this companionable silence, wrapping up breakfast and brewing coffee before the kids come tearing downstairs.

A girl could get very used to this, and I can't let that happen.

"We should head into town later to follow up on the stalker," he says while he's plating the food.

My stomach drops.

Stalker. Right-o.

Here in the happy golden morning with delicious food waiting, nothing feels scary. But I can't shake that feeling of being watched, being *violated*, and how I may never feel comfortable here again come nightfall.

"You're right," I whisper, grabbing a plate to carry to the table. "The sooner we get this done, the better."

X: LOOK HOMEWARD (KANE)

*I*f there's a cardinal rule I've learned after nearly a decade of being a dad, it's when your kid has a shot at a pony ride, you'd be a fool to stand in their way.

Which is why I'm following in their tracks as we ride down Sully Bay's red cobblestone streets, gently curling up and down small hills.

Horseback riding's a great way to see more of the town. The kids were too excited to say no when they saw the place offering rides.

Margot was a little more hesitant with the horses, especially when the attendant said we'd have to share one.

Better that than having her ride alone.

She's not a horse girl.

She's a city girl to the core who never developed a taste for pricey equestrian outings, and she's only ridden a few times in her life.

"Mostly on lead rein," she confessed, half-embarrassed, as the attendant led the horse over to us.

"It's fine," I told her. "I can handle a horse. Used to go riding on my uncle's farm in Wyoming back in the day."

Her eyes sparkled.

I did my damnedest not to think about the fact that she'd be sitting right in front of me.

With her delectable ass now lodged against my cock, it's a lot harder not to remember that with every movement.

"Oh my God! I forgot this can be so warm." She laughs, her back brushing my chest and her fingers half an inch from mine on the reins.

The horse or me?

"What did you expect, duchess?"

"Don't know. Like I said, it's been a while." She leans forward, wedging her ass even more firmly against me, patting his neck. "But you're a good boy, aren't you, Thorin?"

All the horses are named after Tolkien characters, even the ponies, which made the kids scream with delight.

Sophie's perched on Galadriel and Dan's on Boromir. They're so excited they kept butchering the names.

"I can't believe I never tried this here," she says, straightening upright again.

Yeah, unbelievable.

It's a surprisingly warm day, cloudless and blue. Sully Bay is one of those quaint coastal fishing towns that looks like it sprouted up from the landscape sometime in the last two centuries and hasn't changed much since.

Very different from New York.

Different from my uncle's place out west, too, which always had something falling down in need of a fix and people running around to keep up an active cattle farm.

Never thought I'd be one for country living, but here we are.

Today, it's the getaway I needed.

If only Little Miss Sweetass would stop rubbing every time she twists around to catch the passing scenery.

I think it's unintentional, but we've only been riding for

about ten minutes or so, and my balls are blue enough to rival that heap of blueberries back at the house.

It takes *work* to keep her from noticing how hard I am.

Luckily, she's distracted by everything she sees, from the friendly people waving to the jealous boy who makes a face behind his ice cream cone when he sees my kids.

"Why does it look so different on a horse? It's like a whole new town." She giggles and her hair brushes my chin.

Goddamn.

She smells like vanilla and the last hint of summer, and it does terrible things to me as it mingles with the fall smells in the air.

"Maybe you just forgot?"

"Nope," she says with a flick of her hand. "According to Sophie, I only have another few years until I'm half-senile like you."

"Shut it," I say, winking at Sophie when she overhears and throws back a smile.

"Sorry, Dad. You know it's true!"

"If it's true, then you'll be my caretaker. I'm not going off to a damn home."

Dan chuckles and Margot waves gracefully at the people passing by like she's a regal princess traveling her kingdom.

"Let's go left," she decides, waving at a friendly old lady. "Hi, Mrs. Solomon!"

I ease our horse to a crawl, calling to Sophie and Dan to hang back and join us.

"Do I know you?" Mrs. Solomon squints up at us. She's a tiny woman, probably in her nineties with puffy white hair curls around her head and dark eyes that still seem vibrant.

"It's Margot," she says. "Leonidas' granddaughter?"

"*Margot.*" Mrs. Solomon's face splits into a grin, creasing her skin like old leather. "You should've said something sooner, honey. Glad to see a Blackthorn back in this town!"

Margot laughs brightly, shifting against me again.

I remind myself that we're in public, and the last thing I should do is pop a hard-on *here*, right in front of little old ladies and all.

I try like hell to focus on the conversation.

"I was dreadfully sad to hear the news about your granddad," she says, frowning. "Such a great man. It was always so nice when he came around with you and your brother."

"Ethan," Margot supplies.

"That's right. Ethan. How's he doing now? I heard he got engaged."

"He did. They're married, actually. You remember my friend who used to come here sometimes? Hattie?"

"The one with the glasses? Always had her nose stuck in a book, yes." Mrs. Solomon's grin widens. "She used to come into my shop looking for paperbacks and she'd need your help to carry her haul."

"Until we came back the next week, yeah!"

"She's the one he married?"

"That's right," Margot says and laughs again. "None of us saw that one coming."

"Oh my, how lovely. Opposites do attract. It's not just a saying."

My dick throbs in agreement.

"No argument there," Margot says.

They talk a bit more, reminiscing about the past and coming into her old bookstore to pick through stories and relax.

That's the whole atmosphere here.

Must be the reason why I feel like I'm finally relaxing for the first time since we arrived.

"We do like the quiet life here," Mrs. Solomon says. "Sometimes the tourists bring a bit of trouble, but you won't see folks locking their doors or fussing with those fancy doorbell cameras."

Maybe they should start, I think darkly.

"We're lucky this town's more Mayberry than Redhaven. Seriously, I've heard that place has more murders than people," Margot says lightly.

Mrs. Solomon laughs in agreement.

They gab on about some little town in North Carolina I've never heard of, ruled by a creepy family with an iron fist, and a few gory cases that made national news.

Soon, Mrs. Solomon continues on her way, and I start moving us along the path again.

"Was that intentional? Trying to flush out some weirdness by mentioning that Redhaven place?"

"Yep. Sounds like nothing too weird's been going on lately," Margot murmurs with relief.

"Not by the sound of it, no. Worth it to follow up with a few more people."

"For sure." She settles a little more firmly against me, relaxing a little.

Half an hour ago, she panicked at being on a horse, but now she's perched in front of me like a pro.

I try not to feel too smug, or shamelessly horny.

She keeps up the relentless chatter as we pass through the streets, stopping every few blocks to greet someone else.

Somehow, she always knows the locals from the tourists—and their faces must be branded into her brain. She greets the townspeople by memory.

It usually takes them a second to recognize her.

Odd how much she must've changed since she was a little girl, while this town stayed frozen in time.

But the second they place her or hear the name Blackthorn, they start treating her like she's a celebrity.

Sometimes their curious gazes land on me, but few people ask.

Margot basks in the attention, drinking it in. But I think it's more for their benefit than her own ego.

Guess it's expected from a place that clearly revered Leonidas Blackthorn.

But did the old man have any enemies?

That question lingers on my mind.

It's rare for a billionaire real estate mogul who lived like a king to win nothing but respect. People are petty as hell, jealous by nature, and in all his years, he likely stepped on a few toes to keep his empire.

Still, no one mentions anything out of the ordinary.

After we've trotted through the town's main drag on our horses, we stop by a park and what looks like another pop-up market.

Is every little town this spontaneous or are they just showing off?

Then I get a good whiff of the food from a couple nearby food trucks, and my skepticism dies on the spot.

Seafood.

Lobster rolls, fried clam strips, and crabcakes spritzed with lemon.

My stomach growls like a lion, a reminder that we haven't eaten since breakfast.

Dan pulls his pony to a halt, sliding off the saddle like he was born for it.

The pony bends down and starts grazing on grass, unbothered by the laughing crowd swarming around, taking advantage of the unseasonably warm day.

"We can stop here, right, Dad?" he asks.

"Yeah. Good place to take a breather." I swing my leg up and over from behind Margot, sliding to the ground before I extend a hand to her. "You good?"

Her eyes flick from my face to the hand I'm holding out and she smiles. "Thanks. Such a gentleman."

"I've got you."

Her face shines as she takes my hand and lets me help her down.

I'm so relentlessly fucked.

Dan does the same with Sophie like the good brother I raised him to be, and I take the reins in my hand.

By the looks of it, these guys won't go far if we keep them in view, but better safe than sorry. I tie them to the nearby fence next to a horse rest area.

My stomach rumbles again as Margot steps back, her smile widening before she turns to the kids.

"Okay, you're starving. Lunch is on me! What are you hungry for?"

"Lobster roll," I say immediately.

Sophie laughs, covering her face.

"Dad loves lobster," she explains.

"*Fresh* lobster," I correct sharply. "None of that rubbery crap that's been on ice for days. Always in butter. No mayo."

When I inhale the heavenly smell in the air, I swear I can almost taste it.

"Noted," Margot says. "How about you kidlets?"

Sophie casts another vote for lobster, and Dan opts for a plain old cheeseburger. One day I'll teach that boy good taste and opportunity.

I untie our rides while they grab the food. The horse and ponies follow me peacefully as we lead them between the stalls.

Judging by the way everyone smiles and moves out of the way, I figure it's not an unusual sight.

But the sun is shining and Sophie's grin looks wide enough to split her face.

When I get my lobster roll with its beautiful buttery pink meat spilling out of it, I stop caring about anything.

"Shit," I groan, biting into it like the heathen I am. "A man could get used to Maine."

Margot laughs and nudges my shoulder. "That easy? I thought it would take more to win you over than your stomach."

"I'm a simple man. Food's only part of the equation, but it's big."

She blushes.

The rest of it is her, which shouldn't even be implied. But I guess good food ruins my filter.

The light catches her hair, turning it to gold as it frames her face. She digs into her lobster tacos like I'm not enjoying the show.

Sophie eats her half sandwich, too, stopping to look around like she's worried people will judge her for being too into her food.

That's her mom's doing, and I hate it.

Daria, always counting calories and reminding everyone to watch their weight, even in public. The kids are perfectly healthy and too innocent to fixate on their image at this age.

Couldn't tell you how many times we fought about that shit.

No regrets, either.

I'll defend their right to be *kids* all day long until I'm turning blue.

The wolves of adulthood come prowling too soon. For Sophie and Dan, they can fucking wait.

Thankfully, Dan isn't self-conscious. He eats like he's starving, finishing his burger and tots before anyone else finishes their food.

He licks sauce from his fingers, and Margot digs in her pocket for a packet of tissues.

"Here," she says, smiling at him. "You've got a little on your face, too."

"Well now," a woman's voice says from behind us. "Aren't you a sight for sore eyes."

Margot's on her feet before I have time to react, her face wreathed in a smile as she turns to face the little old lady. She's probably in her seventies, wearing a bright print dress and a grin.

"Mrs. Griffith!" Margot says, embracing the lady.

"Margot," the lady says, "Call me Edith, please." She gives me a nod and a smile. "Mr. Saint, I presume. We spoke on the phone. Glad to see you made it up here okay. Hope the house isn't too ramshackle for your stay?"

"It's perfect," I say. "And you can call me Kane."

"I still feel terrible about the mix-up," Edith whispers to Margot. "I hadn't realized you were planning on visiting, dear, and it sure sounded like he needed the place."

"No, no, not at all. It's fine, honestly. We sorted it out." Margot smiles disarmingly. "I told you it wouldn't be a big deal."

"Margot's been great company," I agree, which earns me another smile from her. "The house is quiet, and the lake is huge. Everything I wanted in a nice property."

"Well, I really am embarrassed about the whole mix-up. When they put me in charge, I thought it would be better to have people there—families—rather than let the old place sit around going to ruin. Even if we barely had any takers before you arrived."

"You were right," Margot says warmly.

I nod. "The kids love it."

"There's a *lake*!" Dan agrees, like nothing else matters.

"It's awesome at night. Best stars ever!" Sophie chimes in.

Edith beams at them both.

"I'm so glad you like the place, sweetie."

Margot throws a glance at me, like she can't quite believe Edith Griffith is real.

No one's *this* nice. Except for the folks of Sully Bay.

Still, she must've been around for a while, especially if Leonidas trusted her with helping manage his property. She could know something more about the history around here.

"It's a relaxing place, Mrs. Griffith. Hard to leave." I plaster on a smile.

"Edith," she reminds me, and beckons us back to her stall, where she's selling what looks like handmade soaps. "You must call me Edith. And please take some on the house. I insist, my apology for the messy situation."

Margot's fingers brush mine as we both reach out to collect a handful of soaps that smell like strong lavender.

"Actually, it's great that it worked out this way," I continue. "The kids and I have good company who gives us pointers with the locals. Not sure we'd have gotten off the lake nearly as much without Margot around."

They both smile until it feels like I'm bathed in sunlight.

"Plus, the blueberry farm next door's great." I give Margot a pointed look she finally picks up on. Her eyes widen. "The Babins deserve a medal for hospitality. How many muffins did you make, Margot?"

"Oh, yes, they came over right away to introduce themselves and gave us a year's supply of fresh blueberries," she says. "Such lovely neighbors. I'm kind of amazed Gramps never mentioned them."

The second Edith's face darkens, I know we've hit something.

Sophie and Dan both walk off to be with the horses.

Good. It helps that they aren't around to feel the change in the air.

"Oh, my, the Babins..." The sweet old lady practically grinds their name with her teeth. "I'm surprised they showed their faces after the way they carried on when old Leo owned the place."

Margot frowns and looks at me. Clearly this is news.

"What did they do?"

"Oh, some silly grudge over the land. Only, it stopped being so silly after—and this was years ago—after they started up with their demands. Old Joe's father even sued Leonidas one winter on faulty claims." She shakes her head slowly, still lost in the past. "But they were laughed out of court. Humiliated, in fact."

"They sued PopPop?" Margot looks stunned.

"I'm afraid so, dear. Oh, and that's not all... there was that fire the summer after, before you were born. Torched the old gazebo he'd built and your grams' pretty garden. A real miracle it never reached the house." She sucks in a sharp breath through her teeth. "No proof what happened, of course, but I always had a suspicion who was behind it."

Shit.

My heart drums.

"Fire? Jesus, I never—" Margot clears her throat, rubbing her fingers idly over her collarbone like she's soothing away a bee sting. "He never mentioned any of this."

"No, I suppose not. Leo loved to keep this place pure for you kids, I think. And he wasn't the kind to hold grudges. I'm sorry you had to hear it from me."

Margot's nostrils flare.

"No, don't be," she says quietly.

"It hit Leo hard, that fire. The gazebo was always your grandma's favorite place when she was around, right next to those beautiful gardens. The perennials would come back year after year before the fire." Edith's gaze is distant, and she smiles shyly. "Seems like just yesterday... I'd stop by to pick up a few flowers or bring her a bottle of wine. Sweet woman.

You'd find May Blackthorn painting out there almost every day in the warm months."

"Oh, wow. I found a painting she did in the attic." Margot bites her lip.

"She was prolific! And Leonidas was usually there with her, doting over her shoulder. But he never came around much after her passing, especially after the fire. Just a few times a year when he'd bring you and Ethan around." She heaves a sigh. "Poor man. I'm not sure he ever got over the heartache of losing her last special place."

Margot steps back like she's been punched.

I put my hand on the small of her back, holding her steady.

She gives me a grateful glance, leaning into my hand, and I slide my arm around her hip, pulling her closer.

Her face looks so pale it worries me.

"I had no idea about any of this," she says.

Edith nods seriously.

"It's time you found out about the Babins and your granddad's past. He'd have wanted you to know, especially with them sniffing around."

Margot's brows draw together.

Although she nods back gratefully, she doesn't look convinced.

I wonder if Edith's right.

Maybe the old man never wanted her to know about this stuff at all.

He never told her, after all, and there were plenty of opportunities. He could've left her a note in his will too, instead of sending her on a wild damn goose chase for whatever's buried in the house.

I hate seeing her like this.

She's not crying—I don't think she lets herself cry often—but there's a frailness in her face, her posture.

I hold her closer, and she gives me another grateful glance, her blue eyes dark.

"Whoa, Dad, look!" Dan yells from behind us.

We both turn, and I'm expecting something shocking.

But he's just pointing at an ice cream truck on the other side of the park.

"Can we?" he asks, having missed everything that's just gone down. "Pretty please with sprinkles?"

I turn back to Edith, and she smiles indulgently.

Margot stays silent, still reeling from the latest news.

"Thanks for the soaps, Edith. I should probably get these two terrors some dessert before they go to pieces."

"Go!" She waves us both away with an urgent flap of her hands. "Enjoy yourselves while you're here. And please take care of yourself, Margot, you hear me?"

"Sure will," Margot murmurs quietly.

As we head back to the kids and the horses, I take her hand to steady her.

"You okay?"

"...I don't know. All this stuff about the house, the Babins... Holy shit. I really had no idea. And I still don't get what Gramps wants me to find."

"I know. Have you thought about asking your mom? If you've hit a wall, it can't hurt to reach for new directions."

"Easier said than done. But maybe." She looks pained.

The kids chatter about the ice cream flavors on the menu, bringing us back to the present, but I can tell she's stuck on Edith Griffith's words and the biting mystery in that house.

"You were right about the police report, at least," she says softly. "I know we don't have any proof the Babins intruded, but if they tried to burn the house down..." Her voice trails off.

Yeah, fuck.

My blood boils.

"Don't worry. If they ever show their faces again, we'll be ready," I promise. The weight of it pounds in my ears like a war drum. "No one's getting hurt under my roof, duchess."

A holy vow, and I mean every venom word.

Not my kids.

Not myself.

Definitely not this strange, beautiful woman.

XI: TAKE ME HOME (MARGOT)

I hate to admit Kane was right.

He was right about a lot of things, but especially about the corner I'm in. And the only way out is to call Mom.

I've wasted a ton of time trying to figure out what Gramps left for me and where.

No progress.

If there's a chance Mom knows anything, I just need to summon the courage to ask.

I've been putting it off for a while, but with the tea Edith Griffith spilled about the Babins, it's obvious there's a lot I don't know about this house and the family history.

No, I'm not expecting miracles.

Not in this family.

Mom and Gramps were estranged for my whole life, but maybe she remembers *something*.

I mean, she knew her own mother and loved her until the day Grams died. And before the adult blunders, before the grudges ripped them apart, she knew and loved PopPop, too. No matter how much she likes to pretend she never did.

Honestly, I think she might've changed her name years ago, if it didn't win her so much easy respect. It's even weirder that she kept it after she married Dad, and it's the whole reason we're still Blackthorns.

But still, it's worth a try. It's worth the drama.

If she drops one teensy little nugget that leads me in a new direction, it'll justify picking at old scar tissue.

It's evening now, the sky half-dusky with a vibrant orange sunset fading behind the trees.

Maine is a living painting sometimes, so beautiful even Dadzilla had to admit he's enjoying his time here.

I smile.

Every time I close my eyes, I feel his weight behind me.

His strong arms around me and his massive hands on the reins next to mine.

His hand on my back when we were talking to Edith Griffith.

He knew I needed that silent comfort, the reassurance to keep up a strong front against my worries and the confusion nipping at my soul. That's why I whipped up a small batch of blueberry muffins once we came home, my way of saying thanks.

And I feel like I need his reassurance again now, alone in my room as I stare at my phone.

Yeah, talking to Mom about her father will never be easy, especially now that he's gone. That almost makes it worse.

I think it's one of several reasons Gramps passed on having a proper funeral. He wouldn't put Mom through that —or us.

But there wasn't much of a goodbye through the old man's pride.

Everything we learned this past year about Ethan, about Mom's relationship, about the affair and panic my grandfather's ego triggered, it just made things more awkward.

But she's my mother.

And she answers on the second ring while my breath turns to cement in my lungs.

"Mom?"

"Margot! Darling! How are you?"

I close my eyes. "I'm decent. Still hanging out here at the lake house, y'know."

"That old place? God." There's instant venom in her tone. "How's it holding up, anyway? Last I heard, it was practically derelict. Holden Verity, he recommended extensive renovations, if not a teardown and—"

"Mom, I know, and it's not *that* bad. It's safe and the appliances still work." After a strained second, I decide not to mention Kane and his fixer-upper superpowers that helped make this place bearable. "I was actually just calling to see if you might remember anything special about the house. Anything important, I mean?"

"Important how?" Her voice sharpens.

"I don't know. Just like—anything significant that might've been forgotten? Anything PopPop left behind or just loved about this place?"

I hear her sigh, slow and tortured.

"I should've known. Don't tell me that awful man slapped *more* ridiculous conditions on you inheriting that dive. The way he insisted on bringing you two up there as kids was dreadful enough. I wanted to tell him to—"

"No! Mom, no," I say quickly. "Nothing like that. I told you everything after my little meeting with Jackie Wilkes. Remember? No conditions. No fake marriage funny business like Ethan."

"Well, good. He always did enjoy his little games and riddles, but the time for that ended the day he died. It was childish enough while he was still alive, always spinning stories or adding to his little art collection more than he paid attention to his business. *Idiot*," she huffs out.

My heart sinks.

This is going so well.

I shuffle to the bed, sliding my feet under me, steeling my nerves.

Outside, a large harvest moon rises. I can practically feel its call to the tides and ancient colonial witches and creatures of the night.

The quieter New England gets, the wilder the country.

"Margot, really, what has you so stressed? What did he do this time?"

"...he left me a letter," I say.

"A letter. Oh, *here* we go."

"Hold up, Mom. It didn't say much. Just that he regrets a lot of stuff that happened. But it did say there's supposedly something hidden here on the property somewhere—and I haven't had much luck finding it. I guess I just wondered if you could clue me into anything?"

There's a pause, and I hear the faint click of her heels as she walks through the house. She's angry-pacing like she always does when Gramps is on her mind.

Always heels, I don't think I've ever seen her in flats.

But honestly, Mom's taste in shoes probably helped spark my lifelong devotion. Even so, it's a lot to take in right now.

"There's nothing valuable there. Holden combed the entire property and sent a full inventory about a week after my father died. He was always so meticulous, and I trust him. Far more than the man who was signing his checks," she says distantly.

"Yes, I remember." I roll my eyes. "You sent him on a mission."

My parents were adamant about cataloguing everything that might top off their little fortune at auction.

Mom's main religion is money. Knowing they'd get the bulk of Gramps' collection to sell was good enough, minus a few items at his old house in Portland earmarked for my artsy little cousin.

"Then you know all of his assets and personal property were accounted for when we hashed out the estate."

"I know, Mom. Jackie shared the inventory with me."

"Well, then why would you expect me to know about anything else? Do I look like the kind to hide his secrets?"

"I just thought there could be something off-record. Maybe sentimental. Mrs. Griffith, the lady we had managing the rental, she mentioned how much Grams loved to come here and paint when she was alive, and—"

Mom sighs louder, silencing me.

"Darling, darling, *darling*. Oh, dear." She almost sounds tender. Which isn't very Mom-like, when I'm pretty sure she took parenting pointers from those birds who push their chicks out of the nest to make them fly.

"He's got you chasing ghosts. My mother loved to paint there, it's true. We'd go into that gazebo, and she'd sit me on her knee in front of a canvas when I was little and guide my hand. Just me, Mother, and the lake. I loved it, though I never developed her appreciation for painting. But you must understand, that's all that ever happened. It certainly didn't include *him*."

"Look, I know you don't have the best opinion of Gramps, but—"

"It doesn't matter," she interrupts. "I know the lake house is lovely, even if it's been rotting for years. But you're still so young, Margot. The last thing you need is to waste your time hunting down whatever my deranged father left lying around. Please don't waste the brain cells. Don't give him the satisfaction, wherever the hell he's gone."

A lump builds in my throat.

Just once, I wish she'd give him a shred of respect.

But while we're at it, I wish I could wake up to a Paris runway, where women cut like human statues strut out smiling in my shoes.

"What if it's important? Some piece of art that was too tucked away for Holden to find?"

"If it was that important, darling, he should've been direct with you. He wasn't, and that's on *him*," she bites off. "Of course, I can't stop you. If you really want to fritter away your time looking high and low behind every rat-infested wall, then fine, knock yourself out."

This was productive.

Mom never has a clear head when it comes to Gramps, and she's not the sweet, nurturing presence most people expect with mothers. She can be encouraging, she can be supportive, but she's rarely *kind.*

I used to hate it, the lack of real softness. Almost like she was terrified of being overwhelmed if she offered us any real love.

Now, I know more about her and the reasons she burned her bridge with Gramps. The hard fact that Ethan isn't Dad's child and I am, so yeah, it makes a little more sense.

She's still broken and hurting from Gramps thinking Dad wasn't good enough to marry into the Blackthorn family.

She's also arranged her life in a way that doesn't revolve around children.

Fine, I get it.

But it also fucking sucks for the kids involved.

Not that I'm a kid anymore.

I'm a grown-ass woman, and I'm used to this crap.

"Thanks for the encouragement, Mom. If you can turn the hate machine off long enough to recall anything useful, call me."

I end the call without a goodbye and roll over, frustration burning my skin until it itches.

I swear I'm going to overdose on secrets here.

Whatever secret Gramps left, plus the whole weird business with the Babins. Were they really the monsters Edith Griffith said?

Lawsuits?

Arson?

Potentially trying to scare me and the poor kids in this house.

Kane hasn't said anything else about it, but I know he's on high alert.

Right now, he's downstairs with them, watching a movie and doing whatever bonding dad stuff you do with kids that age.

He's also keeping the evening watch. I just know it.

It's a relief to have him here, but I can't stop the pang of guilt that tells me if he hadn't come, the Saints wouldn't be sharing this mess.

I text Hattie and power up my iPad while I wait for her reply.

I haven't forgotten my other sad little secret.

After Sophie poured her heart out about her shoes, I started looking up orthopedic shoes and their designs, their function.

Turns out, there's a lot to learn.

But Sophie's shoes are the high-support, clunky ones.

Absolute beasts aesthetically.

So, I've taken the design and downloaded it as a base image with a little AI-assisted modeling. I've just started working on something that should have the same support but might look prettier.

Functional, yes, but feminine.

A stab at a statement piece.

Not something bland that will blend in, but not an outlier that draws mean jokes from immature kids.

It's not easy.

These shoes don't go hand in hand with *pretty*. Not in the delicate, flowery sort of way that's stylish. Not with bold, worldly I-don't-care confidence, either.

My phone lights up with Hattie's reply, and I stop working to check her message.

Hattie: *I'm glad you filed a police report! So scary.*

Hattie: *Also the stuff with your neighbors is insane.*

Hattie: *But have you kissed him again? Gotta look on the bright side.*

I chew my bottom lip as I stare at the screen. She's still typing.

Hattie: *Sooo I *might* have looked him up. Because what else do I have to do with my time when I'm not shelving books? Verdict: GORGEOUS. Seriously, if you don't hook up with him, I will try.*

Margot: *Hattie! Remember you're literally married to my brother.*

Hattie: *Kidding! But fr it's your moral obligation to hook up with him before some other baddie does.*

Hattie: *But how are things with you guys? Awkward or chill?*

I think back over the day.

Yesterday, I was *convinced* I'd never be able to look him in the eye again.

It turns out being terrified for your life puts things in perspective. When I ran back into the kitchen that night, I wasn't thinking about the kiss apocalypse much.

Or every wicked thing it means.

Like how his little boy found out and his little girl wants us to date.

Ugh.

I still haven't told him that part.

It might look like I'm asking for a date, but no, that's just my annoying subconscious.

I am self-aware.

And I'm not going to get emotionally tied up with anyone right now.

No more hookups.

No more drama.

Done.

If I have to bring in an army of battery-operated boyfriends to tide me over, hey, whatever.

A cool night breeze drifts in through the window. I inhale it slowly.

A little fresh air always helps me think.

I love the pine-scented coolness here so much I'm not worried about bringing a chill into the room. Hattie, who's all cozy blankets, thinks I'm weird.

Not that awkward, I type back. **We had a nice day in town with the kids. Had some lobster, ate ice cream, rode some horses. Nothing crazy.**

Hattie: *Yet. Just wait until you ride him.*

I drop my phone, press my face into my hands, and groan.

She's so bad.

Before I can tell her this is real life and not another spicy book, a noise catches my attention from the open window.

My heart ticks in my throat.

The low hum of a motor.

A splashing sound?

I stick my head out and look down, scanning the lawn until—

My breath catches when I see him.

Kane.

Huge and godlike, bathed in the low light around the old hot tub.

He just can't sit still. He must've fixed the pump and gotten the whole thing working.

His arms are up, resting along the back of the tub.

His eyes are half-closed as he slouches like a tiger, obscenely content.

I've never seen him like this.

And really, I shouldn't even be watching.

If Hattie saw me now, she'd call me a creep.

And she'd be right.

Normal people don't stare like this, ogling dangerously sexy, older men.

Especially older men they've kissed.

Older men they *swore* they would never kiss again.

I know it's time.

I should just shut the curtains and get back to my designs. Or texting Hattie. Or hell, maybe a cold shower before I face-plant into bed.

But I don't move.

That would be too sensible, and I know he's all alone out there under the stars. Maybe the kids fell asleep early.

I know from experience the warm water feels divine against the cool night.

My brain spins like a hamster training for a marathon on its little wheel.

…there's no harm in seeing if he wants some company, right?

Yes, I'm aware I'm only deceiving myself—it's not him needing company, it's *me*—but I get changed anyway, tying my hair up in a loose knot and finding the bathing suit I always pack on trips out of habit.

My bare feet are quiet as I slip through the house.

The kids must've passed out. I think I can hear Dan snoring on the couch, the TV still flickering as a movie plays.

Kane doesn't glance up as I slide the side door open and step outside. This close, he's so handsome it hurts.

It flipping sears my eyes to look at a man cut straight from the sky.

When he's shirtless, you can tell he used to play hockey. His muscles scream power, loudly and proudly with every ripple.

All sinew.

All solid man.

All big hands made for enticing punishments and whisper-soft caresses.

My brain sucks for getting me into trouble.

I can't help it when my breath catches a little too sharply.

He finally glances up, his eyes shadowy and unreadable. But I can hear the amusement in his voice when he realizes I'm here.

"Margot? What's wrong?"

I undo my robe and let it fall off my shoulders.

His gaze flicks down my body, ravenous, devouring me inch by inch.

I might just self-combust before I reach the hot tub.

The bathing suit I chose is red, a little alluring and a lot daring. It's a one piece, but only the tiniest swathe of material connects the two parts.

The cool night makes me shiver, contrasting with the burn under my skin.

"Nothing's wrong, Kane. I just thought maybe you wouldn't mind some company to try out the hot tub," I say, stepping closer.

He nods slowly and gives me some room to get in.

The bubbling water feels glorious against the cold air.

I almost groan with delight. Thankfully, I'm not that far gone.

Not yet.

"I don't mind," he confirms, clearing his throat. "Got it working this evening and figured I'd try it out. The kids went down fast after dinner. Barely made it through the opening credits, and I figured I'd let them sleep after the ride through town."

"Mmm, good idea." I rest my head on the lip of the tub. "I haven't been in one of these for a while. Usually, I just do pools and jacuzzis in Arizona or Mexico."

"Water hits different in Maine. You ever use this one much?"

"Yeah, when we were kids." I look at him slowly, taking him in. He's watching me with that intensity he often has, like he's never thought about staring at anything else. "Although I never used to appreciate it then. It was too small to swim much as a kid."

"But you do now?"

"Not sharing the tub with a brother who wants to dunk you until you're panicking definitely helps."

He chuckles, then we go silent.

The jets stream against my lower back, comfortingly fizzy.

Why wasn't getting this fixed my first priority?

"How are you feeling?" he asks after a long moment.

I shrug.

Today was a long day, and this helps more than I ever dreamed.

"I finally called my mom. Predictably, she doesn't think Gramps left anything valuable here."

"No? What about sentimental?"

"She doesn't think anything *has* value if some expert can't put a price on it." I dip my fingers into the water, twirling them idly. "I'm not sure Elvira Blackthorn ever had a sentimental thought in her life. I get it, though. Gramps hurt her bad when she was young. He caused a lot of trouble in our family, putting the Blackthorn name on a pedestal, but..." I stop and sigh. "I dunno. It's just a lot. And then there's the prowler stuff and the police report."

"Don't worry too much about that. After I've cleared my head in here, I'll pull the night shift."

"You mean you won't sleep? Oh, wow, is that necessary?"

"Only until we have a basic security system put in. Thought I'd order one and have it sent overnight," he says.

"No, you've done enough. There are a couple local places I can call. I'll work on it tomorrow," I promise.

Part of me wants to argue he shouldn't play watchman, but a man built like a human tank looking out for us feels like a relief.

If someone did try to break in, they'd stop cold and think twice after seeing him.

That is, assuming they weren't armed...

But he's a war machine. Intimidating height and muscles and *touch-us-and-die* attitude.

No one with a shred of survival instinct will mess with this house with Kane Saint around.

"Do you really think they'll come back?" I ask softly. "If it was the Babins, would they be that stupid?"

"Probably not tonight. They'd be dumb as hell to follow up this soon, without thinking it through," he says, propping his arms up on the rim. The space under them looks too inviting. "They know you saw them, and news travels fast in this town. They'll know we alerted the cops soon."

"Well, not like it'll do much. I think the sheriff hands out ten speeding tickets per year."

"It's on file, Margot. That counts. The better the record, the more we'll have if anything goes down and you need to press charges. Not that it will," he adds, searching my face.

"Hopefully."

After a second, he cocks his head.

Protective growly instinct or not, he knows he doesn't need to sweeten the truth with me, unlike his kids. I'm not family.

"Hopefully," he repeats.

I don't remember us getting closer, but my knee knocks lightly against his under the water.

I try to relax and sink down lower, letting the bubbles climb past my breasts to my neck, and his eyes follow the movement.

"It's a damn shame your mom was no help," he says. "Sorry you wasted your time."

"Yeah, it's frustrating. Not really a big surprise, though. I just want to know what he thought was so important and why he wanted me to find it. It feels like my last connection to him fading, going up in smoke."

His knee brushes mine now, but this time the movement feels deliberate.

Just a split-second press that might be for sympathy or comfort, but it ignites my nerves all the same.

"I'm sorry if you feel like you came here for nothing," he rumbles. "I know how that goes, putting in effort, only to walk away empty-handed after driving yourself up the wall."

"I don't feel like that." I half smile. "You remember what I told you about Sophie last night?"

"Yeah. She had to point out how old I am."

I giggle. "Besides that, I mean. I started working on her shoe design this evening."

For a second, I think he's about to shut down on me.

His shoulders stiffen, and for a hot second, I regret saying anything.

But then he draws a slow breath and relaxes again, studying me with cool green lidded eyes.

"I appreciate you helping her out, duchess. More than you know." He sighs. "Soph, she's never been good at being different. When she was younger, it was really hard. Other kids can be fucking brats at this age, and when they know she had a dad on top of it who was—" He hesitates.

"A famous world-class hockey star?"

"Close enough. But yes," he growls. "Yes, they get real nasty. They'd tell her how much she disappointed me. Pure bullshit. I'll never be anything but proud of my girl. Same with Dan, and he got in trouble a couple years ago. Punched a boy who mouthed off about her feet in front of him. That was a fun parent-teacher conference, let me tell you."

And he shifts closer again.

This time, his knee scrapes my outer thigh.

I'm feeling stars instead of seeing them for the first time, even as my heart aches for poor Sophie.

"That's horrible! It must've been so hard for your family. With her feet and the crappy comments, I mean. I never even asked her what's..." I trail off.

"What's wrong with her?"

I wince. "Why does she need those shoes?"

"Ah, yeah." He rakes a hand through his thick hair, and I try—I really try—not to stare at the way his biceps bulge like Hercules' second coming. "The technical name for it's *pes planus,* which just means flat feet. Most folks live just fine with it, but hers is severe. Her arches should've developed around age six, but they didn't turn up like the doctors hoped."

"Oh. So she's been wearing the ortho shoes since then?"

"Basically. A few more years, and I might try taking her in for surgery, if she wants, but she's a skittish girl. She hates hospitals to hell and back, and the procedure we could try isn't a total guarantee."

"They *are* stressful. Especially for a sweet little girl."

My heart swells with empathy.

"When I took her in to speak with the specialist last time,

she nearly had a panic attack and we had to leave. He said surgery's an option, but there's also a slight chance she'll grow out of the worst of it. I'm still hoping it might fix itself and we won't need to do anything."

"Does that happen?"

"It has. There's a chance, or so they say."

I nod hopefully.

Poor Sophie.

She's definitely the kind of little angel who doesn't deserve this.

"So the shoes help support her feet, right?" I ask.

"Yes, and manage her pain," he tells me. "She's unlucky. Like I said, a ton of people have flat feet and don't wind up with problems at all."

"I'm so sorry."

I dwell on his words.

She's blessed to have a lovely supportive dad and a caring brother, a stable home, but it's so unfair that she has to go through this.

One day, I'll have questions for God.

Nice questions, but still…

"As far as disorders go, it could be worse," he continues. "She had claw toe when she was a kid early on, and there was no way around that surgery. Her hospital experience wasn't the best. My ex insisted on flying her to Minnesota for it because she didn't like how short the NYU doctors were, so what did they know? Completely stupid shit, going all the way to Mayo, when Soph could've been back at home the same day, recuperating."

"There's the anxiety," I say sympathetically.

"Yeah, right the fuck there." He stares into the water. "The shoes are more of a temporary fix, a wait and see. If it gets worse, we'll have no choice but to consider the corrective surgery."

"But if they get better, like you said, then there's no need to put her through another ordeal."

"Glass half full. I like that, especially if it's beer," he jokes.

My smile burns my face off.

"Whatever, though. I just wish she didn't need the damn shoes while we're waiting. It's hard on her emotionally," he says, his expression dark.

"Does she still get bullied?" I ask.

"What do you think?" His eyes flash darkly.

My face flares, hotter than ever.

"Oh, sorry. Kids can suck when people are different. Same for adults. But at least they have time to grow out of it," I say. "I don't think I know a single person who hasn't been bullied at least once when they were little."

"Even you? Or did the Blackthorn name scare them straight?"

"I wish!" I cover my face briefly. "You think I've always been this glamorous? My brother was the cool kid. I didn't learn how to stand up for myself until my boobs grew in—and then I had to figure out how to deal with boys leering and girls whispering jealously behind my back."

Kane's eyes heat when I mention my breasts, though he doesn't break his gaze.

"I try like hell to do right by my kids and teach them respect. Wish everybody else would put in half the effort."

"For sure. But I survived the teen years, and Sophie will too. Especially if I can come up with something to help her… They'll just be a design, though. They'll have to be sent off to be custom made with her specs in mind. But it's a start."

"Her shoes are already special orders," he says. "I'm sure that can be arranged."

"Oh my God," I tease. "You have her shoes specially made and you made them black?"

The water swirls around us as he makes a sudden move toward me. Laughing, I fall back.

"There were *three* color choices: grey, white, and black. Or are you telling me I have the fashion sense of a rock?" he asks, moving closer now.

Humor gleams in his eyes, fanning the wicked blaze I've been fighting in my core since the moment I slid into the water next to him.

"Just a little. But you know what, you can learn. And you're doing a great job as a dad."

"Yeah? Hell of an endorsement, duchess." He settles beside me, close enough so our arms touch.

"It must be hard work, being such a good man. You should let go sometimes, you know? This stalker thing has everyone rattled, but we're still on vacation. Both of us."

"Let go how, woman? You sound like you have suggestions." When he looks at me now, there's no more humor in his eyes.

And there's no mistaking it.

The stark bright question in his eyes.

The warmth of the water whisks through me, melding with my pulse, and I twist closer to face him.

His hand drops to my waist, and even though I can't feel the heat of his fingers through the water, it lashes hot need through my bones.

"Maybe this," I whisper, swinging my leg over his thigh.

Growling, his other hand lands on my hip.

You could cut this night with scissors, so thick with desire.

And when his eyes close, I press my body against his.

Underneath, he's already hard as a brick, and it feels like acceptance.

He's letting me make the move even though he could easily pin me down with no objection.

"You're fucking crazy," he snarls.

"I'm okay with crazy." My voice is so small.

His hand squeezes my hip—*hard*—and his other hand moves to my back, molding me against him, tormenting my skin with a hunger to connect.

We both know what happens next, but there's still that delicious, slow drop.

The very second my heartbeat starts to drum too loud in my ears, when my legs shift apart for his hand, when time itself freezes and we're just simmering in possibility.

Maybe, baby.

Tonight, maybe I don't want to think.

Maybe I want to be destroyed.

Then he makes a guttural noise that might be a groan, a growl, or something unspeakable. Either way, it's animalistic, chaotic, and when he kisses me, it's an earthquake.

Holy shit!

Kane's restraint snaps, and then he's everywhere.

His mouth is soft, but he nips my bottom lip as I rock against him, already drunk on his kiss.

His tongue slides into my mouth.

He tastes like blueberries and thyme.

Heat floods me.

"Seriously, did you—"

"Yeah, I'm addicted to your muffins, woman. I ate another one after dinner. But only half as obsessed as I am with finding out what that mouth does besides sass." His finger slides over my lips, silencing me.

God, I'm in pieces.

And I grind my hips more deliberately this time, settling against him until the pressure intensifies.

I moan helplessly.

He swallows the sound, pulling it out of me, drowning me in a growl.

"Keep it down. The kids are sleeping," he whispers against my jaw.

Oh, crap, yes.

The kids.

Before, that was enough to throw me off of him like a ten-thousand-volt shock, but now I just tilt my head back, giving him access to my neck.

This man doesn't need to be asked twice.

Kane's cock grinds against me as he goes to town, huge and pulsing and needy.

Every thrust of his hips makes me feel him, his length dragging over my thigh like he's marking me.

Sweet Jesus, I have to bite my bottom lip.

The stars overhead blur like diamonds as my eyes roll.

"Kane, Kane… don't stop!" Under a minute and I'm already begging.

Yikes.

And as the hand on my hip slides up to my breasts, as he sucks my throat, as he delicately kisses the shell of my ear and breathes more molten lust into me, my surrender deepens.

His fingers tweak my nipples before he pinches them.

A fire burst zings straight to my core.

My pussy throbs until my thighs clench his other hand, teasing and so close to bringing me home.

"Shit. You know I've been thinking about these since the day you barged in?" he whispers gruffly.

"You did the barging, but—really?" I'm frozen. "I wasn't even wearing anything that showed them off."

"Wasn't that a shame? You teased my dick to oblivion without trying, duchess. Bad." He pinches my nipple until I gasp. "And this bathing suit. *Fuck.*"

"It's more like a backup. I've got way better at home."

"I want to see you in all of them. Then I want to tear them off and fuck you senseless."

Ohhh, no.

He licks down my neck, and I shudder, rolling my hips against his cock, climbing him in the water.

I think I could come from this alone, and that's insane.

Normally, I need some manual help on my clit.

But Kane Saint's touch is pure sorcery of the darkest kind.

When his big hand touches the small of my back as he pushes me up and his mouth descends onto my nipple, I'm not prepared.

My bathing suit already feels so warm on my skin, but his mouth is searing.

Blindingly hot.

I'm a gasping mess, biting my lip when he pinches my other nipple. A loud moan spills into the night.

Holy hell, I've got to be quiet.

The munchkins *really* can't see us like this.

"Kane, hey?" I whisper to the night sky. "Are you *sure* they won't wake up?"

"Positive. Movie's still going. And if they do, they'll either head upstairs to crash or wait for me in my room. They don't change routine much when they're this tired."

With his hands on my hips, he grinds me against him, turning me into his toy and I don't even mind.

"They won't see anything. Promise." He kisses me softly.

"I—I hope so. That would be a disaster."

"Enough fussing about the bad, duchess." He flicks his tongue over my other nipple again. "What do you want? Don't tell me you want to stop before you've felt me."

No, no.

I want everything.

His hands carving my shape in his memory, his mouth reducing me to a prayer, his dick inside me.

Tonight.

Now.

Tomorrow, too.

I reach between us, grabbing his mad erection through his trunks.

"I want this. You don't get to be a prick just because you're part oak tree," I whisper.

"Fuck!" he rasps against my mouth as I squeeze him.

Holy flaming hell.

Somehow, I find the wit to tease, just like he did to me, stroking his impressive length through the slick material and adoring the way he jerks and throbs with every pump of my hand.

Kane leans back like the beast he is, his eyes hot and heavy even through the darkness as he watches.

He vibrates with tension, but his hands stay riveted to my hips, holding me as he lets me rile him up.

I quicken my strokes, faster and faster, until he knows my torture.

"Damn you," he says, low and insistent. There's pain in his expression as his chest heaves. "Duchess, if you don't stop, I'll—"

"What?" I grin innocently.

Then I reach under the elastic of his shorts and wrap my fingers around his seething, rock-hard skin—or rather, I try.

He's so huge it's actually a struggle to close my fingers.

But it works.

Because Kane breaks with a feral groan, snapping his head back.

Oh, the perverse beauty.

It does something evil to me, watching this stonehearted hulk falling apart in my hands.

My pulse throbs between my legs.

Tonight, I'm Medusa, and I'm shameless.

His body turns to stone with every slick pump of my fist.

The water isn't the best for this, and after a few seconds—or minutes or hours or whatever—he grabs my wrist.

"Upstairs," he commands. "We go now or I'm fucking dragging you."

Whoa.

No objection.

I just stand, and he joins me, tugging his shorts back in place over his seething hard-on. Nothing can hide the tent, and I swallow a muffled laugh.

"Hush," he whispers.

We take turns toweling off, and then he grabs my hand, leading me through the back door. The house is silent and dark as we hurry through it, practically tiptoeing past the great room, careful not to wake the sleeping kids.

Straight to his room.

No question.

Unlike mine, there's a bathroom attached, and he takes me inside, perching me on the sink as he shoves off his trunks.

He flicks the bright light on, and it shocks me so much that I spend a few seconds blinking at him.

Here, I see the tiger again, this apex hunter with dizzying green eyes.

His pupils narrow, then dilate again.

His dark hair hangs in damp snatches, fiendishly messy from dragging my hands through it.

He only has the one tattoo on his arm, and the rest of his skin is the same honed muscle built to destroy a woman's sanity.

He has abs for miles.

A freaking V of pure honed muscle pointing to his large erection like he's the reigning king of sex.

Not fair.

It isn't right that there are men who can make you very stupid, very fast, and leave you very heartbroken the next day. All because they're model gods.

And he's staring at me with his dark, drugged eyes, his breath ragged as he takes me in.

"I wasn't done with you." I wrap my legs around him, dragging him closer before I take him in my hand again.

His cock twitches, and he exhales sharply, resting his forehead on mine.

"Go fucking slow. I'm not popping off like champagne."

"Isn't that the point?" I smirk.

"Wasn't planning on coming in your hand." He reaches for me, pushing aside the soaked material between my legs. "Your wet pussy says you agree. I'm not wasting your hot little cunt when it's dripping to be ravaged."

No freaking argument here.

Just his fingers, stroking slow, hypnotic circles around my clit, edging me until my breath hitches.

Grinding on him earlier felt good, but this is something else entirely.

I wipe the bead of moisture at the slit of his cock and he groans raggedly.

His fingers don't slow—if anything, they work faster.

My core clenches.

If it's a competition, I don't know who'll win.

I'm not sure I want to.

"Kane," I whisper.

"Yeah?" When I don't reply, he groans. "Say my name again. Just like that."

"Kane." I moan it this time, breathy and wanting. "Kane— I need you in me."

Another groan, and his lips brush my cheekbone, tongue hot against my skin.

I pump him again, slowly this time, feeling his entire body shudder.

We're both poised on the edge, this delicate balance.

Seeing him struggle to keep himself together makes me proud, too.

How can a man like this want me so badly he can barely hold back?

"Condoms," he spits like it's a curse. "Don't know if I have any—let me check."

Oh, crap.

If he leaves me like this, I might actually die.

"It's... it's okay. I'm clean," I whisper, arching into his touch as he pushes another finger inside. Full, but not full enough.

"Yeah?" He crooks his fingers, and I lose my train of thought.

It's a big ask when we're strangers and there's always some risk.

But I *need* him inside me.

My mouth moves, open and silently pleading.

"What's that, sweetheart?" He nips at my neck. "What were you going to say?"

I retaliate by tightening my grip on his cock, stroking faster, watching his chest heave.

"You could just fuck me without a condom," I gasp. "If you want."

He bares his teeth, inhaling roughly.

"You have no fucking clue how much I'd love that." His thumb smothers my clit as his fingers work deeper, and liquid heat floods the base of my stomach, growing and swelling. "Is that what you want?"

"*Yes.*" I clutch at my last fluttering train of thought. "I'm on birth control."

The last thing either of us need is an accidental pregnancy, but I'm so far gone even that sounds hot.

No judging.

I'm a little twisted.

I'm in a daze but I'm not crazy.

I've never, in all my life, had a one-night stand without a condom.

It's not the smart or grown-up thing to do.

And when you're used to casual flings with men who'll ghost you after a few times at most, you need to be sensible.

Sexual health is no joke, I know that. I do.

But Kane just feels different.

His lightning eyes feel familiar in a way they shouldn't after barely a week together.

It's like I've spent half my life staring into them, losing myself willingly.

Or maybe I just love seeing him, the man behind the bluster.

I've seen the good dad, the grump, and the fearless beast when there's a threat to his family—or me.

Yes, it's stupid to trust his word that he's also clean and everything will be fine. Perhaps it's also dumb to trust my birth control, even though it's never let me down in the past.

All I know is, I can't bear the idea of losing this moment.

Not for a second.

"Okay," he says finally. I feel the words through the rumble of his chest. "I'll fuck you, but first you're going to come for me, duchess. Come so hard I'll have to peel you off the floor."

Holy shit.

…that won't be a problem if he keeps talking like that.

I'm already so close my legs are shaking.

And knowing he's close too, the idea of him being inside me, the way he's rubbing my clit and following my body's rhythm to give me exactly what I need, bringing me right to the cliff...

This can only be the best kind of brutal.

"That's right," he says, holding me against him. "Good girl. You're Kane's good girl now."

Oh my God, I am.

I bury my head in his shoulder effortlessly as his fingers quicken and his thumb sends me into tomorrow.

My orgasm rips the fabric of space.

This isn't just another O I need like my next breath.

Not another predictably good, run-of-the-mill climax I get with my favorite toys, or maybe a few of the good ones Kelso used to give.

This is different.

This is *floating.*

An out-of-body experience where I liquify like molten gold.

I'm falling and spinning and coming apart.

He's holding me up while I come undone a dozen different ways I can't describe.

All I can do is *hold on.*

Hold on to Kane as he keeps working me over, sending wave after wave of sensation washing over me.

He knows when to start and when to strum, when to stop and leave me ruined, sagging against him.

"Kane." I whisper his name with awe.

He laughs against my temple, proud and light.

I slowly crawl back into my own body again.

His hand lingers between my legs, and when he moves it, I whimper again wordlessly. He's so gentle as he scoops me up, carrying me over to the bed.

His eyes glint in the shadows, all dancing desire as he

pulls my swimsuit off. I've never been so nervous in my life, but just like on horseback, his hands reassure me.

They're firm as he lifts me onto the bed, hovers over me, and takes a heady moment, just breathing me in.

"Are you ready for me, duchess?"

So achingly ready.

But all I can do is nod, holding my breath as his eyes turn feral.

Then he pushes the blunt head of his cock against my entrance.

Time stops.

His mouth covers mine like a silent vow, swallowing my rough moan as he eases in, taking and filling and claiming, pulling my legs open with his hands on my knees.

"Fuck," he rasps as his hips notch against mine.

We're flush now, no space left between us, and it feels impossibly good.

"I… I'm not sure I can be quiet for this," I say miserably.

He smothers a laugh, but his eyes are stark raving serious.

"You need to be, duchess. Fight it. Bite me if you have to." His hand cups the back of my neck, and I press my lips against the curve of his shoulder. My teeth graze his skin and he pushes my face into him. "You want to ride the storm, you have to *whisper*. Can you do that?"

"Yesss," I say mindlessly. "O-okay."

"Margot, can you do it?"

Truthfully, I'm not sure I'm capable of breathing like a normal person right now.

It still feels like parts of me are scattered on the other side of the universe, but yes, for him, I'll *try*.

He pulls out and thrusts back in, slowly at first, then gaining speed.

Our bodies fit like destiny, every stroke deeper and warmer than before.

I bite back a louder moan, finding my missing pieces in every thrust.

"Yeah?" He grunts a question, the word harsh and needy, and I lean back.

"Touch me," I demand, urgent and needy.

He brings his fingers back to my clit, finding the swollen, sensitive nub and drawing tiny circles around it. "Like this? Your new addiction?"

My breaths are tiny moans.

The sound of our bodies coming together is too loud in this quiet space, deafening, even if I know it's just in my head.

He laughs as his fingers find my breasts again, cupping them with a possessive squeeze.

The noise he makes is bestial when he rolls my nipple.

My body is a lit fuse, and it's only a matter of time until I explode.

Again.

Right on his bare, pumping cock.

His strokes come fiercer, lifting me off the bed before slamming me into it.

The coiled feeling in my core winds tighter with every thrust, making me a human spring.

By the feel of it, he must be as close as I am.

And his breath turns volcanic against my skin, rough kisses like the ground rumbling before the eruption.

"Margot, damn. Keep up, stay with me before I—" His voice chokes off in another guttural groan as I clench around his cock.

Yeah.

Yeah, I will.

I can't say it, so I wrap my legs around his ass, moaning from the beautiful friction breaking me in two.

That's all it takes.

Force and fire.

My climax slams up through my belly, and his hand covers my mouth, muffling my cries as he thrusts into me one last time.

His hips jackhammer, threatening to break the old bed as he pitches deeper, faster, baring his teeth like the lusting shadow he's become.

I'm breaking apart, shattered and—

Coming!

I can't blink.

I can't breathe.

I can't do anything but feel the deluge when it comes.

This white-hot release of heat and waves where we find eternity together.

The way his face screws up as he strikes my depths and unloads his soul.

We're one silent scream, one wild chorus of breath and rattling bones.

We come together so good I truly think I died, because there's no *way* I'm walking out of here the same woman.

For the longest time, we don't move.

Time restarts and punches holes in my memory. It's a little like being very drunk on the sweetest wine, only this high won't leave a hangover.

I don't remember flopping down on his chest, leaving a steaming mess between my legs.

His hand rests on the back of my neck, stroking me like a kitten.

My nails dig into the skin of his shoulder.

I'm not sure he even notices.

That was…

"Holy shit," I whisper, giggling weakly.

"Holy shit," he agrees. "Shower?"

"Please."

There's something adorably pragmatic about the way he helps me off the bed, touching me softly like he's testing to see if I'm still in one piece. And the way he checks the hot water before sliding me under it.

And then, somehow, even though I really, really shouldn't —I let him lead me back to his bed and pull me under the covers with him.

I don't remember falling asleep.

We fuck again, a few more times until we're slow and breathless, before sinking into the velvet darkness.

XII: LITTLE TASTE OF HOME (KANE)

I startle awake after sunrise, the light streaming in through a slit in the curtains.

It's the first time I've slept in for—damn, it must be *years*.

Hardly surprising after the night I had.

A man doesn't have his soul exit his body along with his balls very often.

Even wilder, I slept like the dead while sharing my bed with a strange woman for the first time in a decade.

It shouldn't be this easy.

It shouldn't be this *dangerous*.

Margot's still half-conked out, too, all curled against my chest like she doesn't think anything of staying the night.

Greed overwhelms me when I see this woman in my arms.

Especially when I see her like this, with her hair slightly wavy around her face, loose and tangled in a gold cloud, her eyes peaceful.

She looks too innocent after the way I fucked her last night. Too sweet to be the same girl I defiled.

Getting up a couple times last night to carry the kids off to bed and check on them was hard enough.

Just because I had a good time doesn't mean I let my duty slip by. I made the rounds alone, checking the whole house, the locks, the windows, and they were all good.

Now, I'm boneless, awestruck and yes, a little scared.

What the fuck *was* last night?

There are no words.

She stirs, stretching like a kitten waking up from a nap. Her eyes flutter open, and I see it when she remembers where she is.

What she's doing.

Who she's with.

Her palm flattens against my chest and her fingers curl.

"Hey, you," she whispers, glancing up at me with a soft smile.

Is there any hesitation? Or is it just my scrambled imagination?

It would've been more sensible to part ways after the gravity-defying sex.

Only, what started in the hot tub and continued in bed kept going like an abandoned fire.

Slow, lazy, half-asleep sex.

Like our bodies instinctively knew what they wanted better than our heads, ignoring our brains when they were dizzy and tired.

"Hey, yourself," I say.

Her voice is scratchy with sleep as she says, "So."

"So."

"Last night got a little heated."

Fucking. Understatement.

A flashback of her little hand on my cock in the hot tub and then upstairs, later replaced with her mouth, zings through me like an arrow.

The way she wrapped her legs around me and held on for dear life.

The tiny sounds she made when she bit me, sinking her teeth into my shoulder, begging me to hurl my seed deep.

Never did I think I'd have my first hookup after the divorce unprotected.

Goddamn, Margot Blackthorn must've driven me insane. The only explanation.

Still, after we were sated, there was no way I could send her back to her room.

"Well, let's hear it," she whispers softly, still not looking at me. "How much do you regret last night?"

"Regret?"

"Scale of one to ten. Please don't say eleven." She holds up her crossed fingers with a pleading look.

Shit.

"How's this?"

I roll her over until she's under me.

Her blue eyes flare when she feels my cock.

Yes, I'm hard already, and she shifts against me.

Eager. Ready. Aching to be reclaimed.

I fucking love how obsessed she is, even if the shared addiction worries me.

"Kane—"

"Woman, stop. Let me give you your answer. Does this look like regret to you? Does this feel like I have the faintest second thought?" I kiss her deeply, pressing my hard-on against her belly.

She meets me halfway with a languid moan, wrapping her arms around my neck.

"Oh. Oh, thank God!" she hisses against my mouth. "I was afraid you'd wake up and tell me we made a huge mistake. You know, just like the kiss."

That would be the sensible thing, yes.

But my senses turn to ash when I feel her tongue flick over my bottom lip and the way her legs open to welcome me.

"That *would* be the rational, adult move," I say.

"But we're not doing it."

"No. Frankly, I'm too crazy for that grown-up level-headed shit. I'm stuck thinking about all the ways I need to touch you," I say.

It doesn't feel real, even when she's under my skin.

"You're in luck. I need to be touched." She arches against me, her breasts flush against my chest.

"See, what idiot could resist that invitation?" I bite her lip until she gasps.

Fuck, she's so soft, so eager.

I knew that already—knew she'd be the perfect mix of toned and feminine cloud—her belly soft and her perfect tits spilling out of my hands, nipples ready to be smothered with my tongue.

"Fuck, duchess."

"That's the plan," she whispers, and I laugh.

Then my dick slides between the slick folds of her pussy without an ounce of humor.

For a second, neither of us speaks.

I'm too busy trying to hold back my inner bull, and her hands are on my arms, gripping so tightly.

"I'm sorry I didn't leave last night."

"No way." I silence her with a kiss. "No damn way am I letting you sleep in your own room after this."

"...if you do that, we won't sleep at all. And the kids might find out."

"If it happens, it happens." I crane my neck down, sucking one of those greedy nipples into my mouth. The way she arches and moans makes my dick jerk. "Quiet," I whisper, watching as she pushes the back of her fist into her mouth, eyes fluttering shut.

I've never been so glad this house has such thick walls and old wooden doors. Just enough sound barrier between our revelry and prying little ears.

I grind against her again, half-mad to be inside her.

It's like I've reverted to eighteen again.

This must be the fourth time I'm about to fuck her in under ten hours, and my dick is a steel pipe.

Maybe all the months of stress and nothing but my hand under a cold shower left me that deprived.

Or maybe it's just the black magic spell Margot Blackthorn has me under.

"You feel so fucking good," I rasp.

"I hope so." She tilts her hips, giving me a sly, desperate look I can't possibly deny.

Enough.

My cock pushes into her desperate little cunt.

And my whole body tenses with pleasure, loving how her eyes go wide with delight.

"How are you this tight? You *kill* me," I grind out, giving a long, slow thrust to open her up.

I love how we have to work to make her little pussy accommodate my size.

Almost as much as I love her grip, the way she wrings me out, pulling every drop of come from my balls.

Her head falls back in the pillows, her hair a splash of haloed sunshine.

"Right there!" she breathes, urging me on.

"Yeah? You like being fucked this hard? You like coming on this cock?" I roll her nipple between my fingers until she clenches, so good and tight I see stars.

"Yes!"

My hips roll, working faster and deeper.

My pubic bone hits her clit, pushing her on to the sweetest apocalypse.

Growling, I grab her chin and tilt her face up until she gives me those sapphire blue eyes.

"Tell me what you want, baby, and you'll get it. You'll take it, good girl, real sweet for me. I know you'll be so fucking good for this cock."

"Y-yes! I will," she whimpers. "So good, Kane. Anything you want."

I do want.

So many things.

There are so *many* awful, indecent things I want to do with her.

But for now, we just fuck, knowing this has to be quick and discreet because the kids will be up in half an hour or so.

Getting involved was a terrible idea—a stupid damn move—but not because it's bound to complicate everything.

Because now all I want is to take her on every surface and beat her pussy to kingdom come.

Because I want to hear my name on her lips like a prayer.

Because I'm addicted to this girl, and every taste leaves me fiending more, burning to mark her down to the soul.

I thought I was beyond this high school bravado shit.

I thought being a thirty-something dad means you don't get in this deep with a woman anymore.

I figured a man calmed down with age and experience, shedding his carnal obsessions and psychotic sexy thoughts.

In one night, she blew that to pieces, scattering everything I thought I knew as a single dad who lives responsibly to the four winds.

Just like the way she's demolishing me right now, her pussy wrapped around my cock, pulling the pleasure out of me every time I thrust deep.

I catch her scream against my hand just in time, and she convulses, pouring raging fire up my spine.

I come so fucking hard I think I'm inside out.

I spill my nut in this woman and face-plant on eternity itself.

No, this isn't regret.

Not even close.

* * *

SULLY BAY ISN'T a big place, but it's lively enough to keep the kids entertained.

After we reluctantly pried ourselves off the bed and cleaned up, the kids were already downstairs, clamoring to go back into town.

It's not a bad suggestion when they'll both get homework credit for the educational sites around the town.

Also not a bad way to help us pretend there's nothing different going on.

Yeah, good fucking luck.

Still, there's a small fishing museum and a historic lighthouse just up the road from the main town. They're perfect to keep the kids busy and make sure they learn a thing or two about old Maine's history.

There's something reassuring about taking in over two hundred years' worth of pioneering struggle to tame this stretch of coast.

Proof that human ingenuity overcomes any uncertainty.

I hope to hell I can be so wise.

This isn't the most stable period for us after my bad marriage was just put out of its misery not that long ago, but I'm not letting their education slip.

I'll never let them think their father puts anything else

first, including a young woman who's very good at making him a total jackass.

Margot's eager to accompany us, and I wonder what's going on in her head. She stares outside the window on the drive up like she's never seen this shore before.

"This is nice. We used to spend so much time at the house when we'd come up as kids," she says as we head to the lighthouse.

It was built in the nineteenth century. Unlike the famous Portland Headlight, it's ugly, grey, and squat.

"Not even at the diner?" Dan sounds mortified. As far as he's concerned, it's the beating heart of the town.

"No, we used to go there plenty." She grins. "My granddad loved his big dinners at home but he couldn't keep up with them every day. And after a day out hiking? We were ready for food to just leap into our mouths."

"Dad's an awesome cook," Sophie says, and maybe it's my imagination, but it sounds a little pointed.

"You think so, huh?" Margot slides me a long glance, and I have to remind myself we're not alone to act on it the way I want. "I agree, he has a knack. If he cooks for you kids at home and it's half as amazing as what he whips up here, you guys are lucky."

My face heats under my beard.

"Can't cook all the time, but I try. I'm glad the diner gives us an easy option. Less dishes," I say.

"Fewer." Sophie pushes her glasses up her nose seriously.

"Come again?"

"She's correcting your grammar," Margot says kindly, her eyes dancing. "Fewer dishes to do."

"Thanks, teacher. We'll see who takes in more history today," I tease.

"I'll remember everything!" Sophie insists with a pout.

"Dan's good at math, but I live and breathe English and history."

"See what it's like with two kids smarter than me?" I let out an exaggerated groan and they laugh.

The museum is a small wooden building next to the lighthouse. The kids sprint ahead of us the second we're parked, skipping all the informational boards so they can look at the old fishing boats outside.

"Guys, slow down. Take it in and read," I call after them.

"Let them go," Margot says. A jolt of electricity spikes up my arm when she brushes against me. "The boats are way cooler for a nine-year-old anyway. They can read anything they miss online, old man."

"Did I feel *old* this morning?" I growl in her ear.

Her red cheeks are the only answer I need.

Inside, there are glass cases bursting with colorful sea glass and bright lures in every shade of green and blue. Plus, a bunch of small plaques with old photos, explaining how vital fishing was to this area.

Sully Bay used to be a serious fishing village, a lot like Bar Harbor. Its trade in lobsters, crabs, and fish practically built the town.

Over the past fifty years, it's pivoted toward tourism as Acadia started drawing bigger crowds, becoming a bucket for the spillover summer crowds.

We turn a corner, coming up to a large wooden rowboat hung on hooks—and come face-to-face with Lee What's-His-Face.

The ceramics guy from the market.

He breaks into a lazy smile when he sees us.

"Oh, hello," he says, holding up his hand casually. "Nice to see some familiar faces."

"Lee, right?" Margot beams right back at him, oblivious to the way I've tensed.

Stupid animal jealousy.

After last night, his chances of bedding her are nil, if they ever existed at all.

I know I shouldn't even let the thought invade my mind.

We're having a family outing in an old fishing museum, for fuck's sake, not dancing in a bar.

"That's right. Good memory." Lee gives her a nod that makes me bristle. "Are you enjoying my products?"

"Oh, yes, they're stunning. We're using the mugs already, aren't we, Kane?"

"Yeah." Now I wish I'd left them wrapped up. I don't take my eyes off the guy, though my voice is friendly. "They're great for coffee and hot cider. Very sturdy."

"Are you big into fishing or history?" Margot asks.

"This place? Yes, I suppose." Lee rubs the back of his neck. "Honestly, I like to come here for the sea glass more than anything. There's a lot of inspiration there, especially when you don't see glasswork like it anymore. Bit of a history buff, too, I guess."

"I wish that was me," Margot says with a sigh. "But after a little while, it just goes in one ear and out the other. I like having the big picture more than the nitty-gritty. And yes, the sea glass is lovely. I can see why this place would make any artist happy."

"We find our muse where we can, Miss Blackthorn. There's so much beauty everywhere, if people would just open their eyes and look, instead of getting it from screens." His voice sharpens, even if his smile remains pleasant enough.

Huh.

And he keeps looking at me while he talks to her, like he's expecting me to say something profound.

I don't get it.

The weirdness only deepens the urge to pull Margot forward and leave him to his day.

Must just be the testosterone still whipping around my veins from last night. Hormones will make a man hallucinate, jumping at threats that aren't really there.

I always had a possessive streak, yeah, but not like this.

Always figured Daria desensitized me with her shit. I mean, how jealous can you get once you've been with a woman who isn't faithful?

Turns out, it's plenty, if the molten heat in my blood's any indication.

"We're here for the kids. The school year just started and they need to learn something on this trip for homework," I say, nodding at where Dan and Sophie are pressed up against a glass case with shells and preserved sea animals.

"Ah, good." Lee draws the word out. "There's plenty of that around here. But if it's history you're after, there's an old fort just a few miles up the road. Goes back to the War of 1812, I believe. Really impressive cannons. Your boy will love it. You shouldn't miss it."

"Cannons?" Dan immediately turns and runs up to us. "Did you say a fort, mister? Can we check it out, Dad? Please?"

Sophie drifts back toward us when she hears her brother pleading.

"A fort would be cool," she says. "Maine had a lot happening in that war. I read about it on my tablet a few days ago."

Margot meets my eyes over the kids' heads.

There's no way we can say no, and she knows it.

"I guess it's history day, guys," she says, smiling up at Lee. "Thank you. I can't believe I came here so often as a kid and we never went!"

"It's worth the trip," he says. "Lots to do and really informative."

"We'll finish the museum first," I tell the kids.

Dan's shoulders immediately slump.

"But the fort would be so *cool*," he insists.

"It won't take long, kiddo." Margot nods at the sign. "You didn't even see the mini aquarium yet."

That's enough to get their attention, and they sprint off again, Sophie slightly behind Dan in her bulky shoes.

Lee nods at us politely and heads for the entrance.

As we follow the kids at a more leisurely pace, I slide Margot's hand into mine. Her fingers curl around mine.

Neither of us say anything.

We haven't talked about what this means or what it's meant to be.

Hell, I'm not sure we need to.

We both know it shouldn't be anything.

It can't last, and it won't.

Like the old sailboat out back, we're two strange ships passing in the night, flashing our lights to feel less lonely.

But her hand feels warm in mine, and for now, it's a good day.

Today, we make our own meaning, however temporary.

That's rare enough to make me stop fussing and live in the moment.

* * *

IT'S RAINING by the time we leave the fort two hours later, which turned out to be larger and more interesting than the fishing museum.

Guess there's no faulting Lee for his recommendation.

The windows are cracked in the back, letting in the fresh, earthy scent of fading leaves, and the kids bicker back and forth lightheartedly.

"I can't believe it closes at one," Dan says in disgust. "Who's done looking around a place that big by *then*?"

"I know, Bud." I flash Margot an amused glance. She has her elbow braced against the door, her hair tossed by the wind.

This is one of those precious moments you only remember after it's gone. Like passing scenes from a movie you barely remember and never get to replay.

Right now, I can't remember the last time we had a day this peaceful.

Getting away from New York and the routine back there was the best decision I've made all year. And not just because of the bombshell beside me.

"The drums were so cool," he says. "Like, so cool with their sheepskins. And so old. And did you *see* the eagles painted on the side? Can't believe they're two hundred years old and not worn out!"

"You're hooked now, little man. Imagine having to play those drums on a battlefield. They were important," I say.

"Yeah, it's crazy! I love history when it's cool like that with soldiers and battles. Way better seeing it than just reading about it in some old book. We need more field trips where you can get to see how people used to live."

"Careful, or you'll wind up a history professor like your great uncle," I tease. "Or maybe a rock star who makes people love the ballads of 1812 again."

And I'll be damn proud of him, either way.

"As long as I can drum," Dan agrees.

"Hey, look!" Sophie holds the windup Army drummer they bought from the gift shop.

They were right on the verge of closing, and it was an effort to hustle them through in time to get something.

In the end, they settled on their little prizes, and they pass the shared figurine back and forth.

"So GOATed," Dan says as the drummer's arms move. The tiny sticks make a tapping noise.

It has so much charm it's distracting.

"Eyes on the road," Margot says, laughing and pushing the hair back from her eyes. "You can play with it when you get home."

I snort, braking and turning onto the road that will take us back to the lake house.

"I have it under control."

"Sure you do, big guy."

My dick loves the way she says that a little too breathy, low and teasing with a hint of promise.

Even if this thing between us has an expiration date, it's damn fun in the meantime.

We pass a speeding pickup truck with one side dented in as we turn down the home stretch just before the gravel road.

I swerve to avoid it, just to allow extra room, distracted by thoughts of Margot later.

From her glance, she knows.

"Sure," she says in that throaty voice. "Under control, right?"

"Sophie, give it back," Dan whines from the back seat. "Come on, you're hogging it!"

"Guys," I say sharply as the house comes into view. Weird how somewhere so new can feel like home. "That's enough for one day, don't you think?"

"We should've gotten them two drummers," Margot says.

"There was only one left." I lower my voice. "Soph will lose interest as soon as we're back inside, anyway. She only wanted it because Dan did."

"Yeah, kids." She snorts. "That sounds about right."

As we pull up, I meet her gaze for a heated moment.

Rain splatters the windshield while they continue razzing each other in the back, thinking I don't notice.

I sigh.

This was a good day. We need more like it.

"See you inside?" Margot snatches the keys from the central console and grins at me.

I don't have time to answer before she's unbuckled her seat belt and sprints out into the rain, holding her jacket above her head and laughing.

Dan's next, the little 1812 drummer boy firmly in hand.

I'm last. I lock the vehicle after Sophie gets out and follow them to the back door.

Everyone's still laughing until Margot walks into the house and screams.

XIII: HOME SECURITY (MARGOT)

I knew something was off the second I walked in.

But it wasn't until I saw the ceramic plate smashed on the kitchen floor that I understood why my senses were tingling.

The air was wrong.

Dan's sneakers by the front door were nudged to one side.

The pantry door is open, when I distinctly remember closing it.

But the sight of that colorful shattered plate tells me beyond any doubt what my instinct whispered.

Someone paid us a visit.

And not for a friendly hello.

I don't remember screaming, just the scratching in my throat.

My legs feel unstable, my hand trembling as I reach out to steady myself against the wall.

Holy shit, I should've known this day was too good to be true.

Too happy, too relaxed, too easy.

All the fear behind us, shrinking in the rearview mirror.

Idiot!

Whoever came lurking around the house before wasn't done.

The danger isn't over.

"What is it?" Kane pushes past, pressing his big, warm hand to the small of my back as he coldly assesses the scene.

I'm sure he feels it before he notices the plate, the *wrongness* that hit me from the second I opened that door.

It's like watching a lion turn defensive.

His jaw tightens. His eyes narrow. All his features sharpen, stiffer and angrier and ready for a fight.

That makes me feel a bit safer, at least.

"Was it locked?" he growls.

There's a feral edge in his voice that makes me shiver.

"Yes. I'm... I'm sure of it." I stoop down to grab the keys I dropped on my way in. "I didn't realize anything was wrong until—"

My voice chokes off, not quite a sob.

"You're okay, duchess," he whispers.

"Dad? What's wrong?" Dan whispers cautiously from behind us.

Kane eyes me, and I suck in a breath. The keys are clenched between my fingers now like little blades, just like Ethan taught me years ago.

I guess it's an old habit after years of doing that on late nights in New York City parking garages or outside at night when I'm at the curb, waiting for a lift.

I'm not helpless.

If push comes to shove, I *can* defend myself.

I can even protect his kids.

Kane must reach the same conclusion. He nods curtly.

"Stay with them," he tells me, then looks behind him, ushering the kids into the house and shutting the front door behind us. "Dan, Soph, hang out with Margot while I check the house."

"Daddy?" Sophie's voice is high and unsure.

She's seen the plate.

"We'll be just fine, kidlet," he says, casting a fierce look over his shoulder. "Margot has you guys covered. Stay put."

I nod back at him, wishing I had his intense confidence.

For their sake, I'll find it again.

For a second, I panicked, but these adorable children give me good reason to harden up.

I *need* to keep it together.

"We're cool, guys," I whisper, holding out my arm and pulling Sophie closer. "Kane, be careful... okay?"

"Don't worry about me. Odds are we're alone," Kane says sharply, already stalking through the great room, scanning every corner.

Sophie wraps her thin arms around my waist, but Dan tries to follow his dad.

"I'll come too. Backup," he announces.

"No!" I catch his arm. "Dan, I know it sucks, dude. But your dad asked us to stay here. It's better to have strength in numbers, right? Plus, we can use an extra strong man around while Kane checks things out up there."

"Yeah," he says with a determined look. "I guess you're right."

Thank God.

I'm glad it's easy to flatter a little boy's ego.

We huddle awkwardly in the kitchen, pressed up together near the island.

Dan doesn't want to admit he's worried, but his silence says everything.

Meanwhile, Kane prowls through the house, a wall of bristling muscle with the lightest footsteps.

What did he do overseas, anyway?

Wherever he learned to charge into danger, I'm grateful.

And I almost feel sorry for any reckless intruder he finds.

Almost. But they've invaded my privacy and that's unforgivable.

It's the second time this creep violated my safety, and worse, they've made these lovely children feel rattled in *my* home.

I breathe slowly, my nostrils burning as my blood simmers.

Fizzing anger replaces the fear.

Just who the hell do they think they are?

Breaking into my house, scaring my renters? My friends? My—

No, they're not my kids. Even if they kinda feel like it.

I swallow thickly.

All this craziness must be going to my head.

When Kane reappears on our floor after checking upstairs after what feels like forever, it's so sudden I jump.

"They're gone," he says tersely. I sigh with relief. "Let me have a look outside. If there's a footprint, any evidence at all, that'll only help us."

"Be careful," I whisper.

His eyes meet mine, and he gives me a nod as he heads out the back door.

For a second, we don't break our huddle.

Not until Sophie raises her head and looks at me, her little brows knit together. "So... we're safe?"

"Yes," I say before I can question it. "We're safe, Soph. It was probably just some idiot pulling a prank. Who knows. People do crazy things for attention these days, especially if they can show off on TikTok." I wish I believed that as I walk through the rest of the kitchen, looking for anything else out of place.

Aside from the plate, everything seems untouched.

That's not much relief when I'm avoiding the mess of ceramic fragments scattered across the floor, sweeping a few stray pieces aside before the kids step on anything. They're both wearing their shoes, but still...

It's not a pretty scene.

The sheer force involved tells me this was no accident. It looks more like the plate was *hurled* at the floor intentionally.

But why? What the actual fuck?

Who would be that angry? Who would do such a thing if they were just looking for stuff to steal?

Because maybe they weren't.

And my hands shake when I think it might be more personal than money.

Please, please don't let this be about me or Gramps. These sweet kids can't be scared for their lives all because of some dumb grudge I had nothing to do with.

"Guys, be really careful where you step. I need to sweep this up," I say, guiding them to the table through a clear path. "Take a seat. Let's have some hot chocolate while I clean up, okay?"

It won't fix everything, but maybe it'll help clear their heads while I try to breathe.

"Want some help?" Dan volunteers eagerly, his shoes tapping the floor. I'm glad they forgot to take them off once we came home to stranger danger.

I almost turn him down, but there's something urgent about the way he asks.

"If you want to, you can sweep the edges, wherever I show you. Just don't walk over anything until I say it's clear. There's a broom in the pantry."

"On it!"

Outside, the rain picks up, pounding the windows.

Fall means darker, earlier nights. This normal weather only compounds the claustrophobia inside the house.

I shiver.

"Here, hold it open for me," I say, passing him a big black trash bag from under the sink. After putting two mugs of milk in the microwave for chocolate, I start sweeping.

By the time Kane returns with his shirt plastered to his shoulders and his hair damp, the floor looks clear, and the kids each have a hot chocolate in hand.

Dan fiddles with the windup drummer boy. I'm glad he has it so he's not hyper-focused on the break-in, even if the little toy feels a touch creepy right now.

"Did you see anything?" I ask Kane the second he's through the door.

"Nothing." He shakes his head. "A half-smeared bootprint in the mud by the driveway and some tire tracks, but nothing real useful."

A flash of the old pickup driving past skips in my memory.

The distinctive dent on the side.

At the time, I hadn't noticed much—but I recognized that vehicle.

"That truck," I say, and Kane flicks his gaze to me. His eyes are dark with swirling fury, a forest at night. "The one we passed on the way in… it belongs to the Babins. I saw it when I went to their place."

His jaw clenches.

I can tell he wants to rain brimstone on these 'neighbors' of ours.

That makes two of us.

They lied to my face, claiming they respected Gramps when they've been fighting him all this time. They flipping *sued* him.

Supposedly, they tried to burn the whole place down.
God.

"We should call the police," I say.

"Yeah, better now than later. The kids will have to go home if the cops can't find anything useful," Kane agrees.

"What?" Sophie nearly spills her hot chocolate as she shoves her chair back.

"Dad, that's not fair!" Dan shouts, glaring at his father. "We never go anywhere nice and now we gotta go *home?*"

"Nooo, I don't wanna be stuck with Mom." Sophie's bottom lip trembles. "She's always dragging us on modeling trips and they're so boring."

"Yeah, her new boyfriend doesn't even like me. He sucks at Minecraft too." Dan snorts, shaking his head with disgust.

Poor munchkins.

My heart aches for them. I hate that they have a mother who makes them play second fiddle to her glamorous life.

Maybe because it feels familiar.

Our parents treated us like accessories growing up, just another thing rich people should have along with personal chefs and perfectly trained purebred dogs. Oh, and we never *got* to have a puppy.

Just Ares, PopPop's ancient basset hound. These days, he's napping away his long evenings with Ethan and Hattie.

Maybe my parents regret their distance now, but they've never changed their lifestyle. No big moves to reconnect with us as adults, either.

That's whatever.

"Your mother can take you somewhere warm for a few days," Kane says softly. He smiles, but his eyes are steel.

"We never like going away with her and you know it. It's not like here!" Sophie pouts, her eyes glinting with tears.

Dan nods, folding his arms.

"Dad, this place is cool. We love it here. There's a lake and a fort and I get to play my drums as much as I like. We get our homework done early and no one ever tells me to shut up so they can watch their dumb dating reality show or pose for another Reel."

Ouch.

Kane scrubs a hand through his rain-dark hair.

"Little man, I hear you," he says after a second.

"So can we stay?" they both ask.

He holds up a finger.

"For now. But you have to listen to everything I say, and you never leave my sight or Margot's. You want to hang around with the adults, you'll act like one."

"Got it! You can count on us," Dan promises.

I'm almost expecting him to fire off a crisp salute.

Kane ruffles his hair. "You're a good kid."

"Can I hit the drums now? I finished my chocolate."

"Run along," Kane says.

It's like the danger is half forgotten with the way Dan bolts upstairs.

Kane watches him go, his posture tight and his mouth turned down.

My heart stings as he glances at me, holding my gaze for a long moment before looking away.

I can't imagine how much it must hurt to hear his kids talking about his ex-wife that way, how complicated their situation must be.

Knowing that every time he delivers them to her, they feel so unwanted. Unloved.

Especially when he does everything he can to put them first.

Today, I was able to forget reality for a few heavenly hours.

This was a nasty wake-up call.

Kane Saint has a life beyond our little small-town fever dream.

He has kids to raise and an ex-wife who's still part of the picture.

Danger aside, this situationship isn't healthy.

We can't keep playing make-believe without serious consequences.

* * *

The sheriff arrives just before dinner with a deputy at his side.

They don't stay long, just an hour or so, enough to ask a few questions and photograph the vague mud prints before heading to the Babins to clear things up.

They're sure it's a misunderstanding.

I want to believe that so bad.

I still don't want to believe small-town drama can balloon into real menacing crime.

After they left, I threw together dinner, a frozen lasagna while Kane went outside to get the new security cameras working.

The entire time he's gone, I'm on tenterhooks.

Sophie draws at the kitchen table while Dan brings his drum pad downstairs and plays in the living room—oddly quietly for him.

We all pretend we're fine, but we're obviously still jumpy whenever the house creaks or pops with the wind on a cool night.

By the time Kane returns, I'm a twitchy mess.

Sophie runs up and gives him a hug. Dan talks loudly about the music he's been practicing, some old American military marching songs he found online.

"Everything okay?" Kane asks.

I nod. "Just peachy. Dinner's ready."

He helps me plate the lasagna and apple-gorgonzola salad I threw together and we take our seats around the table.

Dan stays weirdly quiet, picking at his food.

It's like we're still listening for a break-in, a jittering lock or a scraping window.

I can't stop thinking about what might happen if someone was that determined to charge in while we're here.

All the doors and windows are locked, but Kane found a tampered lock on the back door. Possibly a sign someone had a lockpicking set.

The only good news is having the muddy prints on record. The police photographed them.

Also, the truck sighting heading back from the lake house.

But with the small-town attitude, will that be enough?

Will they really think the Babins invaded this house without a smoking gun?

I have to look into a restraining order.

Seriously, I'm done being scared.

Kane stays silent, too, chewing mechanically as he thinks heavy thoughts that show on his face.

He couldn't protect us from the asshole coming back. I'm sure that's hanging on his mind like burrs.

It must eat him to the bone when the man's a protector.

I just wish I knew what to say to make it better, but all my words feel patronizing, so I keep my mouth shut and eat quietly, barely enjoying what should be a tasty dinner on a cold night.

Once we're finished and I bring our plates to the dishwasher, he lays out his expectations for the evening.

At least an hour of schoolwork for the kids, writing up what they learned about the fort and Sully Bay for school. They can work together in here on his laptop.

They don't even protest.

My heart stings.

That's how I know they're shaken up, trying so hard to be brave.

"I'm going to test those cameras," he tells me as he helps load glasses into the dishwasher beside me. "Nothing else is happening in this house on my watch."

"Let me help." I look at his strong, tight jaw and the hard, unforgiving shine in his eyes.

"Sure. Let me make sure they're settled first."

I hate how sour the whole vibe feels.

If I'm stuck here watching our happy time playing house going up in smoke, so is he.

At least he doesn't turn me down, I guess. But it was like he looked straight through me.

I don't know how to bring him back, how to ground us to the moment. Or even how to reassure him.

I don't even know if it's my place.

Especially if I'm the reason his vacation gets ruined. The selfish, stupid Babins, clawing at Gramps' ghost for revenge, and all for some ridiculous grudge from generations ago.

Seriously.

Just how small are these people?

"Are we going to be safe tonight?" Sophie's voice is so small.

"Safer than ever, Soph. Once the cameras are up, we'll see everything. They're motion sensing, even in the dark." Kane gives her a reassuring smile. I ache at the deep worries he's hiding. "We'll be sleeping like logs. No one will get past. I have notifications set up to ping me awake."

"No one? Really?" She brightens.

"Absolutely."

"So with the cameras, does that mean we're good to stay?" Dan asks, more cheerful again.

"For now. After tonight, we'll see, Danny boy," Kane says.

The twins whoop, but Kane's face settles back into a hard line when they're not looking.

At least the kids are happier, I suppose, but I want to believe we're better off with this fancy security system. I don't bother staying mad that he went ahead and got one before I could call a local place.

In this case, I'm glad he acted.

I just want yesterday.

I want Kane to smile like he believes it'll be all right.

I want to get back to kissing him without a care, before our time runs out.

I want to believe we're fine—and dammit, we will be.

I just need to be patient.

Wait for cameras, wait for the cops to update us, and wait for this man to keep screwing me up against my better judgment.

Just for a little while longer.

XIV: THE LONG WAY HOME (KANE)

As the kids peck away at their history papers, Margot and I head outside to check the cameras one more time.

I bought the best stuff money could buy, Enguard grade units shipped in from a world-class security firm out of California. They're damn near bombproof and impeccable with their AI-backed night vision, but the bells and whistles still don't stop my gut churning.

If the Babins were behind all this, they're persistent.

They also planned their break-in, watching the house so they knew when we left.

Also, let's face it, people gab in this little town, so they easily might've known where we were, how far away.

And I left us wide fucking open.

I download the app on Margot's phone and set it up for her. She frowns as she searches for the signal, waiting impatiently for it to connect.

"There!"

"Is it working now?" I eyeball the last camera discreetly mounted above the front door.

Having them peppered across the property makes me feel a smidge better.

No, they aren't armed. They won't magically stop anyone hell-bent on breaking in, but if they do detect movement, at least I'll catch them in the act.

I chose the subscription plan that saves all footage uploaded to the cloud for two weeks before deletion.

That's enough to hand rock-solid proof to the police if this prick makes a third visit. And if they come, I will nail their asses to the wall with charges, assuming Margot doesn't beat me to it.

No one threatens my kids or my woman.

No, I don't care if I'm talking her up into something she isn't.

The way she frowns, her bottom lip twisted in a pout as she focuses, just makes this too real. Headstrong or not, she's a rich girl with zero experience dealing with nasty fucks willing to break the law and get physical.

She's lucky I'm here, and I'm going to make sure her luck translates into action.

If anyone wants to get to her, they'll go through me, and they will need a hell of a lot more than mere fortune. They'd better come fucking dripping four-leaf clovers.

"One more sec. Looks like I can flip the first few streams. We put up eight cameras, right?"

"Yeah, eight."

"Okay." She swipes through her livefeeds, then turns her screen to face me. "Number eight. Looks clear. I think we've got it."

Once I've confirmed all eight feeds work on her phone, I go through and help her label them the same way I did so we'll know where they are.

"Thanks for your patience," I say, glancing up.

"No, thank you. I should've been the one buying these

cameras." She teases her bottom lip between her teeth. "I'm so sorry. This isn't what you guys came here for."

"Duchess, stop. You shouldn't be apologizing."

"But being here puts you guys at risk. You can't just kick back and enjoy yourselves, and it's because of me. I just know it. The bad blood here..."

"Shut it," I say gently. "The Babins made their choice, or whoever the fuck. Nobody twisted their arm. You can't blame yourself over something your grandfather never let you in on."

"Well... maybe." She clears her throat.

My phone buzzes in my hand and I glance down to see Daria calling.

Damnation.

She always did have the world's shittiest timing.

Margot's eyes widen when she sees the name on my screen. I'm sure the little hairs on the back of her neck stand up like thorns, and I don't blame her.

"Um, it's okay, Kane. You should probably answer that," she whispers, stepping back.

"Right." I'm practically vibrating with tension, but we have an agreement never to ignore each other's calls.

I texted her about the trouble in Maine a couple hours ago.

The kids want to stay, of course, but I'm not set on keeping them around in a situation that's less than secure. No matter how much they hate staying with their material girl mom, I'd rather have them annoyed than hurt.

"Daria?" I press the phone to my ear, unclenching my jaw.

"Really, Kane? Is it always such torture to speak to me?"

Yes.

"Did you get my message?" I ask flatly.

"Duh. Why else would I be calling? You have the cupcakes."

My shoulders go rigid, watching Margot fiddle with her phone. She's pretending not to listen in, giving me plenty of space, but I know she's in earshot.

I'd do the same thing if the roles were reversed.

I'm no damn saint, whatever my name says.

I wonder what she's thinking. If she regrets hooking up now.

Somehow, I doubt the other men she's dated are single dads dealing with their ex-wives.

Shit, are we *dating*?

No, too far.

But I've always been bad at labels, especially with this casual stuff.

Becoming romantically illiterate must be the price of marrying young.

"Right. And that's a problem with everything going down in this house." There's a long pause. "Daria?"

"Hang on," she mutters. Her voice goes distant as someone speaks behind her before she comes back on the line. "Sorry, I only have a few minutes. The photog wanted some late-night shots by the fountain. But yeah, if they're in danger, just get them out of there! Go home. Like, it's not that deep, right?"

"Daria." I forget how damnably annoying she is, always expecting easy solutions. I pinch the bridge of my nose. "You need to take them if I have to send them home. You understand? I already gave their tutor the week off, thinking we'd be on vacation."

"What? Me?" She makes a strangled sound. "Jesus, I can't just take them when you snap your fingers, Kane. I'm leaving LA for a shoot in Cabo and it's totally not kid friendly. I mean, what would they even do all day? You know how stir-crazy they get, and the beaches are rough this time of year. They'll be safer with you. You can just check out early, right?"

Not if I want to throw Margot to the wolves.

I can't.

I won't.

"That's the problem, Daria. I already told the owner I'd step up and help secure this property, at least for a little while. I can't just ghost her and—"

"For fuck's sake!" she hisses under her breath. "Dude, why aren't you taking them back to New York? You can figure out a sitter and then go back or whatevs."

She doesn't get it.

She doesn't get a lot of fucking things.

But when it comes to their safety, she has a point.

My blood simmers.

I glance at Margot, unable to help myself.

No, I'm not stranding her in this house to face whatever the Babins have planned with nobody but the lazy-ass Mayberry cops around to stop them. If she got hurt or—

No. Not happening.

Fuck this entirely.

"Hold up. Is this a woman thing?" Daria inhales sharply. "Holy shit, are you *seeing* someone, Kane?"

Her scorned giggle splits my ears.

"It's not like that," I lie.

She laughs again like she can see right through my pathetic words.

Damn.

It's not that Daria cares about me dating.

She's had more boyfriends than I care to count since we split—and probably before, too. And even if she wasn't okay with it, that wouldn't matter.

Trouble is, Margot's right in front of me, listening to every word.

This thing with her is so new, so fragile—and it's not

really a thing, definitely nothing that I care to share with my ex.

"It's complicated, Daria. I can't go just yet and you need to trust me on that," I say. "There's crap to sort out here, and I'm the best man to do it."

"Oh, yes. Right. I forgot you need someone to feed your big hero complex twenty-four seven, and I guess you've found her. Look, I'm sorry, but I can't have them right now. I'm going to be in Cabo for almost a week. Kyle has a pickleball tournament, too."

My jaw pops hearing Kyle's name, her surfer-dud boyfriend.

That joke of a relationship won't last—they never do—and her awful taste in men remains unmatched.

It's not jealousy, I just hate the thought of the kids being around the one-dimensional losers she brings home. Last time, Surfer-dud yelled at Dan for drumming while he slept off a hangover.

Burnout piece of shit.

"It's not fair to spring this on me last minute," she whines. "My schedule is *so* busy lately, Kane. Can't your mom—"

"Forget it," I snap. "I should've known better than to expect you to step up."

"Hey, I—"

"No, you're right. I'll have my mom on standby instead, just like I figured. She's having a spa weekend with her friends, but I'm sure she can reschedule, under the circumstances."

Then I end this worthless call.

Margot stares at me in stunned silence, this compassion in her gaze I don't deserve.

At some point I started leaning against the wall, raking a hand through my hair until it's twisted like a bird's nest.

Goddamn, how did that marriage last more than two years?

"Are you okay?" Margot asks carefully.

She walks up and lays a hand on my arm. Hesitantly, like she's not sure if I want her touching me.

There's nothing I want more.

That may be the scariest surprise today.

"I'm sorry you had to hear that. Daria can be... difficult sometimes."

"Mm-hmm. How'd you guys meet? Just curious."

I snort, winding my arms around her waist and pulling her closer. "You mean, you're wondering how I was ever dumb enough to wind up with a woman who puts her own children last?"

"...am I that obvious?" She bats her eyes and tips her head back innocently. "She just doesn't seem dedicated. Not like you, I guess, and that's weird."

"She's not. I wish it were different. Not for my sake, but for the kids." I find bare skin where her sweater rides up, and I run my fingers along it absently, tracing the waistband of her jeans until my fingers slip under the fabric. "It was a young marriage. Very young and incredibly stupid."

"I guessed that. If you have a couple nine-year-olds at your age, I mean."

"I'm over a decade older than you, duchess."

"I know." She doesn't sound fazed by the age gap and she kisses my jaw. "But to have met her and married and had kids—that still makes you about twenty-seven when they were born?"

Yes, a fucking lifetime ago.

"Twenty-six," I say. "One year older than you."

She shrugs lightly. "I feel old sometimes, but also clueless. You're way more grown-up with a family to look out for."

"Yeah. Thought I knew everything there was to learn the

day they were born. Like hell." I rest my chin on top of her head, and she slides against me.

It's insane how easy this feels, like we've been doing it for years instead of days.

"So what happened? How?" she whispers.

"It was practically arranged. I was young, fresh out of the Army, still at the height of my hockey career. Hell, if anything, the time overseas made me a hotter commodity. Everybody wanted Kane Saint. On paper, Daria was the perfect daughter of a family friend. She was vetted, future eye candy for the cameras."

"Cameras?" She shakes herself. "Hockey, you mean?"

"Hockey, then politics. My father had it all mapped out, and I was too inexperienced to say no to it. He never went higher than his House seat in government and he wanted me to live his dream."

"It's hard to say no to that kind of pressure," she says like she understands. Maybe she does, being a Blackthorn and all. "What did he want you to do?"

"Everything. Taking his old House seat and then sliding into the US Senate, for starters. After that... who knows? He wanted to be Joe Kennedy, only he just had one son to groom for office." I laugh, but there's a bitter edge to it. "I had a taste of that world early. Figured out fast I'd rather chew glass than go into politics and serve shady fucking interests, always lying through my teeth and pretending I work for anybody else."

She takes a moment to digest it, her expression pensive in the faint light from the windows.

The sun set with the rain a while ago. Frogs and crickets fill the night with their songs.

"Were you married by the time you knew you didn't want a political career?"

"Unfortunately." I run my hand through her soft hair,

absently rubbing it between my fingers. "Daria was with me for my status, my potential. Just like I was with her for pretty photos, and I guess my lack of ambition was the last straw."

"I'm sorry."

"I don't regret anything. Without her, I wouldn't have my kids. They're the reason I finally slammed the door on politics, you know. So I could spend more time with them. And when I got hurt and had to retire…"

"I read about that," she murmurs, her arms winding around my neck tighter.

"She was a model who put her career first. You do the math. I was turning into the sort of man she never would've married. The kind of guy who knew his limit and who stops chasing fame and power once he's had a taste. No surprise, she was done with me. Shit, with all of us."

"That's not fair. She had kids—she should always put them first."

"You'd think," I whisper, tucking her hair behind her ear. Unlike Daria, Margot's beauty looks effortless, and it makes her more appealing.

"It must have been brutal."

"It was a lot of change. Hard to stay focused on what matters sometimes for sure. And not everyone was on board."

"Your dad?"

"Furious. I threw away the future he'd planned out down to the last detail, the war chest of money he'd raised and everything else. You already know how Daria felt. After hockey, I chose a start-up instead of jumping into the primary for the open seat in Congress. Our marriage went from checked out to total shit real fast, and I'm not sorry. I can't be. We never should've gotten married in the first place."

"But then you wouldn't have the twins," she reminds me.

For a second, I just stare at her.

Awestruck because she *listens*.

"That's why I don't regret the disaster. How can I? Without Dan and Sophie, I don't have a clue who or what I'd be." Though there's plenty I wish I'd done differently, yes.

I never should've wasted so many years entertaining what other people wanted, trying to jam their enormous square dreams through the smaller round hole of mine.

"Did you ever love her?" Margot hesitates, like she's not sure she wants an answer.

"I thought I did once. Before I knew any better or knew what kind of person she was. But now, looking back... I don't think I ever did. She certainly never loved me. If it's love, you don't fucking cheat. Not hard."

"That's so shitty." Her eyes glisten, and she makes a little sigh of agreement.

"It was. But it's not so bad now. I'm not limping around wounded or anything. I'm just glad to be out of there."

"My ex cheated, too," she says.

I instinctively pull her closer.

"Tell me his name and I'll make sure he's sorry."

She laughs.

"No need—he's not with me, so that's payback enough. He actually thought I'd just forgive him because how was he supposed to limit himself to 'only one person'? Jackwad. Like it was no different than morning coffee." She laughs bitterly, then shrugs. "I thought I'd be heartbroken forever, but I'm doing pretty well these days."

"You're better off without him, duchess. No question." I can't control the jealous thorns in my voice.

"That's what I realized. And I hope you did, too."

"Definitely," I say. "Daria was a drag on my life."

"But you shouldn't keep blaming yourself for her behavior," she tells me now, leaning in to kiss my neck, soft lips fluttering against my skin. "Everyone makes mistakes, and you did the right thing. You put your kids first."

As I hold her, I wonder if I'm doing anything right now.

Falling for this strange woman who drips false promises like honey, bringing her around my kids, knowing there's no future.

If only she didn't feel this good.

If only I could think in her presence.

She says I put my kids first, but hooking up with her is a time bomb.

When it explodes, I won't be the only one mangled in the wreckage.

Sophie, she's already on her way to worshipping Margot Blackthorn and her talents. Dan, he's brighter than ever with a woman around who listens, taking his jokes in stride and throwing them back.

They *like* her so much they're welcoming her into our little family unit without question.

Hell, Sophie even went to her alone and asked if she could help with her deepest, darkest fear.

Not me.

Margot.

What the fuck am I doing?

I don't even know if I'm cut out for another relationship.

I thought I'd spend years licking my wounds after finalizing the divorce, and I swore off women entirely. Everything was easier that way.

Now?

Now, I'm the asshole making it hard.

She feels the way I tense and she leans back, looking up with questions in her pretty eyes.

We've never talked about what this is, what I'm doing with her, and those words feel crushing.

But I also feel her studying me, asking without uttering a single word.

I wish I had answers.

I'm just as stranded in the dark as her, stumbling around.

"I'm glad you're here," I admit roughly. "Even if it's just for another week or so."

"Hey, me too!" Her fingers graze my cheek, gentle enough to make me shiver.

Neither of us needs to mention what happens after that.

Prowlers or not, we already know.

We have lives to get back to.

Lives too complicated for a random wildfire that can't keep burning forever.

Goddammit, though, I don't want to put it out.

I don't want her with any man who won't cherish her like gold.

I don't want her to settle for another fuckboy—or worse, an arranged marriage based on money or status or value proposition.

She smiles up at me, soft and reassuring, breaking through my haze as she stretches on her toes.

I sweep her closer, pinning her against me as I kiss her so reverently I try to forget the fuckery that's happened today.

Here, there's only room for two beating hearts.

There's just duchess, me, and an F5 spinning heartache.

She's so soft, so sweet, but for once I'm not desperate to haul her off to bed and fuck her this instant.

This is enough right now.

More dangerous, maybe, because this kiss says a lot of the things I can't put into words right now. And I can't avoid the tenderness.

Not when she's whisper-soft and it tastes like we're signing a secret pact in quiet, lingering kisses.

This thing with her is unholy.

This thing will skin me alive when it ends.

Until then, I mean every silent word ensouled in my lips.

I'm damn grateful she's with me, and I get to stay in this house, protecting her from lunatics.

Predictably, just as the heat creeps to my balls, the door flies open behind us and Dan comes bounding onto the porch, followed by Sophie. They both laugh at catching us in the act.

"*Seeee?*" Sophie croons. "I knew they'd be doing it."

"Hey." I don't let Margot go even though she jerks back from me. There's no point pretending we weren't just kissing when we've been busted by these nosy little hounds. "What are you two doing?"

"We finished our homework!" Dan says smugly. "Sophie said you guys would be *doing it*. So I had to come and see."

"You're too young to know what that is, little man, and too old to not understand the concept of privacy." I snort loudly.

"Kissing!" Sophie supplies, her face red. "That's what he means."

Margot giggles, one hand covering her mouth, and I can't help the smile that sneaks out.

The rest of the day's woes fade as I grab my son in a headlock and ruffle his hair until he's begging for mercy.

"Dad! Dad, no! I swear I won't mess with you again. It was Sophie's idea!"

Big promises from a boy who loves drama more than a seventy-year-old barfly.

"Okay, you two," I say. "Now that you're done sneaking around, how about a movie?"

XV: HOME STRETCH (MARGOT)

*I*n the end, we settle into *Moana* and a nice sense of normalcy.

Kane gets the kids hunkered down with blankets, the doors and windows firmly locked, while I whip up a quick blueberry sauce for ice cream.

After I heard about the Babins and their crazy business, I wanted to toss all the blueberries they gave us, but that seemed like a waste.

Now, as I bring the blueberry sundaes into the room, I'm glad I kept our stockpile. Dan and Sophie's eyes light up like Christmas.

"It's not Dole Whip fit for the movie, but it's pretty tasty," I say, handing them both heaping bowls.

We share grins.

I think it helps ground them back in Maine, quieting their chatter about jetting off to Hawaii or French Polynesia to live out their adventure fantasies as Maui belts out songs on the TV.

Oh, to be nine years old again.

Also, it's official, I'll do *anything* to keep these kids happy.

"Come the hell here," Kane whispers under his breath, holding out his arm, and I snuggle underneath it as the movie rolls on.

Sophie sneaks me a shy knowing smile I pretend not to notice.

Yes, they're basically in on the big secret—and they'll know we're lying if we pretend we're not 'doing it,' in their innocent little words.

I bite back a laugh.

On one hand, it's a relief. Sneaking around for kisses made me feel eighteen again, like something fun and dirty and illicit. Something to keep from prying little eyes.

But Kane admitted we only have a week left.

Hardly enough time for us to *be* anything. I'm worried that little Sophie especially might get the wrong idea.

She said 'girlfriend' when she came to see me that night.

But I'm not his girlfriend.

I'm not anything.

And Kane, he's just safe, all delicious scruff and calloused fingers playing absently across the skin of my arm as we watch the film.

Less than an hour in, Sophie looks like she's drifting off. She jerks awake every time the music blares with another song.

Dan keeps his eyes glued to the screen, no doubt dreaming of far-off journeys, even if they won't be as wild as Moana's.

I miss this age, though.

Back when an animated movie could stir a thousand hopes and magic still felt real.

They're not trying to grow up too fast like so many kids. That's wonderful.

In a couple more years, things will be different, I'm sure.

Social media throws children into adulthood.

Soon, they'll hit puberty and start caring a whole lot more what people think about them. They'll worry about every selfie and dumb comment, and whether it'll sink them if some other little brat decides to record it and post it in a group chat.

They'll measure time in friends and followers.

They won't count the good days—not consciously—when there isn't another care in the world besides the next laugh with their awesome dad or close friends who feel like extended family.

I know I didn't with Ethan, Hattie, and Gramps.

Feels like only yesterday when we'd hunker around the fireplace with PopPop here while he read us dramatic stories with Greek heroes and scary minotaurs. Honestly, I think he made up half the tales he told or heavily embellished old myths.

Kane brushes his lips through my hair, snapping my attention back to the present.

The kids are half-asleep now.

I'm not as close to him as I could be, and he tugs me closer.

His hand grazes my ass.

A shiver lashes us both.

At this angle, with the blanket and everyone facing the screen, nobody notices. But it's close enough to stay hyper-aware.

We're not going to do anything more and ruin this cute family moment, of course.

Family.

There's a heavy word.

I'm not part of this family and I shouldn't start thinking I am.

That's not what this is.

We're just two consenting adults having a good time,

looking for a little heat between the cold void of our own relationship trauma and the asshole neighbors breaking into the house.

We're just two people cuddling on the sofa.

Kane feels me tense and his hand slides up my back.

His fingers find a sliver of skin, tracing it absently.

"You good?" he murmurs.

"Yeah. Just thinking."

"Don't do that. Not while Maui's singing."

For joking around, he sounds so serious I laugh.

And I hear all the things he doesn't say.

Don't make this out to be more than it is. Or less.

His embrace deepens. I close my eyes for a second, relaxing in his warmth without guilt.

"Margot." His lips brush my temple again, breath hot against my ear.

Even my bones tingle.

"Mmmm." I press my face into his chest, loving the reassurance, before I look back at the screen. He exhales sharply, and we're silent again until the movie finishes.

As the credits roll, Sophie yawns herself awake again, rubbing her eyes and blinking.

"You were snoring," Dan says, suddenly wide awake and poking her side.

"I was not!"

"Yeah, you were loud. I've heard quieter jets take off!" Dan insists.

Kane claps his hands.

"Pipe down, kid. It's been a long day." He's in no mood for a five-minute argument over snoring. "I'm getting tuckered out myself."

As he sits up, I unfold from my spot under his arm.

"Are you turning in early too, Dad?" Dan asks, curious.

"Soon. Come on, guys, let's head upstairs." He picks Sophie up effortlessly.

She smiles and clings to him.

Holy hell.

Watching Kane parent his kids is one of the biggest turn-ons I've ever seen.

I'm not sure if I even want kids, but seeing this man's fatherly appeal smacks my ovaries like a cat with a ball.

He's so calm with them.

Firm, but reasonable and endlessly gentle.

Kind, without being too indulgent.

Fierce when he needs to be.

I remember how checked out and distant my parents could be, and I envy them a little. Growing up attention starved only makes me respect Dadzilla more.

As he leaves the room, his gaze swings back to me, and the air crackles with electric possibility.

"No, I'm not sure Maui was ever a real person," he's saying as he heads upstairs with them. "He's more like Hercules, I think, but there's always some truth to the legend. Every culture needs its heroes. That's how we stay inspired."

"Aw, man. I thought I'd see his fishhook when you take us to Hawaii next year." Dan sounds disappointed.

"*If* I take you, little man. That depends a lot on you and your sister slaying it in school this year and keeping out of trouble."

"But the canoes are real, right? I wanna sail in one of those."

"They're real, yeah." There's a smile on his face in the darkness. "Never forgot the first time I climbed in an outrigger with a few of my guys after our season wrapped up. It was February, and you couldn't go more than five minutes without seeing a humpback whale blow water or a sea turtle surface."

"Wow." Dan blinks up at his dad in awe.

I shake my head and start moving before my head explodes.

I take my sweet time prepping for bed, pouring a glass of water and standing in the dark kitchen, staring at the icemaker light and idly wondering what the hell I'm doing.

None of this is sensible.

I know I'll pay for it later a hundred times over.

But as soon as I've finished my water, I decide I don't care.

I walk to my room and strip, wrapping a robe around my shoulders.

Kane stays with the twins in their room for a while, until I'm sure they feel extra safe tonight.

He really is father of the year material. If they have to head home tomorrow, he's giving them one more night here, without what's coming weighing them down.

No one mentioned the break-in since dinner, but I know they're facing the dark and trying to fall asleep.

I'm still jittery myself.

It doesn't help that my feelings are so jumbled.

If I was here alone, I'd be pacing the room with every light on in the house—if I could stick it out at all without fleeing to a hotel.

As it is, I sit on the edge of my bed impatiently, waiting for his approaching footsteps.

When I hear them, it's no question where he's heading and no hesitation when I open the door.

We stare at each other, barely breathing.

His dark hair matches the shadows on his handsome face, his jaw tight and his eyes smoldering like green witchfire.

I already know it's a mistake as I pull him into the room, shutting the door behind us, but that's life.

The best things are always terribly messy.

"Are they sleeping okay?" I ask as I work off his shirt.

His hands are already on my hips, rough fingers running over the silky material.

"Out like lights. Wasn't hard after I told them a few more stories about my trip to Kona."

"Good." I tilt my head back as he kisses my neck, his lips branding me.

My room is farther away from theirs, at the other end of the house.

"Holy shit, don't stop."

"Not on your life," he growls.

And he pushes me back until my knees hit the bed, my legs buckle, and I fall backward.

His large body eclipses mine, and his mouth smothers my lips until I'm deliciously dizzy, ready to lose myself in the dark silk heat of his passion.

I'm already a little lost.

I dig my fingers into his hair, urging his mouth to my breasts.

He goes down sucking, tongue hot and ready, teasing me through the opening in my robe.

"Love this robe. Easy access," he whispers. "Did you wear it for me, duchess? For this?"

I try to answer, but the way he pulls my nipple with his teeth renders me speechless.

"I... I thought it'd be faster."

"Didn't ask about fast. I asked if you wore it for me, woman." He flicks his tongue over my nipple again and I gasp.

"What do you think?"

"I think you've been waiting with your greedy little pussy, counting down every second."

I laugh at how ridiculous this is.

He's an ex-hockey star with two innocent kids sleeping

down the hall, and we have a freaking psycho out there who might not be done with the house.

Yet the only thing I can think about is his touch.

"Are you wet for me, duchess? Tell me," he demands, sliding a hand down my belly.

"Maybe," I lie.

Lame.

Like my body isn't just one big pulsing cactus, full of needles and so, so thirsty.

"It's only fair. You put me through two whole hours of hell downstairs during that movie. Had to keep my dick on a leash," he rasps, tearing my robe fully open.

Yes, I'm naked underneath.

He rumbles his appreciation.

"If we were alone, I'd have made you ride my face on the floor."

He's. Killing. Me.

Then he parts my thighs, pushing my legs open, kneeling down and breathing warm teases against my pussy.

Instant goosebumps.

"Kane!" I grab the duvet for dear life.

His lips are so soft, yet infinitely wicked as he kisses his way up my inner thigh, biting along the way.

"Goddamn, you smell like sex. You're going to come so hard on my tongue you'll go blind."

His words are a spell.

So I do the only thing I can.

I close my eyes and give my body to Kane Saint and the sweetest torture.

One hand on my knee, holding me open. The other across my stomach, pinning me down, like he knows how much I'll writhe and how self-conscious I get with oral.

Only, with him, I barely notice.

He makes me feel that good, too drunk on sensation to do anything but feel.

It's crazy that just this morning I woke up in his bed after our first night together. The way he touches me now makes me feel like he was made for this.

He was built to sweep away my senses, leaving a dangerous addiction and nothing else.

"Kane," I whisper as his tongue sweeps my folds, tormenting my clit.

He takes his sweet time, mouth and scruff pressed to my hip, his hot breath caressing my inner thighs, my pussy, alternating until I bare my teeth.

I'm flipping panting.

I need him to bring me home more than I need oxygen.

"What do you want, woman? Use your words."

"Stop teasing," I gasp as he finally buries his tongue where I need him most.

He parts my folds, sucking and licking, fucking his way deeper until he reaches the spot on my inner walls that makes my legs shake.

Holy shiiit!

"Yeah, give it up. You taste so good, little duchess." The way he groans is everything.

His eyes are feral daggers, cutting me open as he runs his tongue slowly over his lips.

I need a moment.

I need a thousand years.

The sheets feel soft under my clenched fingers, and he's holding me down firmly.

He *has* to and he knows it.

I can see his muscles and veins bulging as he makes me his prisoner, forever willing, aching to be destroyed.

I don't know why that's so sexy, but it is.

He's commanding like other men only wish they could

be. I've been with boys before who tried to be dominant, but with them it was over the top. Forced.

With Kane, it's as natural as a slow, relentless summer storm.

"Are you warm?" he whispers against the skin of my thighs.

"You're... you're asking me now?"

"You're all goosebumps." His fingers skim my flesh, caressing up my waist to my breasts. "Just wanted to make sure you're not distracted. When you come for me, I want it all. Zero interference."

I suck my bottom lip.

While it's tempting to flip over and push him down on the bed and let him sink inside me now, the curve of his cheek tells me this is another tease.

One more part of the buildup to the revelry that might break me.

He knows what the goosebumps are for.

And he knows that after tonight, he'll have my soul.

"Why don't we just skip to the part where you fuck me?" I whisper, grabbing his hair and giving his head a little tug.

"Careful. That filthy mouth could get you into trouble." His green eyes glow as he looks up my body like the hungry wolf he is.

"You haven't heard anything yet, Mr. Saint."

"I'd like to."

"Then you know how to make me talk."

He chuckles roughly, sucking my thigh hard enough to mark it before sliding two fingers deep.

"Fuck!" I arch my back, helplessly grinding against his face.

"I want to taste you in my goddamn dreams, duchess. If you don't squirt, you'll learn."

Oh, shit.

He grunts with rough delight before his mouth goes to work again, sending me to heaven.

No resistance now.

No more teasing.

I'm so close already it's like a raging fever about to peak and break.

It's almost shameful how fast he throws me off the cliff.

No one else could ever do this.

Certainly not this easy.

But my breaths go shallow until I'm panting, frozen, waiting for that magic moment.

The cool air kisses my bare breasts when his mouth can't, still damp from previous kisses.

His arm sears me as he holds me down.

My knees fall open, shaking, and he meets my eyes as he looks up at me with his mouth on my pussy.

This is the wild divine.

A slow, arrogant smile I feel against my flesh, unleashing a flood that's biblical.

Coming!

My climax barrels through me, a rushing current of white-hot fire.

Three seconds in, I'm writhing, straining to cope with the enormity of what he's done to me.

My psyche splits in two as my body convulses, all wet heat. I can't tell where his face ends and I begin.

And I hear his command in every ruthless sweep of his tongue, centered on my clit and utterly merciless.

Come for me, Margot.

Come like you're fucking mine.

I do.

God, yes, and I fall apart so beautifully the universe melts away until there's just his magic kisses, my delicious torture, and endless green eyes.

He rides out every screaming convulsion before his head rises again, lips and chin damp with a primal look in his eyes.

"Now," he whispers, stopping to swirl his tongue against my nipple as he travels up my body. "Now, I'll fuck you."

"Now? Don't you want me to return the favor?" Somehow, I sit up, my robe pooling under me.

His cock presses against my stomach, hot and heavy, and I reach for it desperately.

He breathes a curse as I wrap my fingers around it.

"I'd rather fuck you," he growls.

"And I'm pretty good with my mouth." I push him back against the bed and position myself between his knees. "Don't worry, you'll still get to fill my pussy up."

"Fucking deal." He watches me with dark eyes as I lick the bead of moisture from the slit on his pulsing head.

With one last grin, I go to town, pushing my lips down his shaft, taking half of him—everything I can manage.

In no time, I'm *gagging*, but I love the mangled sound he makes, bucking his hips like a bull before he regains control.

This blow job isn't elegant or slow or sweet.

It's disgustingly hot.

Deliciously messy.

I *love* seeing him lose control, and I bring every trick in the book to ruin him.

Using my hands to follow my mouth, I stroke him deeper, swirling my tongue around his head like I'm licking an ice cream cone.

He fists my hair until he's pulling.

I think he might want to guide me, but he just holds me as I work until his huge balls strain, tighter with every stroke, and he swells under my tongue.

"Duchess," he grinds out.

Slowly, slowly I back off of him again.

He swears viciously, head dropping back as he fights the urge to finish.

But I knew he wouldn't.

I climb back up his body to kiss him again.

He grabs my waist, supporting me as he gives me another deep kiss, tugging my bottom lip with his teeth.

It's easy to fit his full, angry length against my wet center.

I try not to tremble and fail miserably.

His eyes are hazy with arousal as he looks at me.

"Dammit. I think I need a second," he says with amusement. "Fuck, Margot. You've got me wrecked."

"Yeah?" I rub my pussy, and my body sparks back to life, ready and aching. "I like you wrecked."

"And I want to last longer than two minutes before I bust in you. I'm not looking for a third kid, but you should feel this nut in your womb."

Holy hell.

Wrecked doesn't begin to touch what that extra thrill about breeding me does to my system.

I'm *starving* to feel him buried so deep, hurling his seed in my belly.

"Make me feel it. Everything, mister."

His swollen head slips inside me without another word, and we both groan.

Sweet relief.

Lunatic need.

Urgency.

It's tempting to sink all the way down on him and throw my hips into milking him dry. To make myself his fuck toy with a single-minded purpose.

But he's led our rhythm before.

Tonight, it's my turn.

"Goddamn." His fingers dig into my skin. "You look so fucking perfect. Love watching you take this dick."

I roll my hips, changing the angle slightly as he tenses, every muscle hardening.

I think he forces himself not to bruise me.

He reaches up to cup my breast, rolling my nipple before pinching hard.

Fireworks.

He already has me seeing stars.

I take it slow, teasing him like he teased me as I slowly, gradually, sink down on him. His eyes are locked on my pussy as we fuse together, and he's so big, stretching and invading, all the way to my womb.

I can't breathe.

Before, my plan was to tease him, keep him on the edge, but my body involuntarily folds around him.

There's nowhere like home.

Nowhere like Kane.

Nothing like his ten brutal, girthy inches.

Those stars in my eyes become snowflakes in a shaken globe.

He's so *deep* now.

Somehow, today, I forgot just how big he is, how much he fills me, how good he feels.

When I move, the burn intensifies, building to the very edge of pain.

His face screws up more with every breath.

I plant my hand on his chest for balance as I slowly lift off him, then sink back down, my rhythm slow.

Glorious agony.

My hips jerk more, plunging him deeper, my pussy hugging his cock.

"Keep fucking going," he grinds out, his eyes locked on mine.

There it is.

Permission.

To have the illusion of control, even if we both know he has full power to make me come into next year.

"Fucking obscene how good you feel," he whispers. "Come on my cock, duchess. Come soon."

He inhales sharply as I pick up speed.

His eyes are ocean depths and shadowed turquoise.

I squeeze him again, helpless to the motion.

"Don't come yet," I tell him, leaning forward, pressing against his chest and moving again.

The friction is unbearable.

Too much, but not enough.

Everything, and nothing.

His jaw clenches.

But his hands are so soft, even when they're ready to tear me in two.

"*Margot, Margot,*" he grinds my name under his breath, warning me this stalemate can't last, and he's going to make me pay dearly if I make him lose it first.

That makes two of us.

I love the way he looks at me—all heavy eyes and parted mouth and sharp, staccato breaths.

Like no one else has ever made him feel this incredible.

Like I'm sexier than any woman he's ever known.

"I'm close," he warns, stilling me. "Fuck, where are you?"

Deliriously close.

Determined, too.

And I rock my hips—just a little more friction as his fingers reach up and work my clit.

My pussy grips him, needy and insane as our breath goes mad.

Oh, shit, shit, shit!

My head falls loosely as I press on his chest.

He moves like a human earthquake under my hands.

His hand on my hip guides me in slow, rocking, rolling motions, grinding myself on him.

No more, no more.

There's no holding back when that wave crests and hits me like a tsunami on fire.

Coming!

I think I cry out.

Maybe I say his name, maybe I try, or maybe it's just a sputtering string of expletives.

But I feel his fingers digging into my hip as he pushes into me one final time with a throat-ripping roar.

The wave takes us, thrashing and ravenous and deranged.

We come together like water slapping the rocky shore, and his hot come fills me, sending me to a new high.

We blow our sanity to confetti and go down in a whirlwind of color.

Later, I'm the first one to move, untangling myself and curling under his arm.

I'm lighter than air but my limbs weigh a ton.

Another contradiction.

And there's zero talk of him going back to his room or either of us pretending we want to do anything besides sleep next to each other tonight and then wake up for another round of ecstasy with the sun.

Oh, this is bad.

So stupid and predictable.

Warning lights flash in my head.

Every sensible part of me protests giving myself to a man who has to ghost me, and I know it's coming.

But Kane, he's not Kelso.

Our heaven has a time limit for reasons beyond our own selfish desires, and it makes me more jealous. I want him, every bit of him, for as long as I can get it.

"You good?" he asks gently, tucking me firmly against him. I fit so well against the curve and crook of his body.

"So good," I whisper back with a lazy yawn. He tugs the duvet up over our naked bodies. "Night, Kane. And thank you for everything today."

"No choice—and no regrets either. Sleep well, duchess."

I do, and his voice follows me into my dreams.

* * *

My phone goes off on the counter beside me after I shuffle downstairs to put a pot of coffee on.

Sleeping with Kane has side effects.

I'm not getting a ton of *sleep* and I wake up weirdly early, so I'm still groggy, trying to find the will to grab my phone.

When I finally have the wits to put it to my ear, I suppress a yawn.

"Yes, hello?"

"Is this Miss Blackthorn?"

"That's right. Who's this?"

"Ma'am, I'm Detective Peter Albright from down in Bar Harbor. I'm helping the Sully Bay police out with their investigations."

"Oh, okay." I slide into a chair, instantly more awake. "Did they have a chance to visit Mr. and Mrs. Babin yesterday?"

"That's what I'm calling about, yes."

I scrub the last gritty sleep from my eyes.

Kane's still upstairs, half-asleep and showering after a lazy bout of morning sex. I can hear Dan starting his drumming practice upstairs, and Sophie's probably reading. Either way, the kitchen is empty and I'm alone.

"What did they say?"

"Sheriff paid them a visit, and I spoke with them over the phone to corroborate," Detective Albright says. "We also checked their shoes against the prints we took. I'm sorry to say they didn't match. The Babins also have a rock-solid alibi for the time in question."

"What?" I suck in a breath. "What alibi?"

"Turns out they were delivering blueberries to a local pie shop one town over," he says. "We talked to the owner, and everything checks out."

Yikes.

I was so sure.

I never considered the possibility it might be someone else.

And if it is, *who?*

"I see," I say slowly. "So, no other leads?"

"Not at this time, ma'am. We'll follow up on a couple other theft reports in the area to see if we've got a connection."

"Sounds good. Thanks for letting me know," I say weakly.

"We'll keep looking, don't you worry. And if anything useful turns up, you'll be the first to know. If you have any questions or new information, please don't hesitate."

"Right. I won't. Thank you." I force a smile into my voice, but my stomach flips upside down before I end the call.

Last night, Kane did such an amazing job helping me forget. But it's impossible not to remember now.

Stumbling into the house and finding that broken plate, the pretty ceramic shards thrown everywhere like violent art.

That was hatred, plain and simple.

But if the Babins didn't do it...

That begs another question.

We sent the police to the Babins' house, having accused them, and if they weren't behind this, should we apologize?

Ugh! Awkward.

My vision spins.

A quick look through the new camera app says there were no new disturbances last night, either. We were safe, nothing captured outside besides a deer moving around the edge of the property.

A shiver arcs down my back.

It's just confusing and none of this makes me feel safe.

But there are footsteps on the stairs, so I grab a mug and pour him some coffee.

I won't tell him. Not yet.

Poor Kane, he's already worried sick for the kids—and I don't want to make it worse. He won't like the uncertainty, the creeping danger in not knowing.

Later, of course he'll find out, after I've had time to process the shock.

He steps into the room a minute later, his hair hanging wet and a burgundy sweater painted on across his broad shoulders.

His eyes heat like green lamps when he sees me.

"Coffee already? Must be my lucky morning."

"We both need it after last night. Especially you, Mr. Saint, at your age." I giggle.

"Smartass, don't think I'm above tanning your ass in this kitchen." He kisses my cheek as he passes by.

I push the stressful call away.

"Don't pretend you don't like it."

"I like when you call me Mr. Saint," he growls.

"You're insatiable."

"For you, hell yes." He takes the chair beside mine and grabs my hand, bringing the mug to his lips. "Being around you without touching violates the laws of physics."

"Then this must be how you get arrested by the cosmic police." I say it without thinking.

We both stop and stare, thinking what *else* gets people arrested.

His hand travels up and down my back, tender and soothing.

"I already checked the cameras. Nothing new last night," he says between sips.

"I saw."

"Then you know we're okay." His hand stops at the small of my back, and he brings me closer for another kiss. "I won't let anything happen to you, Margot. I promise."

"Okay."

"Yeah? I want you to trust me." He leans back to look me in the eyes.

Really, I do.

I trust him to protect me as long as we're both sharing this house. The trouble comes if that changes and I decide to stick around a little longer, but I won't dwell on that for now.

"After breakfast, I want to check out the garden. Looks like decent weather today for another run at Gramps' mystery," I tell him, getting started on some waffles. "Not sure I'll find anything, but I should at least check."

Plus, focusing on our mystery will give me something to do besides worry about more burglars.

"Sounds good. I'll give you a hand. I also promised the kids some time on the lake, and you're welcome to join us," Kane says.

"No, you guys go ahead." I shake my head gently.

He doesn't say it either, but we're both thinking the same thing: distraction.

Before this day ends, I wonder if I'll need them by the bushel.

* * *

I'M SHOCKED AND SAD.

The garden is just as large as I remember, but way more

overgrown, abandoned since PopPop's death and left to go wild.

The only building is the old storage shed, and that's where I head after breakfast.

Inside, it's dark and dusty, the air stale with cobwebs splayed between windows.

When I was little, Gramps had people keeping this place nice and tidy, but like everything else, it's been derelict for years.

There are ghostly gaps in the dust where Kane stepped, where he's taken out tools and replaced them.

Weird.

For all his money, Gramps was pretty handy when he was younger. He could patch up the fence or hang pictures or paint, and he'd always come in here for his tools. Sometimes we'd catch him on lazy evenings pruning trees or weeding.

Having Kane show up with his money and fame with the same willingness to swing a hammer feels like a strange coincidence across time.

Like maybe this old house still attracts a certain kind of person.

Yeah, I need to get out of here before I go all sentimental.

One last scan to make sure there's nothing out of place, and I shut the door, glancing at the lake.

Kane and the kids are out on the canoe, a distant shape far from shore.

It's the kind of lazy boat ride to nowhere we'd do all the time, and their shrieks of laughter carry across the still water.

They've been out there for a while. I think they'll be coming back for lunch soon.

Smiling, I turn back toward the house.

That's when I remember what Mrs. Griffith said. I can picture it tucked in the trees and overgrown grass.

Bigger, grander gardens. A flat piece of land, and on it—

The gazebo.

A chill zings down my spine.

The grass catches in my legs as I walk forward, a few scattered branches tripping me up, and then I'm at the old stone base half-covered in dirt.

When I look closely, there are still a few black marks from the fire.

Just like she said.

An occasional chunk of damp, rotted wood from the gazebo itself, but it's mostly been burned to nothing.

But there, right in the middle of where the gazebo once stood, my foot scrapes the unexpected. A little dip in the grass that has me digging, pulling out clumps by hand. And then—

An overgrown door straight from a dream.

It's the kind of thing you'd find on an old storm shelter, metal and rusted, sunk into the ground and overgrown.

I swallow roughly.

This wasn't on the property description. Holden Verity and Jackie Wilkes are detailed to a fault, but I've read the thing at least a dozen times and there was nothing about a hidden door.

Gramps never mentioned it either.

In fact, now that I think back, this little plot of land was fenced off when we were little. Just a few small wooden stakes, like something thrown up as an afterthought to keep rabbits away from a vegetable patch.

We always figured that's all it was, but now...

What is this?

What was under the gazebo?

An old-timey storm shelter? A root cellar?

I crouch down, scraping away the loose plants growing around the sides. I must spend twenty minutes ripping up grass and weeds, tossing the debris to one side until the door looks clear.

The handle feels rusted shut.

When I try yanking the door open, it snaps off in my hand, staining my fingers brown.

"Jeez!" I yell, wrinkling my nose with disgust.

"What did you find?" Kane calls from the dock.

He must've brought the boat in while I was clearing the overgrowth.

Dan's squirming his way off the canoe, not bothering to take off his life jacket in his enthusiasm.

"Not sure yet!" I call back. "Underground cellar, maybe? The door's stuck."

Kane grabs Dan's arm and points him at the work shed, then motions Sophie to follow them.

They head over while I finish clearing a few more plants around the edge.

When they return, Kane has a crowbar, and Dan has a couple cans of WD-40.

"This dungeon was here the whole time? Crazy!" Dan whistles.

"It's where the old gazebo used to be," I explain. "I decided to walk through here and the ground felt funny. So I started digging."

"You've never been down there before?" Kane asks, studying the dusty door.

"Nope. Never knew it was here. Nobody ever mentioned it."

His eyes search mine, and I know we're sharing the same thought.

This could be it.

The big secret I'm supposed to uncover to keep my grandfather happy in the Great Beyond.

"Okay, give me some space," he says, rolling up his sleeves. "Let's see if we can bust this open."

"Dad, do you need a flashlight? I can use my phone." Sophie already has her phone out.

"What do you think is in there?" Dan asks quietly, standing behind us. His eyes light up. "You think he left buried treasure?"

"Leonidas wasn't a pirate, little man," Kane says.

No, but between his love for sailing, Mediterranean adventures, and pulling together the largest private art collection in Maine, he had the heart of a buccaneer.

"I don't think there's real treasure down there. Not like antiques or valuables," I say. "But it's exciting, right?"

The kids nod briskly, their little eyes gleaming.

My nerves spark as Kane works to force the door open.

Yes, I'm letting my hopes gallop away from me.

I desperately, *desperately* want to find something meaningful.

Even if it's just some sappy old box of fishing lures or something.

Then the door pops with a loud reverberation that stalls the air in my lungs.

"I've got the flashlight," Dan calls, handing Kane the phone with its beam switched on. "Do you want me to go down first?"

"Nah, Bud. Relax," Kane tells him, ruffling his hair. "I'll go down there first and scope it out. No telling what we might find."

"Snakes? Scorpions? Evil interdimensional clowns?" Dan suggests way too eagerly.

Kane throws him an indulgent look.

"How would scorpions survive in Maine? And *It* isn't real! I told you on the way up. It's just a book by Mr. King," Sophie says firmly. Like she's totally old enough to be sneaking horror classics.

I bite back a laugh.

"Yeah, well..." Dan scowls. "Maybe there's a new species or somethin'. Or a crazy guy dressed up in a clown mask!"

"Stop trying to freak your sister out. We don't need more uninvited guests around here," Kane warns.

Good luck with that, Sophie tells her brother with a glance.

I love them so much.

Kane's eyes flick to me wordlessly. He rolls his eyes, but he smiles before a grave look falls over his face.

One good, careful grip from the sides lets him lever the door open.

A dull blast of stale air greets us, along with a set of concrete stairs going down into the hole.

"Wait here," he tells the kids, who are still bickering about the possibility of snakes and bears down there.

I follow Kane down slowly, pressing one hand to the wall for support since there's no railing.

His flashlight illuminates worn brick walls.

It's sturdy enough, by the look of it, aside from a few loose bricks.

No snakes or spiders or bears.

Oh, my.

"Looks like underground storage," Kane muses when he reaches the bottom, swinging the light around. He's so tall his head almost brushes the ceiling. "Or maybe a fifties bomb shelter? They were popular, even in little towns like this."

"Gramps wasn't much of a prepper. It's weird that it's here." I swipe a finger along the rough brick.

Slightly damp, but not as bad as I thought it would be.

The beam swings again, revealing a small, unfinished statue on a long table beside the stairs. The only thing in the room.

My pulse slows.

"You recognize that?" he says.

It's like a massive workbench with a lamp and an old leather chair pushed in front of it. Of course the lamp doesn't work, and neither does the small switch on the wall Kane tries for the overhead light.

At first, I'm not sure what I'm seeing.

There are drawings of tiny shoes.

A small box of round objects, either clay or stone. Tools for sculpting, I think. A few round things that vaguely look like shoes, but small and indistinct, no bigger than my palm.

Then on the other side—a bigger statue.

People.

It's a couple locked in a loving embrace.

"Hold up. I think..." I step closer, and Kane hands me the flashlight. "I think that's Gramps?" Despite being incomplete, I recognize my grandfather's younger profile in the clay. "Holy crap. Was this my grams' workshop?"

"Could be. You said she painted, didn't she?"

"Yeah, and I knew that. But nobody ever said a word about her sculpting." I trace the unfinished model gingerly.

This isn't some deep dark secret, no, but it feels like I'm closing in on some hidden truth.

"They look happy," I whisper. Then I look at the pile of little clay statues again and frown. "The little shoes, I don't get. They were in that painting we found in the attic, too, what looked like baby shoes. I wonder if it's part of a bigger project Grams was working on..."

"Is this what your granddad wanted? The stuff he left you?"

"Maybe?" There's hope in my voice, but I'm not convinced.

Not yet.

If these odd, unfinished statues are the big finale, it feels unsatisfying.

The letter made it sound like there was a lesson here, something clear and obvious, a little like the doozy he left Ethan.

The couple statue looks beautiful, despite being abandoned.

Or I might just think that because they were my grandparents. On its own, it doesn't offer much insight into his life.

It doesn't enrich my world.

At the end of the day, it's just a pretty sculpture, and the unfinished shoes are hardly even that.

My throat stings with disappointment, though I should be ecstatic.

It's the first real meat we've found since I showed up here.

Too bad it feels so lacking.

"There must be more," I whisper, sweeping the flashlight around the room again.

I'm looking for paintings, something else Grams left behind, completed artwork.

Nothing.

The wall behind the statue glints sharply in the light, and I grab Kane's flashlight for a better look.

There's a beautiful stained glass window in the wall. The light can't quite filter through it when I stop and focus the LED beam.

Still, the colored light scatters gloriously in the brightness.

"What's that?" He's already standing over me, running his fingers along the sides of the window. As I get closer, I see what he means.

It's like some kind of old artsy cabinet, more like the type of thing you'd see in a church than some strange underground cellar.

There's even a handle on the side.

But when I pull, it won't budge.

Disappointing.

For a hot second, I thought this was it.

Our great mystery.

"Was your grandfather religious?" Kane asks softly.

"I don't think so. He had his beliefs, but he wasn't too serious."

"Huh. There's a real chapel vibe here with that window." He tries the handle, but again, it doesn't move. Almost like it's locked.

I exhale sharply, one long deflated sigh.

"Guess we should leave it alone for now," he says. "I don't want to risk breaking anything. And if we can get more light down here, all the better."

"You're right."

"We'll come back," he promises, running a hand down my arm. "I just don't want to force it. They don't make glass like that anymore."

I nod in agreement.

The glass is beautiful, all bold colors set in irregular patterns. For all I know, maybe my grandmother made that, too.

There's no denying she was multitalented.

It hurts a little, knowing I'll never be able to ask her or Gramps. These are just breadcrumbs, scattered for us to find.

Kane kisses the side of my head as he grabs the flashlight from my lifeless fingers.

"We're getting warmer," he says as he heads to the bottom of the stairs. "Okay, guys, it's all clear," he calls. "No snakes, bears, or evil clowns. Careful on the stairs coming down."

Dan moves first.

Sophie, with her shoes, comes slower and more carefully.

But a minute later, they're both poking around the old workbench, touching the statues and marveling at the stained glass.

Kane could be right—we must be *close*.

I just don't know if that's wishful thinking.

I want to believe it and put this to bed so much.

Just like I want to believe that this man watching me so intently with his adorable kids could stay, rather than winding up like this cellar of artifacts, buried and forgotten.

XVI: DRIVE IT HOME (KANE)

*T*he September sun warms my back as I walk down Sully Bay's main strip with an Americano in hand that smells good enough to inhale through my nose.

Dan and Sophie are captivated by a couple street musicians.

There are three of them. One guy strums a guitar, his partner plays the accordion, and a girl belts out an emotional song with a violin tucked under her arm.

Her voice is haunting, but when Guitar Guy joins in, Sophie's eyes start to shine.

Damn.

I might have to start worrying about her and boys sooner than I think.

Dan grins too, loving the way Accordion Man bangs a snare drum with his foot as he plays, perfectly synced.

"Super cool, Dad. Do you know how hard it is to play multiple instruments like a boss?" Dan asks.

Guitar Guy has long shaggy hair pulled back in a ponytail, and whenever he leans closer to the mic to sing, he closes his eyes.

"It's something," I agree, scanning to see where Margot went.

She came into town with us and ran off to the nearby craft booths to look for more info on stained glass and a safe way to pry that door open.

We figured the kids would be entertainment. They love the candied apples, too.

I couldn't say no at the coffee shop when I saw the huge green balls on a stick slathered in caramel.

Soph bites into her half-eaten apple, smacking her lips.

I sip my coffee and *goddamn, is that good.*

We needed this today.

Especially with more unsolved mysteries piling up.

Even so, Margot's taking her time, and I crane my head, trying to spot her through the swirling crowd.

A lot of older folks crowd around us, making the most of the sunny day and easy atmosphere.

The woman crooning into the mic grins at us and winks at Sophie.

Finally, I see Margot—talking with Viola Babin.

They stand like alley cats, shoulders tense, their hands locked into fists by their sides, and—

Fuck.

"Stay here," I tell the kids, who just give me absent nods.

I trust them to listen—or at least to stay hooked on the music—as I bolt over to avert a standoff.

"—I should've known. Just the kind of nasty shit you expect from a Blackthorn!" Viola spits, her mouth twisted. Gone is the kind, folksy blueberry farmer, replaced with this venomous snake. "You always treated us like redneck criminals!"

"*I* never treated you like anything," Margot throws back. "Your beef was with Gramps. Maybe he had a good reason to—"

"Hey," I say sharply, grabbing Margot's arm.

Her gaze flicks to me and she jumps, like she was expecting a physical attack.

Just seeing her this on edge makes me want to wrap her in my arms and rip Viola Babin a new mouth she can't bitch with.

"There a problem here?" I look at Viola sharply with knives in my eyes.

"She sicced the cops on us," Viola snarls. "Imagine, making us feel like petty criminals in our own *home*. People talk, y'know? And guess what they'll say? It should be the Blackthorn brat for once getting dirty looks and whispers—not us!"

I stare at her coldly, just long enough to start melting the hatred off her face.

"If you didn't do the break-in, then you didn't do it. Let the evidence speak for itself," I say flatly. "Even if you feel targeted, that gives you *no* damn right to go harassing Margot in public. Don't you think she has enough going on right now with the house?"

"You think I care?" she huffs loudly.

"Clearly not. Let me give you a good reason to start caring, Viola." I step closer, all quiet fury now. "If you don't start keeping your distance, then I'll have to start getting lawyers involved. Your shit-fight with the Blackthorns affects my family as long as we're here. Maybe you didn't break in, no, but I can nail you for harassment and child endangerment. Maybe dig up an old arson case or two while we're at it."

"Arson?" Her eyes widen. "What the hell you think you're—"

"Don't think we don't know. And don't think I won't defend Margot Blackthorn like my own if you keep this little grudge rolling. Stay away from them, and keep off the damn property, too."

"You people are all the same," she snarls, "thinking your fancy money and ten-dollar words solve everything."

"Let me make myself crystal clear." I walk closer again, and she takes an automatic step back. "I look out for good people. For folks with less than noble intentions, you don't want to find out what I do. Understand?"

"I—"

"Simple question, Mrs. Babin. Yes or no."

She grits her teeth, but nods, her face streaked red from holding in a thousand curses.

"Good," I clip. "Have a blessed day."

Without giving her another second to yap, I take Margot's hand and lead her away.

Yes, I'm fucking erupting, but I know my girl wouldn't want me to make more of a scene.

She stops short before we reach the kids, not ready to face them. Her eyes are too dark and disturbed in her pale face.

"I think that went well," I joke bitterly. "You okay?"

"I'm fine, yeah. I just hate that I've made another enemy here—or remade an old one. Or whatever. I thought the Babins were just trying to scare me into selling the place. But if it's someone else... I *wish* it was that simple."

"Not your fault, duchess." I grab her shoulders until she meets my gaze. "The ugliness, the refusing to accept an apology, that's their problem. And even if they didn't do it, it's no surprise our minds went there, knowing the history."

She almost smiles.

"I can't believe she went off on me here."

"I can. She's got a lot of resentment toward Leonidas. Since he's gone, she's firing her salvos at you. Are you sure you're okay?"

"I mean, I could've done without the public freakout, but..." She gives a little angry laugh. "Can you believe I ever felt bad for them and wondered if we should apologize? I actually tried. For all of ten seconds before she went nuclear. God."

"Come again?" I frown. "What do you mean, you felt bad for them?"

"Oh." Her cheeks flush red. "The cops called yesterday and told me they didn't do it. The boots didn't match. Ditto for the tire tracks. I guess they had a solid alibi, too."

What the fuck?

"You didn't tell me?" My confusion boils into frustration.

"I-I'm sorry. I didn't want to worry you." She sighs, turning her face down. "With everything going on, I just thought..."

Right.

She thought I'd stress the fuck out if the Babins aren't our culprits—and she's right. Because that means someone else *is*.

"Margot." I clasp her chin and tilt her face up. "This is the kind of shit I *need* to know. No excuses."

She sighs again, leaning into me.

"I know, and I'm sorry. I just... Everyone's been on edge lately. Including you. Especially you. I know you've got a lot on your mind with the kids."

And you.

I don't say it, but she knows.

I slide a hand around her waist, pressing her against me.

"You know I can't protect you *or* the kids if I don't know who the hell I'm protecting you from."

"Yeah. But we don't know anything right now. The detective was a guy from down in Bar Harbor, and he said they'll keep looking into it. He wants to follow up on some smaller crimes outside Sully Bay. Until then, we just have to be careful."

"Next time, you tell me if something comes up, okay?" I growl, meeting her gaze. "Even if you think it's news that'll ruin my day."

"Okay." She nods slowly. "You're right. It was selfish to keep it to myself."

I look at the kids. They're still right where I left them, fixated as the musical trio launch into another song.

Blissfully oblivious to our dilemma.

Just as it should be.

If I could, I'd keep them like that forever, but we all grow up.

"Try not to worry," I tell Margot now, noticing the lines around her eyes. "Viola Babin won't start more shit. If she gets in your face a second time, I'll make sure she's behind bars."

She shakes her head. "I dunno. It's not worth it. It's not even your problem, Kane."

"I meant what I said. I protect the people I care about, whatever the cost." That absolutely means Margot Blackthorn too.

I'm not afraid if she knows it.

I also don't care if she knows how precious she's become.

"Easier said than done. I don't want you having to back that up," she mutters. A small smile pulls at her lips.

"Trust me." I swipe my thumb across her jaw. "While I'm around, you let me do the worrying for both of us."

I realize my mistake the second I say it.

While I'm around.

She straightens and turns away from me.

I hate how accurate that is.

She might be safe for as long as I'm here, yeah—but that isn't long enough.

Less than a week to go.

Less than seven days before we're back home, separated with nothing but ashes of kisses and dead promises.

"Right. Well, thanks for the reminder. I appreciate everything you do."

"Margot," I start, but she's already shaking her head.

"It's cool. We both know it's coming eventually. I mean, neither of us live here. We can't turn everything upside down for... for this." Her throat ticks as she swallows.

Now isn't the time.

There are people swarming around.

Still, I see the way she's closing off, reverting back to the pretty, remote woman I first met, before she softened up and showed me the person inside.

Less than a week.

Less than a fucking week.

One day at a time, though.

While I'm here, I'll damn sure make the most of our time, even if I have to spend it keeping her safe.

I hate that she might have to stay longer, just to make sure the place doesn't burn down mysteriously.

Maybe I can figure out some workaround.

She doesn't even have to tell me that's what she'll do if it comes down to it. But with the kids, I can't risk staying much longer.

I can't be her personal shield when I have a family and handing them off to my mother only works for so long.

But leaving her alone, without worrying about her here?

Fucking impossible.

With the pissy way the Babins keep acting, I don't trust them not to do something, no matter what the police said.

"Shit," I whisper, taking her wrists, pulling her into me again.

She doesn't ask what I mean.

She doesn't need to.

Her forehead rests in the hollow between my shoulder and neck and her hands tangle in my shirt.

For a few heady seconds, we just stand there, filling the silence with thick, needy breaths.

"It'll be fine," she whispers again when I pull back.

"Margot," I start, and I don't know how I'm planning to finish that sentence when someone taps me on the shoulder.

An older man I don't recognize.

"Excuse me, I don't mean to interrupt…" He grimaces apologetically at Margot, who steps back with a smile.

I look at her, but it's obvious he's talking to me.

First time anyone in this town has shown me the slightest interest over her. I'm not sure I like it.

He looks like he's in his late fifties with a gut and greying scruff on his cheeks. I've never seen him before in my life.

"Yeah?" I try to hide my irritation.

"If it's no trouble, I was just hoping for an autograph," the man says, handing me a napkin. He winces again. "Sorry I don't have anything better on me. If I knew I had a chance to meet *the* Kane Saint today, I'd have come prepared."

Autograph?

What the fuck?

"It's for my grandson. Kid's a big fan of all the greats," he explains awkwardly.

That's not the problem.

The *problem* is no one should know I'm here.

That was one good reason to head to upstate Maine.

For most people, I'm not a household name anymore. I've been out of the game long enough to tarnish my celebrity status.

Only the bigger hockey fanatics still recognize me, but still. I wasn't expecting to find anyone here, up the ass end of nowhere.

Margot looks at me over the guy's head and reaches for her phone.

"Sure, pal. What's the name?" I force a smile, icily calm.

"Little Nick! I mean, Nick works fine. Man, thank you! He'll be so excited."

Still smiling until it burns my face, I slash my signature across the napkin with the pen he holds out, then pass it back.

"Here you go."

"Helluva favor, Mr. Saint. You're a real inspiration and a class act, too."

"I try. Thanks." I hope like hell it ends there.

But one quick look around shows me he's not the only one staring at us.

Behind him, there's a kid with a baseball cap, his mouth hanging open. He offers me the hat without a word, his little face turning red.

"Dude, you're Kane Saint? You're my brother's favorite! He's off at college, so uh, would you sign it? If you don't mind..."

It's a frigging baseball cap.

How the *hell* did my cover get blown here of all places?

As I sign the hat for the boy mechanically, Margot scrolls on her phone, her face suddenly pale.

"Um, Kane?" The moment the kid leaves, she shows me the screen.

There's an article with my face from a couple years ago. I'm laughing after speaking at a tech conference with the cockiest fucking people I'd ever met.

Margot's photo is right next to mine. She's standing casually with a man who must be her brother, all of them in black, somewhere in Portland not long after Leonidas died.

Then the brutal headline:

New power couple? Tech king and retired hockey hunk Kane

Saint caught hunkering down in small-town Sully Bay with Blackthorn heiress!

Fuck me blind.

Not good.

The article was barely posted an hour ago, but news flies once every gossip hound and celeb-obsessed gremlin gets a hold of it.

Margot's already royalty in these parts.

The street musicians play on, ignoring how they're suddenly not the center of attention. Sophie and Dan haven't noticed anything yet.

Let's keep it that way.

"The kids," I whisper, and Margot nods.

"Let's get them home," she agrees.

I don't make eye contact with anyone as I push through the crowd to them. They're still swaying to the music and finishing their caramel apples.

I vowed early on to keep them out of the spotlight once I realized how corrosive fame can be.

I chose this life, knowingly or not.

My kids should never face the consequences.

They don't get to pick when people fire off unwanted photos like gunshots, let alone if they show up in lurid stories about the divorce.

It's not fair.

Everyone should get a choice, and I hate that the world doesn't work that way.

I also don't want them to face the constant invasion of privacy before their lives have really started.

The lies people tell because it sells or generates clicks.

The fucked up lengths people will go for their next scoop or million views on Instagram.

All your worst secrets, all your insecurities, all national news fodder in soulless gossip rags.

It's worse that they're not just print magazines anymore and the dirt goes supersonic speeds online.

"Hey, guys." I touch their shoulders to get their attention. Margot's at their other side, watching them intently.

It dawns on me that she's no stranger to this shit.

She knows exactly how to handle it, possibly better than I do.

And maybe we both knew this thing between us was a ticking time bomb.

I just never thought it would detonate publicly.

"We need to head home now," I tell them firmly, keeping my voice calm. Outwardly, I'm smiling, but inwardly I'm cursing myself breathless.

This shouldn't be happening.

Not here.

Not now.

"Dad, what's wrong?" Dan asks, still watching the trio.

"I remembered something important at home. Come on, guys," Margot says, and I throw her a grateful glance.

When Viola laid into her, I could see her rattled, but now she's pure efficiency.

If they want a fight, they'll be sorry for ever going against a Blackthorn scorned.

"Meet you at the car?"

"Sure," she says.

A second later, she's back in the crowd, smiling her pretty face off as people flash photos and yell questions and compliments.

A few phones swing in my direction, too, so I hustle the kids toward the rental vehicle parked on the street.

To their credit, they don't protest once they figure out it's serious. They just follow.

I wish I could say this has never happened before, but it has.

Fuck my life entirely.

I just never thought it would matter here and complicate everything *more*.

What the hell am I doing, dragging Margot down worse?

We could still share the place, do our thing, go our separate ways, and that would be the end.

Instead, sex happened, and then feelings.

I clench my jaw, shaking my head.

She meets us at the SUV a few seconds later, sharing the same grim resignation on her face.

Our Sully Bay disaster just grew ten times bigger.

XVII: FAR FROM HOME (MARGOT)

As soon as we're back at the house, we check the locks on all the doors and windows.

That's becoming habit now, nothing out of the ordinary, but there's a fresh urgency.

Somehow, I still have my hair.

Kind of miraculous when I've been fighting the urge to rip it out for the better part of an hour.

Thankfully, the kids are fine. They settle down in front of the TV in the living room, and I've made us this orange blossom tea I picked up at the market.

Not blueberry.

After this sad experience, I'm going to be over it for the next decade.

We're in the library now with our tea, both of us trying to hold it together.

I just feel like I'm waiting for a crash of thunder. It's like watching a storm rolling in every time he moves.

Kane stands with his back against the oversized leather chair, his head bowed and his shoulders stone as he scrolls his phone.

His vicious scowl says everything.

There are only a couple articles about us so far, but it'll be everywhere soon. Molehills turn into mountains so easily in the media world.

"Hey," I whisper, rubbing his arm as I hand him the tea. He sets his phone down, but he doesn't pull me in closer for a hug.

"Hey, yourself."

"It's not so bad. We've both been through this song and dance before." I've said the same thing three times since we got home, and each time I've been met with an indifferent grunt.

This time feels different.

Almost shameful.

Because we're not a real couple navigating how to deal with the press so we can build our lives together.

We're just two strangers with great chemistry and sheet-ripping nights.

Nothing intended to last—and definitely not under acid speculation from outsiders.

"I'm sorry as hell." He slurps his tea so fast I'm surprised it doesn't burn his tongue.

"Don't be. It's fine, honestly. I'm a Blackthorn." I laugh as I lean beside him. "This kind of stuff happens when you have an interesting life. Nothing new. I probably would've gotten a mention or two anyway just by being here and poking my head into town. This other stuff, it's just—" I shrug. "It's drama. Clown stuff."

"No." He sets the mug down with a *clink* and faces me, his green eyes blazing. "It's not business as usual, duchess."

I swallow hard.

"If you're mad that they think we're dating, I get it. I—" I stop. I don't know. This is the awkward part where I fidget in place, sipping my tea so I don't have to look at him. "It's happened before when I've been hooked up with guys. It'll pass."

His nostrils flare, and I know I've said the wrong thing.

"Is that supposed to make it better? *More* unwanted attention when we don't even know who tried to fuck with the house?"

It was.

But I can't say that now.

"All I'm saying is, the hit pieces are old hat for me. I'm fine. We're fine."

"I'm not," he snaps. "This is a load of horseshit."

"They're just rumors, Kane."

"And they shouldn't have found us to run their mouths." He paces between the tall bookshelves against the wall, and I watch the hard, angry line of his mouth, the tension ripping through him.

The way he moves, all power and intention.

So gracefully intimidating for such a large man.

I want to comfort him, but I don't think I could bear being shoved away.

"They shouldn't have known shit," he snarls. "I've kept my head down and no one knows we're here."

"People talk. You know that. Pretty much all they do in sleepy little towns like this." I shrug.

"Hunkering down with the Blackthorn heiress?" He shakes his head in a short, sharp motion. "What bullshit."

I try not to be hurt.

It makes sense that he's angry being ambushed, watching his not-so-peaceful family vacation go up in smoke. What little was left of it thanks to me.

It also makes sense that he feels he can talk about it openly.

"I never meant for this to happen," he says raggedly,

looking back at me. Every inch of his body is taut. "Never meant to drag you into this."

"Seriously, stop. If we start pointing fingers over who's more newsworthy, we'll be here all night." This time, I head for him, placing my hands on his chest and looking up into his face. His heart drums too fast. "It's *fine*, Kane. Worse things have happened. I've lived through far uglier whispers, and I bet you have too."

"That's not the point." His hand finds the back of my arm, but his grip feels loose. "I hate that it ruined our time here. Almost as bad as that prowler."

"It hasn't ruined anything. Not yet."

He exhales roughly.

"And fuck—all the rumors around me could smear you, too. You've got a life and a career."

"What rumors? That we're dating?" I smile unevenly. "And we'll worry about my career when my designs give me one."

Still, I'm so confused.

"Goddammit." His eyes glaze as he stares into space over my head. "We never should've come here."

Ouch.

My heart shatters like a frozen ball of ice.

"Now you're being ridiculous." I reach up and pat his cheek. "Look at me. Look at you. We're cool. We're not at anyone's mercy besides ourselves."

He shakes his head severely.

"I can't have my shit affecting you."

"How am I affected, Kane? Am I missing a limb?" I reach up, fingers tangling in his scruff until he looks at me. "Dude. I'm more resilient than you give me credit for. This isn't the end of the world. We'll just keep a low profile until it's time to go."

"Time to go," he repeats bitterly. His fingers fold around

my wrist and he slowly pushes my hand away. "You make it sound so simple."

I don't like the bite in his voice.

"It *is* simple. The only thing this crap ruined is having lunch at the diner. We just need to be careful hopping around town. Here, we're safe."

He levels a look that reminds me how *unsafe* we might be in this house.

Me and my stupid mouth.

But finally, his lips curl, though his smile doesn't reach his eyes. "I should've been more careful."

"Stop that. No more blaming yourself. This is what fame is, and I'm sure the kids know it. We got them out of there ASAP. Plus, you set the cameras up, so it's not like any ballsy reporters will show up creeping around the house."

Too optimistic, maybe.

Some people definitely could trespass for a big story or a few candid photos, but I'm hoping we're not worth the risk.

His eyes harden.

I wish I could take back trying to make this bear of a man feel better.

"It's complicated with the kids," he says. "And with you. Shit." He's still holding my wrist like he's forgotten he has it. "If it wasn't for the stalker crap, we'd probably be on our way back to New York right now."

My veins turn to ice as the reality of what he said sinks in.

The only reason he's here is to keep me in one piece.

Not because he wants to stay, necessarily.

He's just too worried about leaving me alone, in danger.

Oh, I should be relieved that he's this good. But all I can feel is my hurt heart pounding and my brain going dizzy.

I'm used to being the summer girl. The temporary fling.

But holy shit, I'm not good enough for him to say it?

To tell me he stayed because he loves my company? He loves—

Oh my God, no.

He doesn't love me, and I have no business thinking he might.

I stagger backward.

"You know what, don't bother. If that's how you feel, maybe we should all leave."

His eyebrows lift.

"Margot, that's not what I meant." He growls, raking a hand through his hair. "I just meant—look, cutting and running would only be worse."

Worse than hanging around out of pity?

Out of obligation?

I don't think so.

"I can be out of your hair by tomorrow," I say.

"No, wait." He takes my arm, stopping me as I'm heading for the door. "I can't keep making stupid decisions. You hear me, woman? I can't fuck things up again."

"Again?" I rip myself free from his hold.

So in his mind, I'm one more item on his long list of mistakes.

"Where are you running? Will you stop taking everything I say the worst way possible?" he snarls.

"I'm not running anywhere, Kane Saint," I say, stopping at the door. "Maybe you should stop running and figure it out."

* * *

NOTHING WILL EVER TAKE away the peaceful nights.

It's one of those rare fall nights where the wind sings, the trees creak with whispers, and the stars wink down from moving curtains of clouds.

Below, muffled voices float through my open window, softly bruising my heart.

Mostly the kids.

They're talking and Dan's drumming—just a soft patter. I'm sure he's trying to keep it down.

Occasionally, Kane's deep voice cuts in with encouragement and stories about the constellations crisscrossing the sky.

He knows a lot about stargazing.

I wonder if he's had it for years or if he just looked up the myths so Sophie would have a little help from her loving dad.

That's totally Kane.

An explosive human contradiction who can shift from tender to torrid in ten seconds flat.

Our argument stings.

He never came up to find me since I stormed out, and I've been sitting in my room all afternoon, only sneaking down for food after I knew they'd eaten.

Of course, he left me a plate.

Of course, this rich beef stew with thick broth served over delicious sticky rice hit the spot.

He's murdering my low carb routine along with my better senses.

I don't know how to feel about that.

I don't know how to feel about anything.

I just know I'm hurt that he's down there having a sweet evening with the kids, while I'm up here like Rapunzel in her tower because that big idiot-lunk can't swallow his ego.

But yes, I *get* it.

I get wanting to flee and take the kids away from this mess.

He's putting them first like any decent parent should.

Mom and Dad never would've left us in harm's way, even

if they weren't exactly affectionate or attentive or—well, you get the point.

Ethan and I had to figure it out on our own.

Everything we had to learn about being a Blackthorn came from PopPop.

I'm no stranger to the limelight and cameras rudely flashing in my face. Or clickbaity people posting scandalous whispers about me online. It's incredible how much having a fortune makes the world oh-so-interested in who you're dating or just hooking up with.

Spoiler: the whispers are usually wrong.

Sometimes, you wish for the dating crap when the made-up alternatives turn fucking cruel.

One disgruntled personal chef my mother let go when I came home from college on Thanksgiving break turns into an exposé on how Margot Blackthorn is such a finicky eater. Why, she threw a fit until her parents canned a woman with Michelin star experience and five kids to feed.

And yes, I must be a spoiled bitch because I can fly private and work on my 'tacky' shoe designs at forty thousand feet.

Just another talentless rich girl who had the moon handed to her.

Just like her folks.

That one hurt the most, honestly.

When people compare me to Scott and Elvira Blackthorn, and not to Gramps. With Ethan, it's different because he inherited the family empire.

Kane should also be used to the searing spotlight and people falling all over themselves to shred you just so they can walk away with a few pieces of your ego as souvenirs.

That's what being famous is—forking over bloody scraps of yourself so the public can bite and tear and taste whatever they imagine.

Ideally, you choose what pieces they get in their hungry little teeth.

Kane didn't want to give them us—however much 'us' there is—and at some level it makes sense.

He wanted to keep his time here private and special.

With the divorce and the whole leaving his company thing, that's more complicated. People have been speculating, making him out to be some kind of rich supervillain. But that's all surface stuff.

It doesn't matter.

And in all my dealings with him, he's never been the bad guy.

I look up at the stars again through the window, my chest tight.

My eyes burn, but I don't let myself cry.

I'm still light on tears.

When Gramps died, I cried so much I felt sick for days. But I never let myself cry over men who aren't family.

Not since Kelso.

Kane's rich laughter floats up to my room.

He chuckles at something Sophie says, and the ache in my chest threatens to swallow me.

Deep down, I know he's right.

We should've been more careful.

It was a blunder any way you slice it, getting involved with an older, divorced single dad papa bear.

A broken beast who's plodding away from his past, ripping up everything in his path.

But I've gotten *so attached* to the kids.

And so addicted to our sunny, sexy mornings together.

Ugh.

I glance at my iPad on the desk.

Why mope when I could be channeling this pain?

Sophie still needs shoes.

The soft pink skin I laid over a template of her orthopedic shoes doesn't seem half-bad now that I'm giving it a second look.

Candy cloud, I call it.

The airy textures highlight the natural bulkiness of her shoes rather than hiding it.

When you can't change what's etched in stone, sometimes the only thing you can do is own it.

That's the idea here.

No shame.

I want her to own this fragile part of herself she's spent years trying to hide.

Kids suck when they're mean. There's a special place in hell for bullies.

But she's such a happy, shy girl, and I want her to shine without judgment. I want her to see what I do when I look at her, and what her dad must've always noticed since the day she was born.

Hopefully, this redesign will help.

A statement, not a megaphone.

With a little more tweaking, I can send the design off to a supplier who can make a custom model. Then if it looks good, I'll ship the finished product to them at home.

My heart hurts again when I remember I'll never get to see her reaction—if she loves them at all.

Once this is over, we'll have gone our separate ways.

My phone buzzes loudly beside me.

Hattie.

She's probably wondering why I haven't been texting her constant updates.

"Okay," she says the second I answer. "I know you're busy canoodling, but I need to know the situation."

"Canoodling? Who says that?" I laugh despite myself, putting my stylus down and leaning back in the chair.

"Me. I say that. And you're not using it to avoid the question."

"What question, Hat-girl?"

"*Are* you canoodling?"

Kane's voice floats through the open window.

"Nope," I admit after a second. "We're not even on the same floor of the house right now."

"Oh. Crap," she says. "Do you want to talk?"

"Would you let me *not* talk about it?" I get up and flop down on the bed.

"I'd tell you that I love you and respect your privacy and that you have every right not to talk to me about it," she says reasonably. "But then I would ignore you for three days straight while eating Ben and Jerry's."

"Cookie dough?"

"Obviously. Only the best in this house. Now *spill*! What happened with that creepy stalker dude? And what's going on with Hunky McHunkster?"

"Please never call him that again," I say.

"Only if you talk. How can I be your moral support if you won't let me?"

I chew my lip, deciding not to tell her too much about the stalker situation.

She'll just worry, and then she'll probably tell Ethan.

Then he'll show up here and make a scene. Nobody needs my brother dropping in with his worries and adding to the mess.

I also don't need my brother sending Holden to turn this place into a fortress or drag me home. I'm not sure the fabric of the universe can handle two tight-lipped strongman egos in the same room.

"We reported the guy I saw to the police. No big deal," I say. "And Kane, he's…"

"Margot, did you sleep together?"

My breath stops.

"How did you know?"

"I *knew* it!" she crows. "You just seemed like you really liked him. I figured you wouldn't hold back. I mean, I get it. I looked him up, remember?"

"Did you Google him again today?"

"Not since we last spoke. Why?"

"We have a problem," I say slowly. "News leaked that he's here with me, and now our names are linked."

"Linked like dating linked?"

"Yeah. But also, now he's here and everyone's all worked up about it. He thinks he's ruined our time together and potentially dragged me through the mud."

"Huh? Does he know you're a Blackthorn?" she asks carefully.

"Yes. And I've told him that I've been through the rumor mill and walked away alive. But he—"

"He still feels guilty?"

"Right." I pull the duvet over me miserably. "Things got stressful. He basically said we're a giant mistake. Point-blank to my face."

"Ouch."

"Yeah, ouch."

"Maybe he was just upset?"

I scowl at the ceiling.

"Maybe. I mean, that's possible. He popped off because he was pissed and he didn't mean it. But he *said* it, Hattie. Sometimes, people are more honest when they're mad."

"Oh, God."

"It shouldn't bother me so much. I don't even *know* him that well. Not enough to get worked up over this."

"Mm, okay. There's no time limit on feelings. Are you sure about that? How well do you know him?"

Definitely well.

Despite our short time together, I know him like the back of my hand.

I know he's a generous handyman. A selfless grouch. A very conflicted ego.

I know he can cook like a stove god, he has a fraught relationship with his ex, and he's a top ten finalist for father of the year.

I know he handles his son's overactive imagination gracefully and fusses over his little girl fitting in.

I know he came here because he wanted to heal *them*. He wanted a badly needed mental break from his family taking too many kicks to the gut.

He wanted shelter.

And I know that even though this thing with us is temporary, even though he tries not to care too much, he'll shelter me too.

But still—*still*, I want to lie.

I want to tell Hattie I barely know him because that means he barely knows me, and somehow that would make this emotional derangement over him less embarrassing.

Only, that's so brutally honest the lie stalls in my lungs.

"What am I supposed to do?" I whisper. "He doesn't open up. He's kinda stuck on his ex, I think, and he won't give his heart a chance."

Hattie purrs her sympathy.

"Oh, that's a tough one. I dunno, maybe the only thing you can do is put some distance between you? Let him work it out. Give him space. You can't do much else."

Wise, unwanted words.

"Yeah," I say once I've gotten my voice back. "Yeah, you're right."

"Will you be okay, though? Do you need me to fly up there?"

"No!" I clear my throat, catching myself. "No, it's fine. I'm not sure I'll stick around much longer anyway. You know me. I'm always okay."

"You always *pretend* you're okay," she says seriously. "Just call me if you need me, m'kay? Anytime. I'll always pick up for you."

"I love you."

"Love you more." She blows a kiss through the line and I disconnect, fighting the lump in my throat. My eyes sting.

Space, space.

Oh my God, just give him space.

Exactly what I was afraid she'd say.

You can't do much else.

I know.

Just like I'm painfully aware I've fallen into a self-baited trap, trying to fix a man who has to fix himself.

But right now, space feels like total isolation.

It's bigger and colder than the gulf between stars.

XVIII: HOUSE DIVIDED (KANE)

The night is a window to a dark ocean called eternity.

There's barely a cloud obscuring the stars, blinking lighthouses on shores we'll never see.

Out here with the kids, my worries should be just as distant, even though they're really just a few feet away.

I can't dwell on that.

Not with Sophie peering through her telescope, mapping what she can with her stargazing app.

Dan has his drum pad outside, tapping out an old Van Halen song with his headphones on. The kid's got good taste, all thanks to yours truly.

It should be peaceful. Quiet. Clear.

And I really am trying my damnedest to be present and listen to my fatherly instincts.

"Hey, Dad? You awake?" Sophie snaps her fingers in front of my face.

"Huh?" I grunt.

Shit, so maybe I'm not listening well.

"What planet is this? Do you think it's right?"

I take the phone from her hands and look at the screen. It shows us an overview of the night sky overhead with nice labels. You can narrow down any section, easily zooming in and searching the names of the major stars and planets named to track with the sky.

There's more on constellations, too, which Soph has spent a long time working on. She wants to know them all by heart one day.

"Which one do you mean, honey?" I ask.

"Look here. I don't know if it matches." She drags me under the telescope, and I look through the lens.

It's too faint to be Jupiter, but the telescope captures the faintest fuzzy rings. Definitely Saturn.

"Should be there on the app. Bet you five bucks you can't find it."

"Daaad," she whines, but she's smiling. "I wanted you to get it for me."

"Where's the fun in that, baby girl? And how will you learn if you don't do it yourself? Look harder, then you tell me what that is."

"Not *fair*," she hisses as she takes the phone and dips her face back under the telescope.

My mind goes back to what Margot said.

About running.

About how I mouthed off, calling it a mistake.

A heat of the moment slip. Almost inevitable when I was pissed off and frustrated and she tried to reason our way out of a bad situation.

If something goes to shit, just say so.

I can handle the truth.

Now, our names are linked in public, and the ugly all-seeing eye makes everything more complicated.

The truth is, I can't fold her life into mine. It's too complicated and we're too incompatible.

That woman deserves better than more rumors breathing down her neck.

And I didn't mean *she* was a mistake.

I don't regret our time together.

The thing I regret isn't Margot Blackthorn—it's how this fuckery could hurt her while she's boiling over our stalker stress.

I damn sure regret having no idea how I'm going to make it better.

"Saturn! Found it!" Sophie says triumphantly.

I beam her a smile. I hope it doesn't look too absent.

"Great job, Soph." I mean it, though.

Dan looks up from drumming, his little face tense with focus as he pulls off his headphones.

Sophie goes back to stargazing with her phone in one hand and her face pushed to the telescope, but Dan watches me with a seriousness that seems older than his nine years.

Normally, I'd laugh.

Tonight, I just wonder if he knows his old man royally fucked up.

That makes me ache, thinking he could have that awareness.

They're both growing up so fast and I can't keep up.

Every time I think I'm used to the stage of life they're in, they grow a little more and time skips forward.

These kids are turning into well-rounded people. I feel like I'm meeting them for the first time every few years.

"Dad," Dan says, leaving his drums and coming to sit beside me.

"What is it, Bud?"

"Something's wrong," he says, regurgitating a phrase I use on them all the time. "Why are you worried?"

Damn.

Of course, I've told them the media hounds know we're

here. Not to scare them, but because I don't like keeping too many secrets.

I want them to trust me, and I need them to feel safe.

They're too young and thankfully too innocent to understand the scummy dark side of fame and money, but they do know not to ever speak to reporters.

"Is it because people know you're here?" His forehead pinches. "So what? Why should we care what they say?"

"Not that simple, little man," I say gently. "It wouldn't be so bad if it was just us, but we're complicating Margot's life, too. And that's on top of the intruder crap."

"Oh, yeah? Is that why..." He trails off, glancing up in the direction of her room, his face clearing.

"Yeah. It's a big deal," I tell him.

"But why? I mean, aren't you complicating it in a *good* way? Maybe she doesn't like people taking pics of her, but she smiles and laughs and she's nice to us. I don't think she cares about the burglar anymore and neither do I!"

"That's not all that matters," I say, even though it's true.

Margot obviously enjoys the time we spend together, and she's instinctively good with the kids.

Hell, kinder and more attentive than their own mother, even if the bar's set so low it scrapes the grass.

"Then what else does, Dad?" Dan asks. "I bet she likes you. Way more than any crush I've seen at school. You get all grumpy when she talks to that ceramics dude. Lee or whatever."

"I do not," I growl, prodding him in the side. "Take that back, boy."

"See? Busted! You know you do." He laughs. "Gah, why do grown-ups have to make everything so confusing anyway?"

I wish I fucking knew.

Since I don't, I tickle him until he's red-faced and begging for mercy, and I'm the one who needs it tonight.

When did my own son get wiser than me?

Everything feels complicated as hell, sure, but maybe I *should* pull my head out of my ass and try again.

Maybe we should talk, and I should explain what happened back there.

The rest is up to Margot.

Assuming it's not already too late for her to hear more of my excuses, my worries, and everything I wish I could control.

That's not fair.

The least I owe her is an explanation.

* * *

WE SPEND the night apart and it's a restless goddamned absence.

Best to give her space, though, and by the time I'm padding downstairs to brew some coffee the next morning, I'm ready to lay my cards out.

But there's a noise in the hallway that stops me cold.

Another intruder?

Impossible. None of the cameras went off and pinged my app.

Only, when I hustle into the kitchen with my fists ready, it's just Margot.

She's standing there, dressed in olive slacks and a crisp white blouse, with those big suitcases behind her.

She stops and stares at me, eyes wide. Her heart-shaped lips twitch.

What the actual fuck?

We gawk at each other for an eternity.

Her mouth is tight, her face almost as pale as that shirt.

She looks like she got about as much sleep as I did, and I hate it.

"Margot," I grind out. "What are you doing?"

She stiffens. "I didn't think you'd be down yet."

"Obviously." I gesture at her luggage. "Is that why you're sneaking out without a goodbye?"

Her mouth opens, closes, and then her face falls.

"Duchess, are you shitting me right now?" There's a jagged lump in my throat. "You weren't even going to say goodbye to the kids?"

Her nostrils flare and she folds her arms.

"I... I figured you could do that for me."

"Yeah, because they'd love that." I snort. "Whatever your beef is with me, I thought we were better than that."

"What else do you expect, Kane? Should I just stick around, waiting for you to realize you fucked up? We had less than a week left anyway."

Less than a damn week, yeah.

Still more time than this exit would be.

And it hits me like an uppercut, I'm not ready for our time together to end.

In the silence, her red-rimmed eyes flick to mine and away again. "I didn't think you'd care."

"Where were you planning to go? Home?" My voice is hoarse.

"I was going to catch the next flight out of Bar Harbor to Portland. From there, not sure," she whispers. "You're welcome to the house as long as you'd like, if you think it's safe enough. I'll be out of your hair and you guys can—"

No.

Fuck no.

She stops talking as I stride forward, catch the back of her neck in my hand, and pull her into a violent kiss.

Her hands flatten against my chest like she wants to push me away, but we both know she won't.

That isn't what we want.

Not when her mouth softens.

Not when she melts into me.

Not when this pitiful mangled sob boils out of her.

"Kane," she strains out, but I shake my head.

"I know. You feel like you have to go because of the bullshit I said last night. I take it back. I'm sorry. Just hear me out first? Please, hear me out, and then you can decide if you still want to leave."

Her eyes fill with tears. I fucking hate that she's crying because of me.

"You don't have to explain anything. Really, what's the point?"

"I do," I insist. "You don't know everything about me yet, and I want you to understand what happened." I smooth my thumb over her cheeks and the tear trails there. "Let me have a chance to give you the truth."

XIX: HOME SWEET HEARTACHE (MARGOT)

Oh my God, we've been starved.

It's like I've been fiending for his touch my entire life.

Kane watches me for a second, his eyes slitted, before bringing his lips to mine in another manic kiss.

Too much and not enough.

The truth can wait.

Raw, tangled emotions snarl on my bones as he drags me closer, closer, and still not close enough.

All I can do—the only thing I can—is cup my hand around the back of his neck and surrender.

Stay.

God, I didn't realize how bad I just wanted him to ask me to stay.

He doesn't even have to do it with words.

Not when this kiss is so potent and clear it leaves me dizzy.

It screams how much he wants me and how big of an idiot I am for trying to sneak out without a goodbye note.

His hard-on presses against my belly, an angry reminder.

I couldn't truly know thirst until I felt his flood.

The heat, the urgency, the electric need zinging through my body.

I sigh as he cups my breast, rolling my nipple between his fingers.

He groans when I reach between us, running my fingers over the front of his shorts, feeling the punishment I deserve.

Thick and heavy and pulsing with promise.

Yes, we need this.

We need to lose our minds a little before this ends.

And if it does—when it does—at least let it fade with one more sweet memory.

One last soul-spinning send-off worthy of goodbye.

His greedy hand slides under my shirt and finds bare skin under my bra.

With a dark growl, he pulls with no mercy.

Buttons go flying.

Blouse, ruined.

But I can't be mad.

I wrap my hands around his neck again and he understands what I want. He feels the intensity as his free hand finds my ass for support a split second before I jump.

Yes, I'm climbing this man like a tree.

My legs pinch his waist, and before I know what's happening, my ruined shirt is on the floor.

The cool morning air pulses against my skin, and he flicks open my bra clasp.

I'm liquid now.

So clumsy from the lust storming my veins.

Neither of us needs to say another word as he turns, carries me to the pantry, and throws me against the wall.

His hands go to work, tearing off my slacks.

A second later, there's nothing between us except his shorts and my thin, soaked panties.

"Fuck, duchess," he rasps against my mouth.

"*Now*," I plead.

"Now." He squeezes my wet pussy.

I almost combust.

Kane's breath comes muffled, heavy as black smoke pressed into my hair, and I arch into him.

Now, now.

Destroy me, now.

The bed upstairs feels like it's on another continent.

I can't bear to wait that long.

I need him in me, filling me, looting me and inflicting the sweetest insanity.

It's the kind of need I've never felt before, this fever bordering on desperation.

If I ever had any control, it's gone in a kiss.

And with Kane, I don't think I do.

"Stay. Right the fuck there," he mutters, shoving my panties to one side.

I nod, gripping his hair, panting.

"Do you have any clue, Margot? Any earthly idea how crazy you make me?" he whispers.

Then his fingers push inside me, delivering an answer.

I gasp, still pressed against the wall, rapidly losing my mind.

Another kiss smothers my moans.

So good, but still not enough.

His hands grab my ass, kneading and squeezing, imprinting his fingers on my flesh.

He shakes me like a doll with a feral growl before turning me over and hoisting me across the room.

When I blink, I'm sitting on the counter.

"Better leverage. Plus, I won't knock a duchess-sized hole in the wall," he explains.

I nod again, leaning back slightly, bracing myself on my hands.

"Please," I whisper, shaking to my core. My legs fall open. "Please, Kane."

He's already shucking off his shorts, and his single-minded cock springs free, swollen and ready, veins tracing its landscape like lightning in the sky.

The bead of thick moisture at his slit makes me smile, knowing how undone he is.

"No clue. No fucking *clue* what you do to me, woman," he says, his eyes burning me down as he mounts me and pushes inside.

Foly huck!

We both become instinct, inhuman, just two gasping shadows spiraling into ecstasy.

Quiet, quiet.

I remember at the last second we need to be quiet. There's no guarantee we'll be alone if the kids wake up, and we need to hear them coming before they catch us.

But it's always the same when he claims me, that fullness of being stretched until it almost hurts so deliciously.

Full, so full.

So joined.

So *owned*.

I love his cock too much for my own good.

"Good girl." His words rattle like broken glass now as he pulls back and thrusts inside again.

Soon, he's going faster, harder, pressing his forehead against mine, bringing the thunder, the wind, the destruction.

One breath.

Delirious with lust.

But his thumb seals my bottom lip, a reminder to shut it and be careful.

Oh, but I can't.

Not with him *pounding* me like this—not even if I want to.

"Kane!" I shudder around him.

Snarling, he pulls me closer, closer, burying my face against his shoulder, marking the back of my neck with his teeth.

I bite him back, branding him in turn.

He claws my hip in retaliation, though we're too far gone to remember anything except the need to keep it down.

I'm going to come faster and harder than I have in my life.

"Too fucking good," he grinds out.

"So good." I hold on tighter.

"You're going to break for me, duchess."

"*Yes.*" I don't have another word to tell him how *much* I want that. I want everything right now and it's terrifying. "Please, Kane. Please!"

"That's right, baby." He sounds disembodied, more animal than man.

We're that mindless, getting high off the other, lost in the sensation, overwhelmingly sinful and desperate.

He's desperate, too, I can feel it.

The heat gathers, my orgasm pulling tight.

"Quiet," he warns, shifting us so his hand is over my mouth as he picks up speed.

A good thing too, or I wouldn't be able to hold in my cries.

My eyes roll back as the wave crests, picks me up, and hurls me down again like a giant chucking a stone.

To call it an approaching orgasm would be an insult.

This is unlike any sex I've ever had.

On the edge, sharp, needy in a way that kills me.

"I'm going to—" I don't have time to finish before it hits full force.

Coming!

The wave sweeps in, blasting my entire being, making me one with the current.

I shudder against him as I convulse, my loud moans stifled against his palm as he fucks me through it, his eyes sharp as he admires me.

And he slows, tender again, just enough for me to recover right before he picks up the devil's speed.

I hold on, fingers white and nails digging into his skin, staring down at his cock pounding me, and then his face, jagged with strain.

His mouth splits open and his face screws up in a silent, strangled roar.

Just before he finishes, his eyes flick to mine.

Perfect green, alive and primal.

Then he's a mountain falling down.

His jaw clenches so he doesn't make a sound, and he's so deep inside me I can feel his throb, his heartbeat, his unforgiving *heat.*

Ohhh, shit.

The flood.

The magma flow.

The eruption, his seed all lava as it overflows my pussy and runs out between us.

His grip bruises my hip, trying to draw me closer, though there's nowhere to go with him bottomed out as he empties his balls deep inside me.

I wrap my arms around him and hold on tight.

"Fuck," he says hoarsely.

An entire universe in one gravel word.

I press my face against his chest.

He smells like cologne and Kane and forbidden sex.

I think I'm still trembling.

His hand brushes my hair. "You good?"

"I… I think so."

He tilts my head back so he can kiss me. "We should clean up. Hurry."

"You mean before we have company?"

"I mean your bags, duchess. I really don't want them to see them. I'll take them up while you fix yourself." He kisses me again, slowly and thoroughly.

Just like that, it's decided.

I'll stay because I can't imagine doing anything else.

"Can you walk to the shower?"

"Y-yeah. I just need a minute," I say, half laughing.

"No time."

The next thing I know, he's pulled out, thrown his shorts on, and he's shuttling me upstairs in his arms. I laugh against his chest.

"I'll go back for the bags in a minute," he tells me quietly. "I don't want you going anywhere. We still need to talk."

"I won't."

He puts me gently down in the bathroom.

He brushes my hair back from my face with a tenderness that's not exactly new but still makes my chest ache. Even though he told me what he wants, I know he'll respect my decision.

If, after he tells me everything, I still want to leave, he'll let me go. No question.

This morning, after crying half the night, I thought for sure I had to leave. I thought it was my only real adult decision.

Now, in his arms, I can't escape the glaring fact that it's the *last* thing I want.

Cutting him short just means hacking up our hearts, and if they're going to hurt, it should only happen naturally.

* * *

The steamy shower chases away all the bad thoughts that followed me upstairs.

Kane joins me after pulling my luggage back up. He takes the bar of soap and washes me in a way that feels reverent.

"So, breakfast might be late today," I say as he massages soap bubbles into my chest.

"Yeah," he says. "Worth it, though."

"Better hope the kids agree."

"They'll barely notice." He brushes my wet hair back from my face and maneuvers himself so he's standing under the blast.

I take the soap from him and start rubbing it across his tan skin.

Broad shoulders, firm pecs, and ridges forming a six-pack. Or maybe it's an eight-pack?

I count them as I go, letting my fingers trace his ridges and valleys.

Yeah, definitely eight bullets in this human gun.

I've hooked up with men who were built before, sure, but they spent half their lives in the gym.

Body sculpting was their life.

For Kane, it's just who he was. The warrior he still is at heart.

I love that.

"I'm sorry," he says as I wash his neck.

"For which part?" I grin up at him, the water from the shower dampening my eyelashes.

"Funny girl."

"I know I am." I press a kiss to the damp curve of his shoulder. "But what are you apologizing for?"

"When I thought my shit would blow up your life, I panicked." His warm hand clasps the back of my elbow. "You said I'm the one running, and you were right. I *did* try to run by pushing you away. But that hasn't gotten me anywhere."

I want to argue back.

It got him here in the first place. Running away brought him to Maine, and to me.

And it was also going to take him away from me again.

One deep look into his eyes tells me that's not what he's thinking right now though.

"When my last relationship burned up, it wasn't the only problem," he says. "I had to walk away from her and my company."

Finally, the mysterious OptiSynth.

"And you don't think you made the right call?" I ask.

He turns off the water.

The sudden morning cold against my too-hot skin almost feels overwhelming. Together, we step out of the shower and wrap ourselves in fluffy towels.

Instead of drying, though, we both walk to the bed and sit on the edge of it.

"It's complicated," he tells me, folding his hands in his lap. "You deserve to know, but it's not a story that reflects well on me."

I take his hand and hold it in mine.

"It's okay. Just start at the beginning. What did you do there?"

"It's what I didn't do. The worst part is, I joined it on a whim. With my hockey career buried and no love for politics, I figured I'd take my money and try a few start-ups. I always had an interest in technology. When a friend mentioned OptiSynth, I—"

"But what *is* it? Some AI thing?" I interrupt.

I've looked it up, of course, but I want to hear it in his words.

"Oh. Right." He sighs. "They originally promised to revolutionize interior design. They'd be a tool for designers to upload original concepts and then build tons of variations with AI. Not just images or crappy five-second videos, but full-blown 3D modeling."

So far, so good.

That's what I gathered, too, and I have to admit it's a nifty concept.

Everyone and their dog talks about AI these days if they aren't actually using it. It makes sense to jump on what's popular, a guaranteed road to riches.

Only, from Kane's face, that's not what happened.

"But you didn't like it?" I guess.

"For a couple years, it was good. Really good while it was in the development phase." He lifts his gaze to mine. "I still had a lot of celebrity cred back then, and I used it to bring in more investors. We were getting off the ground fast, beating our competition off superior capital."

"Nice," I say, releasing his hand as he pulls it free.

With his towel still wrapped around his waist, he stands and paces the room.

There's something oddly compelling about the way he moves now, tattoo bristling on his arm, his muscles tight and defined.

"My intention was never to replace designers or put them out of work," he says shortly. "You have to know that."

"I believe you."

"People have been talking shit about me because I was the one to bring so many people onboard. My presence got the big money interested, the kind that could push us forward. Not just money, the art world came too. Hell, I did the outreach, connecting with them in a way the business and tech types couldn't. We made this incredible software because I made it possible. And that's where I fucked up."

"Kane," I whisper, getting up and crossing the room until I'm in front of him, still in my towel, hair wet down my back.

I don't look as majestic as him, but he stares at me like I'm the sunrise. "It's okay. I promise."

"I should've seen it coming from ten miles away," he whispers, his fingers tracing my jaw. "You can tell me it's not my fault, but it is. Because I should've known this was exactly the kind of tech people use for pure fuckery."

I lean into his touch. "What do you mean?"

"It was just a few cutthroats who wanted to save on costs at first. They showed up just as the project really took off, and the new executive team decided to plot a new direction. They scrapped the plan to roll out tools—they decided it was good enough to pitch it as a 'designer replacement' to major firms."

"Oh, yikes." I flinch.

"I was fucking livid. Felt double-crossed as they shrugged and rewrote our vision and white papers. But there was nothing I could do. Then word leaked out, and all the artists I'd worked with were furious, blaming me for the knife in the back. Even though I was just as much in the dark about it as them."

"Holy shit. Kane—"

"They had a right to be mad." He shudders, like he needs to get this out and doesn't want my sympathy. "But I couldn't live with empowering a company that lied to me so they could fuck over people's livelihoods. I was done. I left, leaving a big hole of rumors behind."

"Kane." I catch his face and bring it down to mine, kissing him tenderly. "It's not your fault."

"I wish I could believe that."

"You had good intentions. You brought people together for something they might not have ever noticed. And you did it all to help artists, not ruin them."

"Whatever I intended, it blew up in my face. You know

the controversies with AI? Especially with creators?" he asks tonelessly.

"I know enough."

Like how tons of hardworking artists are up in arms about it.

Too often, AI isn't just a supplement or a helper—it's a devious hijacker. Creative works get scraped and fed into the engines to train the system to think better, until eventually it beats human talent at its own game.

Even as a budding shoe designer who doesn't need to worry about money, it makes me worry.

Will there ever be a place for my designers if they're good enough? Or will they be mowed down by machines that can vomit a hundred new concepts per hour?

No, you can't stop progress, but you also can't change the facts.

And when inventions start chipping away at the human soul because they're faster and cheaper and easier, well...

"You know you have to stop blaming yourself, right?" I hold his face between my hands. "I know that's just talk. But you can either choose to believe that, or you can choose not to, but you're carrying a burden that isn't yours. If you're going to blame someone, blame the guys who screwed you. Blame the people who took what you tried to do and twisted it."

"Margot—" His voice is rough. Angry.

"No. A man with the best intentions, who refused to stick around to support a company he doesn't believe in, doesn't *get* to fall on his sword for their BS."

I kiss him again, and this time he kisses me back. Hard.

"Don't know what the fuck I did to deserve you. But I'm going to keep on doing it."

"Then try to forgive yourself, okay?" I stare at him fiercely. "And you never know... maybe there'll be a time when the truth comes out. People will forgive you if they hear your side of the story. But first, you have to forgive yourself."

His hand slides down my back, sealing me against him.

We're still damp and cool from the shower, but none of that matters with the feel of his skin against mine.

"Does that mean you'll stay?" he asks between hungry kisses.

"I can't believe you took this long to tell me."

"Margot, I ruined people's lives." He leans back to caress my cheek.

"No, Kane. Greedy *assholes* ruined lives. Not you. And maybe the OptiSynth hacks made you feel like it's your fault, but they need to take a good, hard look in the mirror, and stop smearing the name of the one man who had integrity." I stop, breathing heavily.

His smile warms me like the sun.

"I love it when you get worked up. My little defender."

"If I don't, who else will?" I warn. "Seriously, anyone who tries to make you responsible for this—"

"Go easy. I won't put you in a place where you need to fight on my behalf," he says, kissing me again.

But before he can push me back on the bed and undo the shower, there's a soft thud from downstairs.

"They're up," Kane whispers against my mouth.

"Then the only thing we need to worry about now is breakfast." Laughing, I rest my thumbs on his cheekbones, stroking his face until he relaxes.

XX: GLASS HOUSES (KANE)

The kids don't know how close we came to losing the woman they're wild about.

By the time we made it downstairs and found Dan waiting impatiently at the table, all evidence of Margot trying to leave was gone.

I'm glad we moved those damn suitcases in time.

Yes, I could've explained it, and they're good kids. They might have understood.

They know our time hasn't gotten any easier between the break-in and the town gossip mill, so if she went home for safety and sanity, they'd get it.

But that wouldn't have been the whole story.

And I'm glad as hell I don't have to lie through my teeth.

I make breakfast while Margot chats with Dan about the War of 1812 and the drummer boy figurine he's still obsessed with.

A few minutes later, Sophie comes down, having finished her fantasy book, and she takes her usual spot next to Dan.

We eat as one family again.

One big, cozy, loaded word I can't believe I'm enjoying.

It's been too long.

Even when I was married, we didn't eat together often with our schedules. Even when we had the time, Daria would usually skip out with a smoothie on her way to the gym and then a photo shoot.

For her, spending little moments with the kids was just a chore of married life. Like everybody else in her circle, we were accessories, and we could wait while she came and went.

Sure, she loves them, in her own weird way.

The trouble is she'll never love anyone more than herself.

That's the bitter truth, a hard damn horse pill to swallow.

The kids are old enough to accept it now. I'm sure they'll have sharper, more bitter questions for her when they're older, and when that day comes, I won't be part of my ex-wife's regrets.

I want them knowing they had one parent who always put them first and last.

But Margot, she's fallen into our life too easily, laughing and joking with them so effortlessly. Sometimes I just stop and stare like a deer in the headlights.

Dangerously good.

Comparing my ex to this temporary fling can't be healthy.

She might've agreed to stay for now—just like I agreed to stop freaking out—but there's still an end date coming we haven't discussed.

In under a week, we'll go our separate ways.

Maybe we'll talk about seeing each other again.

That's a big fucking *maybe* with razor-sharp teeth.

But we both want to figure out if this thing is worth fighting for, don't we?

Me, I already know the answer.

I'm just not a reckless enough jackass to say it to her face. Not today and not yet when we were hanging by a thread.

"I have an idea," Dan announces as we're finishing our plates of pancakes, scrambled eggs, and bacon.

"More drumming? You're going to learn every ballad from 1812 and put on a show for us?" Margot asks teasingly.

"No! Uh, I mean, not yet. It's sunny outside!"

Sophie looks out the window at the shimmering lake, breaking into a grin. "Bet you five bucks I can read your mind."

"Of course *you* can," Dan huffs. "Dad, are you in?"

"Depends what it is, Bud. Let's hear it."

"It's such a nice day and we were already out in town, so... I think we should go canoeing again." There's a sly look in his eyes.

He knows I usually banish them after breakfast to get some schoolwork done. Even on vacation, they're building good habits. Duty first, then leave the rest of the day free.

"Dad, he's got a point," Sophie joins in. "If we wait too long, it might not stay sunny like this. It's Maine and you never know with the fall weather."

I bite back a smile as Margot looks at me. There's a happy question dancing in her eyes.

"What do you think, Dad?"

"Hmmm." I take my sweet time, playing it up and leaving them in suspense as I look at their hopeful faces. "I suppose we should take advantage of this weather."

The kids whoop, and Margot starts clearing the table.

"You guys head out," she tells me. "I'll catch up, after I've finished tidying up."

"You don't have to—"

"Go!" she insists, giving me a playful push. "It won't take long to throw these in the dishwasher and wipe down the table."

I reluctantly give up because the kids are already running for the door.

"Guys, get changed first," I yell after them.

They skid down the hall, stopping just short of colliding with the wall.

"Ugh, really?" Dan says, but he turns and races upstairs with Sophie behind him.

Outside, the lake ripples in the breeze, one large mirror spinning the light overhead into gold.

It's painfully gorgeous, but I wonder if we should expand our horizons. This could be the last good day for the water.

After a quick Google search, I settle on the other side of the lake down the road, the part we haven't seen. I bump into Margot on her way out of the kitchen.

"Are we ready?"

"Yeah. There's a place with boat rentals a little ways down the road. Thought we could explore a different part of the lake in something more durable than the canoe we brought."

"Oh yeah, I know the place. Good idea." She glances upstairs and then looks back at me. "You're not scared something will happen while we're gone?"

"That's why we have the cameras. They're still watching like hawks, last I checked," I say grimly.

It's not my main reason for choosing somewhere away from the house, but if anybody's watching and waiting for us to leave, this could be an opportunity to find out who's behind this shit.

She nods after a second. "We should make sure we don't leave anything too valuable here, then."

Right.

I hate that I almost wish something would go missing.

So far, they haven't stolen shit, and that's unsettling.

But she's right, there's no good reason to take any unnecessary risks.

"Pack up anything you don't want to lose. Laptop, tablet, jewelry, whatever," I say. "I'll do the same for the kids and we'll stow it in the trunk to bring with us. Can't imagine anyone will try a vehicle break-in in these parts."

"Yeah, okay." She leans up to kiss my cheek. "I'll be quick."

She's not wrong.

By the time I've packed away a few last odds and ends like Sophie's telescope and put them in the trunk, Margot's ready, and the kids are practically foaming at the mouth.

The rental place is just a short drive along the lakeshore. Once we get there, I grab us a bigger family canoe and we get out on the water.

Looks like a nice chance to explore the channels and the smaller connected lake that's closer to this side.

Amazing what a difference one day makes.

We still have our burglar fuckwit hanging over us, along with our emotions, but I feel lighter every time I look at Margot Blackthorn. It's easier to breathe.

I can't stay pissy when I'm basking in her smile.

"Hey," I say as she settles in next to me. Her hair is tied back and she's wearing a bulky life jacket, but she looks ridiculously beautiful.

"Hey, yourself," she says.

"Thanks for coming. The kids are having a great time." I nod at where they're sitting at the front of the canoe, chattering too fast for me to hear.

Every time they spot a small island, they're making up stories about buried treasures and ancient dragon bones on the fly.

I miss having that much imagination.

And I've missed having a day this easy, bright and cool and soothing, one of the rare times that makes it worth living.

"Of course," she says like it's nothing. "It's good to see them so happy—and even better when it's you."

"It's been a rough season."

"It's over now. If you give it a chance, life turns over, just like the leaves out here." She rests a hand on my knee. "Onward and upward, right? This is your year, big daddy. I can feel it."

"Hope you're right." I watch them as I paddle along, steering us into one of the bigger channels next to a sandy beach. "That reminds me, I had something to ask you."

I clear my throat as her eyes sharpen.

Why the hell am I *nervous*?

"If it doesn't put you out too much, how'd you like to come visit sometime?"

She tilts her head, a tiny smile playing across her mouth. "I have an apartment in Manhattan."

Of course she does.

That's only a half answer and good reason to keep my poker face on.

"I'm spending a lot of time in Portland these days, but... my shoe stuff will take me back to New York sooner or later." She taps a finger against her chin, her smile widening. "Especially if I have friends to visit."

"You do, woman. We want you there."

"I'd love that." Her blue eyes soften. "Before today, I thought you'd never ask. I wasn't sure if you wanted this thing to..." She trails off.

"Until now, I wasn't sure either," I admit. "But hell, watching you try to skip out made me realize I'm not ready for that. Not tomorrow and not next week. We can go our separate ways, but we don't *have* to."

Her eyes ignite, putting the blue lake to shame.

"Then it's settled. No big goodbyes. Just see ya later." She nods.

Sunlight crisscrosses her face, and she squints in the light.

"Dammit, yeah." The kids are distracted, so I lean forward and kiss her lightly on the lips.

The softest moan spills into my mouth and her fingers dig into my thigh.

Just a peck, innocent and quick, wrapped in a dark and dirty promise.

No lie, I'm addicted.

I'm going to need her back not long after we put Maine in the rearview mirror.

It's a struggle to hold in how addicted I am.

"Ew, you guys." Dan turns around to see us just in time, his nose wrinkled.

"Ew yourself, little man. I'll make you regret your words someday when you're old enough to do more than pull a girl's pigtails."

To be fair, I suppose I never grew out of that myself.

I chuckle, though, leaning back.

Margot's cheeks flush as she giggles and mutters something about how embarrassed he'll be.

The rest of our outing passes in a happy haze. The heat in my gut grows heavier by the minute, and it has nothing to do with the sun.

When we get back to the dock for a bathroom break and lunch, the warmth fades.

There's a slip of paper on my windshield.

A ticket? All the way out here with no one else in the parking lot?

Didn't see a meter or sign of any sort asking for a fee, though.

My instinct tells me that isn't it, and I don't like the other possibilities.

Margot and the kids wait in the boat for me to bring back lunch from the cooler, so I grab the note and look it over.

Send the kids and the woman away. You'll face your destiny alone if you're still a man, and not just a grubby little thief.

Now we know.

My heart picks up, thundering with rage.

Our asshole stalker was never after Margot. He's got a beef with *me*.

And *thief*? What the hell?

This must go back to the OptiSynth disaster. Nothing else I've done would leave anyone so irate, so willing to follow me here and raise hell.

But the kids, shit.

Margot.

I don't know how I'm going to break the news and shatter a perfect morning.

Still, now there's no choice. I need to get them out of here.

Back to my mother.

Away from Sully Bay.

Whoever this creepy fuckroach is, they're not going to stop without good reason. I can't risk putting my family in their crosshairs.

I promised we'd stay as long as I was sure they'd be safe.

Now, I'm not certain of anything.

And Margot, fuck—how do I tell her?

How do I drag her off her own property when she's just at risk?

Every breath sears my nostrils.

I take a few tortured seconds to calm down before grabbing lunch from the trunk, raiding the cooler like an angry grizzly.

No, cool it. Let them have the lake for a couple more hours.

When we get home, I'll break the bad news.

* * *

THE SECOND we're back at the house and settled, I drop the bomb on the kids.

Things have changed and they're going off to Grandma.

I've texted my mother, explaining the situation and why I'm sending them home. She was already on standby since Daria turned us down.

"No way!" Dan whines, folding his arms defiantly. "Dad, you said we could stay."

"I said for now, Bud. We're way past 'wait and see,'" I tell him. "You know better. I don't play around with safety."

He opens his mouth again and closes it, twisting his lips.

"I don't wanna go." Sophie's stubbornness surprises me today.

She's normally the skittish one who shows up at my bedroom door for comfort during thunderstorms.

"I know, Soph. It's rotten luck, but we don't have much choice. I'm not budging on this, guys. Hate me for now. I'll live, as long as you're okay." I start upstairs after slipping Margot that stalker's note plus one of my own so she understands the severity. "Let's get your stuff packed. You've got a flight to catch."

"If it's so dangerous, why don't you come with? Why are you dropping us off?" Dan demands.

"Because I need to sort this out once and for all. Last thing I'll do is let this problem follow us home," I say, heading to his room first.

I look in and shake my head. Clothes everywhere in a messy explosion. Typical preteen boy.

Also, I need to look after Margot. If she won't leave, neither will I.

That's the part I don't say.

Sophie hovers in the doorway like she can feel it. "Is Margot coming too, Daddy?"

"You'll see her again," I promise, walking over to hug her. "Maybe this old house someday, too. This isn't the end. I just need to make sure no one's being targeted."

"But who? Won't you tell us anything?" Dan flings his clothes on the bed, and I fold them.

"Don't know. Still working on that part," I say.

"Sophie? Want some help packing?" Margot offers from the hallway.

"I just... I don't want to go!" Her little face wilts. "Tell Dad you want us to stay."

Margot throws me a wry look. Judging by the anguish in her face, I know she understands how serious this is.

"I wish I could, honey," she says gently. "But this time, you'd better listen to your dad. He's doing the right thing, even if it sucks a lot right now. Come on, let me help..."

Thank you. That's the only thing I can mouth.

Then Margot takes my daughter and leads her off to help get her stuff sorted.

The entire time I'm packing up Dan's belongings, my phone is out, lying on top of the bed. I keep my ears peeled for any notification dings from the camera app.

With this fucker decloaking with his direct threat, I can't afford to let my guard down.

Not for a split second.

Dan stares at his packed luggage with a frown that cuts across his face.

"I still don't get why you're not coming if it's sooo dangerous," he whines.

"Because it's my problem. This person, they're angry at me, and that means I need to make sure there's nobody else in the way if this guy wants to meet and the cops can't find him first."

He sighs, closing his eyes.

"Well... when you're done, can we come back?"

"We'll see. Probably not for now, but next year? It's possible." I ruffle his hair. "I'm proud of you for taking it in stride. Look after your sister and grandma, okay?"

He nods glumly.

Then there's a knock at the door, and Sophie pokes her head around the corner, a packed suitcase trailing behind her and her pink backpack slung over her shoulder.

"Where's Margot?" I ask.

"She said she had to grab something from her room," she says. "But she told me to tell you she's ready."

I scroll through my travel app for available flights.

The airport in Bar Harbor is small, just puddle jumpers and a few private planes, but I know there's a flight out to Portland later tonight. I'll have my mother waiting to pick them up after she flies up to Maine.

It also means a slight wait at the airport to make sure they get on the plane, but better they're out of the house ASAP. No one will target us there.

"Come on," I say. "Let's go downstairs and wait for her in the living room."

"We're not saying goodbye," Dan tells Margot gently. "More like 'smell ya later.'"

Sophie cracks the weakest smile.

"Margot said the same thing," Sophie says, wiping at her face with her cuffs. "She says she'll see us again no matter what."

A fresh warmth erupts in my chest, despite feeling like we're being dragged across thorns.

It doesn't take away the crippling fear and uncertainty, no.

But it helps.

And when we get back down to the living room to wait for Margot, so does the sight of her standing in the doorway.

She's everything.

Even now, even after the menacing note, she's not showing an ounce of fear. Not in front of the kids. Not with me.

It makes me want to wrap her up in my arms and never let go.

She flashes a reassuring smile before kneeling next to Sophie.

"Hey, I have something for you. I was going to work on it a little while longer, but with you guys heading out…"

"It's cool. Really." Sophie wipes her nose and sniffles.

Margot unlocks the iPad in her hand and tilts the screen at Sophie, showing off what looks like shoes.

They're still clearly orthopedic, but unlike any pair I've ever seen in her medical supply catalog.

They're light pink with brighter delicate flowers etched along the sides with a white stripe running through them. The color obscures the bulkiness, giving them a sleeker appearance as Margot rotates the 3D model.

"I made this for you. I mean, they're not made-made yet, but the design's ready," she says. "You can have them made to order soon. They use existing ortho shoe specs so they won't have to go through any red tape getting them approved. I emailed a copy to your dad for safekeeping. We just need a manufacturer." She darts me another look, and I flick through my emails where, sure enough, there's an attachment from Margot. "Do you like them?"

Two big tears roll down Sophie's face. Her lips tremble.

"Oh my God! I—yes! I… I can't believe you *made me shoes.*"

She doesn't need to say another word.

"You asked for my help, remember? I'm still no expert in orthopedic shoe design, but I can make them look pretty."

Her face caves in with happy sobs as she throws her arms around Margot's shoulders.

I look at the design in my hands, holding in a breath denser than fog.

Insane.

This gesture's kinder and more motherly than anything

I've seen Daria do in nearly a decade of phantom co-parenting. Sophie's never had anyone go out of their way with her shoes before.

Hell, not even me, because I didn't know how.

I don't think Margot can fathom how huge this is.

Her eyes meet mine over Sophie's shoulder, and I wonder.

Does she know how generous she is?

Does she get that she's an angel who rolled off her cloud?

I fucking don't deserve this through my huffing and puffing and emotionally stunted confusion. But Soph, she's had this coming her whole life.

All I can do is stand there in awe, holding myself together.

"I just want you to love your shoes and love yourself," Margot whispers, leaning back to look Sophie fully in the eyes. "And I want you to *own* them, okay? They're a statement to the world. Every girl deserves a wardrobe that screams pretty."

"Wow! But if my feet get better, can you do shoes for me then too?" Sophie asks shyly.

Margot nods and smiles.

"Of course, honey. Anytime. But let's not keep your dad waiting, okay?"

"We're gonna miss you," Dan says firmly, pushing Sophie out of the way so he can steal a hug. "You staying here with Dad?"

We share another look.

That's something else to figure out, but I let the kids get their goodbyes out first.

"Keep him from doing anything stupid," Dan warns, and Margot laughs.

"Do you think he will?"

"You never know. He's a tough dad but sometimes they're

too brave to know better. They bite off more than they can chew," Dan says, so seriously I haul him back gently.

"Okay, buddy. This Neanderthal says it's time to get in the car."

Their faces harden as they look around the house one more time, like they're still saying some dramatic goodbye in their heads.

I take the opportunity to pull Margot aside.

"Hey." I take her hand, squeezing gently. "Come with us. There are extra seats on the plane. I could buy us tickets right now to go with them."

Her brows knit together as she stares at me. "This is my house, Kane. I'm not done here. With Gramps, I'm so close."

"I know," I say gruffly.

"This person, they're after you, right? The note said it."

And I'm not sure why the fuck I should trust a monster.

I want to drag her to the vehicle and back to New York, but I have no right. This is her inheritance, her house, her life.

It isn't my place. Especially when my presence here has gotten in her way.

"If you won't come with us, head to Portland," I say, almost pleading with her now. "Just for a few days. Enough time to let the clown who left that note know we're gone. You read it," I whisper. "He wants you out of the way so he can face me alone. I'll stay here and watch the house, and wait for—"

She reaches up, grazing my jaw and silencing me.

"You, Kane," she says, "are an adorably dumb Saint."

"Margot—"

"I'm not leaving yet. This is my house, and I'll stick it out until I find whatever Gramps hid behind that glass door. Maybe I'm not Army trained or whatever like you, but we have the security system, and I know this town. I'd be crazy to bow out now."

"Just a few days. Less than a week," I mutter.

It's a losing battle, but I have to try.

"That's a no from me. If you're so determined to come back here and help before some unhinged weirdo follows you home, then so am I."

Damn, I hate her logic.

If there's one thing you learn in the Army, it's knowing when to make a tactical retreat, and that time is now.

"Fine, duchess," I growl, kissing the tip of her nose. "Stay here and check in with me. I'm coming right back."

"I'll be fine. It's just a few hours," she promises.

"Every half hour. Text me, or I'll call the cops," I tell her, holding her gaze until she nods. "I need to wait with them until they're on that jet, but I'll be back ASAP."

She pats my cheek.

"Go," she says. "And when you're done, come back so we can tie this up. Everything."

She doesn't need to elaborate.

I don't want to leave her, but there's no damn choice.

The sooner I get them off to Portland, the quicker I can be back here, ready to face the storm.

"You know I will," I whisper.

With a parting glance, I give her one last kiss.

Then I grab the kids' luggage, lead them outside, and leave her standing in the middle of the living room, watching us from the door.

XXI: HOME ALONE (MARGOT)

*I*n front of Kane and the kids, it was easy to look fearless and chill.

That's what you do when you're a mature adult who gets how important it is to look brave for everybody else.

But alone?

I'm a plucked chicken.

Being on my own doesn't usually bother me, but tonight, it's *terrifying*.

All the doors and windows are locked, of course, but I still patrol the house, triple-checking to make sure they're holding up and haven't mysteriously moved.

Thankfully, Holden did a good job when he'd stop in to check the place, tightening the locks and checking window seals.

"Right down to the last hinge, Miss Blackthorn," he tells me now over the phone.

Yes, you know it's bad when I've called up Gramps' ice-cold former bodyguard for company. I used a made-up loose door as an excuse.

"Anything you need checked again? Say the word, and I

can be there this week. I'd rather earn my keep, seeing how the old man was so generous to keep me paid." His voice is so low—almost scorched—I think he could give Kane competition in the smolder department.

"Holden, no way. What did Ethan tell you last time?" I smile, knowing he's the only one who ever got away with calling PopPop 'old man.'

"Relax." He spits it like it's a cursed word.

"Uh-huh. So you should listen. It's totally gorgeous this fall, why don't you take your daughter out to an orchard or something? Perfect bonding weather, even for a guy who sleeps in his suit."

"I do *not*." He snorts.

"Say, while I've got you, though, you're positive he never mentioned anything weird here? Like, no secret storm shelters, no stained glass? No weird paintings or sculptures with baby shoes?"

"Miss Blackthorn, no. You're being evasive. I can't help you if we're playing this game. When did you decide you were done being the easy one?"

"Hey, man, I'm messing with you. If I need your help, I'll ask." I smile and sigh. "But isn't this better than getting in the middle of Ethan's fake engagement? Or whatever Gramps left for Cleo? I bet that'll be *fun*."

"Unfortunately, yes. Don't make me regret choosing you over your reckless cousin and your punk-ass brother," he snarls. I swallow a laugh, remembering how much trouble they used to cause when we'd stay. "However, come to think of it, you mentioned baby shoes. There was one time."

"Yeah?" I wait, holding my breath.

"It was years ago, back when you were kids. I walked into Mr. Blackthorn's library in Portland with a tray of black tea we'd occasionally share and found him distraught. He had this little mangled clay object, and he was muttering to himself, clearly frustrated."

My heart flips.

"Whoa. What was he doing?"

I hear him drumming his fingers for a second before he answers. "If memory serves, he was sketching it. There was a small book in front of him with drawings, what looked like the little statue from several angles. It was a broken pair of small shoes."

I'm nervous now, and it has nothing to do with the situation here.

"Did he... did he explain what it was all about? Anything to do with my grandmother?" I ask carefully.

"He had his secrets, and this was one more. I never asked, not directly, but he saw the look on my face. And he pulled out a small bottle of whiskey he kept in his drawer and spiked our tea. 'Something to take the edge off being frozen,' he said." Holden pauses, his voice losing its edge. "It was summer. I noticed the phone was slightly lopsided in its cradle—like he'd slammed it down—so I fixed it. Probably another attempt to contact your mother."

"Oh."

My heart dives like an elevator. It wouldn't be the first time Mom hung up on him. But even though I knew it happened, hearing what it was like, from his side—

My throat hurts, thick and raw.

A little girl squeals in the background then, and I hear Holden mutter a few stern words to her.

"Sorry. Regrettably, Miss Blackthorn, that's all I can remember."

"No, that's super helpful. Thanks, Holden. I'll let you go be a dad. If anything else comes up, I'll give you a shout."

I end the call and check my notifications before I start crying over family drama I'll never fix.

But what's up with those little shoes? And what's waiting for me if I do get that glass door open?

The security feed from each camera still shows nothing out of the ordinary.

Small comfort.

To pass the time, which runs slower than molasses, I start cleaning the entire house from top to bottom. It's kind of therapeutic since cleaning has always been a choice.

Growing up, we had hired help who came in every day, keeping the family properties sparkling.

I didn't start doing my own deep cleanings until after college, even when I had my own people.

There's a ritual feel to doing laundry, folding clothes, putting the dishes back in place, and giving the kitchen a good wipe-down.

The movement helps quiet my chattery brain.

After an hour of light stuff, I decide to go all-in, scrubbing the kitchen floor on my hands and knees with a tile cleaner I found under the sink.

The rubber gloves feel cold against my fingers. They keep me from obsessively checking my phone more often than every five or ten minutes.

Still nothing.

At the hour half mark, I text Kane to let him know I'm alive, then dive right back into scrubbing.

Once the floor rivals a mirror, I head into the living room and start wiping down the trim boards, cleaning the windows, and spraying a little fabric cleaner on the furniture.

That pulls up a surprising amount of filth.

Kids are precious and dirty.

I go from room to room, hunting cobwebby corners and spritzing fresh lemon.

Then there's a deafening *snap!*

A twig.

I hope.

Even though I'm on the second floor, I race over to look out the bedroom window.

Predictably, there's nothing.

Just a bitter fall wind tossing the trees around like bones. Branches will easily come off in that wind, which must peak around thirty-mile-per-hour bursts.

God, I'm a mess.

With a shameful sigh, I abandon my last project—sweeping under the bed—and pace through the house one more time.

Seriously, can we keep it together? Just for a little while longer.

I wonder.

It's a struggle not to march through every room with a knife in hand. I'm ninety percent sure I couldn't stab an intruder if I had to, but let's pretend I could.

I might put on a brave face and say all the right things, but when it comes down to it, violence isn't my thing.

"Settle down. We're halfway there and he won't be gone *that* long," I mutter.

It definitely sucks when a girl has to talk herself down from turning into Courage the Cowardly Dog. Watching that cartoon as a kid was way more fun than imagining ghostly mummies and psycho barbers lurking outside in this wind.

I swallow thickly, hating how Kane would laugh if he could see me now.

Another look at the app.

No movement. No people. No cause for concern.

So I lean against the wall, exhaling roughly in the hallway.

I shouldn't have asked Holden about the past when I could've saved it for another day.

But how would PopPop handle this?

Hard to say, but he'd probably not give a crap about some

weirdo threatening him. And not just because he had a brawler like Holden around when he got older.

With his money and influence, I'm realizing he must've had enemies. Maybe even people who would threaten his life.

I mean, the Babins literally committed *arson* on this property, and he still came back. He brought us here as kids.

Was that a giant *fuck you* to anyone who messed with him?

Time to channel a little Leonidas Blackthorn and stop slinking around like a scolded cat.

I head downstairs, find the flashlight in the kitchen drawer, and make sure it turns on.

Yes.

The bright light floods the dimly lit halls.

Just a quick look outside to make sure nothing's blown loose. It can't hurt for peace of mind.

I nod to myself as I step outside and—

Holy crap!

The wind slaps my face, whipping my hair into my eyes. I struggle to brush it back with my fingers so I can see straight.

The lake sounds rough tonight, slapping the shore. A blanket of clouds drift in like stampeding elephants.

Ugh.

Hopefully their flight isn't delayed.

Of course, the kids' safety comes first, but it would really suck if they get tied up at the airport waiting half the night while I'm stuck here alone.

For now, let's not think about it.

Besides, for all I know, the storm is localized and might just graze Bar Harbor.

I ignore the pulsing anxiety as I walk down to the site of the burned gazebo and the old storm shelter before the rain starts pounding.

Since it's been opened before, I'm able to yank the doors wide enough to stare down into the darkness.

They creak like a coffin.

Silly.

It's only scarier now because I'm here alone.

But I have my phone.

I might as well take a quick look.

With one hand braced against the wall, I descend the steps one at a time.

They're steep, but sturdy, and soon I'm at the bottom without breaking my neck.

The same stale scent I noticed before rubs my lungs and I try not to cough. This place needs to be left open one day to air out.

I swing the light around, taking in the old clay pottery figures of my grandparents, half-finished, and all those little shoes on the table.

Why did he leave them like this?

Did Gramps ever come down here much after she died? After the fire?

If he didn't, that would explain the staleness, I guess.

I swear there's a hint of scorched smoke, but it might be my imagination.

Turning the corner to the back wall, behind the stairs, I shine the flashlight on the stained glass.

It's so pretty. The colors glint vividly in the light.

As I admire it, I notice something behind the glass, just a dull blurry shadow.

There must be something inside that cabinet.

I can't tell what it is when I get closer, pointing the beam at the tinted window.

Another painting, maybe? A book? With a small round rock on top of it?

It looks like a few treasures trapped behind there. No way of getting to them without smashing the beautiful glass.

Sigh.

Another family secret waiting, even if it's not the priority tonight.

Does it have anything to do with the shoes that had Gramps so upset? My mind drifts back to Holden's story.

I idly let the light drop to the floor, running a hand through my hair, barely breathing.

My fingers still feel stiff and wrinkly from my cleaning blitz despite wearing gloves the whole time.

I just wish I knew what Gramps was thinking when he left this place behind.

Back when he was alive, I never imagined he had so many layers.

He was just PopPop, a human lighthouse built to weather any storm and shine like the stars through the darkness I've only started to understand.

That darkness was his.

And now the lighthouse is gone.

Here I am, mentally and literally wandering the stormy night, wondering if for just a split second, maybe I can find one last dying ember he left behind.

This can't be unique.

Every family has a few ugly mysteries, sure.

But Blackthorn secrets only burble up to inflict pain.

It's a miracle Ethan put down the bottle and finally chose to fight for his future.

My phone buzzes then, scaring me to death.

Jesus!

I pull it out to send Kane another *hi, I'm not dead* text.

Kane: Kids are on the plane. Just took off and I'm leaving now. Might be slow going in this weather.

Right.

Thunder growls down at me through the open storm doors. I wince.

It's a big enough storm to hit Bar Harbor and snarl any traffic on the small windy backroads to Sully Bay.

Hurry back and stay safe! I send before shoving my phone back in my pocket.

There's a steady pelting rain now.

Pretty much inevitable with clouds this dense, but I didn't think it would hit so quickly.

Time to get moving.

I climb back up the stairs carefully since they're already slick, shielding my face as I look at the sky, which rips open and drops its grief.

Another squall soaks me as I'm fumbling back to the house, making my clothes wet and heavy.

Holy shit, this sucks.

I'm a shivering mess by the time I go pounding through the front door, drenched and tingling from the cold.

I'm so disoriented I don't notice it at first.

The pantry door half-open.

The small, slightly hunched shadow moving out of it.

I only realize Viola Babin is in the house when I smell the smoke.

She stops by the wall in front of me, a glowing cigarette in one hand and a thick wooden club in the other.

Her hair is dry.

She must've got here before the sky split, and there's a hard darkness in her eyes so much worse than the restless night.

Distant, yet determined.

A little sad.

A lot cruel.

"Awful night for some justice, don't ya think?" she hisses.

I make a strangled sound, scrambling back into the hallway until I hit the wall in the mudroom.

"Stay back!" I throw out my hands, doing my best to sound scary as I look around desperately for somewhere to run—or at least for a weapon.

What did she say?

Justice?

There's a nasty smirk on her lips, like she hates the taste of the smoke she's inhaling, but she needs it anyway like a vampire needs blood.

And I'd guess she needs something darker and thicker than nicotine tonight.

My lungs stop working.

Even worse, she's blocking me from the kitchen, reducing my chances of grabbing anything useful.

Not good.

Oh, sure, I could make a run for it and try to sprint around her, but there's no guarantee I'll get past before she starts swinging that club at my head.

Also, I doubt she's alone.

If she's here, odds are Joseph Babin isn't far behind.

She shifts the club in her hand, smacking it against her palm as I stare at her.

If she hits me with that thing, it's going to break bones. A head strike could kill me.

She's not a large woman, but she's wiry and lean from years working the blueberry fields.

One good hit and it's lights out. Or at least so much blistering pain I'll wish I was unconscious.

Crap, crap.

Last I checked, Kane has at least thirty minutes until he's home. Maybe more in this mess outside.

Another rainy gust shakes the window, reminding me how screwed I am, and Viola smiles.

I can't stand it, I have to look away.

Just in time to see movement outside the window.

A bigger silhouette stalking the darkness, and I think there's something bigger and more deadly in his hands.

A baseball bat? A rifle?

Shit.

So that's where Joseph is, then.

Not in the kitchen. Not yet.

But in less than a minute...

What are they *doing* here? What do they want? They wouldn't be crazy enough to just kill me in cold blood... would they?

I don't realize I'm straining forward, my body reacting faster than my brain, searching for a way around her.

"Don't even think about it, missy," Viola snaps, striding closer. "I can read you like a book. Let's just say you did get a knife, what do you think you're gonna do? Gut me like a fish?" She holds up her club again, brandishing it. "Don't bother. It'll only make it worse if you wanna go out kicking like a scared rabbit."

My breath stalls.

"What do you want?" I force out.

She just sucks her cheek as thunder vibrates the house.

"Like I said, awful night for this, but I bet this old place will still burn in the rain with enough good kindling."

"*Burn.*" I echo it without meaning to. "Like the gazebo, you mean."

She throws her head back and laughs, an evil, tinny sound.

"Oh, so someone blabbed about that, huh?" She gives me another carnivorous smile, stepping forward so I'm forced to back up, closer to the door. But there's nowhere left for me to go with Joseph outside. "Half the folks in town thought we were behind it. But there was no proof, was there? Things are harder now, but not when you're smart. Those fancy cameras you put up don't work half as well as you think."

Oh my God.

I don't even know if they knocked out the one by the door or if I was too distracted by the storm to notice.

There'll *be* proof this time, if I have anything to say about it.

Only, that hinges on survival first. I have zero doubt she intends to leave me beaten or dead to burn up with the house.

My phone hums in my pocket, but with that club in her hand, I don't dare reach for it.

My heart hammers in my throat, so fast it's sickening.

Every time the wind moans, I think it's Joseph lighting a fire.

But he wouldn't do it yet.

Not with his wife still inside.

"Why?" I whisper. "Why get this crazy over—"

"Crazy? Girl, it's been a long time coming. You know what that's like, spending your whole life staring at land that was stolen by some rich cockadoodie who don't even live here? Tonight, we're putting it right. We're reclaiming what's always been *ours*." She stares straight through me. I keep my eyes fixed on the club in her hand. "The storm'll prevent anyone from coming to the rescue, knowing how bad the cops get tied up on nights like this."

The worst part is, she's right.

Any small-town police force will be busy with accidents and cars run off the road. There won't be anyone on the little road by the lake house. No one will notice the blaze and call it in until the house is toast.

That is, unless I can get in touch with someone, which I can't without my phone.

She's closer now, almost pinning me against the wall.

Then lightning flashes, and I see my chance.

Screaming, I rush forward, darting under her arm as I plow into her.

Maybe she's stronger, but I'm younger and faster.

I knock her off-kilter for the tiniest second.

Just enough time to swerve, avoiding her club.

Then I go pounding through the kitchen, the living room, and then beyond to the study.

A few more steps. Come on! Come on!

I slam the door shut behind me, turning the lock.

Behind it, Viola howls with rage.

Her hateful scream merges with the pounding storm, even when she starts slamming her fists against the door.

Whatever state the rest of the place is in, the doors are solid slabs.

Thanks, Gramps and Holden.

At least there are makeshift weapons in here.

I look around wildly.

Antique chairs, but they're the old-fashioned kind, way too heavy for me to lug around and throw easily.

A solid lamp, maybe. A club of my own.

And beside it, on the desk, I see Dan's little drummer boy from the fort. He must've left it behind in the rush to pack up and leave.

I feel the big key on the back, and I start winding it as she hisses obscenities, trying her best to break down the door.

All I need is a quick distraction.

Something to draw her attention for a few seconds, and I'll have the upper hand. That lamp is solid brass and must weigh ten pounds.

One good swing and she'll go down.

The door shakes. Hinges groan as her kicks get louder.

The wind rattles the old glass window behind.

My hands are shaking, but I've never been more ready in my life.

"You feisty little bitch! Get back here!" Viola shrieks, slamming her boot at the door again, the wood creaking under the strain. The hinges wrench, only held on by a few loose screws. "I was gonna make it quick, but now you'll *pay*!"

Drummer boy, let's go!

I set him down a couple feet in front of the door and unplug the lamp, hoisting it in my hand as I stand to one side. I'll be behind the door when it breaks open.

The little metal figure bangs his drums as he marches forward, just as the door gives one last miserable *crack!*

Viola charges through it like a mad horse.

She instantly sees the tiny moving figure in the middle of the floor and stops, this puzzled look on her face.

Bingo!

I raise the lamp, ready to wait one more second until she's in range, but she pitches forward before I swing.

Huh?

She crashes down on top of the toy and there's a metallic crunch.

What happened? With the lamp still clutched in my hands, I turn to the large, dark figure in the doorway.

"Kane!" I gush out, running forward, relief coursing through me. "Oh, thank God. I didn't think you'd be back yet. Viola and Joseph, they're planning to..." I trail off as lightning flashes in the window, revealing his face.

Not Kane.

"Lee?" I whisper, fumbling for the light switch and flicking it on. The clear view only proves what I knew—it's Lee Glazkov, the ceramics guy.

I don't understand.

"What are you doing here?" I croak. My voice has rusted shut.

Instead of smiling, he looks at me coldly. No hint of the same warmth whatsoever at the craft fair or the museum.

No smile.

No compassion.

No relief that I'm okay even though he just whacked Viola Babin to the floor.

He had to know she was trying to hurt me.

I'm so confused.

"You know, Miss Margot," he says flatly, "you really should have left with the kids when I told you."

Oh no.

Oh *fuck* no.

"You... you left the note?" I whisper, backing away, horror gripping my throat.

"I thought I made myself clear, yes. You *and* the kids had to leave. They're gone, yet you're still here." There's a sadness in his tone that scares me.

"But what do you want? Why are you doing this?" My voice rises.

With a disinterested sigh, he nudges a limp Viola away with the toe of his boot.

"I warned you, didn't I? Just look at this. You and your 'friends' have made my life very, very complicated."

Friends.

Does that mean he found Joseph, too?

But what the hell does he want with me?

I have to warn Kane.

His eyes flicker darkly the second I reach into my pocket, touching my phone.

His thin, vacant smile tells me one thing: he's no savior, and the Babins were the easiest part of this nightmare.

XXII: HOME TURF (KANE)

*T*his fucking storm.

Between the slanted rain and shrieking wind, the traffic getting out of Bar Harbor has slowed to a crawl.

I tap my fingers on the steering wheel, impatiently checking my phone every few seconds.

It hasn't been thirty minutes since Margot last texted. No need to worry yet.

Fuck, I should've left sooner.

But it was too important to see the kids off until their plane was in the air. Sophie can be a nervous flier, especially without me there.

For now, they're safe.

Mom will meet them as soon as they get to Portland, and there's a flight attendant keeping an eye on them until they do.

Meanwhile, Margot's alone at that house, and I'm still nearly an hour away, if my Google Maps are accurate.

Damn.

Call it illogical and I won't disagree.

She was sure she'd be fine, but she doesn't know what this stalker freak might be capable of.

Honestly, neither do I, and that's the problem.

You can't prepare for a shit scenario when there's too much uncertainty.

Better the devil you *know*. There's a reason they say it.

How I wish I knew this fucking devil.

Traffic inches forward, red lights blazing through the sheeting rain and horns blaring every time a car tries to cut through the snaking line of vehicles.

Time becomes excruciating.

I listen idly to the radio with a single-minded focus, trying to tune into the local Sully Bay station just in case there's any news about the storm.

I don't know what I'm expecting, but not knowing drives me berserk.

This person wants me. Not Margot.

She's not the target.

She's safe.

I repeat that mantra until it's etched into my brain. If only that made me believe it.

Still, she's a sensible girl. She's not Daria and she won't leave the doors unlocked.

Once on a family trip, my ex did exactly that, and we came back to our vacation rental with a beach bum stoner crashing in our bed.

Margot isn't that stupid.

I can see her making the rounds, glued to her phone for any notification hinting trouble.

Everything's fine.

If only I could convince my gut.

And at the thirty-minute mark when she should've texted me passes, I do my damnedest not to panic and try mudding it through the ditch.

She's probably watching TV, you jumpy fuck.

Working on more shoe designs.

Cooking something delicious that'll punch me in the nose the second I get back.

Yeah, that's the sort of thing she'd do because my woman has a spine.

That doesn't stop me when I can't stand the radio silence a second longer.

I punch out a quick message asking for an update.

Last message from her was forty-three minutes ago.

That could mean nothing.

She probably put it down while she was cleaning or cooking or just lost track of time.

After all, I told her I was leaving, and the traffic would suck.

All thanks to this dick-dragging weather.

Another ten minutes limp by and she doesn't message me back.

Shit.

I'm a patient man, but everyone has their limits.

So I call her, wrenching my way around a car and creeping along the edge of the asphalt in a dangerous sprint that gains me a few extra feet of road.

The call goes straight to voicemail.

I start talking before the beep, but there's a catch like someone picks up.

"Margot?" Nothing. "Margot? You're scaring me, woman."

Static.

A burst of mindless distortion, and then two distant voices.

I can't make out the words, but there's a man's voice, and a higher-pitched one that has to be her.

A scream.

Definitely Margot.

My heart leaps up my throat.

"Please." She's pleading and I grit my teeth, tightening my fingers on the wheel as I wrench it to one side, narrowly avoiding a collision as I swing around another car.

"Shut it," a man growls, and the call disconnects.

Shit. Shit!

All this time, I've tried to convince myself she's okay, when she's actually in very real danger.

I tell Siri to call the police. It takes forever to connect, minutes of the connection glitching.

Will this fucking traffic *ever* let up?

I pound the horn with my fist, slowly muscling through the wall of cars in front of me.

"Hello… what's the location of your emergency?" The dispatcher's voice is still distorted when I finally connect.

"Sully Bay, Fleet Street. My girlfriend's being assaulted," I snarl, describing it the best way I can.

"Can you repeat that, sir? I'm sorry. Due to the weather, there's been a high number of incidents tonight and communication issues—"

I spit the full address as calmly as I can, which is about as chill as a raging moose.

"Copy that," he says quickly. "I'll get someone out there soon. Please be advised all our local officers are tied up with accidents, so officers will come from the next town over."

"Next town? Fuck." I close my eyes, knowing that probably means Bar Harbor. "ETA?"

"Forty minutes. I'm patching through the details now."

Far too goddamned long.

"Thanks," I clip and disconnect, focusing on cutting through the traffic, one hand hovering over my horn.

Give me ten tickets, suspend my license, I don't care.

As long as I get to the fucking house.

Knowing she's in trouble glazes my blood. I never got a chance to tell her—

No.

No, you can't afford to get emotional now.

Long dormant instincts from half a lifetime ago in uniform leap up and bite me in the ass.

You never forget.

Never, never, and not when it's more than your life on the line.

I swear, if I make it in time—if God is that kind—if I'm angry and cruel enough to keep her safe, if I have my chance to dismember the snake threatening her, I'll never hesitate again.

I'll never hold back.

I'll never let Margot Blackthorn out of my sight without her knowing she's madly and truly loved.

* * *

IT TAKES AN ETERNITY, but eventually I'm squealing down the road to the lake, my wipers slashing hopelessly at the rain.

Instead of rocketing up the driveway, I park by the side of the road at the end. I reach into the back seat for a loose hammer on the floor I used on the dock.

Not a good weapon, but for now I'll have to improvise.

The rain smacks me in the face, soaking me as I prowl to the front door.

My eyes slowly adjust from the glare of my headlights, and I maneuver carefully.

Someone's still in there with Margot.

They sure as hell won't leave here alive if they've hurt her.

A few lights in the house are on, blazing against the dull night, mostly upstairs.

No sign of anyone near the windows.

The curtains are open, and I can see from this angle that her bedroom window is cracked, though there's no light inside.

Moving through the gloom, I approach the porch from the side. Gnarled bushes scrape my pants.

I see the front door cracked open and a lamp on, though from this angle, I can't see inside.

My gut knots.

Margot would never leave the front door open, especially in this situation.

I stop to listen, holding my breath. I can't make out anything besides rain hammering the house.

I need to get closer, dammit.

Wind whips around the house as I stalk across the porch, keeping out of view and—

Fuck, that's a smear of blood.

Like dark ink against the light wood, already being washed away by the rain.

A shadow moves in front of me, all slow, halting motion and a low curse.

I'm on them before I can make out who.

Joseph Babin, I realize a second later.

He's staggering along the porch like he's been thrashed within an inch of his life.

A second later, I have his collar in my fist and I've hurled him against the house. In the near darkness, I can just see the bleary whites of his eyes.

"W-wait," he says hoarsely, scratching at my wrist. "Wait!"

"Fuck you." I push my face close to his. "What the *hell* are you doing here? Where is she?"

His breath smells foul. I don't bother hiding my disgust.

He looks like he's about to piss himself.

I hope he's scared for his pathetic life. It's very much

hanging in the balance right now, depending on what he says next.

"It... it wasn't me," he gurgles. His fingers shake weakly as he tries to free his wrist. "I didn't do it. Please, you have to—"

"Why are you here, asshole? Where's Margot? Tell me!" I shake him like a piñata.

He turns his head slightly, and I see the bloody gash at the back, like someone smacked him with blunt force.

Relief washes through me.

If he was damn near crawling across the porch, that means the blood I saw is his, not Margot's.

"I don't know," he babbles. "I'm telling you, I-I... I didn't do anything."

"Did she do that? Did Margot hit you?" I glare at him, and when he doesn't answer, I shake him again. "Fucking talk!"

"Wha—no! No, she never saw me. It was the other man."

"What man?" I growl.

He shakes his head again, mouth opening and closing like a stunned fish out of water.

Goddamn.

The rain pounds on, spraying his face, but I don't give a flying fuck about his comfort.

I want answers to the only question that matters.

And if he's here at all, it can't mean anything good. I'm sure his evil sneak of a wife will be slinking around here somewhere, too.

But that's not what concerns me most—what other fucking *man* is he talking about?

The man who left the note?

The man who wanted Margot and the kids gone?

I rear back and power-slam Joseph into the wall again until his head bounces.

"Where is she?" I bite off. "You have five seconds. Then you'll wish I wasn't carrying this hammer."

"That man, he's got her!" he snarls. Fear flickers in his eyes now, his face hollowed out like a jack-o'-lantern past its prime. "Storm cellar, I think. Last place I saw them."

Fuck me.

Without a second glance, I toss him on the porch face-first and go sprinting through the sleeting rain, rocketing toward that ominous hole in the ground.

XXIII: HOMESICK (MARGOT)

Twenty Minutes Earlier

$\mathcal{I}$ think my kidnapper might be the dumbest man alive for thinking I'd go out easy.

The second Lee grabs me, my fight instinct wakes up.

There's no one close enough to hear me, but I scream my lungs out anyway.

I read somewhere once that you can't always scream if stress puts you in a choke hold. That's why people carry around whistles, I suppose.

Whatever the science—and I am *stressed*—I don't have any problem making noise.

Piercing, earsplitting, eagle screech loud.

He swears and grabs my arms, wrenching them behind my back.

I throw myself down, resisting.

And I'd keep doing it, if only his boot didn't find my stomach.

Blinding pain.

I hate it as much as I hate him because it smothers my resistance.

The next few minutes are a blur as he drags me through the house and out into the rain.

We almost trip over the limp, groaning body of Joseph Babin. He's alive, but who knows for how long.

Even with my stomach in sick knots, churning, I don't give up.

Raw, animal instinct takes over, fear and adrenaline swirling in a lethal cocktail until I'm acting on sheer impulse without any higher thought.

He's taking me to the cellar, into the damp and darkness.

No!

I bite his arm. Claw at his hands.

Attack, attack, attack like a crazed wolverine, wherever I can find some skin to bruise or bloody.

I'm on the ground now, barely avoiding his feet as he tries to crush my skull.

Writhing.

Screaming.

His boot slams into my ribs and presses down, knocking the wind from my lungs.

Only when I'm truly cornered, that's when I start begging.

It's not a conscious decision, but it's inevitable as he reaches down, growling, and starts lugging me toward the storm shelter again. I wonder if he saw me emerge earlier or if he found it when he came creeping around.

"Enough," he snarls, digging his fingers into my arm.

Galaxies of nerves light up in agony.

"Stop, please!" I strangle out into the storm. My wet hair slaps my face, the wind tossing it into my mouth as I try to breathe. "Please, just let me go."

"Shut the fuck up, little girl," he snarls as he releases me with one hand to reach down for the shelter doors.

I take the opportunity to buck free. He curses as he catches my arm and swings me back around.

I collide with his leg.

Copper explodes in my mouth. I bite my tongue.

Between the blood and that savage kick to my belly earlier, I'm going to be sick.

Holy shit, can this *get* any worse?

"Knock it off. Get down there," he orders, pushing me toward the steps.

Oh, God.

They're still slick from the rain, and I almost slip, catching myself against the damp wall.

It's the first time he's let me have any space.

I'm not done yet.

I know I can't beat him in a fight, not when I'm hurt and weakened like this, so I grab my phone.

There's a call coming through and I swipe to answer as I stumble forward into the darkness. I mute it just in time.

Kane.

He must be worried sick, and he should be.

I want to cry with relief, but the second I hear his voice, Lee will know the cops are on their way.

Still, I press the screen against my chest so that square of light doesn't give me away.

Lee has his own flashlight, and he slams the door behind him, shutting us both in the killing darkness. The storm's roar dims.

There's something glinting and metal in his other hand —a gun?

Not that surprising, really, even as my bruised stomach drops to my knees.

I don't know why he didn't use it before, but there's no denying this could get really messy, really fast.

I regret answering Kane's call now.

He can't help me with this, and all I'm doing is luring a selfless single father to his death.

Fresh nausea flips my stomach over.

"Please." I turn to face him again.

"Shut it," he growls, walking toward me.

I disconnect the call a split second before my knees buckle and I'm dry heaving.

Miraculously, I don't vomit.

God, I need air.

My breath comes too fast, too loud, echoing in the small space as he marches down the steps toward me. His gun points through me, aiming at my future grave down here.

"You finally get it out of your system?" We lock eyes. "Not another peep from you, princess. I don't have the time or patience. You've made me very late."

It's the way he stares at me through the shadows, I think.

Those eyes, they aren't human.

They're so empty.

Seriously, how can this be the same guy who flirted with me? Who sold us his lovely plates and mugs we've used for meals?

Why has he gone total psycho?

"Please," I whisper, my voice cracking pathetically. "Please, don't—"

His gun comes up to my face and clicks.

I wince.

"Maybe you didn't hear me when I said 'shut it' before?" He bares his teeth. "Since you've insisted on being part of this, Miss Blackthorn, I'll let him see you alive again. But only if you're silent." He glances down to where I'm still clutching the phone against my chest, and his expression hardens. "And you'll hand that over. Right now."

I don't mean to scream when he rips it from my hands, hurling it down and stomping the screen, but I can't help it.

My only connection to the world, obliterated before my eyes.

I suck my bleeding lip, staring at the smashed glass and metal bits.

His gun never flinches, so ready to end my life in a heartbeat. I slump against the floor, shivering and cold.

I look back up at him, replaying his sinister words.

"Part of what? What did I do to you?" I whisper bitterly.

"Don't play dumb with me. You can't be that stupid."

"What... what's this about? Money? Is that it? Because I have that. If you'll forget about me and Kane, I can fork over whatever you want. I know about crypto, you can have it in a few hours. Totally anonymously. You can go start over on the other side of the world if you just—"

"No! Fuck you and your money." Suddenly he's too close, growling in my face, the barrel of the gun biting my cheek with a freezing sting that makes me jump. "I know this is news to a spoiled brat like you, but there's more to life than the billions you've robbed from everyone else. You're just like *him*."

His voice drips hate.

I don't need to ask.

I don't dare answer.

I just hold myself as still as I can, willing myself to become a disembodied lump of clay, no different from the little shoes abandoned on the worktable.

When one wrong move could leave you dead, sometimes it's best not to play at all.

Lee pulls back with a vicious smirk. His face looks like a

mask on a mannequin, no one and nothing behind those cruel grey eyes.

I'm just a messy complication to him. Not a sworn enemy.

Just a nuisance he didn't plan for.

He isn't even enjoying my horror. He's sizing me up, calculating how fast he can dispose of me so he can get back to the real mission.

"No wonder you wound up with Kane Saint," he grinds out.

"We're not—" I stop because there's no point in lying. "What does it matter? Why is that so awful?"

"Why do you think, princess?"

Oh my God, Kane.

Kane.

I start shivering. He knows I'm in trouble. The cops might be on their way right now, but between the storm and the madman pointing a gun at my head…

Does it matter?

I swallow more blood reluctantly.

This place is so deep in the ground the walls are probably soundproof. No way anyone hears anything, if I'm still alive by the time they—

Shit.

Shit!

I need to think fast. Delay him from pulling that trigger.

What if the best thing to do is to keep the devil talking?

Listen to his venom, his threats and promises, his deranged grudge against a man who couldn't have possibly done anything to drive him to violence.

"Why are you here?" I whisper when he takes a few steps away, slowly studying the abandoned art, the small glass door.

Enough space so I can breathe.

"To right a wrong," he whispers darkly before facing me again.

"What's wrong? What did Kane do to you?" I shake my head, showing my confusion. "Did you know him in his hockey days?"

"Hockey?" Surprise flashes across his face before that lifeless mask drops again. "He really didn't tell you, did he?"

"Jesus, no. Please. Help me understand."

He hesitates, fondling the gun with his free hand before he drops it at his side.

"Kane Saint took my life." He slides down the wall in front of the stairs, gun held more loosely now but still pointed at me. "As soon as his company launched that fucking software, I was out of a job in months. My clients, ghosting overnight. I had to limp back to the ceramics work I did in college before I ever consulted on a multimillion-dollar home. And no one buys this shit—not nearly enough to keep food on the table, much less live."

Oh, OptiSynth.

I should've guessed.

Because Kane gave me a very good idea how many lives were thrown into turmoil with the corporate betrayal.

Still, I didn't think too deep. I couldn't visualize how much it must've wrecked good, hardworking, talented people on the ground.

And some of them were clearly unstable.

Neither of us could've guessed how deep the damage went.

Yet here it is, all sharp teeth, ready to tear through me, through Kane, through the *kids.*

I draw in another deep, shaky breath.

It's all I can do to keep from breaking down on the spot.

"I was at the top of my field," he whispers, lost in his own mind. "My work won awards. I made homes out of blank slates for rich people like you. Years of service, many awards—and when I had a chance to sign on to a new pilot program in its testing phase that promised to make everything I do faster and better, how could I say no? And even if I had, there was no stopping the inevitable. My career was destined to die. A sacrifice for the gods of AI."

Finally, a spark.

Something human.

Something hurt.

Something dangerous.

I believe him, too.

I believe he was the rock star he claims to be because he's taken this so personally. And if his ceramics weren't paying the bills, he didn't skimp on the quality. They have this attention to detail that's so rare.

Crazy or not, the man is gifted—and now that gift is useless.

All because he was born in the wrong time.

All because we live in a time where art can be fabricated by an algorithm.

"I'm sorry," I whisper, trying to find sympathy. "I really am. You didn't deserve that, Lee, but you can't believe it justifies this. Don't you see? You can't put that broken piece of your life back together by carving away someone else's."

"Like hell." He snarls, flicking the gun up again. "What do you know? Kane Saint's company took my soul. He took it, he used my work to train his beast. Just coaxed it into his palm like a butterfly and then he *squashed* it." He makes a fist, rattling it until I see the veins bulge up his arm. "And all I could do—all I could fucking do—was watch it get murdered in slow motion. Gone in a few weeks. All so heart and soul and beauty could be replaced by a zombie running on a prompt. It's not just a crime against me, Miss Blackthorn. It's an atrocity against humanity—and it's up to me to make it right, starting tonight."

Yikes.

The last piece clicks into place.

Robin Hood level delusions of grandeur.

There's nothing worse than when someone believes they're the victim, taking up a noble cause.

It's the kind of thought that creates assassins, tyrants, and terrorists.

I bite my lip so hard it hurts, realizing I'm face-to-face with a loose cannon.

"And you know what happened next?" he growls, lowering his gun again and pacing the small space. The wind whistles overhead, howling against the doors above. "My whole fucking *life* imploded."

"I'm sorry," I whisper, but he's not looking at me anymore, too lost in his own shredded ego.

Then his face twists and there's more than tormented rage.

"The people who were *supposed* to care—friends I knew for years—they blamed me for feeding my work into the training engine."

Oh, no.

I see it now, the picture he's painting. The poor artist whose life work has been destroyed, transformed into a hated laughingstock on top of it.

"My wife." His voice scrapes like rust. "When I needed her most, she told me she couldn't deal with it anymore—with *me*. She took the kids. And guess what, princess? The courts sided with her. No visitation rights. They said I was out of work. They called me unstable." He spits on the floor.

"That's awful," I say. *Awful and a hundred percent true.*

His gaze snaps back to me.

"That's nothing coming from you. You crawled into his

bed. You played house with him, one big happy family after he destroyed mine." He swings the flashlight, illuminating his face for a heartbeat. Not so empty anymore. There's a crazed, violent spark in his eyes. "But maybe you sticking around isn't an annoying mistake. What if it's karma?"

I don't know if he's seeing me or my dead body.

It's terrifying, watching him unravel more by the second.

He's not remotely healthy.

It's not hard to see why his wife must have fled. I'm sure the income and social humiliation didn't help, but the mild-mannered interior designer and dad turned dangerous.

He became *consumed*.

All that killer obsession fixed on Kane and anyone close to him by default.

Not the company.

Not the executives or investors who decided to twist their own founding vision.

That poor woman must've been so scared for their kids if he started lashing out like this.

There's no room for revenge in any relationship.

Holding my breath, I move slowly, pushing my hands up in front of me as I stand haltingly. I treat him like the unpredictable wild animal I don't dare frighten.

"What are you doing? Don't move!" he screams.

"My leg was cramped. Sorry. I'm staying right here." I press my back against the wall. *Not a threat, not a threat.* "It sounds like you've had it super rough."

"Yeah, well…" He scratches his neck. "It never would've happened if it wasn't for that money-grubbing jockstrop bringing in enough cash to turn OptiSynth into a monster. He was the face of it, you know. The one they trotted out to bring more investors in. Dumb fucking ice-freak can't be good for much else."

I nod, inwardly wincing.

"He fed the monster. He brought it to life. He robbed us blind!" His gun jabs the air and I jump. "Fuck, if he hadn't gotten all the wrong people on board, if it hadn't launched, I wouldn't be ruined. At least, I wouldn't have been tricked into slashing my own throat. And not just me. So many people, kids just starting out who'll never get to live off their creativity. The children, lifeless, and their children's children."

...is he sobbing now?

This man is a human land mine.

Trembling, he wipes his face.

"This... this isn't my revenge. I'm not that selfish," he whispers, shaking his head. "No. It's collective vengeance. I'm just the instrument. The moral arrow always bends this way, you know. Justice. And sometimes justice can be very, very painful."

Justice.

It's creepy how he echoes Viola's favorite word of the day.

I don't know how much longer I can keep a straight face, but I have to try.

For Kane.

For the kids.

For my life.

"Lee," I whisper, keeping my voice low like he's a stray dog I'm trying to coax from the corner. "Listen to me, okay? Kane told me everything."

"I bet he did. Did he also tell you how he abandoned us after they picked our bones clean? Did you know he had conference calls with artists in the pilot, dozens of us?" He curls his lip, teeth glinting white in the the flashlight. "Were you impressed how he made his money?"

"It's not like that."

"Bullshit! He didn't give a flying fuck what happened to

me or anyone else. He was just in it to eat and run. Now, he'll taste lead."

"That's not fair!" I throw back.

If there's one thing I've learned from living with Kane, it's that he doesn't flaunt his wealth.

He doesn't fear getting his hands dirty doing things most people with his money would hire folks for.

If I had to guess, he cares more about the kids' college funds than whatever big nest egg he has sitting with a wealth manager.

"You still think I'm the villain, don't you?" Lee snorts roughly, leaning forward, gun hanging loosely in his fingers as he takes my chin in his other hand and stares down at me with hollow eyes again. "Just because I'm the one holding the gun?"

"I don't think you're a villain, Lee."

"Fuck yourself, princess. After I've dealt with your boyfriend, you'll see. I'll turn myself in. Guys like me get a lot of fans in prison. I don't care about winding up behind bars. I hate violence."

Oh, I wish he hated it now.

I reach up to touch his wrist, and he releases me.

My chin throbs from his grip, another bruise guaranteed.

"Kane didn't know about the software replacing people until it was too late," I venture, rubbing my chin. "He didn't run away. He left because the other people wouldn't listen. The way they screwed you over broke him. Honestly. He's been beating himself up ever since."

"Liar," Lee spits. "You expect me to believe that?"

Up comes the gun again.

My palms sweat furiously and my pulse rocks my bones.

If I push too hard, he could kill me before I can blink.

After all, what does he have left to lose?

His life is in shambles.

And if he's surrendering when it's done, he's already expecting a life sentence. Prison. What's a little more for one more murder?

I can't win.

But I can't give up, either.

"Whether you believe me or not, Kane didn't know what happened until it was too late to stop it. Then he walked out when there was nothing more he could do. He's almost as mad about it as you are. You should've seen him when he told me about it—it *killed* him to be part of something that disgusting."

"He *was* responsible."

"Not for making the calls. They decided to make the AI a replacement rather than a tool, not him. The software was meant to help designers originally. You know that, or you never would've joined."

"You know nothing!" Lee slams his fist against the wall, scarily close to my head.

That shuts me up.

"You don't get it. You can't. You won't. The world must know that *no one* is safe from this anti-human monstrosity. Not while it's in the hands of people like Kane Saint." His words are mangled, his voice torn. "It's an abomination. No matter how rich or famous or powerful, there must be consequences. Saint will help me demonstrate that."

"Demonstrate what? That you have a vendetta?"

His face curdles.

"People will understand why. It's time the world started standing up for artists rather than fucking billionaire tech lords."

"Look, I agree with you," I say desperately, the tears building behind my eyes. Crying won't help anything, but I'm only human. "I'm sort of an artist too. I design shoes. I've been feeling the pressure from AI myself, even when I use it.

The way it invades your creativity and slowly takes over, it's *wrong*."

"If you know all that," he says, staring me down, "then why are you siding with Kane Saint? Are you that goddamned dick-matized?"

At least he isn't looking at me like he wants to set me on fire now.

I think I'm getting through to him.

The rough brick scrapes my hands as I tuck them behind my back.

Keep looking, dude. I'm not a threat.

"Because I believe him when he says he's not responsible," I say. "Kane is on *your* side, and if you want to make a stand against OptiSynth for ripping you off, I think he'll help you. They called him once, asking for a favor, and he was so angry... I've never seen him like that. He's a good man. He doesn't want it to be like this. But Lee, this isn't the way. You need lawyers, not bullets. Not blood."

He stares at me for a few more seconds, the flashlight fixed on my face, blinding me.

Please, please believe me.

"I wonder, did he give you this little script?" he asks at last. I want to cry. "Or did you come up with it on the spot? Maybe they should've hired you for PR, Miss Blackthorn."

"This isn't a stunt—"

"Just shut up. Shut the fuck up, and I won't need to hurt you. Believe it or not, I don't want to. I'm not bloodthirsty. I'm a peaceful person. But if you defend Kane Saint one more time—if you keep making excuses—they'll have to write your obituary next to his."

I shake my head, feeling my face screw up.

"Please, you don't have to kill him."

"I do, I do." His voice is impassive, freed from the passion from before. "That's what I came here to do and there's no turning back. I can't buy my way out of this like a Blackthorn."

That's it then.

The only question is if I die with Kane.

Then the storm door flies open, tossing in the wind.

Lee whips around, gun swinging at the opening.

There's nothing there.

Just indifferent rain and churning grey clouds and the dull growl of thunder, though the rain looks lighter than before. A faint patter on the steps rather than a death drum.

I press a hand against my chest, trying to breathe.

"Who's there?" Lee calls, unsure, inching closer to the stairs. He has the gun in both hands now, trained at the patch of restless sky.

The dim light shows off my grandmother's statue, and I stare at it, grounding myself and trying to breathe.

Lee stays preoccupied with whoever lifted the door.

Someone must've yanked it open.

There's a reason this is a storm shelter. It might be old with rusted hinges, but no wind short of a nor'easter is hauling one of those heavy doors open.

"I'm warning you!" Lee barks at the sky. "I'm armed and I'm not afraid to shoot."

Come on, think.

Think while he's distracted.

Could I even lift the statue? What about a lump of little shoes? Or would Lee notice and shoot me first?

A real possibility, but I can't just stand here.

Especially if Kane's up there, unarmed.

I can't bear it if rescuing me gets him shot and killed.

I *have* to try.

So I peel away from the wall slowly, slinking toward the worktable as Lee treads up the stairs carefully. He's too high to see me now without looking down, all his attention fixed on whatever's waiting outside.

But what if it's not Kane?

The Babins probably aren't dead.

Lee beaned Viola on the head pretty bad, but how long will she be conked out? Maybe she's already back on the prowl, lurking with her club and a thirst for revenge.

God, I hope not.

I'm done with this monster of the week thing tonight.

Also, I don't want her to die, even if she's an awful, deranged woman.

Lee reaches the top of the stairs and pokes his head up into the night.

I'm closing in, ready to reach for the statue and test its massive weight, when a hammer flies past him and clatters down the stairs, breaking off a chunk of concrete.

I stumble back, narrowly avoiding the impact as it spins by my feet. There's barely a second to glance at it.

What the—

Lee fires.

"Kane!" I shriek.

Because Viola wouldn't bring a hammer to a gunfight.

My gut knows.

And if anything happens to that brave man, I'll never forgive myself.

When he hears my voice, Lee whirls around and sprays hellfire.

But I'm already flat on the ground before the bullets come zinging overhead.

Behind me, there's a deafening crack. A shot goes bouncing around the room.

The sound of shattered glass.

Fine tinted shards explode like confetti as I scramble to cover my face from getting sliced.

When I open my eyes, I'm still in disbelief.

A blurry shadow cannonballs Lee with a primal roar.

Two men go down like lions, snarling and tossing, two tornadoes of limbs at war.

Kane's on top—for now—crashing his fists into Lee's face.

Then Lee flips him over and slams an elbow into Kane's ribs.

Oh, no.

Kane grunts with pain, and I cover my face again.

Neither of them notice the glass shards under them. There's a larger fragment by my hand, about the size of a spoon.

I reach out to grab it, but it falls apart in my fingers, the fine cracks split through it giving way.

So much for an easy weapon.

Then Kane levers up and throws Lee into the brick wall with so much force it feels like the whole space trembles.

Lee's face smacks the wall with a sickening *thud*, but he pulls back, twisted and bleeding.

Just in time to jab his thumb into Kane's wrist, breaking his hold.

I can't stand this.

My fingers tremble over my eyes as I look between them, wondering how I can jump in to help.

But it's too late.

Lee's gun swings up, a death promise aimed at Kane.

I'm about to scream, but Kane knocks his arm aside and punches him in the face so hard something cracks.

Do something! Before they kill each other.

My pulse beats so fast it turns my hurting stomach.

Lee dropped his flashlight and it rolled across the cellar. Now the light burns against the wall, showing two thrashing shadows.

Thankfully, Kane's military training and muscle gives him the upper hand.

After a few more blows so fast I can't see them, he has Lee pinned against the wall again.

The lunatic's face looks battered, smeared with blood and dust.

For a second, I think it's over.

But I see the way Lee's hand moves, twisting the gun toward Kane's stomach.

And Kane's hands are too busy holding Lee down to notice. There's nothing he can do to stop the gun's slow, snaking journey.

His face is slick, straining, his eyes wild with effort.

I have three seconds.

I pop up quickly.

I don't care about the danger or the glass cutting the palms of my hands as I lunge for the statue.

Yes, it's just as heavy as it looks.

A freaking boulder.

Muscles I never knew I had scream in my back as I heave it up, high over my head.

"Margot, no!" Kane warns. "Stay back!"

Lee smiles, more reptile than ever with new gaps in his teeth.

"Fugg you, Saind," he slurs. "Gonna kill you."

The gun inches closer.

Kane's neck muscles bulge in stark relief.

My arms are shaking.

I can't hold this statue much longer, I—

"Drop it, you asshole," Kane rasps. "Last chance."

"Nodding else madders," Lee gurgles.

The gun barrel digs into Kane's stomach.

Lee's bloody smile widens.

"Y-ou you're the reason my life's shid. They'll know shoon. The whole wide whirld."

"Go ahead," Kane snaps, right in his face now, pressing his bulk into the gun. "Shoot me. Won't change a damn thing. Nothing will do that when you chose violence. You chose to be a slave to your past."

"No!" I whisper.

I know what he's doing.

He's still redirecting him.

This brave, beautiful man will die ten times just to keep a madman's gun away from me.

Kane cranes his neck and looks at me.

"That's something I'll never be again thanks to this woman," he whispers softly.

Oh. My. God.

Lee coughs and spits blood on the floor next to Kane.

"Shud the fugg up!"

"No. I heard what you told her. I lost my life once, too." Kane looks back at Lee again, and I slowly lower the statue. The gun hasn't moved, but Lee frowns, hesitating. "Took me forever to find it again, but I did. I filled that chasm. After meeting Margot Blackthorn, I can die happy if you shoot me tonight. I found the woman I love."

Love.

He loves me and I'm so freaking gutted I can't move.

That's why he stayed.

That's why he put his kids on a plane and rushed back for me.

That's why we're both here, staring death in the face.

That's why he's prepared to die any second, to give up his life for mine.

It's all a violent blur now.

All the early mornings in the kitchen.

Late nights under the twinkling stars and glowing planets.

The laughter and kisses.

The sweetness, the standoffs, the memories we made with Sophie and Dan—of course it meant something.

Only the entire world.

"If you kill me," Kane growls, "then you're giving up on your only way back. You can still be human. You can stomp out that fire, that hate, that ugliness before it ruins you, Lee."

Silence.

There's a massive lump in my throat as my lips twitch and I whisper, "I love you too."

Not how I ever imagined we'd say those words.

Absolutely the most messed-up timing.

But that just makes it truer, holy vows written in adrenaline and blood. If this maniac murders him in front of me, at least we—

The statue starts to slip in my hands and I lunge for the ground.

Lee slumps against Kane's hold with a groan, his head hanging.

It's like he's a human balloon deflating, a long ribbon of blood and saliva drooling from his mouth.

His chest heaves out a sob.

Then after the longest second, his gun falls to the ground.

Amazing it doesn't go off.

Kane reaches for a loose brick beside Lee's head and with one swift hit, he knocks him out cold.

"Just in case. He'll live," he tells me, letting the man slump to the floor next to his gun, lifeless.

I'm still on my knees, gripping the statue, staring in wide-eyed horror.

He gently pries my numb hands away, and he still somehow has the energy to carry it back to its stand.

Battered, bruised, and bleeding, he's perfection.

The most wonderful man alive.

And miraculously, he *is* alive.

Holy shit, we survived!

"Never walk up to a man with a gun again, duchess," he says with a thin smile.

"No choice. I thought he was going to shoot you," I whisper brokenly, giving in to rest my forehead against his chest.

He smells like blood and sweat and stone, mingled with testosterone.

It's like breathing pine needles, but I don't care.

This scent is quintessentially Kane, and I'm about two seconds away from losing my last thread of self-control.

"Nah," he says, embracing me. "Nah, he was just angry. Full of mindless pain. Did he hurt you? Are you okay?"

"I'm okay."

His hand sweeps my hair, holding me against his wall of a chest.

For a second, we both breathe, inhaling each other and the wonder of being alive and in love.

"Got your call," he says over my head. "I thought he was hurting you."

"Only a little. He wanted you. I don't think he planned to kill me."

"I'm fucking glad he didn't." His voice goes pitch-dark.

"Thank you for coming back." I run a hand up his back and he flinches. "Are *you* hurt? I'm so sorry you took a beating, I—"

"This?" He leans away and glances at a nasty gash on his forearm before wrapping his arm around my waist. "Just a scrape. Come on, woman. Let's get the fuck out of here."

Even though we're both okay and I'm so grateful I didn't have to crush a man's head, my legs are still weak.

It's Kane, and only Kane that keeps me standing as we stumble up the stairs.

The rain has slowed to a drizzle by the time we finally surface.

We're greeted by a reassuring blueberry-cherry flash of lights.

"Better late than never," I whisper.

Kane chuckles in agreement.

I take a long, rough pull of the cool night air.

It's over.

This ugly chapter is done, and now comes the rest of our story.

XXIV: HOME TO ROOST (KANE)

One Week Later

Sometimes, I still can't wrap my mind around waking up next to this fuck-hot woman, alive and whole and hopelessly in love with me.

How?

Just how?

The early morning sun spills through the gaps in the curtains, painting her in soft gold like she belongs in heaven's VIP room.

Never thought it would be so easy to get her into my bed in New York.

I thought there'd be more to figure out, more time to process the hell we just lived through.

More arrangements, more negotiation to reshape the pieces of our lives to fit neatly.

Surprise. It turns out attempted murder really fucks with a person's priorities.

And no, we haven't figured out everything yet.

We're working on that, one day at a time.

But after everything that went down, we needed to share our space.

We needed to be *whole*.

And we made it happen, faster than I could blink.

Margot left with me the day after the Babins and Lee Glazkov got taken into custody after endless sit-downs with the police.

Not that it needed much detective work.

Lee had social media posts scheduled with a thousand-word manifesto about what happened and why. What he intended to happen, my murder in cold blood.

Looking back, it felt obvious that his will to kill was weakening.

Yes, he was irate and fighting hard like the depraved psycho he is, but it still takes a special ruthlessness for a man who's never killed anyone to pull the trigger.

Anger alone can't always cut it.

Now, though, I wonder if I read him wrong.

Or maybe I just figured out there was a small buried part of him who wanted another chance at life.

I smelled his desperation—too much like mine—even if his was twisted into deranged violence.

Thank God I wore him out before he let his anger shoot first.

One day, after a lot of justice and years of hardcore mental treatment, he might even have a second chance.

I certainly have mine.

Margot snoozes beside me, an eye mask over her face to block out the sun, and her blonde hair splashed across the pillow.

It's adorable watching her sleep like a kitten.

She shifts in her sleep, pressing against my side with a

sleepy groan.

I pull her in and reach for my phone, just like I do every morning.

Margot says it's a bad habit to read the news before I've had coffee. Before the stalker-killer episode in Maine, I wasn't the kind of guy to get too hung up on social media.

Hell, I know half of it isn't true, especially the shit they write about me.

But this is different.

None of it feels real yet, and I need to make sure.

With one hand, I punch in the Babins' names.

There's not much fresh. Nothing new since yesterday.

But they're out of the hospital, already in front of a judge for attempted assault, trespassing, arson, and a litany of other charges that'll keep them locked up for years.

Especially if I have anything to do with it.

The cameras caught everything their confessions didn't before the Babins took them out. Viola was caught walking into the house with a club, and Joseph doused the front porch in gasoline.

The rain has probably washed it all away by now, if it wasn't cleaned up by the Blackthorns' bodyguard, who rushed up there the day we left.

There's no way they'll crawl back to their blueberry farm after this.

The Babins didn't make many friends in Sully Bay.

And Margot?

She made a hell of a lot.

As for Lee, he's only at the start of a very long, rough road. My name is big enough, and his vendetta personal enough, to make his attempt on my life a big splash in the press.

Ironically, about as big as he wanted.

And now there's a simmering stir about AI screwing over designers and other creatives.

Part of me hates that Lee's message didn't just die in that cellar.

Only, a bigger part of me knows it had to happen, for reasons that have nothing to do with one enraged almost-killer.

More importantly, it's brought up legal questions about how the OptiSynth software learns, how it pulls so much material from existing designers and artists without compensation.

I'm not the guy to sort it out, so I'll leave that to the judges.

The crack in the armor is there. OptiSynth will face the issues I tried to warn them about—big questions and a crisis they can't just sweep away.

The world is talking.

Morals are shifting like desert sands.

I don't know if Lee Glazkov will ever walk free again, but it won't be for many years.

For now, that's enough.

And if he ever does, I sincerely hope he turns his ruined life around.

There's nothing like opening your eyes and seeing the world right-side up.

Margot stretches sleepily in my arms, her eyes opening in lazy slits of blue.

"Kane." Her voice is thick with sleep as she pulls the phone from my hand. "What have I said about brooding alone this early?"

"Only after coffee."

"*After* coffee. Actually, only after coffee you've made."

"Isn't that implied, duchess?" I ask, dropping a kiss on her head.

"Mmm. Any news?"

"Nope. Guess some people speculate we broke up because we haven't been seen together since the dustup."

"Screw them!" She snuggles closer. "Who cares what they say? They don't need to know I wake up in your arms wet every morning."

I like that.

I like that a fucking lot.

"The rest is all good news," I promise. "Everything we'd hope for."

"Mmm." She kisses my shoulder and rolls over, grabbing the worn, bound journal off her nightstand.

It's one of the final gifts her granddad left for her, tucked behind that stuck glass panel Lee shot out in his fury. On top of it, there was a broken pair of little shoes. Beautifully painted clay and far more intricate than the other lumpy, unfinished sculptures down there.

They were barely held together too by this crude attempt at gluing them together. At one point, they must've been fractured into half a dozen pieces.

After the crime scene was cleared, the police handed Leonidas' stuff over, saying it wouldn't be much use as evidence.

I don't think she ever imagined she'd wind up with the old man's treasures.

She's been glued to the journal ever since, flipping through the pages to soak up the wisdom, a different entry every single day. He kept it going for years.

Sometimes the entries make her sad, sometimes happy, and sometimes wistful.

It's the connection she always wanted from the Great Beyond, and I'm happy as hell for her.

She flicks through the pages again, stopping on a random

one. I prop my chin on my fist as I watch her read, her forehead lining with focus.

"Now who's brooding?" I tease, reaching up to smooth away the lines with my thumb. "What's he telling you today?"

"Do you want to read it?"

"Read it to me."

She reaches over for my hand and our fingers twine as she starts at the beginning.

"*My darling wife,*

You were always right, even when I was too blind to see. Lately, my pride has kept me from seeing anything except the beautiful baby shoes you made—the same ones I savaged in a fit of rage a few months ago.

You must know I'll restore them. I just need time. I need to practice my technique and hope my arthritis doesn't make art impossible.

I don't have your talent, May, but I'll try to do you justice. I won't stop until they're the perfect memory of what our Elvira wore in happier, easier times.

Yes, I know.

She deserves to know how sorry I am, too.

One day, she'll know the truth, and she'll have the little shoes we lost in that fire. I hated seeing you in tears. The precious shrine to our children was the one thing I could never replace after those goddamned devils turned your studio into ashes.

If I had more proof, you know they'd be in jail. I would rename their lot May Blackthorn Blueberry Farms in your memory.

That's why you made the shoes she wore as a loving testament. That's why it was your last project.

I miss you, May.

I miss the easy times.

I miss the old Leonidas you loved, before a tortured old man smashed our daughter to pieces, just like I smashed up the lovely shoes you made.

I pray you'll forgive me from the other side. Just like I pray she'll understand how deeply I regret the ways I tore the heart out of this family.

"On the bright side, the grandkids are fine." Margot's voice wavers. I squeeze her hand, giving her the space to keep reading. *"They're too young to understand this nasty rift. One day, before it's their problem, I will mend Elvira's heart. And I will copy your shoes down to the last detail, so help me God.*

You were the only one who could ever suffer a stubborn old fool.

Even when you're gone, you're still my guiding light.

One day, no more night.

One day, Elvira will know she's been loved with every step of her life.

If there's one thing I wish I'd learned when you were still here by my side, it's how there's never enough time to say the things that truly matter.

The words settle between us like lead.

She already knew about her grandfather's hand in trying to break up her parents, Elvira and Scott. One of the many things we discussed when we came back to New York.

I understand how crazy it must've been, learning that the man she looked up to the most was flawed.

Your heroes in life are ultimately people, riddled with human flaws.

And now, hearing his remorse, his determination to put things right, her eyes are misted.

"He never finished the shoes, did he?"

"I don't think so," she whispers. "His arthritis *did* get worse. A few years after he wrote this, he could barely stand to write. It must've killed him that he couldn't do it. He could never get his sculptures up to my grandmother's level before his body gave out."

I shake my head. There are times when biology is so fucking cruel.

"Your mother doesn't know yet, does she?" I say softly.

"No." She wipes at her eyes, sitting up.

"Do you think it might be time to tell her? Show her this letter and the shoes?" I tap the journal. "It's never too late to make amends. He couldn't make it perfect, but he put in a ton of effort."

"I know, I know. She hated him so much. But God, it's beautiful, isn't it?" She traces the words on the paper. "I counted at least a dozen shoe sculptures. Holden said he found twice as many back in Portland. He spent years on this, and he could never get it right. He always carved his signature and the date into the bottom."

"You think your mom will never forgive him?"

She hesitates.

"I don't know. She spent my whole life bitter. She'd barely agree to let us see him. I don't know if she really knows how to forgive." She looks up at me, her eyelashes wet. "I'll bring it to her soon, though. I have to." She heaves a breath. "But Ethan needs to see this stuff first and read the journal. It's only fair."

Ethan, her brother, who had his own demons, if I understand the family history right.

"It's so stupid—and so complicated." She leans back into me. I wrap an arm around her shoulders. "Once he sees it, I think he'll help me bring this to Mom. I just don't know how she'll take it. They were estranged for over twenty years, until the day he died."

"Yeah, but she didn't know how much he hurt. She didn't know how sorry he was and that he knew how much of a mistake he made with your dad, your whole family."

Her dad. *Not Ethan's.*

It's a dire, fucked up family situation for sure, but I'm not here to judge.

Hell, I'm just getting back on track myself.

"I'll be there too, if you want me to be," I promise. "For you, I always will be."

Her face smooths and she leans up to kiss my jaw.

The journal settles on the blankets as she shifts so she's on top of me, holding my face in her hands as she kisses me, all soft lips and searing tongue.

I'm hard enough to split rocks.

"I love you," she tells me fiercely. "I love you so much, Kane."

"So fucking much," I agree, and I find the silk bottoms of her pajama shorts. I slide my fingers under them, and she shudders against me. "Is that what has you this wet? Love?"

"I like it when you tell me you love me," she says shyly, smothering her moan as I rub her pussy.

"I love you."

"Oh!" Her teeth scrape my neck, just enough to make me throb. "I love you, Kane. Always."

"Always," I growl, pushing my fingers deeper inside her.

She clenches around me, and my greed is overwhelming.

No matter how many days it happens like this, I still want to reclaim her.

I want her ruined.

I want her marked, inside and out, with red marks on her throat and my seed leaking between her legs.

Mine, dammit.

Mine and forever.

My growl doesn't even have to form the word.

My sweet, needy duchess already knows.

And she takes my hand and moves it to her breast, shifting so she's got my cock at her entrance.

"Kane, holy shit. Don't make me beg."

I curse under my breath, and she laughs, seriously considering it.

Her clothes are gone in a whirlwind.

Then she's on top of me and I shove her legs apart to mount her just right.

Lucky for her, I'm so thirsty today. I push the fuck in.

I'm balls deep and she's moaning helplessly, the sexiest music I've ever heard in my life.

Sometimes, like now as she's moving above me in slow, languid movements, I think I'm drowning in a dream.

Like I'm not lucky enough to have a woman this beautiful worshipping my cock, opening her legs and aching to be fucked into next week damn near every day.

She laughs.

She shudders.

She grinds down until her clit gets my friction.

And I forget about anything besides how fucking awesome she feels, the slow roll of her hips, the way she knows how that shy smile destroys me—like she has some big secret, and I'm the lucky prick she gets to share it with.

"I could keep you chained up here all week," I snarl.

"Deal!" Her head tilts back, exposing her throat.

I flip her over, arms around her back, and brace myself over her.

"I love you, Margot."

At this angle, I take her from behind, pumping deep until I bottom out, pushing my balls against her.

In to the hilt.

I love watching her eyes widen in the mirror on the wall when she feels the head of my cock against her womb.

I reach around and find her clit again, driving faster, finding that little nub and bringing her to ruin.

"Fucking wait for me," I growl.

Her eyes roll, huge and glassy.

"I... I don't know if I can. Oh my God!"

"Wait, duchess." I slow, keeping her on the edge as I thrust deeper—hard long strokes that only feed the fire, and fuck, it feels divine. "Need you to come with me today."

"Kane." Her mouth falls open and I push my thumb into it, her lips closing around me and sucking automatically. "Kane!"

"Good girl."

Her trembling eyes tell me she's close, but I don't need the hint.

I've spent enough time learning her body.

All the wicked ways her flesh worships me, a candle to flame.

Knowing she's on the brink sends lightning through my nerves, and I slow down, pinning her against the bed.

For a second, we linger on the edge, lost in each other's gaze, this killing balance of *almost* and *not enough.*

Then her body shudders and she loses it.

My spine becomes a lit fuse.

My balls heave, a split second from erupting.

"Fucking come!"

And she does.

My girl comes so beautiful in a shuddering, desperate, breathless orgasm that splits the morning.

Her body clenches around mine, small waves fluttering as I come too, turning myself inside out, heart first.

I empty myself inside her like a man turned human flood.

"Kane," she whispers my name with a reverent kiss.

"Margot," I whisper back, sucking her bottom lip with my teeth.

As long as she's here, as long as she's alive, she's my property.

And I'll carve out hours every day just to remind her how glorious that can be.

* * *

THE RIGHT WRONG PROMISE

For a nine-year-old, Dan has an ego bigger than the Moon when it comes to his games. Mostly because he beats me every time.

"Dad, you're too slow! You gotta *move* to keep up." He loves to rub it in.

We're playing *Beat Saber* with his VR headset, smashing through colored boxes with our swords to techno music that must be meant to make hearts explode.

If you think it's a game I'd be naturally good at, you're wrong.

The kid leaves me in the dust with his quicker moves, beating me so decisively he makes it look effortless.

At the end, he rips off his headset, and I hold out my fist for a bump.

"Nice round, little man. If it were archery, you'd be in trouble."

"No fair! You said I'm not old enough yet." He grins up with his messy hair.

"We'll see about next spring," I promise, a sly grin spreading across my face. "*If* I can finally beat you at this one time."

"Dad, you suck! You know you won't." He paces the room in frustration. "You're old and slow. Why don't you see if you can beat Margot? She's closer to your age."

"Watch it." I pull him into a headlock. "Life's not fair and we're not always up against our equals."

Of course, whether I beat him or not, we'll be taking up archery once he turns ten. That's the age when I first picked up a bow.

I can't wait to do it again with him and Sophie.

Judging by the relaxed look on his face, he knows it, too.

"You're my *dad*," he says matter-of-factly. "I'm supposed to pick on you. Way of the world, like you always say."

"Close enough, little punk." I rub my knuckles against his head and release him.

We sit down on the sofa next to each other and grab our water bottles.

"So," Dan says. "When are you gonna get Margot a ring? It'd be a shame if she goes back to Portland first."

What?

It's no secret the kids adore her, but the question beans me on the head like a rock.

"You really like having her here, huh?" I play it cool.

"Well, yeah!" He blinks at me like I'm the biggest bonehead he's ever met. "I *like* Margot. Sophie loves her, they're closer than she ever was with Mom."

Fucking ouch.

I wish I could deny it.

"Bud, listen." I sigh. "We're working through some serious stuff. It's mandatory after the trouble we had in Maine. Might take us some time, but once I've figured it out, you'll be the first to know."

"Cool," he says. "I can help you figure out how to ask her, you know. When the time comes."

Without another word, I reach down and ruffle his hair.

Between us boys, I'll be fine.

Still, I can't say I mind the moral support from my little wingman.

Just then Margot sails in, a sunny smile on her face as she leads Sophie into the den.

My daughter's wearing the most extravagant soft bubblegum pink shoes I've ever seen.

The shape's barely thinner than her basic black shoes. I've seen the specs a dozen times while Sophie talked my ear off, counting down the days until they arrived.

Only, the shade Margot picked with soft white stripes running along the front and the colorful flowers splashed on the sides create an optical illusion. It makes them look smaller and prettier, and the color draws the eye away from their bulky size.

Damn, I'm impressed.

These aren't shoes meant for blending in.

They're a pastel pink spotlight, and Sophie spins in them, beaming with pride.

"I see the Candy Cloud shoes are here. How do they feel?" I ask.

"Dad, they fit perfect!" she chirps, giving us another twirl.

"Those are *so* pink and girly." Dan laughs. "But for you, it works, I guess."

High praise from her punk brother.

"I'm in love. I think I wanna marry these shoes," Sophie says.

Margot bites her lip as she glances at me, her eyes dancing.

"I think they turned out fabulous," she says. "What do you think, Dad?"

"Yeah, Dad." Sophie bounds up to me, a little ball of pixie sugar I haven't seen for some time. "Tell me what you think!"

"Hmm, let's see… They seem safe. They help you walk without falling over. Everything good shoes *should* do." I rub my chin, drawing it out.

"Daaaad!" She claps her hands to her cheeks and pulls her face down.

"Okay, munchkin. I think they put Dorothy's ruby slippers to shame. If you walk in wearing those, everyone will think you're pure wizard. They're you, Soph. Right down to the little flowers."

Her face scrunches with a smile before she nods solemnly. "They really are, aren't they?"

"Hell yeah." I lift her up in a hug until she squeals before I set her down again.

Then I catch Margot's eyes over the top of Sophie's head.

Genius, I love you, I mouth.

Hiding a laugh, she mouths *I love you* right back.

Dan might've had a point earlier.

I don't want to rush into anything crazy, but what else will ever match this sweet insanity with Margot Blackthorn?

What else ever could?

I can't wait forever.

Her grandfather went to his grave watching his hourglass run out. I'd be painfully foolish to make the same mistake.

Not in this life.

Not with this woman.

Definitely not when she's as perfect with my kids as she is with me.

XXV: DADDY'S HOME (MARGOT)

Weeks Later

*I*f I keep holding my breath, I'm going to pass out.

Here, right now, in my parents' extravagant living room, before we accomplish anything.

Right in front of Hattie and Ethan, who flew down to be with us today. Right in front of Ares, too, Gramps' adorably ancient basset hound who now lives with the happy couple. He sprawls at our feet, somewhere between napping and giving us the saddest puppy dog eyes.

They're on one side and Kane sits on my other side, holding my hand. Not caring that I'm gripping his palm so hard it would be bone-crushing with a man who doesn't have tiger paws for hands.

God.

Waiting, that's the hardest part.

At least Hattie looks happy today. Her hair's pulled up in a messy bun and she has the widest grin on her face. Probably because they've been spending plenty of time hitting the New York bookstores to find more inspiration for her shop.

She's an easy girl and she loves to rattle off her bookish finds.

All it takes is books and a doting husband.

"I honestly didn't see it taking off as well as it did," Hattie says, her shoulder leaning against Ethan's in silent support. His hand rests on her thigh.

I try not to smile.

I've never seen my big brother act the way he does with her.

She's softened the first-class asshat, turning him back into the boy I remembered, before he became a teenage dickhead sideswiped by tragedy.

But those days are behind him, and his eyes flick to mine, then to Kane, cold and assessing.

It's the first time they've met.

Not under ideal circumstances, either.

"But get this, I got Gwen Lynn *and* M.E. Court coming in to do a mother-daughter signing next week! Two famous authors," Hattie chatters.

I love her, and I don't mind her book freakout today. It helps things feel less awkward.

"That's going to be a big signing, Hat-girl. Are you sure you'll have the space?"

"Oh, man, I hope! You wouldn't believe how far some people will travel to get their books signed," Hattie says. "Not just fans, but other authors and influencers." She sighs, stars dancing in her eyes. "Gwen was *so* cool on the phone. Her latest hero is based on her hubby, Miller, that hardass whistleblower from that weird organ harvesting thing? He's got the daddy vibe down, a lot like your—"

Kane stares at her.

"Um, never mind." Blushing, Hattie beams at me knowingly.

"I wish real estate moved on TikTok half as easily as books," Ethan grumbles. It's the first time he's said more than three words since we got here.

"I keep telling you guys to up your social media game," Hattie says pointedly. "People love pretty places almost as much as they do books. You need to send your Reels to fewer rich dudes and more to their ladies."

I laugh and shake my head.

It's too adorable, watching my best friend lay on the business advice for my billionaire brother. They make a good pair.

I can see the amusement flashing behind his stern eyes.

"But he'll figure it out. Blackthorn Holdings is killing it lately, like Leo never left. Right, hubby?"

"Yes, even if my wife might wind up more famous than I am," Ethan says, dropping a kiss on the tip of her nose. "Never change, Pages. Don't give me a chance to keep up."

When Hattie stops batting her eyes, Ethan gives me a guarded look.

We both remember why we're here.

Hattie and Kane know what this is and what it means, but they can't *feel* it like we do.

Only Ethan and I can sense the hundred-ton boulder on our backs.

Kane's shoulder nudges mine gently.

I grip his hand in both of mine.

My hold tightens when we hear footsteps.

Mom's clicking heels and Dad's heavier shuffle coming closer.

It's so unbearably formal, but that's the only way my parents do it.

The door opens and Mom walks into the room, followed

by Dad.

She quickly flings herself into the chair across from us, with Dad forming up by her side with his hands folded behind his back.

Of the two, it's Dad who smiles.

Mom is too careful with her face. Sometimes, I wonder how much she really *can* smile with the endless treatments she'd had to cheat aging.

But when she looks at us, everything she needs to say is in her eyes.

She read the journal.

I handed it over last night along with Grams' painting and said we'd be here to talk—if there was anything she wants to talk about.

That's why we're here for this big family reunion.

To see if there's anything she wants to say.

To find out if this family can even try to bury its bitter, ugly past.

"Well? Let's hear it," Mom says.

"Did you read it?" I ask.

She nods, then shakes her head. "Not all of it, of course. But enough. God knows, I was up half the night with it." Oddly, she isn't wearing much makeup today.

She rubs her eyes in a tired, soul-weary way I haven't seen since childhood.

Ethan looks at me, practically vibrating with tension. Hattie puts a calming hand on his shoulder.

"And?" he asks.

Mom looks between us both.

"What I can't fathom," she says, her hands gripping the sides of the chair, "is why that ridiculous, tight-lipped old idiot had to send Margot on a wild goose chase looking for his feelings instead of sharing them while he still *could*."

"Mom, that's not fair. You sent back every letter he tried

to give you," I start, but she holds up a hand.

"But," she says, "I never imagined him being so... honest, either. Or so eaten up with guilt." She looks at Dad, who watches her with a soft, worried expression.

"You don't know the half of it," Ethan growls, grabbing the small box by his feet and thrusting it at her. "Take a good, long look. He worked his ass off, trying to rebuild the baby shoes your mother made. If you read the journal, you know they lost the originals in the fire."

Mom takes the box with a sigh and unfolds the loose cardboard on top. She looks down.

For the longest second, her face is completely unreadable.

Dad's face goes white and he lays his hands on her shoulders.

Look, I still get mad at the way they treated us as kids.

The way we never felt like a priority, but there's no doubt that they adore each other in their own weird way.

Learning Gramps forced them apart when they were young and Mom defied him and went back to Dad and he accepted the baby she'd conceived with another man in a reckless fling tells me how much love is sacrifice.

Loving Kane taught me the rest.

"All that guilt, all those years," she hisses to herself. "It must've driven him mad. I'm not sure how he was ever good with you kids."

"He was," Ethan says sharply, leaving no doubt.

She's right, it *did* make PopPop crazy.

He just hid his agony very well.

It's obvious from his journal, from his obsession with the shoes he broke, that he was consumed with finding a way to repair the family rift created by his pride.

If only to regain a little of the deep, everlasting love he clearly had for my grandmother.

Half the entries in that journal were pondering what he

could do to fix all the hurt he caused. Whenever he wasn't journaling about his art collection or a day out on the water with us kids, he was bleeding.

Ink doesn't need to be red to look like a murder scene, and this poor, damaged man died a thousand times. He relived losing his wife and his daughter over and over.

No, there won't be any easy answers about why he makes everyone's inheritance so difficult. That's just the kind of tortured weirdo he was.

But he was *our* weirdo, and I loved him.

Also, I can't wait to find out what's in store for my little cousin soon, last on the list to inherit his kind of crazy.

In the end, he was a teacher, and he left us lessons he couldn't just give us in life.

Gramps couldn't have known I'd meet Kane at the lake house, but he knew I struggled to slow down, to stop and breathe and find myself.

He called me May. Not just because I resemble Grams, but because he'd laugh and tell me I don't slow down.

Being at the lake house made me hit pause.

And yes, it brought me Kane, but if he hadn't been there, I think I still would've walked out of there in a better place emotionally. Assuming the Babins didn't burn my body, of course.

Gramps made a lot of mistakes, no question.

Yet there's no doubt he loved fiercely.

Just as fiercely as Ethan and Hattie.

Just as fiercely as Kane and me.

Reading his journal with time and space to reflect taught me a lot. It's given me the chance to understand Gramps in a different way.

The way he and Mom left off, too. She wouldn't even look at him or come to his big house in Portland to pick us up when those long summers ended.

Ethan leans forward, his hand covering Hattie's on his shoulder.

"Does that mean you forgive him?" he asks.

The trillion-dollar question.

My breath stalls.

Ares perks up and whines, his thick tail slapping the floor.

Mom dabs her fingers at the thin, wrinkled skin under her eyes. When she drops her hands, I see the moisture gleaming there.

Unexpected and scary.

"Not today. Not yet. I can't," she whispers, but there's something in her voice. Genuine regret? "It's still too raw. Reading this book, looking at these shoes, they—they beat me to a pulp again. And that man has done enough of that for this lifetime."

Devastating.

Kane tightens his grip on my hand, his thumb stroking my skin.

Mom looks at me, and her face softens.

"But someday... someday, *maybe*," she says. "Maybe I just need time."

Holy crap.

Nodding, I wipe away a tear with my own shaking hand.

Time.

I can give her that.

We all can, if that's what she needs.

This isn't a slamming door.

It's an opening, one tiny step in the right direction.

"We wanted you to realize how much it meant to him," Ethan says.

Mom smiles.

"Thank you," she says simply.

It's not what we wanted.

No big, dramatic, heartfelt conclusion to tie up everything real neat, but that's life.

For now, someday is enough.

Someday, we'll have true closure. An end to the hate, the heartache, and tears between the people we love most.

Someday, she'll accept his apology from beyond the grave.

Dad massages her shoulders, and Mom leans up, kissing his hand.

They trade a glance I don't quite understand.

"This was important, Evvie," he says after a few moments. "It's a fresh start."

"Whatever it is, it's left me famished."

She reaches for her phone. Less than a minute after she types out a text, the chef rolls in.

He's a tall man, pushing a trolley across the floor, and he starts unloading covered silver dishes onto the sideboard against the wall. Ares lumbers up and sits, ready for head scratches while he watches the food intently.

I should've seen this coming when we came over for 'breakfast.'

"Mom never cooks," I whisper to Kane. His eyebrows are halfway to his hairline.

He's no stranger to wealth and comfort.

But as a man who still cooks for his kids a lot, this must be *weird*. Even if it's always been an expression with money.

Love, in Mom's own odd way.

Today, it's an olive branch.

"I know the past year has been difficult. Years, really," Mom says.

Ethan just nods, large and brooding from his seat. Hattie stares wide-eyed at the breakfast extravaganza, which is almost laid out now.

Dish after dish, piled high with everything from Belgian

waffles and their fixings to small red smoothies in shot glasses and perfectly folded omelets.

Say what you will, but Elvira and Scott Blackthorn never half-assed hosting a meal in their lives.

"But," she continues, "I'd like us to move on from the drama and his will." She looks at me. "Especially you, honey. I want you happy, just like Ethan and Hattie here."

Hattie giggles as she looks at my brother, who gives Kane the protective big-brother stare.

Dude, enough.

I tug Kane's hand onto my lap. "Thanks, Mom. You know, I think I'm getting there, and it's all thanks to Gramps."

She studies me for a long moment before giving Kane another assessing glance.

"The lake house," she says.

"The lake house. He didn't know—he didn't plan anything—but he made it happen all the same." I squeeze Kane's hand. "It's pretty eye-opening, meeting the love of your life."

For a second, you can hear the lights hum in the room.

"So I've heard," Ethan says abruptly. "I wondered when you'd get serious and stop dating losers, Sis. It must be serious if he's here to pass the smell test."

Ethan leans in like the Neanderthal he is, making a big snorting show of sniffing the air.

I'm so dead.

"I'm here for Margot," Kane says gruffly, leaning back in his chair, unfazed by my dumbass brother.

Ethan's big, but Kane is just as broad, and right now they're two bull moose locking verbal horns.

"Ethan," Hattie hisses. "Behave."

"Kane, it's okay," I whisper, firing him a glance.

Kane relaxes and smiles. "Your brother's protective. That's a good thing."

"Oh, I'm too hungry for bickering," Mom says, already moving toward the chef and the food.

"It's good to have you here," Dad says, holding out his hand to Kane. "We haven't met properly yet."

Technically, they met yesterday when I brought the journal, but that was intense and quick.

No more than the briefest introductions, not with everyone laser-focused on the journal.

Kane levers up out of his seat and takes Dad's hand with an easy smile. "Kane Saint."

"Scott Blackthorn," Dad says. "This spoiled miscreant's father. Trust me, I made her this way."

He's so shameless.

I roll my eyes.

But at least his eyes aren't flashing with skepticism like with the handful of other guys I've brought home. Dad might not have a nose for much besides luxury and investments, but he can tell a man from a boy.

And Kane Saint is no freaking fuckboy like Kelso.

Dad's warmth tells me he sees a better man.

A real *man*.

I think that's why my father's face tightens and his knuckles turn white as he grips Kane's hand.

"I must warn you," he whispers, "if you hurt my daughter, I'll make sure you pay dearly."

"Dad, seriously? Can we just be civilized?"

"Scott, listen to her." Mom glides back to greet Kane with a hug and a kiss on both cheeks. "Don't listen to him. We just want to see our little girl happy. There's been too much turmoil in this family for a long time."

"For Margot, anything," Kane promises, shooting me a smile that makes my heart flutter.

Only the love of this man saves me from wilting with embarrassment.

Later, Hattie curls up on the sofa with me and stares across the room at Kane.

"Wow, he's way taller in real life! I knew hockey guys were big, but man..." She whistles dramatically.

"I mean, he's basically like Ethan, give or take a couple inches."

"Same for the ego, I bet." She giggles and blows my brother a kiss. "I told him to play nice, but you know how it is."

"Let me guess," I say, my voice dripping with sarcasm. "He doesn't like him."

"You're his little sister. He's just having a hard time getting over it," Hattie says apologetically. "Of course, I *told* him the age difference literally doesn't matter, but he insists it does."

"Would you be okay if I hit him on the head with a croissant?" I hold up my pastry, narrowing my eyes. "It's been a while since we had a food fight."

"Be my guest," she assures me. "Maybe you'll knock something loose that reminds him he's being ridiculous and overbearing."

Ethan and Kane are still squaring each other up as they move closer to us.

For a second, I think Ethan wants to embarrass both of us. It's like watching a loading screen spin, just waiting for something awful to come out of his mouth.

Then he stops and sticks out his hand.

"I wish you both luck, brat," he says.

"Oh my God," I mutter, standing to prod my brother in the side. "Really, Ethan?"

But I take his hand anyway and shake, knowing this is about as nice as my brother gets.

Kane slides his arm around my waist. I can practically see him holding in a belly laugh.

"He's not half-bad," he tells me. "Frankly, he's cooler than I'll ever be the day Sophie brings a boy home."

Hilariously, I know that's no lie. I'm just grateful I'll get to be there for it.

Hattie comes up to Ethan's other side.

"All this dick waving is making me dizzy," she says, ruining the effect by giving Ethan the soppiest glance I've ever seen.

"We're only in New York for a couple days." Ethan slides his arm around Hattie's waist. "Want to come to dinner before we head out?"

"You can bring the kids," Hattie tells Kane quickly. "Margot says she designed some really cool shoes for your daughter, and I'd love to see them."

"See?" I say to Ethan, pointing at my best friend. "This is what support looks like."

Kane kisses the side of my head.

"Dinner sounds great," he says. "Sophie can't get enough of showing off her favorite shoes."

I sigh.

It's so sweet how much she loves them. I almost tear up every time I think about it.

"Feels like a good time to bury bad memories," Kane says as we all head for more from the breakfast spread set up on the bar. My mouth waters at the delicious smells.

"Cheers to that," Dad says, holding up a glass of black iced tea.

While he's distracted, Ares trots over and steals a sausage off his plate.

"Good boy," I whisper.

Dad gives the dog the stink eye.

"I'll always be around to help Margot any way I can. As long as she'll have me." Kane looks at Ethan, the words falling like a solemn vow.

Forever, you lunk.

I can feel the brushfire on my face, slowly rising up my cheeks.

I load up my plate more than usual, if only to hide the embarrassment.

I love my fam, but we've never been good at being vulnerable.

Even when Ethan was spiraling, locked in a little cabin with empty bottles strewn around the floor, he wouldn't face his feelings. Not until I gave him a serious reality check.

But now here we are.

Kane, cutting through the Blackthorn family freeze with his honesty.

Telling everyone how devoted he is, how much he loves me, without even dropping the big L-bomb.

"Okay, Gigi," Hattie whispers in my ear as she joins me. "It's official. You're getting married."

"Um, *what?*"

She just grins.

I glance back at my family, my parents talking with Ethan and Kane and the over-the-top breakfast Mom arranged for us. All in her ridiculously fancy living room.

Sometimes, you have to scratch the surface to find the love, especially in a dysfunctional mess like ours.

But if you look hard enough, you'll find it.

And sometimes you'll accept it like new skin over scar tissue.

PopPop would be proud of us today.

As Kane looks up, I smile.

All teasing aside, my bestie might be right.

If the day comes when this rock of a man pops the question and wants to make me one with the mountain, with his kids, with eternity, I can't imagine any reason why I'd ever say no.

XXVI: DON'T TRY THIS AT HOME (KANE)

A Few Months Later

The lake house has a different vibe in the winter.

The fall was an explosion of colors and vibrance.

Now, as I drive Margot and the kids up the familiar gravel road to the front door, everything sparkles under a pure white sheet.

There's snow everywhere, casting a thousand shades.

The lake looks iced over, the center still cracked, the water dark and still as ink splashed on a white page.

We've only been back once since everything went down with the Babins and Lee Glazkov. Just the two of us. Margot came up to see the property to take care of it, and I insisted on being by her side.

I wasn't having her go alone, even with the danger neutralized.

THE RIGHT WRONG PROMISE

Yes, the Babins are locked up and waiting for trial, but they tried to burn the place to cinders along with my woman.

Better to play it safe.

Coming here now hits different.

The expectancy in the air, the excitement seeping in from the back seat.

"See, kids? Your old man told you we'd be back," I say as I park.

Dan and Sophie are already flinging off their seat belts and throwing their doors open.

"Don't go down to the lake," I call after them, but they're already gone, sprinting around the back.

I'm sure they know better than to risk falling through the ice. I pounded it into their heads ten times over the past week.

Margot stops and stares at the wooden porch. The dusting of snow gives the place an added shine under its tired paint.

"You okay?" I ask. "Tired from the drive?"

"It's just *weird*. Coming back here in the winter, I mean," she says, smiling. "But it's nice to see the kids so amped up."

"They love this place. Almost as much as I do." Since the munchkins aren't watching, I give in to my obsession, taking her face in both hands and kissing her.

"Already? We just got here!" She laughs as she leans back, but I know she's feeling it too.

From the corner of my eye, I see Dan heading back to the front. He ducks behind one of the deer-chewed bushes beside the porch. Sophie's already on the ground in front, making a snow angel.

Damn. Guess I should've had them dressed in snowsuits rather than jeans and jackets.

Oh, well.

"Keep your eye on Dan. He'll probably whip a snowball at you the second you step out," I warn.

"He can try." She opens the door and puts one leg out. "He probably forgot I have an older brother, too."

I watch as she walks to the house, scooping up some of the thick snow in her bare hands and patting it into a ball.

Dan, busy hiding, doesn't notice she's armed and ready until he jumps up, snowball in hand.

The boy wins a nice fat snowball to the face.

I chuckle as I climb out. The frosty air nips my skin, but I don't care.

Margot doubles over, laughing, her breath coming in soft puffs around her and a couple strands of blonde hair escaping from her bun.

"Not fair!" Dan yells as I approach.

"Fair. Don't pick fights you can't win, little man," I say. "Especially when you're not paying attention."

Dan hurls his snowball at Margot, hitting her on the side as she turns.

Sophie comes running into the commotion, her hair already damp with snow and her face flushed from cold.

"Cool it," I say, clapping my hands together. "We need to get unpacked before I have to watch you guys for frostbite."

Predictably, they groan, and so does Margot.

"But *Daaad*," they all say in unison.

"Don't make me say it twice."

With another groan, they all turn and start trudging back to the car.

"Not you." I catch Margot's wrist. "Let's check the house before they blow in. Make sure everything's okay inside. I know Mrs. Griffith was here for a quick check last week, but you never know."

"Like just checking or checking for trouble?" She frowns.

"The house, duchess. It's always good to have peace of

mind." I tap the end of her pink nose. "I'm not worried. Worst thing waiting for us in there is the cold. The cameras are still working."

"Oh, yeah. Right." Her shoulders loosen. "And yes, it'll be *freezing*. I bought a bunch of heating pads and blankets for a reason. Let's get a fire going, though."

Hand in hand, we move, and I'm glad we're ahead of my little tornadoes.

That ice on the porch needs salt. Margot skids on a slick patch from the eaves overhead and almost loses her balance.

I catch her, folding her into my chest.

She looks up with heated eyes.

"Wow. We really *are* back," she whispers. "Feels familiar already."

I smile back to that time in the attic, when we wound up in a similar position.

Hell, I think I fell for her right then.

"That time we kissed," I growl.

"You can relive it."

That's all the invitation I need.

I swing her back up, kissing her long and hard before I see the blur in my peripheral vision.

I break away, holding out a hand, just in time to stop Dan from sprinting up the steps.

"Careful, Bud," I say. "It's icy over here. Why don't you pass up your bags?"

Predictably, the very first thing he brought up was his drum pad. I take it off his hands.

With the door unlocked, Margot helps pass our luggage inside before heading in.

The place looks just like we left it, except we can see our breath.

She flicks on a light, and everything comes to life.

"Sooo cold! You can throw a penguin party in here." Dan shivers.

"Won't be for long," I say, giving him back his drum pad. "Why don't you move around while we crank the heat up? It'll help. Go get settled upstairs."

"You can choose your own room," Margot adds. "Any room except for your dad's room."

"Our room," I say.

She smiles then, her eyes dancing. "Our room, I mean."

Dan doesn't notice the exchange and shoots up. Sophie runs up after him, her suitcase flopping.

"Wait for me, Dan!" she yells, charging up the stairs.

I wince at the sound of the suitcase hitting every single step on the way up.

"Shit, sorry about that," I say.

"What's a few more scratches on the old wood?"

"I'm sure I can buff them out."

"Oh, no. You're not playing handyman this time, Kane Saint. We'll find someone to fix it *after* we leave."

The look in her eyes says there's no argument.

Chuckling, I catch her around the waist, pulling her closer.

Amazingly, our hunger hasn't slowed down a notch in our months together.

Hell, if anything, it's growing like a beanstalk, ever since that kiss.

The fact that I can have her morning, noon, and night some days only makes me fucking ravenous.

If she's not busy on calls with designers and physicians who want her Orthique line of shoes in production by summer, and I'm not investing in my latest start-up projects with mountains of vetting, we're either with the kids or I'm locked up with her under me.

"Your job is dog food now," she teases.

I snort. "Come on, it's *one* start-up I decided to fund. The owner's a nice guy and hungry for a win. Big social media presence with lots of dogs all over social media. Zero chance Brady Pruitt screws me over."

I mean it, too.

After the debacle with OptiSynth, I'm never getting tripped up again.

"Exactly. This is my house and my responsibility. If you're under my roof, you just worry about your updates with cute dogs." She taps my chest with her finger playfully.

That wins her my teeth when I kiss her again.

"What the hell will I do with you and our kids and no work?"

Our kids.

Her eyes blaze, and I think she gets it.

They don't call her *Mom.*

Not yet.

It hasn't been long enough, and they still have a real mother who pops in and out of their lives when she starts feeling guilty.

Margot won't ever replace Daria, no, but there's no hiding how thrilled the kids are to have some motherly affection at home.

No hiding how awestruck that makes me, either.

We're becoming the family I always wanted.

Whole.

Undamaged.

Somehow, a living miracle.

"It really is freezing in here," she says with a shiver. "Can you turn the heat up and start the fire? I'll go make sure the pipes haven't frozen."

"Sure."

She heads off through the house while I go to work.

First big improvement here needs to be better insulation.

We already have a list for this year.

"Kane?" she calls once she's back in the kitchen. "Is there any salt in the toolshed? We should get the ice off the porch before we forget."

"I'll check in a sec."

I stand in the doorway, watching her ass bob as she bends down to look under the kitchen sink.

One day, we *will* come back here alone, minus the kids.

All so I can bend her over every surface of this kitchen and fuck her to ruin.

Upstairs, the kids whoop.

I'm sure they're bouncing on their beds.

Whatever.

Today, I don't mind too much, especially if it keeps them busy.

"No frozen pipes in the bathrooms?" I say as I stroll toward her.

"Nope. Mrs. Griffith did her job." She turns, ass perched on the edge of the counter, and I step between her legs. She grips me with her knees as she says, "You know, Mr. Saint, this is very risky."

"And very necessary. I had to fuck you here sooner or later. And I prefer fucking *soon*," I mutter, leaning down to kiss her.

The bloodlust is instant.

My body overwhelms my brain, urging me to take her now, even though I know that can't happen.

"You're forgetting something," she moans against my mouth, digging her nails into my neck.

"Making you explode on my mouth?"

"Your children."

"Dunno. They're busy upstairs," I growl.

"Not busy enough," she says firmly. "And they're definitely not old enough to catch us like *this*."

"We need more locks on the doors," I snarl.

"You can't lock your children in their rooms, Kane."

"I can and I will." But I'm laughing as I pull away. "We'll have it your way for now, I guess."

Just in time.

Dan comes pounding downstairs and darts past us, out the front door.

"Careful on the steps!" I call, squeezing her hip. "Why don't you set your old bedroom up as your new office? I'll bring in the rest from the car."

Sophie tumbles down the stairs next, hair flying loose from its ponytail.

"When we're done unpacking, can we play outside?" she asks.

Having them play outside is exactly what I want, but I pin on a stern expression.

"Only if you layer up. Coats, hats, gloves, the works. It's bitter out there."

"I know, I know. But can we, Dad?"

"Sure, Soph. As long as you don't go anywhere near the lake."

"They wouldn't be that stupid," Margot says from my other side, giving them both a wink.

"Yeah! We don't wanna *drown*," Sophie says with a quiet dignity as she heads for the car and Dan, who's back hauling the next load of stuff in.

"See you upstairs," I say to Margot and head back out to the car for a few last things. We're not here for that long, so we shouldn't have that much stuff, but somehow, we still have a carful, more than half of it for the kids.

When I get back upstairs, Margot's in her old bedroom, the window cracked and a viciously cold breeze sneaking through the gap. There's something charming about the beauty of her silhouette against the white landscape outside.

I'm lost for words.

Some people are worth the fight.

Worth the fuss, the blood, the sweat, the tears.

Worth the road to forever, paved with hell.

I know that deeply now, just like my failed marriage taught me some people are worth cutting loose.

Margot showed me how good it feels to love, if you can find the right person.

"Thinking about how it feels to be a famous designer yet?" I ask as I go into the room fully, and she laughs, turning around.

"Just checking some emails. And I don't feel famous yet."

"You're on your way." I hold up her iPad. "Especially once Blackthorn Wings launches Orthique in a few months."

She's still so shy.

She blushes adorably. Like she can't believe the whole design world noticed Sophie's bubblegum shoes.

"It feels too good to be true," she admits, glancing up from her tablet.

"What does?"

"To do something I'm actually passionate about."

"You've always been passionate about shoes," I say.

"No, I mean *orthopedic* shoes."

It's crazy how lightning can strike ten times overnight.

Her new partners even offered to make Sophie one of the faces leading the marketing campaign. Daria was disgustingly thrilled, but my little girl said she needed time to think about it.

Whatever she decides, I'll be proud as hell, knowing my daughter will never have to feel shame over her feet again.

"It's not what I imagined. But it's way better than making any other shoes," she says, leaning into my chest and tipping her head back.

"You're too good at this," I whisper, kissing her again.

"I know! Crazy, right? I'm not even *trying*." She shakes her head. "And none of this would've ever happened if Sophie hadn't walked in late one night and asked for help. I couldn't let her down, Kane. Not for anything."

There's a fucking brick in my throat.

Not just because there's an angel in my arms, but because I know this is it.

"Can I steal you away from your designs before dinner?"

"This is a working getaway for me," she says, staring at the tablet I've put back on her desk. "But for you, okay."

Without letting go of her hand, I lead her downstairs and out into the back garden, where the frozen lake glows pink under the winter sunset.

The kids are outside, decked out in all the layers I asked.

I think they're having a snowman-making competition now, passing the time.

"Wait, where are we going?" Margot asks as I lead her forward.

"You'll see."

"You're not taking me out on that lake?"

"If I was going to murder you, sweetheart, I wouldn't fall through the ice with you."

"So romantic." She laughs. "Seriously, you're taking me to… the storm shelter?"

"There's something there I want you to see," I say, reaching out and opening the huge metal doors.

She hesitates as she looks into the darkness. "I haven't been down there since Lee…"

"I know." I touch her face, turning it to face mine. "I promise, there's nothing there to scare you. Just something you'll like. We're replacing the shit memories with better ones today. Trust me."

After another second, she nods. "Okay."

First thing I do is bring out the blindfold, slipping it over her eyes.

"Um, how will I get down the stairs like this?" she asks, holding still. "I can't see anything."

"That's the point. I'm going to help you. Are you ready?"

"Nope!" She laughs.

"Perfect." I take her hand and flick on the new light I had installed.

No more flashlights. I want this place to feel safe, welcoming. The same way it must've felt before for her grandparents.

We've come full circle, and I want her to appreciate how special that is.

After the showdown, this place was covered in dust and glass shards. The beautiful stained glass window was destroyed.

It took a long damn time to get it cleaned up while she was sleeping during our last trip.

But now the floor is bare. There's a stained glass panel back where it originally stood, and this time it's made so it opens easily.

I lead her down and stop in front of it. The backlighting gives off an ethereal glow, like it belongs in an old cathedral.

"Okay," I whisper, reaching for her blindfold. I slip my fingers into the band and stop.

"You're really milking this."

"Only because you'll freak."

She leans into me a little. "I'm already happy."

Slowly, I ease the blindfold off and stand back, watching her reaction as she comes face-to-face with the stained glass.

The stained glass image of us.

Her blonde hair and my dark, her blue eyes and my green, her head on my chest and my arms around her.

"Holy—Kane!" Her voice breaks. "*Kane.*"

"Yeah?" I barely breathe.

"What? How? *When?*" She turns to face me, eyes glistening with tears. "Oh my God, did you do this?"

"Took five years off my life," I admit. "A lot of late nights. Months working with the best back in New York until I felt like I could do it justice."

"You *made* this? Are you freaking serious?"

I nod firmly.

"Leonidas Blackthorn wouldn't have settled for anything less in your grandma's old studio, would he?"

Her bottom lip quivers.

Slowly, shakingly, she nods, and then she wheels back around to the glass.

It's not as intricate as the greats, no.

Not the sort of rustic beauty you'd find in a church—that's not us. It's vivid and bright and the colors are a little chunky.

Still, it's a statement piece, as she'd like to say.

Just like Sophie's shoes.

It's mine. It's ours.

It's fucking everything.

I slaved over each inch of glass down to the last detail.

"I thought you'd want it replaced one day, and this seemed fitting."

"It's us," she whispers reverently.

"Us."

"God, Kane. Have I told you I love you?" She almost charges into my arms, and I catch her, holding her softness against me. "Because I love you. I *love* you."

"I haven't even gotten to the good part yet."

"What good part?" She looks around the empty space. "What, are you going to carve our names into a tree? Write them in the sky? Bury us alive together?"

"Sometimes, I worry about you."

"I'm serious, Kane. What more *is* there?"

"This." I kiss her, then step back.

Without hesitation, I drop to one knee, reaching in my back pocket for the little box I spent hours picking out.

Hattie helped me, and I know it caused the girl physical pain not to be able to blab it to Margot five seconds later.

"Holy shit!" she squeals, one hand coming to her mouth. "Are you serious? Oh my *God*."

"I haven't even asked yet," I say, trying not to laugh.

"Oh, yeah, right, I'm—sorry. Sorry! Ask away. Ask me. I'll pretend I never said anything."

"Don't want you pretending, duchess. Not today and not ever. This proposal couldn't have gone any other way if it wasn't real." I flick the box open.

Inside, there's the tiny emerald ring nestled inside, set in brilliant gold. Something small and elegant and stylish, just like my wife.

Fuck me, *my wife.*

The diamond-clustered emerald felt perfect, delicate and stunning like her.

When I showed Hattie, she agreed, so I went ahead and bought it.

"Margot." I say her name reverently, and she meets my gaze, the tears spilling over. "Before I met you, I told myself I wouldn't ever marry again, because I didn't think anyone else would ever fit into my family. But you came along and you proved me wrong, and I've been thankful every day."

"I didn't think you'd ask," she says through her fingers, releasing a long, shuddering breath. "Not this fast. Not so *soon*."

"When you know, you know," I tell her. "And I knew almost from the first week in this house that you were the exception to every rule. I knew since I kissed you in the attic. So, Margot Blackthorn, will you be my wife?"

She laughs wildly and holds out a shaking hand.

"You know I will! You know—Kane, you know, and so do I."

"Hell yeah," I say, taking the ring out of its cream satin and sliding it onto her finger. The perfect fit still feels like a relief. "But I had to ask."

"I know we've talked about the future, but I didn't think you were ready." She's half crying, half laughing, cupping my face in her hands. "I thought you wanted to wait a while, and… and I was cool with that."

"Wait for what?" I take her hand and kiss her finger—the one with a glittering ring sitting on it like a star. "I told you, I knew since the moment we met."

"Liar," she says, tipping her head back to reveal her throat. "You hated me when we first met."

"Didn't hate you."

"No, but you didn't think I was the future stepmom of your kids." She stops, thinking about that for a second. "Oh, do you think they'll—"

"They'll love it," I assure her. "They love *you*."

"Oh well, I know that. But I've never tried to be anyone's mom, you know?"

"It won't be hard. Nothing different from what you've been doing every day for months. You're my wife and their friend and yes, an authority figure when you need to be, but you don't push it. They respect you for that. That's what matters."

"I love them," she admits, crying all over again. "But you're right. If I didn't think I could, I wouldn't say yes, no matter how much I loved you."

"And if I didn't think they'd love you, if they didn't *already* love you," I say, sinking my fingers into her silky hair, "then I'd never ask."

"You make me so happy, Kane. It's kinda scary." She holds

out a hand, watching wide-eyed as the ring gleams elegantly in the low light, colorfully tinted from the stained glass.

"That's okay," I tell her, sliding my fingers between hers and holding our linked hands above my heart. "You can be scared. I'll still be right here to hold your hand."

"I. Love. You." She laughs and turns back to the glass. "It's almost a shame this is down here where no one will see it."

"It's our special place. Our little secret."

"I mean, that's nice, too." She turns and presses her head against my shoulder.

For the longest time, we just stand there, lost in each other.

If someone had asked me before coming to the lake house if I thought I'd be proposing in the new year, I'd have laughed in their face.

I was done with love and all the trouble that came with it.

Then Margot streaked into my life like a comet, and it's been one hell of a ride ever since.

And I wouldn't change a single damn thing.

I just think what kind of romantic clown I've become, knowing her and wanting to make her happy to the letter of the law.

The man I was a year ago would've called me whipped.

The man I was ten years ago wasn't half the man I am now.

Now, that last missing piece falls into place, and I've met the man I was meant to be.

"Should we head up?" I say, and she nods, this time being the one to take my hand and lead me upstairs into the grey, washed-out light of the day.

It's clouded over, the sky threatening more snow tonight. The wind whips her hair across her face.

"We should tell them," she says, but I just point over her shoulder.

While we were down there, the kids' snowman making competition turned into something a little more elaborate.

I don't know who wins—Dan's depiction of me with a large carrot stuck in my face—or Sophie's Margot, with branchy arms dragging on the ground.

Neither of them are world-class artists yet.

But they also grabbed our clothes.

The snowman has my hat, and Margot's scarf is wrapped around 'Margot's' neck. The snow woman has bright-red berries for a mouth, pressed into a heart shape. Dan even scrubbed some shredded bark onto my snowman's chin for stubble.

I scratch my short beard with a smile.

"Congratulations!" Sophie screams, right before cannon-balling herself at Margot.

Margot looks at me helplessly as she's practically tackled to the ground by two small kids. "Did you tell them before we—"

"No," I say, wrapping my arms around them from behind. Sophie squeals with laughter, and Dan makes a noise a bit like a chicken. "But I guess I let something slip to Dan."

"I knew the whole time, Dad!" he says smugly. "I figured he was going to ask you to marry him. Sophie said you'd say yes because you love him and you already live with us, so why not? It just makes sense!"

And it does.

Margot laughs. She tips her head back and laughs at the sky so hard the tears roll down her face.

"What?" Dan asks anxiously. "Did I say something wrong?"

"No, Bud," I say, holding my family tighter. "Nothing you could say right now could ever ruin this."

XXVII: NO PLACE LIKE (MARGOT)

Three Months Later

𝓘 thought the proposal would always be the happiest day of my life—and I was *wrong*.

Nothing on God's green earth will ever beat our wedding day.

We spent the winter renovating the lake house, bringing in contractors for the big stuff and doing the little fixes ourselves, slowly making it into a home.

Our home.

A special family place like PopPop always wanted.

No, we can't settle in permanently with the kids going to school in New York and both of us taking frequent business trips. We've been to LA more times than I can count over the past few months while fashionistas and tech savvy marketers planned out how to launch Orthique into orbit.

Sure, I'm endlessly grateful for the shoe dream becoming a reality, but it has nothing on becoming Mrs. Kane Saint.

And just like Ethan, I have Gramps' whimsy to thank for that.

What better way to honor him than by making the old house into a stunning new place worthy of becoming our home base?

For real.

I don't know how to process being this happy.

It feels wrong.

Like I can't possibly keep smiling this much without some big, scary thing coming around the corner to crash the vibe.

Today, though, that scary thing is just me standing in front of a hundred people and hoping I can get my heart out in the vows we've rehearsed before I seize up.

Hattie adjusts the pale-blue dress she's wearing. Who else would be my maid of honor?

If I wasn't the bride, I might say she outshines me in the sleek satin, all her curves on display.

"Okay, here we go." Hattie brushes my dress down, making sure there are no flaws. "Ready to walk the aisle, princess?"

"Hattie. I'm not five."

"It's your wedding day! Every girl's entitled to the royal treatment," she says firmly and unhooks the dress from where it's resting on the closet door.

"You heard the lady. Everyone's a princess." My little cousin, Cleo, nods from the corner, slouched in a chair with her massive sketchpad. "Them's the rules and I don't make them."

"Just wait for *your* wedding day, Clee. You'll love the rules I make up then."

"Oh, no." She flushes and shakes her head like the shy little art geek she is. "I'll let you and Ethan have all the fun. I don't need that much crazy in my life."

I shoot Hattie a knowing look.

"You haven't chatted up Jackie Wilkes about the will yet, have you?"

Cleo shakes her head, the bright-pink highlights in her hair flashing.

"Man, I just wonder if Gramps saved the best for last. What if he sends you off to a dinosaur dig and you wind up engaged to a hot archaeologist or something?"

"Oh my God, can we stop?" Her face is a ripe tomato.

"She has a point. Let's get back to your wedding day, Gigi." Hattie looks smugly satisfied as she studies my face in the mirror for any touch-ups needed. "The rules say you have to be smack-dab gorgeous, and I'm not letting you walk out there looking like anything less. I have to return the favor."

"True, you had some help from yours truly," I say with a grin. "Your mom wasn't half-bad either."

Her eyes meet mine in the mirror, and she grins back, nodding to the makeup brush in my hand.

"Yet here you are, doing your own makeup like a pro. You *know* how good you'll look when the dust settles. I'm here for moral support."

It's true. I didn't want to bring anyone all the way out here just to make my face a wedding mask.

Besides, if there's one thing you learn from growing up famous, it's how to do makeup quickly and efficiently.

Kane said he'd leave it to me, yes, but he's also a minimalist at heart.

For my hubby, I've kept it simple, going for a subtle spring glow that brightens my features.

Light-brown liner, just enough to emphasize the shape of my eyes.

No false lashes.

Soft coral-pink lipstick.

The same shade painted on my fingers and toes.

"Okay, how are we doing? Incredible yet?" I ask the peanut gallery.

"Smokeshow," Cleo clips.

"*Showstopper!*" Hattie agrees, brushing a hand down the sleek satin of my skirt. "Holy crap, it's almost time. Are you ready?"

Ready or not...

I check my phone.

Mom sent me a pic of some flowers and says she'll be up in a sec.

"Mom's coming," I say. "I think she'll want to help me put on the dress."

"Mom's privilege," she agrees carefully.

I know where she's coming from.

Hattie's relationship with her mom also wasn't the best until recently, so she gets how complicated it can be. But in the end, family's family, and if they're willing to step up, we'll let them.

Ever since Ethan found out he wasn't Dad's last summer, and ever since I turned over Gramps' stuff to Mom, she's been stepping it up in the parenting department.

It's a little weird, honestly.

But it means a lot to see her try.

"Whoa. That's a ton of flowers." Hattie peers over my shoulder at the message.

"I asked her to pick them up. Hopefully she has the bouquet so I can see if I can even carry it. It's *huge.*"

"Gorgeous, though!" she says.

She's right.

Beautiful daisies, roses, and dahlias.

They'll be a vibrant splash of color against my cream dress.

"Very you," Cleo adds, standing over my shoulder. "Kinda important to make it all jive."

It's a relief to hear that, knowing I let Mom pick the flowers without much discussion. Of course, she went for something extravagant and over-the-top because that's Mom, but she chose something I would like.

A statement.

Not the elegant, insanely pricey Black Baccara roses she'd have picked and had flown in from Europe. Like she actually did for her own wedding, I mean.

There's a knock at the door, and Mom comes in, dressed in a pale-yellow dress that she somehow pulls off. I'm surprised the flowers piled in her arms doesn't pull her over.

"This is for the altar," she gasps, a little winded.

We're in the room I first stayed in when I met Kane.

Somehow, it felt right—and it gives him the opportunity to get ready with Dan and Ethan and his parents.

Hattie hangs the dress back up and takes the flowers, while Mom hugs me so tight I can't quite breathe.

"You look *so* gorgeous, honey," she says, a little choked. "No wonder Kane wants to marry you."

I smile, because I know she means it in the best way. "I thought you were going to be late."

"And miss the moment my daughter steps into her dress for the first time? No!" She shakes her head firmly. "This is too important. I wouldn't miss it for the world."

Having passed the flowers off to Clee to carry downstairs, Hattie hands me my dress again.

We picked it for its simplicity, this modern and elegant off the shoulder piece, airy and bright. It sweeps in at my waist and cascades out again at my feet.

Classic and timeless.

I step into it carefully and for the first time, the tears bite.

Holy hell.

As far as weddings go, this one feels relaxed, but the emotional sucker punch had to come sometime.

So far, I haven't had to do anything except wake up and scarf down the breakfast Hattie brought me in bed.

"Yay, the sun's out! The rain this morning had me worried," Hattie says, bouncing with excitement at the window. "And it looks like they're all set up. Don't look, Margot. You can't see yet and spoil the surprise."

Since I planned the whole thing, it doesn't make that much sense that I'm not allowed to peek, but whatever. I'm too busy eyeing myself in the mirror for imperfections to care about what they're doing outside.

I finally look like a bride today.

I look like I'm getting *married.*

Hattie turns and her eyes widen.

"Oh, Margot," she whispers, her hands flying to her mouth. "How does it look even *better* today than when you tried it on for alterations?"

"Um, I guess because it's really happening." I don't know if I'm trembling from nerves or sheer excitement. "Come help me do my hair."

Hattie and Mom work together to get my hair sorted, both chattering away about the guest list, a who's who of New England power and fame, plus the folks who couldn't make it.

There are a few people I don't mind passing on their invitations.

Daria, for one.

She's down in Key West filming for two weeks and had to decline.

Honestly, I'm relieved.

I knew we had to invite her for the family's sake.

Just like I know how important it is to keep up healthy relationships for the kids. Still, every time I find out another way she neglected them, I want to punch her.

But this is my wedding day, and even my distaste for Daria can't last.

"Everyone's in place," Mom says from her perch by the window. "Ooh, and Kane's walking to the front. That man has a good pair of shoulders."

"*Mom.*"

"It's fine, your dad said as much. Keeping fit, that's important for a man at any age. You need to be sure he takes his health seriously, and yours, too." She touches her hair self-consciously, though it's fresh from the salon and almost blindingly glossy.

"I can look after myself," I say, rolling my eyes at how hopelessly cringe she can be.

She looks at me and smiles.

"I know, honey. You've proven that, what with your near-death incident and all."

There's another knock at the door, and when Mom opens it, Sophie pokes her head through.

Finally, someone who won't annoy me.

"Hey, Soph," I say, putting the finishing touches to my lipstick and slipping a thin chain around my neck. The engagement ring glints on my finger, and like I always do, I have to stop myself from admiring it.

"Are you guys almost ready?" Sophie asks shyly. "The ceremony's supposed to start soon."

"It's a wedding, half pint. Brides are always late." Hattie winks at the little girl.

"Really? Why?" Sophie frowns.

I look back in the mirror.

"You know what? You're right. Why should I be late when I've been *dying* to walk down that aisle?"

"Yay!" Sophie claps her hands.

I give her a quick once-over.

She helped pick out her dress, which is an adorable pink

made from satin to match mine. She's also wearing a pair of adorable white sneakers with gold splashed along the sides, specially designed just for her today.

"Still got the rings?" I ask her.

"Wouldn't lose them for the world! They're in my pocket," she says proudly.

"Then let's go have a wedding."

Hattie takes my arm, and Mom takes the other as my breath stalls.

This is it.

The end and the beginning.

As Sophie leads the way, we head to the back door, where a red carpet sprawls down the steps, flowing all the way to the cute altar by the lake.

Outside, it's heavenly.

The sun shines like liquid gold.

The birds chirp merrily in the trees, the lake gleams like emerald, and all the people I love have assembled to watch me marry the man I love the most of all.

"Oh, no, are you going to cry?" Hattie whispers. "Because if you cry, I'm cooked. I'll cry ten times more."

Actually, there's a real chance I will burst into hilariously messy tears, but I just squeeze her arm.

Mom leans in to kiss my cheek.

"Hang on. I'll check in with the music," she whispers and hurries along the carpet.

The huge, winding red carpet was Dan's idea, and it felt like a little much in the planning stage.

Now that it's forging the perfect path, it's everything.

I start down it slowly, the priest having caught Kane's attention so he's facing away from me.

Good. I want to see the wildfire in his eyes when he notices me walking down the aisle toward him, counting down the seconds.

One.

We step through a wooden arch threaded with white roses. There's a low hum through the crowd as they realize I've arrived.

Two.

Kane turns, and the band starts up.

And there, right in the middle, I see Dan with his drums and the most serious look on his face.

He barely stops to grin up at me as he does a little solo, the rest of the band backing off to give him space.

Three.

Holy potato, here come the tears.

"Good luck—you'll kill it!" Hattie whispers, and she pulls Sophie back gently so I can walk in front of them.

Four.

It's a shorter aisle, which means I'm already close enough to Kane to notice the slack-jawed wonder on his face, the lopsided smile he holds in, and when I take another two steps, the sheen in his eyes.

I stop counting because it doesn't matter anymore.

I'm not freaked out by all the eyes on me.

I'm not second-guessing.

I'm not afraid.

How could I *ever* be anything else than ready to jump into tomorrow with his man?

"I love a man who cries at weddings," I whisper playfully as soon as I'm close enough.

Ethan snickers loudly in the front row. Hattie slaps him.

"I don't cry at weddings, woman," Kane murmurs. "Just mine. I thought you were beautiful before, but now..."

He doesn't finish.

He doesn't need to.

The awe etched on his face leaves me in shambles.

"Y-you don't look so bad yourself, Mr. Saint." I force down the boulder in my throat.

But I do mean it.

There he is, decked out in this magnificent deep-teal suit with a yellow rose pinned on, so vivid it glows—presumably courtesy of my mother.

When he made his color choice, at first I wasn't sure.

But he's handsome and suave and he'd look good in anything.

If he was standing here in worn sweatpants and a jersey, I wouldn't hesitate.

I'd take the hand he offers, just like I do now, locking his fingers around mine until it hurts.

Together, we face the altar, waiting for destiny.

* * *

It's crazy how fast the biggest day of your life vanishes before you can blink.

After the reception, the band—minus Dan—takes over while the guests split up and file in for dinner.

We pose for photos.

Ethan razzes me and Dad tells me how proud he is of his baby girl.

Kane's mother pinches her son's cheek until I think she'll leave a bruise.

Everything goes better than I imagined.

The only missing piece is Gramps, but not really.

There's an empty seat at one table and a lit candle next to his portrait.

I can almost feel his hawkish eyes following us the whole time, finally at peace.

The same look he'd give me after those extravagant scavenger hunts as kids when I'd come in, show off his gifts, and he'd hold me up in his arms, always whispering, *"That'll do, darling May. That'll do."*

This was his home once, half a decade ago.

Now, we went and made it ours, and even if he's not here in person, even if he's somewhere in the afterlife, his spirit lingers.

He'll always be as real as the air we breathe.

And I think he's lighter now, no longer this heavy, sad presence, just waiting for me to stumble over his secrets.

He's just another soul who's glad to have his beloved family back in one piece.

"Look." Kane takes my hand just as I'm about to get out of my own head and thank a few more guests for coming.

He nods.

There, by the shore, beside an old log, I see Mom. She's just a silhouette in the sunset, but there's no mistaking the small bouquet of flowers clutched in her hands—or the meaning.

Roses for Gramps.

Her way of saying 'apology accepted,' and maybe goodbye.

For a second, I break, shoving my face into Kane's chest to muffle my sobs.

"You're okay, wife. We're *all* okay now."

"That's... that was always his favorite spot," I strangle out, nodding at the log. "I think maybe he used to sit there a lot with my grandma, too. I've seen a couple old photos where they're there, their backs turned, just admiring the water."

We watch Mom for a few more seconds, but it's her moment.

I turn back to the reception area. Two huge gazebos and enormous tables of food. Dan keeps gorging himself on sweets long after dinner, and little Sophie tears up the dance floor, blissfully oblivious to her shuffling steps, all thanks to her beautiful shoes.

"Guess we did all right, huh?" I rest my head on Kane's shoulder.

"We fucking scored. Best wedding I've ever been to."

"Hey."

"I never said I was the *groom* at." He laughs and bends to kiss me. "Have I told you how beautiful you are?"

"You always do. But maybe one more time?"

He snorts. "So beautiful I know I'm the luckiest idiot in the universe."

"You'd better." I laugh and drag him to where Hattie's waving us over. "Come on, our people await."

"No rest for the wicked," he mutters, but he's grinning.

"Exhausted yet?" Hattie asks. "I remember when we got married, there were so many people to talk to and so much to do and so much to eat! I looked up and it was almost midnight."

"It's going by too fast, but I'm having the best time. The weather and *this*." I wave my hand around at the crowd that turned out to celebrate us. "What could be better?"

"I saw your latest article," Ethan tells Kane. "Left me with a lot to chew on. I have firms beating down our door all the time with some revolutionary AI algorithms for real estate."

Hattie nudges him. "Seriously? Today of all days you guys have to talk about work?"

But Kane nods, and I roll my eyes at Hattie.

Men, I mouth.

She shrugs, but secretly I think she's as delighted as I am that Kane and Ethan are getting along.

"There's no undoing the tech. We just need to slow down and think before going full steam ahead," Kane says. "People should know the risks and the ways it can screw up the human equation. The more support I can drum up for that, the better."

"I shared it. Not that you needed the help when it went viral." Ethan folds his arms.

"Thanks, man." Kane nods. "It starts with awareness, hands down. This shit should be treated like splitting the atom. If we use it to power cities instead of wiping them off the map, everybody wins."

Despite the heavy subject at our wedding, I smile.

Kane finally decided what he wants to do in the near-term besides investing, and he's charged into it.

His new AI action group leverages his name in sports and his family's old political connections to try to broaden the discussion around artificial intelligence.

Especially the threat to stifling human creativity.

There's a lot I agree with and a lot more that's over my head, but so what?

His heart's in the right place, worthy of the hero he'll always be.

And I'm so proud of him for fighting back and trying to do some good in an upside-down world.

Ethan and Kane talk on about their business endeavors and prospects, while Hattie and I grab more cake and giggle over our party favors.

"Mind if I cut in?"

Kane finds me, scoops me into his arms, and carries me up the red carpet to the lake house, leaving the final few people still in attendance to clean up after us.

"Hey!" I smack his shoulder, laughing, throwing my head back as he strides up to the house. "Did you miss the part where we're leaving our wedding behind?"

"Nope." He doesn't glance behind him.

"What are you doing?"

"What does it look like?" He pauses on the threshold. "I'm

bringing my wife home. Then she's heading upstairs to consummate this marriage until she passes out at dawn."

"Wow. Big words. You really think you can handle Mrs. Saint?" I try and fail to test my new name without shuddering. "That's going to take some getting used to."

"I think I'm goddamned explosive."

I reach up and brush a lock of dark hair from his face. He's almost painfully lovely in the light.

"Go on, then," I say. "Carry me over the threshold, hubby."

"This is the part that makes the marriage valid," he says, taking a giant step over the threshold into our lovely, renovated home.

While we've been busy drinking champagne and living it up, someone came back and weaved white flowers around the banister Kane repaired during our first week together.

Candles burn on both sides of the steps, flanking a smattering of rose petals.

"Can't believe I let you talk me into real candles. That's a fire risk," Kane says, but they've only just been lit.

"You hush. It's beautiful and Hattie will sneak in later to put them out before she leaves." I reach up and take his chin in my hands, turning his face to me so I can kiss him. "So," I tease. "Aren't you going to carry me up the stairs?"

He does it so easily, not even pausing for breath halfway up.

And this human whirlwind doesn't stop there, carrying me to the bedroom, which has transformed into a bridal boutique.

It's ridiculously pretty and over-the-top, which makes me think my mom had to be involved. It also makes my eyes sting.

This is my husband.

My new life.

The right wrong promise.

The forever I didn't think I was ever promised.

Tomorrow, we're grabbing the kids from a sleepover with their grandma and heading to the airport.

We'll be in Costa Rica for the next two weeks, celebrating our first family vacation, but tonight it's just us.

"I've said this before, but I am lucky," he growls, plopping me down on the bed. "You make me blessed."

"Kane..." I hold out my arms so he can get one last look at me before he takes this thing off.

"You heard me. Blessed." He's already looking me up and down with a razor-sharp hunger that tells me he loves what he sees. "And have I ever told you how fuck-hot you look in that dress?"

I gasp a little.

"Yes, actually. But you know I don't mind hearing it again."

"You're too fuckable for life, Margot Saint." He leans forward so his weight braces on the bed and he sucks my neck.

His teeth scrape my collarbone until I shiver, already reduced to a moaning mess.

"I'm blessed too. Because romance isn't dead." I twist underneath him, digging my nails into his chest playfully. "Want to know something even better?"

"What?"

"All you have to do to get me out of this dress is a simple zip."

"Damn. I thought I'd die from blue balls working at the buttons."

"They're fake."

"Do you know how much I love you?" He kisses me, his mouth hot and eager, his tongue delving deeper until there's zero doubt he intends to *show me*.

I go down laughing, long and hard, this happy high that radiates from head to toe.

The kind of deep, lasting joy that blooms from the inside out.

I think I'm at capacity.

Thank you, Gramps.

All because I came to this beat-up lake house with no clue it would end in the man who's made for me ripping off my wedding dress.

For a second, I send up one more thankful prayer.

Then Kane kisses me again, growls into my mouth, and I stop thinking of anything else at all.

FLASH FORWARD: ONE BIG HAPPY HOME (KANE)

Years Later

"Dan?" Margot calls upstairs. She's holding his lunch in one hand and one sneaker in the other. "Dan, hurry, you're going to be late."

There's a thump from upstairs. Probably my son rolling out of bed like he's still trying to figure out how to use his arms and legs after the latest growth spurt.

At the table, calmly eating oatmeal like it's not her first day of high school, Sophie rolls her eyes. "I *told* him to get up when I did, but he said he wanted a few more minutes."

"Dan!" Margot calls.

"I'm coming," Dan calls. "Two minutes. Put some toast on for me, will you?"

"I'll get that," I say, putting the small plastic spoon down and leaving Elliot where he's sitting in his highchair.

His little chubby hands bang against the plastic tray, and I laugh. My baby boy gurgles at me.

"I know, buddy. Patience."

Dressed in a suit and heels, Margot dumps Dan's bag and singular sneaker in the corner and pulls out her iPad, flicking through her new designs. She's going to present them at the annual Blackthorn Wings board meeting.

The company has taken off faster than we could've predicted. In no time, there's a massive online store, brick and mortar sites in Portland and New York City, and plans to expand soon.

My wife's latest designs are part of her expansion project.

I drop a kiss on the top of her head as she flicks through her presentation. "You'll kill it, duchess. You should look more confident."

"You say that now, but what happens if I forget everything?"

"You won't."

"You don't know that. And ugh, what do I really know about the Canadian market?"

"More than you think. You don't forget *anything*. Sometimes I wish you did." I return to Elliot and pick up the spoon. It's a normal breakfast, chaotic and messy, and I wouldn't have it any other way. "How are you feeling, Soph?"

She chews, thinking, and blinks behind her glasses.

I cannot believe how grown-up my little girl looks.

Margot taught her how to do her makeup, and there's a flick of tasteful eyeliner.

Part of me hates it—she looks so much older than my daughter, and interesting enough to start catching boys' eyes.

But I guess that's what happens when every dad has teenage girls.

You don't want to give them up, and no little half-grown broccoli haired punk will ever be good enough.

Makeup or not, I still won't okay dating until she's sixteen.

"I feel sick," she says.

Margot looks up from her tablet.

"You look amazing," she says. "That cat eye really suits you."

"Right?" She preens a little, perking up. "It took me, like, half an hour to get it just right."

Dan finally comes barreling into the room, his hair a mess and his tie wonky.

"Food," he says bluntly, and pops the toast before it's done. "Is there any peanut butter?"

"In the cupboard, where it always lives, big guy," Margot says.

"Tuck your shirt in," I say. He grumbles to himself as he finds a plate, but he does as I say. I scoop up another spoonful of orange goop and hold it to Elliot's face. We eye each other. "I just want you to know that I'm not putting up with insubordination. Not from anyone."

"Dad! Cringe." Sophie rolls her eyes. It's her favorite word lately. "Also, he's a baby. He can't *understand* you, y'know."

"He might." Margot sticks her tablet back in her bag and eyes the kitchen devastation. "How does this happen?" she demands. "I just cleaned up last night so the housekeeper wouldn't have a crime scene to deal with."

That makes me chuckle.

Only woman around with her kind of money who cleans up before the cleaner.

"Kids," I mutter.

Right at the same time Dan, with his mouth full, mutters, "Probably Dad."

I flash him a look and he seals his lips.

That's what I thought, Bud.

"Okay," Margot says, checking her watch. "I have a few before I need to leave. When is band practice till, Dan?"

"Five."

"Great. I'll pick you up then. Soph, you good waiting?"

She nods, eyes shining. "There's an astrology club *on the same day*. Isn't that amazing?"

"Certainly convenient," Margot says, and laughs, giving Sophie a hug on her way past. "It's exciting. But you don't have anything to be nervous about. Everyone's going to love you, and anyone who doesn't has bad taste. Don't listen to them."

"Dude." Dan swallows his final bite of toast. "Just tell everyone your stepmom is a shoe designer and everything will be fine. They'll wanna be friends with you to get in good with Margot Blackthorn."

They both still call Margot by her name, though sometimes they slip up and call her Mom.

Either way, it doesn't matter to her—she doesn't need a title to love them fiercely.

"Okay," she says, plucking Elliot from his chair and kissing his chubby cheeks. He gurgles, clearly in a good mood this morning. "I need to go. Dan, please comb your hair again before you head out. You want to make a good impression. And listen to your teachers."

"Yeah, I will." He smooths down his hair with no success.

"You're going to do amazing, guys. I wish I could see you off, but I'll be late for my meeting if I don't leave now."

"It's fine," Sophie says. "You saw us off for every grade in middle school."

"True," I say. "And I don't have my meeting until one, so I've got loads of time."

Her eyes meet mine with a burst of gratitude.

Margot's business soared the same time as my AI lobbying did, and ever since, it's been a fight to balance our lives.

But it's nothing like my past marriage where careerism and disinterest slowly ate us alive.

Margot always pushes for family first, and so do I.

We make sure we're prioritizing the kids, the dinners, the movie nights, and the vacations. We get 'home' to Sully Bay as often as we can, where we pick right up on the magic we left behind.

Hell, sometimes I think that magic picks us up and carries us with a will of its own.

Last Christmas, we had a moose come sniffing around the house. The big guy even settled in for a nap by the new detached studio I built for Margot, perfectly connected to May Blackthorn's old workshop underground.

After I joked that Santa must've upped his reindeer game, we spent the whole afternoon crafting a life-sized snow-moose.

And when Elliot came along, we had to reshuffle our lives again. I'm damn glad it's one big growing extended family.

Between us, plus Hattie and Ethan, and Cleo and Holden, it's easy trading kids whenever somebody needs a break.

"I love you," Margot tells Sophie, hugging her until she squirms. "I can't wait to hear about your first day, girlie. You'll kill it in physics. Don't let the juniors scare you just because you're smarter than them. Remember, kill them with kindness."

"Mom!" Sophie's eyes spark with amusement. "Is that what you did with your bullies?"

"Well, I didn't get to skip three grades for science like you, but I had your uncle Ethan." Margot drags Dan into a reluctant hug. "Make me proud, boy-o. Don't get in trouble unless you can't help it. Enjoy band practice tonight."

"Yeah, I will." He mumbles with another full mouth, but the moody brat can't hide his loving smile.

Then Margot plants a kiss on my lips. "Love you, Dadzilla. Go kill it today."

"You too, woman," I say, but she's already half out the door.

"I'll let you know!" she calls behind her.

The front door bangs and she's gone.

First whirlwind out the house.

"Okay, guys," I say. "You have ten minutes. Check your backpacks one more time, I don't want to have to turn around halfway there. Do you have lunch money?"

Sophie nods. "You gave it to us yesterday."

Dan looks like he'll argue the point, but by the looks of it, he's realized he's forgotten something, so he goes pounding back upstairs to find it.

Sophie's still sitting at the breakfast table, very still.

"You okay?" I ask her.

"Yeah. Just…" She looks at me despairingly. "What if I have no one to sit with at lunch? It's *weird* when you take classes with the older kids."

Damn.

I remember being her age, how exile from the friend group was the catastrophe feared by every teen.

Dan's always been great at making friends—the trouble we'll have is making sure he doesn't make the *wrong* ones.

Sophie, she's always been a little less confident. Margot has gone a long way toward fixing that, but being bullied half her school life because of her shoes has left its mark.

"Everyone's in the same boat, Soph, whether they're a science whiz or not," I say. "Everyone's going to be a little scared and a little nervous, and they're not going to know who to sit with. If no one sits with you, go find someone who looks shy and sit with *them*."

"What if they don't want to sit with me?"

"Not happening. Nobody in their right mind would prefer to be alone." I flick her braids until she smiles. "If all else fails, you sit with your brother."

"Dan? No way!" Her nose wrinkles. "He'll have his dumb music friends and the jocks who buddy up to him. Totally not my crowd, Dad."

Considering the jocks are the least of my worries, I have to bite back a smile as I say, "He's your brother, Soph. He wouldn't leave you stranded."

I'm backed up by Dan clattering down the stairs, a thick textbook in one hand and a sneaker in the other. He shoves them both in his bag.

"Just stop being weird and sit with me, Soph," he says. "We're twins. People expect us to be all creepy and shit."

"Language, little man," I growl.

"And *stuff*," he corrects. "Anyway, are we ready or what?"

Outside, the sky is a clear blue and the day is shaping up to be a gorgeous one, cloudless and hot.

A shame we're all too busy to enjoy it, but we'll be back at the lake house for the fall colors soon enough.

As I get Elliot strapped into his booster seat in the back, Dan and Sophie exchange a few words with our elderly next-door neighbor, who's spent the past four years watching them grow from kids into teenagers. The lady has a real soft spot for Dan even though he kicked a football through her window.

Probably because he came around to apologize and offered her the rest of his pocket money to fix it without either of us knowing.

Elliot's face screws up as I strap him in, and I pinch his cheek.

"Not today, squirt," I tell him. "It's a big day for your brother and sister. Let's make this easier on them, huh?"

He stares at me with Margot's blue eyes, but by some miracle he doesn't wail like he was threatening to, and I call the kids over.

With the morning traffic, it's a twenty-minute drive to

school. Dan gives Sophie shotgun, letting her sit beside me, while he takes the spot beside a drooling Elliot.

"Babies are so helpless, Dad. It's crazy you had a third kid," he informs me after wiping Elliot's chin with a tissue.

"One day, you'll get it."

He makes an unconvinced grunt and goes silent.

"Or," I continue, "maybe you won't. But Sophie, she'll keep the family line going, and you'd best be ready to wipe more drool and spilled baby food."

"No thanks! I'm gonna live out west," he says, horrified.

Sophie giggles. "No, but you'll still be the uncle. And we'll still visit."

"Uncles don't wipe chins."

"I dunno." Sophie is on a roll now, laughing along with me. "Think about Uncle Ethan."

"He *wants* a baby. He has a baby."

"Yeah, but even if he didn't, he would wipe Elliot's chin."

"He's changed his diaper," I tell them. "Several times now."

"*So* gross," Dan coughs hilariously, but I know he's doing it more for fun.

Once we pull up outside the school, I smile.

Sophie forgot how to be nervous on the ride over. She's laughing at something Dan said, and I know they'll both be okay.

"You know I'm proud of you both, right?" I say.

"Yeah, we know." Dan flings the door open. "C'mon, Soph, let's go. Before he *hugs* us again!"

She's slower, but he waits for her to offer a helping hand. They walk up the stairs to the main entrance.

Of course, I offered to come in as they ran away, but they weren't having it.

Elliot blows a loud raspberry in the back, and I pull away with a chuckle.

It's a new era, and another day in the best season of my life.

I fucking love the life I've built with Margot Saint.

No matter how hard it gets in the turbulent teenage years, these moments tell me it was all worth it in the end.

And when we're reunited later tonight, I'll show my woman just how much I mean it.

ABOUT NICOLE SNOW

Nicole Snow is a *Wall Street Journal* and *USA Today* bestselling author. She found her love of writing by hashing out love scenes on lunch breaks and plotting her great escape from boardrooms. Her work roared onto the indie romance scene in 2014 with her Grizzlies MC series.

Since then Snow aims for the very best in growly, heart-of-gold alpha heroes, unbelievable suspense, and swoon storms aplenty.

Already hooked on her stuff? Visit nicolesnowbooks.com to sign up for her newsletter and connect on social media.

Got a question or comment on her work? Reach her anytime at nicole@nicolesnowbooks.com

Thanks for reading. And please remember to leave an honest review! Nothing helps an author more.

MORE BOOKS BY NICOLE

The Blackthorn Inheritance

Vows We Never Made
The Right Wrong Promise

The Rory Brothers

Two Truths And A Marriage
One Big Little Secret
Three Reckless Words

Bossy Seattle Suits

One Bossy Proposal
One Bossy Dare
One Bossy Date
One Bossy Offer
One Bossy Disaster

Bad Chicago Bosses

Office Grump
Bossy Grump
Perfect Grump
Damaged Grump

Dark Hearts of Redhaven

The Broken Protector
The Sweetest Obsession
The Darkest Chase

Knights of Dallas Books

The Romeo Arrangement
The Best Friend Zone
The Hero I Need
The Worst Best Friend
Accidental Knight (Companion book)*

Heroes of Heart's Edge Books

No Perfect Hero
No Good Doctor
No Broken Beast
No Damaged Goods
No Fair Lady
No White Knight
No Gentle Giant

Marriage Mistake Standalone Books

Accidental Hero
Accidental Protector
Accidental Romeo
Accidental Knight
Accidental Rebel
Accidental Shield

Stand Alone Novels

Almost Pretend
The Perfect Wrong
Cinderella Undone
Man Enough
Surprise Daddy
Prince With Benefits
Marry Me Again
Love Scars
Recklessly His

Enguard Protectors Books

Still Not Over You
Still Not Into You
Still Not Yours
Still Not Love

Baby Fever Books

Baby Fever Bride
Baby Fever Promise
Baby Fever Secrets

Only Pretend Books

Fiance on Paper
One Night Bride

Grizzlies MC Books

Outlaw's Kiss
Outlaw's Obsession

Outlaw's Bride

Outlaw's Vow

Deadly Pistols MC Books

Never Love an Outlaw

Never Kiss an Outlaw

Never Have an Outlaw's Baby

Never Wed an Outlaw

Prairie Devils MC Books

Outlaw Kind of Love

Nomad Kind of Love

Savage Kind of Love

Wicked Kind of Love

Bitter Kind of Love

Printed in Dunstable, United Kingdom